Love
in the
Shadows

by

Linda H. Bost

Love in the Shadows

Cover Art by *Tina Lynn Stout*

The Wild Rose Press, Inc.
PO Box 708
Adams Basin, NY 14410-0708
Visit us at www.thewildrosepress.com

Publishing History
First American Rose Edition, 2016
Print ISBN 978-1-5092-1008-4
Digital ISBN 978-1-5092-1009-1

Published in the United States of America

hand. Her slow heavy steps and sagging shoulders stifled the reprimand Momma Hattie had planned to give her for keeping them waiting.

Silently they walked the worn grassy path that led them by the fields, the click-clank-clink of metal striking rocks and hard dirt breaking the quietness of the morning as the field slaves worked. A plume of red dirt rose and fell in the field just like Abby's hopes of being free and having a normal life.

"The bearberry bushes are beyond the grove of trees." Hattie pointed with her chin. "Just on the other side of the meadow. Mr. Jack doesn't allow us to go this far on the plantation by ourselves, so Abby-girl, you stay close. No wandering off."

Hattie's body stiffened, and pain clouded her dull dark-brown eyes. Abby remembered the time when she did wander off. She never wanted to forget it. Correction: she never wanted to forget him. He had become a part of her dreams the past two years or more. She remembered how the tall stranger's eyebrows shot up to the top of his hat when he stumbled upon her by the creek. He was just a boy, not much older than she was.

"You frightened me! Are you alone out here?" He slowly moved toward her.

She backed up from the creek, her heart skipping beats as she struggled to keep her shaking legs on the ground. He stopped in his tracks, and she could see the curly black hair hanging from under his hat, covering his ears and neck. His kind black eyes sparkled with gentleness as he spoke.

"Please, don't be afraid," he said slowly as he took another step toward her. "I will not hurt you." The

warmth of his voice and his wide smile froze her in place. She knew she had nothing to fear. Her heartbeat returned to normal, and she was able keep her legs from shaking. "My name is Lawrence. What's yours?"

She looked up into his handsome face and tried to speak, but only a grunt formed in her throat. Her eyes fell back to the ground.

"Surely you have a name, little one."

She looked up at him one last time, trying to memorize his kind face before she dashed back into the woods, running as fast as she could.

She never told anyone about the incident.

"Abby, are you listening, child?" Hattie placed her slender black finger under Abby's chin and lifted her face.

"Are you listening?" Abby could only nod her head.

"I know you're still nervous about our noonday meeting. I have laid my heart out before the Lord. He has assured me that everything will be all right. Have faith, child. Have faith and don't worry." Abby rocked on her heels and smiled up at her momma.

Bong! Bong! The bell sang out over the plantation promptly at noon. Heat flushed Abby's cheeks as she and Momma Hattie rushed to the meeting place in the middle of the slave quarters. Her nostrils flared and her eyes watered from the stench of human waste and body odor. She didn't care; she had more pressing things to worry about; her future and the future of every slave on the Bradley Plantation. She and Hattie were greeted by blank faces, soft murmuring, and pairs and pairs of vacant eyes. Abby's face shone as white in the sea of black faces as the magnolia flowers that littered their

master's yard, but they had all assembled for the same purpose—to learn their fate. Hattie wouldn't have to give her a discreet nudge to remind her to pay attention; Abby was ready to do anything to save herself and Momma.

The rumble of horses' hooves echoed through the silence, and necks craned to get a glimpse of their new master coming over the hill, but Abby didn't dare take her eyes off the ground. Hattie grabbed her daughter's hand and began praying in a soft voice. The jangling of the harness could be heard as the carriage drew closer, and dust swirled out behind the wheels as Eli brought the carriage to a stop right in front of the group. At that moment, Hattie saw that Mr. Jack was the carriage's only occupant, and she relaxed her grip on Abby's hand. Eli reached to help Mr. Jack stand, but he gently shook his head. He took hold of the padded front seat and heaved himself up with a slight grimace.

"My cousin is on his way back to Savannah. You may all go back to your homes."

He gave Hattie a slight nod and a half smile as he released his hold on the front seat. The seat creaked under his weight. He signed to Eli that he was ready to leave, and the carriage made its way back over the hill. The people breathed a collective sigh of relief as they watched the carriage until it was out of sight. Hattie wrapped her arms around Abby.

"This is an answer to prayer, child." Abby wanted to yell for joy, but she did not. She could not. She, Hattie, and the other slaves would continue their normal lives on the Bradley Plantation, at least for now.

Chapter Two

Crouched in his hiding place, Lawrence let his thoughts drift to his sister Kathleen, her upcoming marriage to her fiancé, Adam O'Daley, and the love they shared. A surge of longing that surprised him burned in his heart for such a love and a family of his own. At a sudden movement in the bushes, all his senses went on full alert. Lawrence stepped from his hiding place. The fallen leaves and twigs beneath his rawhide-clad feet didn't crunch or snap. He brought his single-barrel shotgun to his shoulders, aimed down the barrel, and slowly squeezed the trigger...*boom*. He smiled. "Right between the eyes."

The long-legged, twenty-year-old Lawrence Mallory leaped over several fallen logs to claim his kill and tied the furry cottontail with the leather cord dangling from his hunter's bag, where it joined its six cousins. "We'll have rabbit stew tonight!"

Smiles and slaps on the back greeted Lawrence when he returned to camp. The hairy, cross-eyed cook, Whistle, whisked the cottontails from Lawrence's bag exclaiming "Lookie here!" As if he had been the one to spend the last two hours sitting motionless in ankle-deep mud waiting for the little critters to return to their burrow, he whooped and danced around in circles.

"How many did you get this time?" Lawrence heard his three companions ask, but he gave no

response, his eyes fixed on his friend. Paul's appearance in camp meant letters from home. As he watched, Paul waved a white piece of paper in the air.

Lawrence took two giant steps and was face to face with his friend. As he reached to snatch the letter, Paul thrust it behind his back. Lawrence did a quick step forward and a fast move to the left, then to the right, before he successfully gained possession of the letter. Laughter erupted. He kissed the letter in a mock salute before he stuffed it into his pocket. A smile lit Moses's face as he joined Lawrence and Paul. "When you boys finish playing, we can go over this brief that I got today from the big boss himself."

The crackling of the fire and the honking of geese overhead faded into the background as Lawrence listened to the report from their boss, J.L., the owner of the Knickerbocker Magazine Company. The four wide-eyed men's rigid bodies leaned forward on their makeshift log stools as they listened to the new directions the magazine owner wanted to take.

"J.L.," Moses said, clutching the letter in his hand, "is willing to offer our readers a cash incentive to settle in the beautiful and wild territories they have been reading about, that we have been reporting about for almost three years. He's offering to double the salary for any man who's willing to accompany the settlers to their new home." The news sent hats flying in the air, broad smiles, and men jumping up and down like a group of giddy females. When the men settled down, Moses continued, "The settlers will travel to Savannah, and from there those of us who choose to be guides will lead them to their new home sites." As the men discussed the news and made decisions about their

future, Lawrence shifted his position on the log stool and reflected on his own future. He and Paul had already decided to return to Philadelphia, Paul as an editor for the magazine and Lawrence—well he wasn't quite sure yet. Of one thing he was certain—he didn't want the life of a wealthy tycoon, pursuing leisure as if it were a fulltime job. He rubbed the calluses on his hands. Scars shone against his suntanned skin. Every one of them told a story of his coming of age, and he smiled. For almost three years he had felt he had a true purpose in life—he was making a difference. A smile crept across his lips as he looked over at his five friends. He wondered what they would think if they knew his true identity, his relationship to J.L.

The aroma of rabbit stew and sourdough bread floated through the air and into Lawrence's nostrils. His stomach growled in response, but instead of giving in to his hunger, he slipped the letter from his pocket and made himself comfortable on his log stool. His eyes twinkled when he saw his sister Kathleen's familiar script. A single letter from Kathleen and not the family could mean only one thing—she was married! He ripped open the letter, scanned the contents, and flung the letter into the air, yelling, "Kathleen and Adam are married!" The clanking and scraping ceased as his friends paused over their meal. Smiles broke out on overstuffed mouths, and cheers erupted in the camp.

"It's about time," the cook sputtered between bites. "I was beginning to think that fellow was never going to marry our sweet girl." The other men shook their heads in agreement. The five men had adopted Kathleen as a sister—or daughter, in Moses's and Whistle's case—even though none of them had ever

met her. Lawrence had often read aloud portions of her letters and those from his family, to give his friends a taste of the civilized world they had left behind.

"There is more. The wedding was moved up by a few months because Adam's father is ill, and they will be traveling to Darin, Georgia, to help take care of him." Lawrence shook his head. "I just can't imagine my sister living on a ranch, certainly not in the South, of all places."

"Darin, Georgia, did you say? I know of a Double-O Ranch in Darin, Georgia. It's owned by a rich and powerful man," Moses said as he twirled his spoon between his fingers. "I wonder if that's the place Kathleen and her husband are going."

"I know the place you are talking about," Whistle piped in. "What's the owner's name?" Whistle tugged at his shaggy beard, speaking more to himself than anyone else. "Naw," he said, still pulling on his beard. "The fellow I'm thinking about is a big-time slave owner. Mean as the devil himself. Besides, I don't think that fellow has any kin, and I don't see our sweet Kathleen getting mixed up with the likes of anyone related to him."

"What's his name?" Moses said, snapping his fingers as if that would help him remember. Jumping to his feet and shaking his finger in the air, he and Whistle spoke at the same time—"Walt O'Daley!"

"Yes, that's it," Whistle added.

Lawrence straightened on his log seat and looked directly at his friends. He spoke in a low, strained tone. "Adam's father's name is Walter O'Daley."

Moses set his bowl on the log stool he had just vacated. "This man we're talking about makes the best

bridles, harnesses, and saddles in these parts."

"He has the finest horses, too," Whistle added, nodding his head as he stuffed his mouth with more bread.

"That sounds like Adam's father," Lawrence said, nodding.

"This Walt is a rich man. If he is Adam's father, what took him so long to get the money he wanted to provide a fine home for our Kathleen? He could have just asked his pappy," Whistle remarked. "You know, son," Moses said, rubbing the back of his neck and pressing his lips together, "this Walt I know is a hard man." He raised his head and looked at Lawrence with sympathetic eyes. "Well, at least he was. He built that fine ranch by enslaving his own countrymen, the Scots-Irish. He about starved them to keep them from running away, but most of them did anyway." Moses sat back down on his log stool. All eyes were fixed on him, and all pretense of eating ceased.

"He got into the slavery business, bought about thirty or forty of them, more than anyone else in that part of the country at that time. I heard his wife died when she learned he had become a slave owner. "Humph." Moses shook his head slowly and tried to keep the moisture from his eyes. "He worked those slaves from sunup to sundown, in all kinds of weather. He didn't spare the whip. I saw men whose faces and bodies were distorted from whip marks. Faces that had been seared with a branding iron…" Moses choked on his words. The memory sent a shudder down his spine. "I was just a boy…" He slowly released a long breath of air. "The faces of those men haunted my dreams for years."

Lawrence cleared his throat to break the silence that had engulfed the camp.

"I know Adam and how he and Kathleen both despise the institution of slavery. His father must be seriously ill if they are they moving south to that kind of setup."

****

Kathleen's elbow banged on the wooden slats at her side. She gripped the handle of her open parasol and pushed her heels against the wooden floorboards to keep from being unseated as the carriage lurched over the rough dry road that led from Darin, Georgia, to the Double-O Ranch. Adam O'Daley turned and saw his wife's wide eyes, trembling bottom lip, and pale face. He leaned back on the reins and brought the galloping horses to a stop, laid the reins in the seat, pulled his wife into his lap, and wrapped his arms around her to hold her tight for a while.

"I'm sorry, darling. Are you all right?"

Kathleen let out a big sigh. "I am now." She threaded her arms around her husband's neck, and he lowered his mouth to her lips.

After a few sweet minutes, he raised his head. "Are you sure you are all right? I didn't mean to frighten you."

"I know you didn't," Kathleen said, sliding down to regain her seat.

"It's just that…" A deep furrow appeared between Adam's eyebrows, and there was a bit of an edge in his voice. "This is not exactly the wedding trip I planned for you—bringing you to a place where slavery is embraced and the diabolical system flourishes because greedy men want an easy way of obtaining riches and

fame for themselves."

He looked out across the rough land, trying to get control of his emotions. He wove his fingers through his wife's.

"I know," she said, squeezing his hand. "I know you won't like being there any more than I will. But your father needs you—us."

"I hope that's true and this is not just another scheme to get me down here."

"Whatever the reason, we will make the best of the situation," she assured him.

Adam pulled his wife to his side and tilted her oval face up to look into her blue-gray eyes. "Have I told you lately how much I love you?"

Kathleen's cheeks flushed, and a delighted shiver ran down her spine. She batted her thick lashes and smiled. "Yes, but I will never grow tired of hearing it." She rested her head on her husband's chest as they resumed their travels at a more sedate pace. The gentle swaying of the carriage soon lulled her to sleep. Several miles down the road, Adam gently elbowed her.

"Darling, you must see this!" Adam brought the carriage to a halt. Kathleen slowly straightened, stretched, and moved her head gracefully from side to side, then froze. Her eyes shot from one side of the road to the other as she tried to take in the riot of color before her. Her mouth fell open.

"This is so lovely! This rivals the botanical gardens in Philadelphia."

Adam nodded. "I know."

They took in the sight of the beautiful dogwood trees of pink, red, and white blossoms peppered among orange-flamed azalea bushes. The sweet smell of

magnolia blossoms filled the air and teased their nostrils, while the tall pine, oak, and maple trees served as a protective canopy over the beautiful landscape.

"Oh, Adam, this is so spectacular!" Kathleen took in a deep breath. "I thought the sunrises and sunsets were magnificent when we were on the steamboat, but this…" She spread her arms and sucked in a breath. "Is anything comparable to this? I am beginning to understand why my brother wants to be an explorer and travel to parts unknown, writing articles about the beauty of God's creation."

Adam nodded his head in agreement.

Kathleen looped her arm through her husband's. "Are we on the ranch?"

"Yes and no. This is on Father's thousand-plus acres. I remember him describing this place to Mother on one of his rare visits home." Adam's face turned red. His tight lips and the set of his eyes let his wife know that he was thinking about all the years his father had spent pursuing riches in the South instead of the love of his family in Philadelphia. She gently rubbed her husband's arm.

Adam gave the reins a light tap, and the couple was again on their way. Kathleen laid her head on the leather seatback and enjoyed the miles of shade from the trees. All that could be heard was the jangling of the horses' harness and the chirping of the birds.

She turned her head in her husband's direction.

"Are you all right?" he asked.

"I'm fine, just thinking."

He leaned over and gave her a peck on the forehead.

Kathleen lifted her head, marveling at the abrupt

change in the landscape. Open land stretched out before them, with mountains and tall hills in the background like protectors. Groves of trees danced across the plains, stopping wherever they pleased. The couple looked at each other and then at the sign just ahead of them. "Welcome to the Double-O Ranch," it read. Kathleen stood and balanced precariously in the carriage before it came to a complete stop.

"This is...this is...oh, Adam." Kathleen found her husband's hand. "I have never seen anything so grand!" She pointed to the huge, beautiful three-story red brick house that sat on a slight hill in front of them. "Your father's house is more magnificent than any of the mansions in Boston, Philadelphia, and Savannah. And look at those trees."

"Crepe myrtles," Adam said.

"I love the way they line the lane leading up to the house." She sighed.

The couple spent a few more minutes taking in the breathtaking sight.

"Hon, we'd better be on our way. We shouldn't keep the king waiting," Adam said through clenched teeth.

The couple got a better view of the house and the grounds as their carriage rolled up the lane. The front porch had tall stately columns that faced formal gardens, fountains, and holly trees. They could see a large gazebo peeking around a corner at the rear of the house, accessible by curving brick walkways. Before they could take in any more of their surroundings, they were greeted by two well-dressed black slaves. Adam helped his wife out of the carriage, and without a word a slave climbed aboard, took a seat, and drove the

and her long silky braid. *Another person wants to harm me?* The words pounded in her head. She lay still in her bed, wrestling with the questions that assaulted her thoughts, until she heard the soft snores coming from across the room. She slipped out of bed and went where she could think and pace. *Oh, Lord, what is to happen to me when Mr. Jack dies? Will we be sold?* Abby paced back and forth in the upstairs room, avoiding the wooden planks that creaked. She stopped suddenly, hands flying to her lips; she shook her head violently and stopped in her tracks. *Oh, no...I might be sold? No! No!* Abby wanted to scream the words. They struggled to get out of her mouth, but they got lodged in her throat and never passed her lips.

Her chestnut-brown eyes stung and overflowed with moisture, and no amount of batting her long lashes could hold back the flood of tears that rushed down her cheeks. Momma Hattie, with the help of their master, Mr. Jack Bradley, had spent all of Abby's life trying to protect her. What would life be like without them?

She rocked back and forth on the stool until darkness gave way to daylight. Many thoughts meandered through her mind, and one kept returning—*What would it be like to live a normal life—to go where I please whenever I please, to have friends, to laugh, to marry... Marry?* She smiled, but her eyes burned with tears. *Who would ever want to marry me? Even if Mr. Jack lives a long life, I could never hope to marry anyone on this plantation. No one would have me.*

"Abby Rose, come down here! We are ready to go. We have only a few hours before noon." Momma Hattie and Eli, their helper and protector for the day, were already outside waiting for her with buckets in

Chapter One

Abby sat on the rickety stool, her face pressed against the windowpane in the upstairs room. The cool surface did little to calm her nerves. She tilted her nose up to take in the fragrance of clover, mint, garlic, and wild onions that wafted through the herb room and surrounded her like a warm blanket. This is where she felt safe—where she came for comfort, to pray, and to worry.

She had slept very little. Momma Hattie had struggled out of bed in the middle of the night to spend time with the Lord. Her groans and soft cries darted through the air and jarred Abby's senses awake. Her eyes flew open, but she stilled herself as she listened to a portion of her momma's prayer.

"Lord, you know Mr. Jack has a kind heart. He has been good to me and my Abby Rose. Lord, you know about his sickness and that my herbs and potions are helping him less and less. I ask that You be merciful unto him and extend his life to help us find a way to keep my Abby safe. I ask that You expose the evil in the heart of his cousin who is coming to help run the plantation. I know my Abby will not be safe with him. Oh, Lord, please hear my plea…"

Abby's heart galloped in her chest like stampeding horses when she understood the meaning of her momma's words. Sweat drenched her white petticoat

Dedication

To my Lord and Savior—
I hope my words captured the scenes
the way you showed them to me.

Abby remembered too. She never wanted to forget it. Correction: she never wanted to forget him. He had become a part of her dreams the past two years or more. She remembered how the tall stranger's eyebrows shot up to the top of his hat when he stumbled upon her by the creek. He was just a boy, not much older than she was.

"You frightened me! Are you alone out here?" He slowly moved toward her.

She backed up from the creek, her heart skipping beats as she struggled to keep her shaking legs on the ground. He stopped in his tracks, and she could see the curly black hair dangling from under his hat, covering his ears and neck. His kind black eyes sparkled with gentleness as he spoke.

"Please, don't be afraid," he said slowly as he took another step toward her. "I will not hurt you." The warmth of his voice and his wide smile froze her in place. She knew she had nothing to fear. Her heartbeat returned to normal, and she was able keep her legs from shaking. "My name is Lawrence. What's yours?"

She looked up into his handsome face and tried to speak, but only a grunt formed in her throat. Her eyes fell back to the ground.

"Surely you have a name, little one."

She looked up at him one last time, trying to memorize his kind face before she dashed back into the woods, running as fast as she could.

"You haven't changed, John.
Always running away when situations became tough.
Even now. I did wrong to believe more of you."

"That was always your problem, wasn't it, Anne?
You never believed in me at all."

"You never gave me reason to." At his growl, she
let her mouth break into a gaping hole making hollow
sounds. "So, thank you, on behalf of the Fernsby Ladies
Literati, for your kind and generous donation." She
paused, letting her eyes rake over him one final time.
She wanted to unglove her hand and hold it out to him,
to have his angry hot lips graze her bare knuckles. One
last touch to brand his name into her bones.

But she also longed to slap him. Hard. To hear her
hand crack sharp against his arrogant stubbled cheek.
To have it hurt him red stinging sore, to leaving him
feeling, but for a moment, some of her pain.

Instead she nodded, turned, and crossed the hall to
the door his manservant held open.

"See you in another twenty years," John said, his
tone full of boredom.

His stick tapped on the tiled hall, and she turned at
the doorway determined to have the last word.

But all utterance died.

Two young women waited halfway on the stairs,
holding their arms out to him, crimson and indigo
dresses falling off their shoulders, disheveled hair,
smiles wide, inviting him up in lewd whispers. He
stretched out his arms to them, then leaned forward to
get his foot balanced on the stair, his vest rising against
his white shirt, as if already undressing.

carriage around to the back of the house to unload their belongings while the second slave escorted the couple into the house. Kathleen's hand found Adam's as they stood in the large black-and-white-marble-tiled foyer, taking in the exquisite imported furniture, beautiful decorations, and elegant curtains.

"There's no doubt Father enjoys his wealth." Adam extended his arm to his wife.

With another glance around the room, she concurred. She had never met Walt O'Daley, but there was one thing for sure—he had impeccable taste.

Kathleen glided up the polished wooden spiral staircase like a princess on the arm of her prince. When they reached Walt's bedroom, the servant stepped aside and allowed the couple to enter.

Kathleen sucked in a deep breath as she stepped through the door. Two Victorian spoonback chairs and a small dark-blue upholstered settee formed a seating area around a huge fireplace; two sets of double windows were adorned in blue and gold damask fabric with luxurious fringe. A large mahogany four-post bed stood in the center of the room, and in the middle of the bed was a very frail man with sagging skin that would have blended in with the white pillows that propped him up had it not been for the brown liver spots that decorated his skin. Adam dropped his wife's arm, rushed to his father's bed, and threw himself upon his breast. He made no attempt to stop the flow of tears dripping from his eyes.

"Oh, Father," he choked out, "I am here."

Walt's thin, liver-spotted hand touched his son's face, examining it as if he wanted to make sure this was indeed his son and not one of his dreams. Adam leaned into his touch. Walt's eyes flooded with tears. "Is it really you, son?" he croaked. "I am so glad you came."

Adam enveloped his father's translucent hands in his. "Yes, Father, it's me."

Walt squeezed his son's hand. Shame penetrated his features.

Walt's voice was low and scratchy. He moved his lips several times before he spoke. Regret laced his voice. "Son, I am so sorry for all the unhappiness I've caused my family...your mother's death chief in that." Tears flowed freely down his cheeks. He cried in his son's arms. Kathleen stepped from behind her husband and placed one hand on Adam's back. After a few minutes, Adam raised his head. "Father, I would like for you to meet my bride, the former Miss Kathleen Mallory."

Walt extended his hand to his daughter-in-law. She ignored it and gave him a light kiss on his cheek instead.

Chapter Three

It had taken Lawrence and his companions well over three months to complete their work and return to base camp in Savannah, Georgia. When they arrived, they learned their boss had arranged for them to stay in one of the city's finest boarding houses, expenses paid, plus receive double pay during their time there, even though they wouldn't start guiding settlers west until well over a month later.

Lawrence smiled to himself at all the praises they had given J.L. for being a kind and generous man. He thought for a brief moment about revealing J.L.'s identity, but didn't. He enjoyed being known simply as Lawrence. How would his friends treat him if they knew he had more money than he could possibly spend in several lifetimes, not sparing any luxuries?

Lawrence and Paul delayed their trip to Philadelphia to help oversee the resettling project his magazine company had undertaken. He had been in Savannah for several months. His work had kept him busy, but the longing he had for love and a family still burned deep in his heart. When his latest letter from his sister Kathleen told him she was expecting a baby, his desire grew even more.

Lawrence gazed out the window as Paul briefed him on the resettling project. He unconsciously drummed his fingers on the desk.

"Lawrence, have you heard a word I have been saying?" Paul shuffled the papers in his hand and smiled at his friend.

"You know what you need…"

A knock at the door interrupted him. Lawrence laughed and jumped to open it. He knew what his friend was going to say to him. They had had the conversation many times before.

"We are working too hard. Young men like us should be out enjoying the company of pretty young ladies."

Lawrence reached the door and took the envelope from the servant. He turned and bowed to his friend.

"Your wish is my command, sir." He tried to quell the grin creeping across his face.

Paul took the letter and opened it slowly, read, and—"Yahoo!" His yell could have raised the dead. "Lawrence, are we really going to the ball at the Mercer mansion?"

Lawrence slapped his friend on the back. "Only for you, friend. Only for you."

When the greatly anticipated night arrived, shimmering lights lit every window in the mansion. Music skipped across the air to tickle Lawrence's ears and set Paul's feet dancing. Lawrence leaned to straighten his friend's cravat, and smiled.

"You'll have time for dancing once we enter the house."

They were ushered into a fantasy world of extravagance, a sparkling, glittering show of elegance and refinement. Ladies in all their finery and men in black tails filled the room, where lavishly laden tables with a rich assortment of food awaited the guests. The two lingered for a moment, taking in the sight before them. Lawrence thought it equaled being back in Philadelphia spying on his parents' guests as they entertained some of the city's wealthiest citizens. For himself, he had long ago wearied of the façade paraded by many of the wealthy. He wanted to leave, but he wouldn't dare deprive his friend of this night of a lifetime.

Paul brushed an imaginary piece of lint from his coat and smiled as he leaned to whisper, "I think I'll leave you now."

Lawrence gave his friend a playful swat on the shoulder. His eyes trailed Paul as he went straight to a group of ladies who hid their faces behind fancy fans. Lawrence lifted his brows and gently shook his head. He was only a few months from his twenty-first birthday, and he had already grown tired of highly refined ladies who giggled too much, flirted with their fans, and spent entirely too much time gossiping. His thoughts were interrupted by a loud giggle. His gaze leaped across the room to find the source of the voice heard over the soft music. A small group of men and women were being entertained by a vivacious beauty with cinnamon-colored hair. They hung on her every word. He wondered what tantalizing gossip she was sharing. Suddenly she left her friends, who stared after her feminine form with raised brows and confused looks. He crinkled his brow. Before he could examine the incident further, he heard his name called out and turned to see his solicitor making his way toward him through the crowd.

"Lawrence, I see you and Paul made it."

The solicitor pumped his friend's arm up and

down. "I'm glad you came, knowing how you feel about these types of gatherings."

Lawrence gave his friend his best scowl.

"Come, I have some friends I want you to meet."

Lawrence followed his friend to the far end of the room, all the time trying to keep a discreet eye on the young lady who had attracted his attention. His solicitor made introductions, and before the small talk ended, Lawrence spied the beauty coming in his direction. Her doe eyes were shining, and she clenched and unclenched her fists. Heading for the terrace, she flung the door open and rushed out into the dim night. He wanted to go after her, but his feet remained planted on the floor as he tried to stay engaged in the conversation. After about twenty minutes, he gave up all pretense of listening, excused himself, and headed for the terrace.

****

Elizabeth paced on the terrace, trying to calm her nerves and wishing her heartbeat would return to normal.

"What must they think of me? I couldn't continue my story; the only thing I could think about was getting out. I could feel the war beginning to rage inside of me. Oh, Lord, what is the matter with me?"

Her eyes spotted a secluded stone bench far away from the terrace doors, and she went to it and sat. After several slow, deep breaths, she pulled her handkerchief from her sleeve and dabbed her face and neck. She was about to tuck the white handkerchief back into its hiding place when her eyes fell on the embroidered initials—D.B.

"Oh, Mother!" She cried into the handkerchief that had been one of her mother's favorites. "Am I going to be like you?"

Lawrence heard the soft cry as he stepped out onto the terrace. The young lady was seated on a bench partially hidden by the foliage. He cleared his throat to alert her to his presence and saw her shoulders stiffen. She quickly wiped her nose and replaced the handkerchief in her sleeve.

"Miss, are you all right?" No response.

He decided to try again. "Can I get you something?"

Elizabeth slowly turned. Even in the dim light it was evident her nose was red from crying. "You are very kind, sir, but I am perfectly fine."

Lawrence took tentative steps toward her. "This is a beautiful night. Allow me to introduce myself." He bowed. "I am Lawrence Mallory from Philadelphia."

Elizabeth extended a gloved hand to him. "I am Elizabeth Bradley from Mason, Georgia."

"Very pleased to make your acquaintance, Miss Bradley."

He kissed her hand. With a slight tilt of her head, she gave him a little smile. "Under the circumstances, you may call me Elizabeth."

"Elizabeth it is, then."

He motioned to the space next to her on the stone bench. "May I?"

Elizabeth adjusted her skirt to make room for him. "Well, Mister— I mean, Lawrence, what brings you to Savannah?"

Lawrence spent the next half hour telling Elizabeth all about his work as a writer and illustrator for the Knickerbocker Magazine Company. Her eyes danced with glee and then with horror as he told her about sleeping out under the stars when he was too tired to pitch his tent, and about snowstorms, tornadoes, and going a year or more without seeing a woman of any kind. Elizabeth told him about her father's illness and recovery, described her life on the plantation, and divulged that they were in Savannah visiting her aunt, her father's sister. There was a gap in their conversation for a few minutes; Elizabeth's dimples twinkled when she looked at Lawrence. He lost himself in her green eyes. Elizabeth placed her hand on top of his. "Would you like to dance with me?" Lawrence threw his head back and roared.

"Miss Elizabeth, I see you don't stand on propriety. I would be honored to dance with you." Lawrence stood and offered his hand to help Elizabeth to her feet. When their hands touched, heat coursed through his body. Her eyes grew wide before she blinked several times and lowered her head. He knew she had felt the same bolt of lightning. With all the pomp he could muster, he escorted the lovely lady to the dance floor, where they danced the rest of the evening.

"What a night!" Paul laughed out loud, then put both hands behind his head and leaned back into the soft leather seat.

"I think I am in love," he said, smiling as their carriage rolled down the lane. "It's a shame I will be leaving all the lovely ladies in a few days," giving his friend a sideways glance. "Did you do anything else tonight other than discuss business, Lawrence?"

Lawrence gave his friend a playful punch in his side. *Yes, I met the woman I am going to marry.* Lawrence leaned his head back on the cool seat and pictured the young lady with the cinnamon hair and emerald-green doe-eyes.

The next day, promptly at two, Lawrence knocked on the door of the home where Elizabeth was staying. A very dignified black servant opened the door. "I'm here to call on Miss Elizabeth Bradley." The man bowed and escorted Lawrence into a tastefully decorated room. Before he could get a good look at his surroundings, he was greeted by a tall man, about his height, with pale, sagging skin. "You must be Lawrence Mallory," the man said, shaking Lawrence's hand with a surprisingly strong grip. "My Lizzie—I mean Elizabeth—talked about you until well into the morning. You left a lasting impression upon my daughter. I had to remind her that I needed my rest," he said with a low chuckle. "I'm Elizabeth's father, Jack Bradley."

"Mr. Bradley." Lawrence bowed before him. "Pleased to make your acquaintance, sir. I was very impressed by your daughter, sir."

The two exchanged pleasantries for a while. Lawrence told Jack about his employment with the Knickerbocker Magazine Company, and Jack in turn told him about his farm. Finally, as Lawrence shifted in his seat, Jack cleared his throat. "Let me see what is keeping Elizabeth."

Before he could exit the room, loud voices could be heard from upstairs. One voice was clearly Elizabeth's. "I'll just check on Elizabeth," Jack said, and, eyes wide, he hastened from the room and rushed upstairs.

Soon Elizabeth descended the stairs. Lawrence could see her from his seat in the parlor. She wore a cute pout that added a certain amount of attractiveness to an already appealing face. She wore a stunning pale blue gown. She looked like a bride—his bride. By the time she floated to the bottom of the stairs, he was there waiting with a silly grin on his face like a lovesick schoolboy. "You look beautiful."

Elizabeth stared but didn't respond. It was as if she had never seen him before.

He waited.

Nothing.

The grin disappeared from his mouth.

Elizabeth saw the man's lips move, and she wanted to speak, but she couldn't. The battle inside her was raging again. She felt herself slipping away. "Lord, no! Please help me!"

"Elizabeth, darling, are you all right?" Lawrence asked again with alarm in his voice.

He heard rapid footsteps coming down the stairs.

"Sure, my little Lizzie is fine." Jack gently took hold of his daughter's arms. "She's just a little tired from our long talk last night."

After a few minutes that seemed like an hour to Lawrence, Elizabeth smiled—a smile as bright as the sunshine. "Oh, Lawrence, you came."

"Of course I came, darling. Are you all right?"

"Yes, yes. I'm fine." Elizabeth extended both her hands to him in greeting. Lawrence never blinked as he looked deep into her big green eyes. He slowly lifted her hands to his lips. He kissed one hand and then the other. Pink suffused her cheeks. She lowered her eyelids, and Lawrence's heart leapt. He was still a little confused that Elizabeth hadn't seemed to recognize him at first, but all questions vanished when he saw her reaction to his simple kisses. "Would you care for a stroll in the beautiful garden I saw on my way in here?"

Lawrence looked in Jack's direction. He smiled and gave a slight nod as Elizabeth responded, "That would be lovely. Do I need my wrap?"

"No, it's a warm day for early February, and if you do get chilled, I'll warm you," Lawrence said with a devilish grin.

Elizabeth was relieved to be outside in the fresh air. She needed to clear her head. *I have to get control of myself. I know I have treated the servants horribly, and I can tell they are a little afraid of me. I have been feeling so morose and irritable lately. So far they have kept my outbursts and horrible behavior to themselves, but I don't know how long that will last.*

"You are mighty quiet. Are you sure you're well, sweetheart?"

Elizabeth could only nod her head in response to Lawrence's question.

The couple spent several hours strolling through the beautiful garden. An abundance of daffodils had emerged from their winter's nap and were now bowing their yellow faces before the sun. Laughter filled the air as Lawrence sat on a stone garden bench with Elizabeth, sharing amusing tales about leaving home at seventeen, to his parents' consternation, to explore the country. He told her about a time when he and Paul had gotten lost when they left Savannah.

"We set up camp. I was to go get wood while he prepared us some food. I couldn't find my way back."

Elizabeth covered her mouth to contain her giggles, but laughter bubbled out through her fingers.

"An explorer who couldn't find his way back to camp."

Elizabeth's laughter grew even louder. Lawrence

pressed his lips together trying to hold back his own laughter. He cleared his throat in an attempt to regain his composure and continue his story. "I came across a young girl at a creek. I think I scared her out of a year's growth. I was hoping she could tell me where I was, but she ran off before I could ask her. It took me several hours to locate Paul." Lawrence chuckled. "My navigating skills have greatly improved since then."

Elizabeth laid one soft hand on top of Lawrence's calloused one.

"I am glad you were able to find your way to me." Lawrence turned her face to look at him. He swept his fingers along her flawless apple cheeks, then traced her lips with his finger. She sucked in a deep breath, and he leaned down and placed a light kiss on her lips.

The couple spent almost all their time together in the next two weeks; he found Elizabeth to be somewhat moody but witty and intelligent and not the least bit shy about speaking her mind, and he loved that about her. They took in concerts, enjoyed plays performed by a traveling troupe, attended church functions and parties. But what he enjoyed most was having Elizabeth on his arm as they ambled around the city taking in its many sights and discussing their future together.

****

Elizabeth's eyes filled with moisture. She coiled and uncoiled the white linen napkin in her lap. Lawrence moved his food from one side of his plate to the other side.

"I didn't realize you would be leaving soon. I thought you would be staying on with your aunt." Elizabeth covered one of his hands with hers.

"I have been here for over six months. Father was

too ill to come after me until now. He has to get back to the farm."

Lawrence stretched his long legs under the white floor-length tablecloth. "When will you come back to Savannah?" Elizabeth took a sip of her tea. "I don't know." She blinked back tears.

Silence punctuated the moment. Lawrence took hold of Elizabeth's hands and gently rubbed the back of each one with his thumbs. His deep voice became intimately low. "I love you, Elizabeth. I loved you the first time I saw you at the ball. I love our time together."

She was about to speak, but Lawrence covered her full lips with his finger. "I want you to become my wife, Elizabeth." She blinked long damp lashes several times.

"Do your really mean it, Lawrence?"

"I have never been more serious about anything in my life."

He didn't care about the crowd around them or propriety. He leaned over, cupped her chin, and kissed her full lips.

"I would be honored to be your wife," Elizabeth said as she pulled her embroidered handkerchief from her long sleeve and dabbed the tears from her eyes. When she had finished, Lawrence wrapped both his hands around hers and placed them over his heart. Her smile and her sparkling eyes were already filling the yearning inside him for love and family.

The next morning, a servant entered the solarium carrying a silver tray on which lay a missive marked Urgent and addressed to Jack Bradley. Jack eagerly took the letter and ripped it open. His mouth drew back at the corners; his eyes danced. This was an answer to prayer. He rushed from the room with the letter crushed in his hand. "Sister!" he yelled. "Can you prepare for a wedding with all the trimmings in four days?"

****

Palms sweating, hands clenching and unclenching, Lawrence paced over the Oriental rug rehearsing the words to say to ask Jack for the hand of his only child—her hand in marriage to a man she had known for only two weeks. Jack entered the room with a big smile on his face.

"Please sit down, my boy. You are going to put a hole in that rug, and my sister will expect me to replace it." Jack chuckled.

Lawrence took a seat on the settee. Before Jack could sit, Lawrence began to speak. "I assume you got my note." Jack nodded. "I know you don't know much about me—" Jack held up his hand.

"I know all I need to know about you." Lines formed between Lawrence's eyebrows.

"What do you mean?"

"I know there's more to you than being an explorer and writer for that magazine company. You got a personal invitation to the Mercer Ball, didn't you?" Lawrence smiled with understanding.

"We both know that no one receives a personal invitation unless they are of certain means." Jack gave a devilish smile before he turned serious.

"I know you love my daughter, and she loves you. You want to marry her?"

"Yes, sir, I do. I love her very much."

"You are a fine young man, Lawrence. I would be honored to have you as my son."

Chapter Four

Adam and Kathleen threw themselves into the care of Walt. He thrived under their prayers and caring ministrations. He experienced fewer bouts of tiredness and dizziness and showed no signs of confusion. Some days he was strong enough to spend time in the harness and saddle shops.

One morning Kathleen sat at the kitchen table with her Bible open, her brows pulled together and her forehead creased as she searched. "Where is that verse?" She thumbed through the pages of the book. Soft voices drew her gaze to the doorway. She smiled when she saw her father-in-law and a servant making their way to the table.

"You're a blessing to an old man's eyes, my dear. You are as pretty as a picture."

Walt took the chair at the head of the table, and Kathleen smiled, squeezed Walt's hand, and leaned to give him a kiss on the cheek.

"Don't let me interrupt you, my dear." Walt nodded in the direction of her opened Bible.

"Oh, Adam and I finished our devotional time before he left. I was just looking up a verse that's been on my mind."

Walt blew on the hot black coffee the servant had set before him. He peeked up at Kathleen. "I wouldn't mind hearing what you and Adam talked about."

Kathleen's eyes sparkled with delight as she opened her Bible and started reading and sharing with her father-in-law what she and Adam had discussed during their devotional time.

That evening, Adam joined his wife out in the gazebo. "You know, darling, I think it's time for us to see more of the ranch." As Adam sat down next to his wife on the swing, Kathleen let out a big sigh.

"What's wrong, darling?"

"I was just thinking…" Kathleen shifted her position in the swing. "Look at all this," she said, waving her hands around. "Being surrounded by all this luxury can lull you into thinking there is no ugliness here."

Adam knitted his fingers into his wife's. "I suppose, but we know better." He kissed her fingers.

"What do you suppose the slaves' quarters will be like?"

Adam stared out across the beautiful gardens. "One thing I do know—they will look nothing like this or the fine house Father had built for my brother and his wife."

Kathleen laid her head on Adam's shoulders. "It's a shame they never got a chance to see it. I know his wife would have loved it."

"Father named the place the Double-O for him and my brother, the two O'Daleys."

Adam put the swing in motion, wrapped his arms around his wife, and kissed the top of her head. The creaking of the swing was all that was heard as the couple sat in companionable silence for a while. Finally Adam cleared his throat. "Tomorrow we will visit the slave quarters—a visit I have put off long enough."

****

The couple rocked back and forth in silence as the carriage took them over the bumpy path that led to the slave quarters. Adam's eyes widened and his lips tightened; disbelief and incredulity distorted his features. Kathleen's mouth flew open as she gasped at the horrific site before them.

"Oh, God!" Adam squeezed his wife's hands. "I have never seen this kind of property even in the tenements of Philadelphia or Boston."

Kathleen's gaze flickered like the flame of a candle as she watched people spilling out of windowless huts. She was unable to find her voice, and tears made a path down her crimson cheeks. The carriage rolled to a stop. Gabe, one of Adam's cousins, came around to Kathleen's side to help her down.

She made no effort to move, and neither did Adam. The couple sat in the carriage staring at half-naked women, children, and men, who stood before flat-roofed, windowless huts made of random pieces of wood nailed in a crisscross fashion. Black iron pots suspended from wooden tripods were stirred by women much too thin. A few older men sat on logs, no chairs being visible, and clothing that was little more than rags hung drying from a rope extended from one tree to the other. Their shocked silence was broken by a naked precocious child who walked up to the carriage, stared at them in turn, and asked, "Are you our new master?"

"I am no one's master," Adam said more harshly that he intended.

Adam stepped from the carriage and addressed the cautious crowd, whose downcast, dejected attitude matched the squalor of their surroundings. "I am Walt's son, Adam O'Daley."

The faces before him showed no emotion. Adam took his wife's hand and helped her out of the carriage.

"This is my wife, Kathleen."

Kathleen gave her head a quick nod in greeting. She kept a tight hold on her husband's hand.

Adam cleared his throat and stammered, "We would like to inspect your homes." The slaves stood stone-faced. "With your permission of course," he added.

No one uttered a word. Gabe was getting ready to speak, but the little boy who had spoken to them tugged on Adam's pants.

"Wanna come wif me." The little boy pulled Adam along the path.

Adam's eyes watered. Kathleen covered her nose and mouth from the stench of human waste. They stopped at the third windowless shack. Two women stood by the door; they slowly moved aside to allow the couple to enter the one-room dwelling. Kathleen shuddered when she saw the dirt floor, the old blankets folded up in a corner, and no obvious source of heat. Adam's mouth formed a straight line when one of the women told him, in reply to his question, that six people lived in the ten-by-ten building. They were ushered into a big barnlike structure that served as a kitchen and common meeting area. A strong wind could have easily blown the big, dilapidated building down, by the look of it. When the couple exited, they came face to face with a few slaves who were willing to answer questions. Adam and Kathleen learned that four older slaves prepared the morning and noonday meals for everyone, but the slaves themselves were responsible for their evening meal. This meal was prepared outside regardless of the weather. Adam's mouth twisted, and Kathleen's eyes teared up when they learned that the people's diet consisted of a small ration of corn meal, salted herring, and occasional vegetables, not nearly enough for the physical labor they were required to do. Judging from the lash marks on the backs of many, the whip was the driving force behind the energy it took to work, instead of good nutritious food.

"Where are your gardens?" Adam asked.

"We ain't got none," one woman said as she looked at the ground.

Kathleen tightened her hold on Adam's arm as they made their way back to the carriage.

"Oh, Adam, we have to do something about the deplorable conditions these people are living in."

"I know," he replied. "I can't believe Father can surround himself with so much opulence but deny decent food and clothing to the very people who make his wealth possible."

Kathleen batted her long wet lashes as she turned to look at her husband. "I have an idea. Mother's charity group collects clothes for the needy. I will write her to see if the group will send their donations here. I can't think of a group that's in more need than these people." Adam leaned over and kissed his wife on the cheek. "*We* need to do more, Adam." Kathleen choked on her words.

Adam patted his wife's hand. "We will do something, honey; we will." He spoke through clenched teeth. "I can't believe Father has bought and sold these people just like he would buy and sell any other merchandise. His treatment of these people testifies that he only thinks of them as dispensable."

"Don't you think he has genuinely repented and is sorry for how he's treated others and how he has lived his life?"

Adam rubbed Kathleen's hand. "I don't know, darling, but we will see what he says when I tell him about the changes I want to make to the slave quarters."

****

Walt fingered through the pages of the book on his desk. He had taken up the habit of reading his Bible every day just like his son and daughter-in-law. He watched Adam and Kathleen as they stepped down from the carriage. He could tell from their faces they had been down to the slave quarters. Adam bolted through the door of the study.

"Father, we need to talk—"

Walt held up his hand. "Son, you can make any changes you want on the ranch. I trust your judgment."

Air rushed from Adam's lungs, and he dropped down in a chair. "You mean it, Father?" He couldn't believe his father would agree so eagerly and without hearing his proposal, but he spent the next hour telling Walt about some of the changes he would like to make to improve the slaves' living conditions.

"I will make sure everyone cooperates with you and follows your instructions."

"Thank you, sir." Adam shook his father's hand, and as he walked out of the room he thought about what his wife had said about his father's transformation.

"Thank you, God, for touching Father's heart," he whispered under his breath.

****

Adam pulled out his pocket watch and tapped his fingers on the desk. He was waiting for the two top foremen to meet with him to discuss his plans for making immediate changes to alleviate some of the suffering endured by the slaves. Maxwell and Gabe entered the study with hats in hand, and Adam waved them over to sit in the two chairs in front of the desk facing him. He looked the men directly in their eyes and got right down to business.

"I need for you to inform the other men that, as of now, they are to secure and supply the slaves with decent food and adequate clothing." The glance the men shared with each other was one of confusion, shock, and something else Adam couldn't read.

"Each slave," he continued, "is to have at least two sets of decent clothing, and a pair of shoes."

The men sat with mouths agape. "Where are we to get food and clothing from?"

"You can start by looking to see what is on hand here at the ranch. Then you can go into town and purchase the other supplies that are needed. Oh, yes, and another thing. You are to furnish the people with seeds and whatever else is necessary to plant and care for a garden."

The men looked at Adam. "Is there anything else?"

Rising from his seat, Adam walked to the window. "Yes. You will shorten their workdays so they have sufficient time to plant and cultivate their own gardens." Adam faced the men. "And something has to be done about their dwellings. They need to be properly built to shelter them from wind and cold, with a stove for warmth and for cooking, and a wooden floor. And furnishings—table, chairs, beds…"

The men looked at each other with raised brows. They were clearly flabbergasted, but when dismissed they quickly left the room to do Adam's bidding.

In the following weeks, Adam visited the slave quarters often to make sure his orders were being carried out.

****

Over the next couple of months, Walt's health deteriorated. It was a great source of concern for him and puzzling for everyone else, since he had been doing so well. Adam arranged for a doctor from Savannah to examine him, and he was diagnosed with a rare heart disease.

Walt died a few weeks later in his sleep.

Adam walked the length of the parlor, one hand stuffed in his vest pocket, the fingers of his other hand combing through his thick brown hair.

"I can't believe it...I just can't believe it! Why would Father leave the ranch to me instead of to Maxwell and Gabe?"

He looked at his wife seated on the settee. "Did you have any idea Maxwell and Gabe wanted to get out of the slave business but only stayed because of their loyalty to Father?"

Kathleen shook her head slightly. "I had no idea."

Adam resumed his pacing. "Father knew we have no desire to live in the South, and he knew how I— we—abhor the institution of slavery."

Kathleen patted the space next to her on the settee. "Honey, please come sit down." Adam slowly walked to the settee, and Kathleen covered his hands with hers. "Honey, I really don't mind staying here for a while"— she rubbed her protruding stomach—"but I will not have our baby born on a slave plantation. I don't care if your father called this place a ranch to appease your mother. It's still a plantation. People are forced to work and are kept here against their will. I don't want our child..." Kathleen's voice faded.

"I don't want that either." Adam brought his wife's hands to his lips. A smile spread across his lips as he looked into Kathleen's eyes. "We have to set the slaves free."

Kathleen smiled in agreement.

****

The rich aroma of coffee swirled through the air, and half-eaten sandwiches and cherry tarts lay abandoned on the silver tray. Adam's and Kathleen's hunched shoulders and bowed heads moved to the rhythm of the squeaky pens that flew across the papers before them. Adam looked up and smiled at his wife when he had written the last word.

"We are going to do this." Kathleen squeezed her husband's hand. "We have to stand up for what is right, no matter what. We know this is the Lord's will. If the Lord sees fit, He will help us through any personal consequences we might face because of the action we are taking today."

Kathleen tightened her hold on Adam's arm when they stepped into the quiet common house in the slave quarters. They were greeted by more than forty bowed heads and tense bodies. Adam cleared his throat, walked to the middle of the room, and held up a bundle of papers.

"We are granting all of you your freedom."

Heads shot up all over the room. No one spoke. Shocked expressions marred faces. Soon low voices filled with excitement, doubts, and confusion reverberated throughout the air. An old woman spoke above the soft noise.

"Master O'Daley?"

Adam held up his hand. "My name is simply Adam O'Daley."

The old woman continued in a shaky tearful voice, "What we 'pose to do? I is old. I ain't got nowheres to go."

Another woman, a little younger, spoke up. "I be slave all me whole life."

Adam heard similar responses throughout the room. He held his hand up.

"Please let me finish telling you about our plans."

Stiff bodies leaned forward on benches, eager to hear what else Adam had to say.

"If you choose to stay here, we will continue to build decent housing with wooden floors and fireplaces for heating and cooking. You will be able to trap your own game and plant gardens. The portion of the cows and hogs we raise will be shared with everyone. Those of you who stay need to understand that we will be working, but as a family. Everyone has to carry his or her own weight. Many of you are skilled laborers, saddle or harness makers, seamstresses, and horse trainers. You will be working to keep this ranch profitable as well as helping yourselves and fellow workers. You will receive wages for your labor, and we plan to open a store so you can buy or trade here, if you wish, or you may do your business in Darin. If you choose not to stay, we will give you money and provisions for your trip."

As soon as Adam finished speaking, high-pitched

conversation erupted in the room.

Kathleen took hold of her husband's hand. "Do you think any will stay?"

"I don't know, honey. If no one stays, we will sell the place and go back home when you are able to travel."

One thin man stood and addressed Adam and his wife.

"I's thankin' ya for what ya wanna do. My wife done been sold. I wanna find hur."

Similar responses were given throughout the room. Some slaves were leaving because they wanted life beyond the South.

At the end of the meeting, Adam and Kathleen still had twenty workers that they would proudly educate on what it meant to live in freedom.

Over the next months, the ranch was a hub of activity. Kathleen gave birth to a healthy baby boy they named Raymon. Construction on the new houses was finished quickly, and so was the establishment of the trade and barter system. The former slaves were getting accustomed to their freedom.

Everything was going just as Adam and Kathleen had planned, until she received a disturbing note from her baby brother. Kathleen flew out of the house, gripping the letter in her hand, as she saw Adam walking up the walkway.

"It's from Lawrence," she said, waving the letter in the air, with tears running down her cheeks.

"What does it say?" Adam rushed to his wife's side.

"He's gotten married to an Elizabeth Bradley, and they're on their way to Philadelphia to meet our folks."

Her body shook from crying.

Adam wrapped her in his arms. "How old is he now, nineteen?"

Kathleen shook her head. "No, he's twenty-one. But he likes adventures, dangers, and being on the move too much to settle down."

"Obviously not any more, darling." Adam chuckled and planted a kiss on his wife's forehead. "Not any more."

Chapter Five

Fear, speculation, and curiosity had dominated the slaves' hushed conversations ever since Miss Elizabeth returned from Savannah six weeks ago with her new husband, the Bradley Plantation's soon-to-be new master. Abby had only peeped at him through thick hedges when he was out at the stable. There was something very familiar about how he stood, his kind voice, his black hair that curled at the end. She had to get a better look at him to satisfy her curiosity. Abby was thinking of the stranger and how she could...

"Abby-girl."

She jumped, dropped the bowl she held, and slapped her hand over her heart.

"I'm sorry, child. You have been as jumpy as a jackrabbit ever since Miss Elizabeth came home with that new husband of hers." Hattie put her hand on her daughter's shoulder. "I know you are wondering what kind of master he will be and will you be safe with him. I have a feeling about that young man—a real good feeling."

Abby smiled.

She wanted to tell her momma that she had a good feeling about the young man too, but she couldn't.

"Abby-girl, after you finish with those herbs, you can take them up to the main house, but not until I make sure they don't have any company up there."

****

Lawrence moved the curtains to one side. "Darling, who did you say lives in the little house surrounded by the trees?"

Elizabeth crawled from her position in bed and went to join Lawrence at the window and peered out.

"Oh, that's where Father's favorite slaves live."

She let the curtain fall back into place and resumed her seat on the bed.

Lawrence frowned. "What do you mean your father's 'favorite' slaves?"

"The healer and her mute, feeble-minded daughter," Elizabeth said, waving her hand in the air.

"So why are they your father's favorite slaves?"

Elizabeth sighed. "The healer saved his life when he was a little boy. If you hear Father tell it, you would think she was sent here by God just to take care of him."

Lawrence pulled a chair closer to the bed and sat down. "Tell me more about your father's angel," he said, smiling.

"There's not much to tell. Father came down with cholera after his family visited Savannah. During that time, few people in this area knew how to treat the sickness. Hattie heard he was dying, and according to Father, she strutted up to the house bold as can be and told his parents that she could heal him."

Lawrence scratched his jaw. "That was a brave move for a slave. How did she heal him?"

Elizabeth hunched her shoulders forward.

"Mainly she had him drink lots of sugar water. Hattie was adamant about cleanliness. Hands had to be washed thoroughly, and everything that touched Father had to be clean."

She looked at her husband, a myriad of emotions passing through her eyes. Lawrence leaned toward her, concern etching his face.

"Is there something else?"

Elizabeth paused. "She prayed. Father said he had never heard anyone pray to God like she did."

"Like what?" Lawrence asked, fingering the silk fabric of her nightgown.

"Like they were friends having a conversation."

"What else happened?"

Elizabeth got a faraway look in her eyes. "She cared for Mother and prayed for her, but she died anyway."

Lawrence took his wife's hands, which had become cold as ice, and gently massaged them with his fingers, but before long Elizabeth rose from the bed to go over and sit at her dressing table. He stayed in his chair by the bed for a while, contemplating what he had just learned about his father-in-law's long-time compassion for a slave and her daughter.

A few minutes later, Lawrence sneaked up behind his wife and planted a kiss on her neck. Elizabeth jerked her head away, rolled her eyes, and used her brush to ward off any further attempts her husband might make in trying to show his early morning affection. Lawrence stood to his full height, shock coloring his features.

"Elizabeth, darling, what is the matter? You have treated me like an unwanted stranger for the last week."

Her wide eyes flashed. She jumped to her feet, almost toppling the chair as she backed away from her husband and bumped into the fireplace mantel.

Breathing heavily, she stared at him. "Leave me alone," she screamed. "Just leave me alone!" Her face turned ashen, and she clenched her fists.

Lawrence's mouth fell open. A sick feeling invaded his stomach. He was speechless as he stared into his wife's vacant eyes. *Oh, Lord, what is happening here? There's that look again. I don't think she knows me.*

He hesitated a moment, then slowly walked to his wife with outstretched arms. He intended to put his arms around her, but thought better of it and returned them to his sides.

"Darling, are you all right?" he asked with as much control as he could muster. "What's wrong?" he asked, in a voice just above a whisper.

Elizabeth covered her face with her hands and sobbed. Lawrence pulled her into his arms and onto the bed, where she cried for a long time. She hiccupped between sobs and wiped tears away with the backs of her hands.

"Lawrence, I love you so much. Please believe me. It's that…it's that sometimes I get a little confused."

"Shh…shh…darling." Lawrence rocked his wife in his arms for a time. He kissed her on the forehead and rubbed her back as she relaxed in his embrace. Finally she lifted her head and kissed her husband with heated passion. The memory of the incident faded into the background as the couple enjoyed a time of sweet intimacy.

****

Lawrence whistled and practically skipped down the stairs as he headed to the study to meet with his friend and solicitor. He found Dave pacing up and down the border of the Oriental rug, leaving a trail of footprints behind in its plush nap and pulling his watch from his pocket to check the time. He had been waiting for Lawrence to make an appearance for almost half an hour. He had stopped pacing and was ready to pour himself another cup of coffee and delight his taste buds with a few more scones when he heard the whistling and heavy footsteps in the hallway, then silence as the whistler stopped at the study's entrance. Dave looked at his friend's flushed cheeks and sparkling eyes and met him halfway across the room, his hand extended, to give him a hearty handshake.

"I see that married life agrees with you, Lawrence, old boy."

A crimson flush crept up Lawrence's neck, and a smile tugged at his lips. It took him a few minutes to regain his composure and voice. He motioned for his friend to sit. "I am sorry I kept you waiting, but I was not expecting you until later. I see you made yourself comfortable while you waited."

Dave grinned and took another scone. "You know these are some of my favorites."

Lawrence laughed and took a seat opposite his friend.

Dave pulled two tickets from his pocket and handed them over. "All the arrangements have been made for you and your bride to travel to Philadelphia."

A wave of sadness washed over Lawrence before he took the tickets and laid them on the table.

"Don't tell me. You still haven't told your family you're married."

"I have, but I should have done it sooner," Lawrence said as he scratched his chin. "I've been a little busy." He raised a brow.

Riotous laughter vibrated throughout the room before Dave's face took on a pensive look. "How are you adjusting to life on the plantation?"

Lawrence leaned his head back to rest it on the high-backed chair.

"I'm a disappointment to Jack. He thought I would take over the plantation one day." Lawrence drummed his fingers on the woodwork that trimmed the upholstered chair.

"Jack was shocked to learn that I loathe slavery and find the institution morally repugnant because of my Christian beliefs."

Dave raised one eyebrow. "Did he give you his best Christian argument supporting slavery?"

Lawrence hunched in his chair, rubbed his long fingers together, and smiled.

"I didn't waver. You know what was strange?" He looked at his friend. "Jack seemed pleased that he couldn't persuade me to change my opinions."

"That's interesting," Dave said, stuffing another scone into his mouth.

Lawrence reached over to move the dessert tray out of Dave's reach, but his friend playfully swatted his hand.

****

Abby hugged herself with anticipation as Momma Hattie told her it was safe to deliver herbs to the cook. She swallowed back a laugh just thinking about getting a chance to see if the boy she'd seen a few years ago was indeed their new master. She wiped sweat from her palms and grabbed the kitchen doorknob. Her heart drummed in her chest as she stepped into the kitchen to deliver the herbs. She put them on the worktable, looked around to see if anyone was watching her, and then sneaked out a door that took her into a short hallway.

She tried to calm the butterflies fluttering in her stomach and relax her frozen muscles as she stood in the hallway trying to decide what direction to go. To the left she saw the huge oak-trimmed stairway. To the right she saw a big room with a large table and an overhead candelabra.

Her eyes grew wide with indecision, and fear swept over her. *What if I get caught? What will I say?* Then she relaxed, a smile tugging at her lips; she would say nothing. No one expected her to say anything. For all anyone knew, she was mute and unable to speak.

Feeling a bit calmer, she chose to go left until she found herself in another hallway. This hallway was longer, with several doors opening into it. Her heart sped up, and perspiration formed above her top lip. She wiped it away to keep it from running into her mouth. She wanted to go back, but her feet kept taking her forward as swift and silent as a cat. She peered into one room, then another, until she came to a partially closed door. She peeked through the crack, and there he stood, his long fingers clasped behind his lean straight back, his broad strong shoulders relaxed before her eyes. She willed him to turn around so she could look into those sparkling black eyes; at least she hoped they were clear black eyes. Her chest tightened when she heard soft footsteps descending the stairs and a feminine voice calling for Lawrence. Her eyes lit up as she repeated the name to herself. She was momentarily paralyzed with joy—until Lawrence turned in her direction and she realized she had to get out of there, and fast. The voice behind her was getting closer. She turned slightly and saw a door right in front of her but several yards away. Without thinking, she dashed for the door, hoping it would lead her outside.

Lawrence met Elizabeth in the hallway. He tapped the tickets on her upturned nose.

"Are you ready for our wedding trip? Dave has made all the arrangements for us to go to Philadelphia."

"I am ready to go anywhere with you, my love." Elizabeth kissed her husband on the cheek.

****

Within two weeks, Lawrence and Elizabeth stood on the deck of the steamboat *Orion*, heading for Philadelphia to celebrate their wedding with Lawrence's parents and friends. He hoped enough time had passed for them to have accepted his hasty marriage.

Once the boat was underway, the couple followed the steward down the hallway to their room. Lawrence's eyes gleamed when the door to their cabin was opened and he looked around.

"Dave, you old dog, you," Lawrence said, just above a whisper, as he took in the large bed, three vases of red roses, and a tray of scones on the small table between the two high-backed leather chairs. Elizabeth pushed past him and entered the room. She turned slowly, taking in the room.

"Is this it?" she asked, her palms turned upward.

"I can't stay in this place for two weeks." She accented each word with a sharp jolt of her hands.

"Dave got this room especially for us. He thought we would love it."

"Dave? What does he know about what I would love? And who is Dave, anyway? Another one of your mysterious friends?"

"Elizabeth, you know Dave."

She held up her hand. "I tell you, I will not stay in this..."

"Elizabeth, I know this is not as elegant as you are used to, but this will be fine for two weeks."

"You'd think anything is nice after sleeping in a tent and out under the stars for so long."

Lawrence raised his hands, intending to place them on his wife's shoulders.

She slapped them away, stamped her feet on the floor, and screamed, "I'm not staying in this tiny awful place! Do you hear me?"

Lawrence stared at his bride with an open mouth and wide eyes. Confusion and disbelief clouded his face. He wondered what had happened to his sweet wife. The steward's face showed concern but quickly returned to normal as he set down the bags he was carrying and backed out the door to give the couple some privacy.

"Elizabeth, darling, calm down." Lawrence spoke in a soft voice, his arms outstretched.

Elizabeth hesitated, then slowly walked into his embrace and wept softly on his shoulder, but her complaints later grew so strong that Lawrence decided to take her on a tour of the first-class accommodations. She saw there was little difference in room sizes or furnishings. Some of her complaining stopped, but she remained irritable and moody. He had become accustomed to her mood swings, and usually his soothing words, caresses, and kisses were enough to

ease her melancholy, but now they were unwelcome—
and so was he. Nevertheless, he waited on her, hand
and foot, to ensure she had a pleasant trip.

He was glad when the journey was finally over and
they safely arrived in Philadelphia. He had decided to
hire someone to take care of his wife during their stay.
Taking care of Elizabeth would be too much for his
mother and the regular servants.

Lawrence's heart raced like a thoroughbred's
heading for the finish line when the carriage pulled up
to his childhood home.

"Oh, Lawrence, the Bradley mansion looks like a
cottage compared to this."

"I hope you will find it comfortable."

He rubbed his sweaty palms on his trousers before
he helped his wife from the carriage and escorted her to
the door. He stood at the door for a moment, wishing
his heartbeat would return to normal before he stepped
over the threshold.

Elizabeth looked at him and smiled. "You do live
here, don't you?"

"Very funny," Lawrence said, giving his wife a
sideways smirk as he pushed the door open. No one
was there. He resisted the urge to yell. He patted his
wife's fingers on his arm and headed for the parlor.

As soon as they entered the room, cheers and
congratulations erupted from the crowd of family
members and servants gathered there. Lawrence gave a
hearty laugh and accepted the handshakes, slaps on the
back, and playful shoving and pushing that followed.
He kissed his mother, shook his father's hand, and
presented his wife to them.

"Mother and Father, I would like for you to meet

my bride, the former Elizabeth Bradley of Mason, Georgia."

Elizabeth was the picture of elegance and refinement as she conversed with her in-laws and other family members. Lawrence was relieved.

"We are so pleased to finally meet you." Mr. Mallory gave his new daughter-in-law a peck on the cheek.

"We wished we could have attended the wedding," Mrs. Mallory said in a stiff tone as she took Elizabeth's hand in hers.

Lawrence glanced at his mother with a slightly raised brow. Elizabeth smiled and threaded her arm around her husband's forearm before she was introduced to Lawrence's older sister, Lauren, and her husband. The couple chatted with the guests for a time, until Mr. Mallory cleared his throat.

"Let's allow the happy couple to rest a bit after their long trip. You're all invited to the after-dinner celebration." He shook his son's hand. "We can catch up later."

"I had your old room prepared for the two of you," Lawrence's mother injected. The couple expressed their thanks to everyone. As he turned to go upstairs, Lawrence whispered to his wife, "If you don't like the room, we can move somewhere else." His mother frowned at the words.

The couple made their way upstairs to Lawrence's old bedroom, where Elizabeth stepped into the large room first.

"This is lovely," she said.

"It looks like Mother has been busy redecorating."

"You mean you didn't like floral designs when you

were growing up?" Elizabeth tried to stuff back a laugh.

"Do you like it?" Lawrence held his breath. "We can move to another room."

"I wouldn't dare, after your mother has gone to so much trouble for us."

He smiled and released the breath he was holding.

****

Early the next morning, Lawrence went searching for his mother.

"Oh, here you are, Mother." He walked into the salon and gave his mother a kiss on the cheek as she thumbed through a stack of papers on the table.

"May I have a word with you?"

"This must be important, for you to leave your bride this early in the morning."

Lawrence smiled as he took the chair across from her in the solarium.

"I need to hire a servant girl to take care of Elizabeth while we are here." Confusion clouded his mother's features.

"What on earth for? We have plenty of help here."

"I know, but Elizabeth likes to be pampered."

"All right, then, I'll see to it right away." Mrs. Mallory slowly put her cup of tea down.

By that afternoon, the new servant girl was busy helping Elizabeth dress and undress, draw her bath water, style her hair, and whatever else she desired help with. Elizabeth seemed happy, and Lawrence was relieved. He had his playful sweetheart back, and he was enjoying the benefits of married life once again.

The couple spent the next few weeks enjoying all the entertainment, private parties, and teas that the wealthy engaged in. Mrs. Mallory and her daughter

Lauren busied themselves planning an elaborate party to celebrate the couple's marriage—until Lawrence intervened. He approached his mother in her study one morning.

"Mother, I know you mean well, and I don't want to disappoint you, but will you consider scaling the party down to a few close family friends?"

Mrs. Mallory bowed her head and fidgeted with the invitations on her desk.

"Mother, I know this means a lot to you since you didn't attend the...well, you know, but Elizabeth is exhausted."

His mother looked at him with relief in her eyes.

"That might explain it," she said, letting out a huge breath.

"That might explain what, Mother?"

"Elizabeth attended one of my charity fundraising meetings with me a few days ago," she said, fingering the pearl necklace around her neck. "I guess...well, I knew after the first two meetings that she was probably not interested." She paused and looked up at her son with moisture in her eyes.

"I left her for a short time, the other day, to chat with some friends. When I returned, she was seated in her chair, just rocking back and forth. When I touched her, she looked confused, and for a time, Lawrence"— she gulped air—"I don't think she recognized me."

Lawrence grimaced and took his mother's hand in his.

"Will you cut back on the number of people for the party for me, Mother?"

Mrs. Mallory slowly nodded. He gave her a quick smile and immediately left the room.

Not being able to host a grand party for her son was a big disappointment, but Mrs. Mallory honored her son's wishes and limited the party to a hundred close family friends. The evening of the party, Elizabeth was a picture of charm and grace. She was the belle of the ball and was having great fun. Lawrence was relieved and happy that everything was going so well.

After that, Elizabeth was her old self again, and Lawrence started going to the office with his father several mornings during the week. One afternoon as he entered the house, he heard Elizabeth screaming and things crashing. He rushed up the stairs to their bedroom. He saw pieces of a broken dish, a few books, and some dry toast on the floor. His eyes locked on two figures cowering in the corner—his mother and the servant girl. Their arms covered their faces.

"What in tarnation is going on here, Elizabeth?"

She dropped the vase in her hand and stared at Lawrence, then dissolved toward the floor. He scooped her up in his arms before her head made contact with the rug, and gently laid her on their bed. The servant girl and Mrs. Mallory still hugged each other as they made their way over to her.

"Are you two all right?" Lawrence asked as he embraced his mother and gave the servant girl a searching look. They could only nod their heads, still in shock and confusion, but at his request the girl left the room to summon the doctor.

The muscles in Lawrence's jaw twitched as he gazed at his wife's sleeping form on the bed. Mrs. Mallory rubbed her son's arm as she spoke.

"Elizabeth was not feeling well, so Sara brought

tea and toast up to her. When she entered the room, Elizabeth started screaming for her to get out and started throwing things. I was on my way to my room when I heard the commotion and rushed in to see Elizabeth attacking Sara. I tried to break it up by talking softly to her, but she got more agitated. We ended up in the corner where you found us."

Lawrence hugged his mother tightly.

"Thank God you are not hurt."

Mrs. Mallory pulled a blanket up to cover Elizabeth before she addressed her son.

"What exactly is wrong with Elizabeth? What she did was totally unjustified and truly scary. How well…"

Lawrence's lips tightened.

"Just stop right there, Mother," Lawrence said, his hand up. "I will take care of Elizabeth. She will be all right. She is just a little high strung."

As Lawrence uttered the words, he didn't believe them himself. But what else could he tell his mother?

Elizabeth was awake and back to her old self by the time the doctor arrived. She refused to be examined. She told him she was just overly tired and had allowed her temper to get the best of her. She apologized profusely to Mrs. Mallory and Sara and asked for their forgiveness for frightening them. They accepted her apology but had difficulty believing fatigue was the only reason for her volatile behavior. They felt her problem was much more serious than that.

Elizabeth was the picture of charm and grace for the next few days, but Lawrence knew that all was not well with his sweet wife. Apparently, his mother and father felt the same way. In the parlor one evening, after Elizabeth had gone up to bed, his parents expressed their concerns about her health.

Mr. Mallory crossed and uncrossed his legs, cleared his throat several times, and finally spoke.

"Son, your mother and I are concerned about Elizabeth's behavior. Your poor mother is almost afraid to be alone with her." He pulled his wife close to his side. "Sara is talking about quitting. We just can't have another episode like we had a few days ago. Things might turn out differently next time." He paused, then asked, "Has she behaved like that before?"

Lawrence blinked his eyes rapidly, but he said nothing.

"We just want to make sure Elizabeth is all right, for everyone's sake," his mother added softly, touching her son's hand. Lawrence got up from his chair and began pacing back and forth, running his fingers through his hair as he walked.

"I think we would all feel better if we knew what was wrong with her, and having a doctor examine her will ease everyone's mind and let us know how we can help her," Mr. Mallory added.

"You can send for your doctor, but we're leaving at the end of the week," Lawrence stated, and left the room without looking back.

In a few days the doctor came to examine Elizabeth; he gave her a good report. A week later, the couple was on their way home, with one stipulation— Elizabeth was to get plenty of rest.

****

Frustration over Elizabeth's health plagued Lawrence day and night. Ever since they had returned to the Bradley Plantation, she'd had little appetite and often complained of fatigue. Lawrence tried his best to get his wife to eat, even attempting to force feed her. He was at his wit's ends when his father-in-law suggested that Elizabeth be examined by the healer.

Furrows formed between Lawrence's brows as he sat on the bed with his wife's head in his lap, wrapping strands of her cinnamon-colored hair around his finger. He caught sight of the full bowl of soup on the bedside table. He had tried for hours to get his wife to take a spoonful, but she had refused, saying she was too tired to eat. Remnants of his own ham sandwich beckoned to be finished as his stomach growled, but he dared not move a muscle in fear that his wife might awaken. He was relieved she had finally fallen asleep.

****

"Since you have been worried about the new master, I want you to go with me to the big house."

Abby mouthed, "Why?"

"It seems Miss Elizabeth took ill on her wedding trip, and her daddy wants me to examine her. Put all of those things in my kit," Hattie said, pointing to the herbs and potions she had placed on the worktable. As Abby carefully put all the things into the kit, she could feel the excitement rumbling inside her. She would finally be able to see the master up close. Her hands stilled at the thought. *Suppose he saw me running from the house and recognized me?* Her face turned ashen, her legs grew weak, and she grabbed hold of the edge of the table, upsetting some of the herbs.

"Abby-girl, are you all right?" Hattie rushed to her daughter's side and touched her forehead with the back of her hand.

"You don't seem to have a fever."

Abby sank down in the kitchen chair.

"But let's not take any chances. You just stay here and get some rest, and I'll be back as soon as I can."

****

Lawrence watched the old woman as she carefully examined his wife. He was impressed by the questions she asked and her attentiveness as she listened to Elizabeth's responses. He thought he noticed something pass over her face when Elizabeth answered some of the questions, but before he could examine it more carefully, Hattie interrupted his thinking with instructions on how to care for Elizabeth.

"I will leave this tonic with you." She gave him two brown bottles.

"Give her a spoonful of this three times a day, and this one"—she pointed to the other bottle—"rub this potion on her and massage her limbs several times a day, especially before bed. I will leave the cook some herbs to add to her food. Miss Elizabeth, you should be fine in a few days." Hattie patted her hand and left the room.

Chapter Six

Lawrence settled into a leisurely routine at the Bradley Plantation. He spent his days going over various documents and papers his solicitors had sent concerning his various business ventures. He discussed politics with his father-in-law, and he spent far too much time reminiscing about his life as an explorer and writer. He was just about to have his midafternoon tea when the butler entered the parlor with a letter addressed to him in a very familiar female script. He was excited to see it was from his sister Kathleen and her husband Adam. Opening it quickly, he read the updates about his nephew Raymon, and about Walt's death, and his eyes bulged and his mouth went slack. He bolted from his chair. "I can't believe it!"

"What's wrong?" Jack said from the other side of the room.

"My sister and her husband are slave owners. Adam's father passed away and left the slave ranch to him and my sister Kathleen."

As Lawrence continued to read the letter, a slow smile formed on his lips. Jack leaned forward in his seat.

"What is it?"

He looked at Jack and blew out a loud breath. "Kathleen and Adam have freed the slaves, and many now work for them as ranch hands and skilled

Linda H. Bost

laborers." He chortled. "Now, that's the sister I know and love."

Jack was incredulous and couldn't believe he'd heard Lawrence correctly. "They freed their slaves?"

"They don't believe in slavery. It's a diabolical system, really." Lawrence put the letter back into the envelope.

"They took a bold stand to free their slaves in the South," Jack said, staring out the window.

Lawrence cleared his throat.

"There's more."

He walked over to place a hand on the fireplace mantel as he looked at Jack.

"They want me and Elizabeth to come and live on the Double-O Ranch to help with bookkeeping and managing the trade and barter system they have adopted for the workers."

Jack rubbed his chin and looked across the room. "What are you going to do?"

Lawrence shook his head. "I don't know yet. I had hoped we would settle in Philadelphia or somewhere up north, but I don't know." He scratched his chin.

Jack rose and went to his son-in-law and laid a hand on his shoulder.

"You have a lot to think about, my boy." He left the room without looking back.

Lawrence knew what Jack said was true. He did have a lot to think about. The possibilities and opportunities Adam and Kathleen were offering him were answers to prayer—a chance to do meaningful work again. He pulled the letter from his pocket and slapped it against his palm as he walked back and forth across the floor contemplating what to do.

60

"Do I take a chance and go to Darin, Georgia, or do I stay here? Here? Here, I am slowly becoming a man of leisure—living a luxurious lifestyle on a slave plantation, of all places."

He snorted. He stopped in his tracks. Then, with a gleam in his eyes, he ran upstairs, taking two steps at a time.

Elizabeth was dressed in her riding habit and sitting at her dressing table. Her maid was arranging her hair when Lawrence entered the room.

"Are you ready to go now, darling?"

"Give me a few more minutes, and I'll be ready."

"Don't rush. I have something I want to discuss with you before we go riding."

"It must be good news, the way you are smiling." Elizabeth's eyes danced with delight as she looked at her husband through the mirror. When the maid had finished with her hair and left the room, Elizabeth turned to face her husband, who was now sitting on the end of their bed. "What's the good news?"

"I received a letter from my sister and brother-in-law today." He pulled the letter from his pocket and looked into his wife's bright eyes.

"They have offered me a job on their ranch, the Double-O." He tried to read the expression on his wife's face, but it remained neutral. He continued, "You will have your own beautiful house with elegant gardens and fountains to keep you busy." Elizabeth turned, stared at herself in the mirror, and said nothing. Lawrence twisted the ring on his finger as he waited for her to respond. He gave her his brightest smile as he looked at her in the mirror from his seat on the bed.

Finally she spoke. "Is the house near the smelly

cows? I don't think I could tolerate that smell day in and day out." Lawrence let out a roaring laugh as he walked over and knelt beside his wife.

"Darling, you will not have to worry about smelly cows. Adam is in the horse business. He breeds, trains, and sells horses. He also makes and sells harnesses and saddles. The finest, I understand."

"Oh," she said shyly, pausing for a few minutes before adding, "I think we should go."

Lawrence was surprised that his wife seemed genuinely happy about the idea.

"I look forward to having our own home and meeting your other sister and brother-in-law. I hope Kathleen and I will become great friends…a sister I never had."

Lawrence pulled his wife into his lap.

"Are you sure you want to do this, Elizabeth? What about leaving your father?"

"Oh, darling," she said, cupping her hand around his chin. "My place is with you—my husband."

He kissed his wife soundly. "Are you ready to go for our ride now?" Elizabeth smiled. The two left the room hand in hand, and he had a skip in his step as they made their way outside.

When the couple was leaving the stable, Lawrence caught a glimpse of Jack ducking into the little white two-story house where Elizabeth had said Jack's favorite slaves lived.

"I do know one thing. There's something strange going on here," Lawrence muttered under his breath.

"Did you say something?" Elizabeth asked as she kicked her horse in the side and raced by him.

****

Jack hummed as he entered the house, grabbing hold of Hattie and Abby by their arms. "God has answered our prayers! Lawrence and my little Lizzie are moving to the Double-O Ranch, a slave-free place owned by his brother-in-law and sister, and you two are going with them."

Hattie beamed, and her dim eyes lit up. "Praise God!" she yelled. Abby swallowed the laughter rising in her throat.

"Sit down and let me tell you the plan," Jack said with a wink.

****

Looking around to make sure Lawrence was alone; Jack stepped out onto the terrace, strolled over, and sat in the chair across from him. He mopped his face with his handkerchief and wished he had rehearsed the tale he was about to share with his son-in-law.

"Lawrence…um…uh…I want to talk to you about going to Darin."

Lawrence looked at his father-in-law.

"Elizabeth has been doing so well ever since Hattie's been giving her those herbs and massages. Wouldn't it be a shame if the treatment stopped and Elizabeth had a setback?"

Lines formed between Lawrence's brows, and he leaned forward to stare into Jack's eyes, thinking to himself, *I know you are not going to tell me we should stay here.*

Jack cleared his throat, caught the lemonade glass he was about to knock over, and rushed the words past his lips. "I would like to send Hattie and her daughter with you to help care for Lizzie and make sure she stays healthy."

Lawrence leaned back in his chair with a puzzled look on his face.

"You are willing to let two slaves go, just like that?" Lawrence snapped his finger.

Jack gave a quick smile and wiped away sweat from his face and neck. "Yes, I can. Hattie is too old to be of use in the fields, and her daughter—well, being the way she is, needs her mother."

Lawrence studied Jack's face. The man appeared nervous but otherwise sincere. "They can go. But understand they will have to be set free."

"I know. I know there are no slaves on the Double-O." Jack rubbed his chin. "Let's not mention this to Elizabeth. I want to surprise her."

"Okay," Lawrence agreed with a frown. Jack let out a booming laugh, shook Lawrence's hand, and trotted inside smiling.

****

The long-anticipated day finally arrived when Lawrence, Elizabeth, and those accompanying them would leave Mason to start their new lives in Darin, Georgia. Lawrence walked into the kitchen, looking for Jack, with a skip in his step and a whistle on his lips, and then froze. His wife stood with hands on hips and her nose inches from her father's.

"If you are going to send slaves with us, why can you not send Evelyn? She has been my personal maid since I was very young. I don't understand why you insist upon sending an old woman who can barely walk and a scrawny little girl who can't talk. It doesn't make any sense, Father. I will not take them!"

Jack embraced Elizabeth, rubbing her back as if comforting a fussy infant.

"Now, now, honey," he said, wiping away her tears with the ball of his fingertip. "If you become overly tired like you did when you went to Philadelphia, they will know exactly what to do. I am just thinking of my sweet girl."

Jack planted a kiss on her forehead and held her for a long time. As Lawrence backed out through the door, he heard Elizabeth give a loud sigh. "All right, Father, you are right. The herbs, special vitamins, and massages have helped me. Hattie and the girl can come with us."

Lawrence blew out a breath. He was glad hysteria had been avoided.

Lawrence looked out the window in the study while he waited for Jack to give him the freedom papers for Hattie and her daughter. He agreed with Elizabeth— there was more to Jack's story about why he wanted Hattie and her daughter to go with them than what he was saying. Elizabeth's personal maid could have been trained to care for her, giving her the right herbs, vitamins, and massages.

He rubbed his jaw and paced the room as his mind raced through possible reasons Jack might have for sending them away. "Let's see," he said out loud. "Jack is willing to let the old woman go and grant her freedom because she is no longer able to do hard physical work. But she seems well respected and accepted as a healer here," he countered to himself as he slipped behind the big mahogany desk.

"Wouldn't he need someone like her around? Now her daughter..." He tapped his fingers on the desk. "Elizabeth said that girl is mute and mentally challenged." Lawrence pushed away from the desk to give his long legs some room. "What about breeding?" He shivered at the word. "Some slave owners do it to increase their population. Does this girl have a condition that makes her unfit to be married and have children, or something else that makes her worthless to a slave owner? If so, then why has Jack kept her this long?"

Before he could analyze that thought, Jack burst into the room, whistling a happy tune. "Didn't mean to keep you waiting, Lawrence, my boy. I'll get those papers for you." Jack went over to the bookcase, pulled out a big red bound book, flipped through a few pages, and took from between them an envelope. He replaced the book and handed Lawrence the envelope.

"Jack, I meant to ask you about the girl…"

"Don't worry about it. I'm sending Eli to help you with my girls. Oh, and I have one more matter to take care of before you leave." He spoke over his shoulder as he rushed from the room.

A frown distorted Lawrence's face. "*His girls?*…and Eli the stable boy?"

Lawrence flew from the room to find Jack. He wanted some answers. When he reached the hallway, noise from the outside stopped him in his tracks. He heard Elizabeth complaining to the servants about the number of trunks and bags in the wagon. He thought, "Please, God, no!"

"Lawrence," Jack called from the porch. "I have one last thing for you." Jack looked at Lawrence, who was running his hands through his hair, a pained look on his face.

"Don't worry about the servants. They can help Elizabeth for a bit longer. I want to make sure you have enough funds to take care of my daughter"—he smiled brightly—"and her guests."

He offered Lawrence a big wad of cash, but Lawrence shook his head.

"Jack, I don't need your money."

"Ridiculous," he said. "Everyone needs money."

"I can take care of Elizabeth." Lawrence smiled and added, "And her guests, a thousand times over. I have means."

"Very well, but consider this and the money I have deposited in an account for you and Elizabeth as another wedding gift."

"But…" Jack stopped him before he could finish his sentence.

"Take it, and let's not speak of it again."

Lawrence took the money and put it in his pocket.

Jack took his hand and squeezed it. "Lawrence, you are a fine young man. The finest. That's why I can trust you with my girls."

The commotion grew louder, and both Lawrence and Jack made their way to the wagon. A servant held a bag that had been tossed from the wagon. Elizabeth settled herself in her seat. Jack went around to her to say his final goodbye.

"Where are my other guests?" Lawrence asked, grinning as he climbed into his seat. "We don't want to miss our boat."

Then his mouth went slack and his eyes widened. He took in a gulp of air. Heading for the wagon was the old woman, and clutching her arm was a slight girl, a white girl, her complexion that of one who had been kissed lightly by the sun. Lawrence's words got stuck in his throat. He could only stare at the pair. Jack quickly helped the two into the back of the wagon and signaled for the driver to go. Lawrence's narrowed eyes met Jack's as the wagon pulled away from the house. Anger burned in his belly like hot ashes. What was Jack up to? That girl was no more that old woman's daughter than he was the King of Persia. Lawrence jerked his head around and gripped his seat. Curiosity and anger consumed him. He kept glancing back at the girl. *Could she be..? She...must be! Jack's daughter?* If so, that would explain why she and the old lady stayed in a nice house and spent almost all their time preparing herbs and remedies. The furrow between his brows grew deeper when he recalled that his wife had referred to the two as her father's favorites. Lawrence's thoughts were interrupted by Elizabeth's loud sighs and shifting in her seat.

Abby bit her bottom lip and squeezed Hattie's hand. She could feel Mr. Mallory's angry eyes on her and her momma. His deep, clear, midnight-black eyes were clouded with anger, but Abby would have recognized them anywhere. They belonged to the young man she had met at the creek so long ago—Lawrence. Hattie covered Abby's hands with hers and began singing a hymn, ignoring Lawrence's questioning eyes. Abby slowly released her grip on Hattie's hand. She didn't care about the anger on her new master's face; she knew anyone could be upset by being tricked the way he had been. But she was determined to enjoy her new experience. Mr. Jack had told her she didn't have to hang her head or drool anymore. Her insides quivered with the thought.

As their belongings were being transferred to the boat, Lawrence noticed Eli's bulging muscles flexing even when not in use. Jack had sent him as a protector, obviously. Lawrence shook his head. Anyone would be a fool to tangle with this giant of a man. Lawrence blew air out from between his teeth. Why would Jack want to give up someone like him?

Once they were on their way, Lawrence sat so he could observe the girl and her mother without being conspicuous. They cuddled so close; he doubted air could pass between them. When the boat swayed, the girl gripped the rail so hard her knuckles turned white. Her mother spoke to her, and she raised her head and slowly released her death grip on the rail.

Abby swallowed a giggle. The sheer joy of being out and tasting a bit of freedom made it almost impossible for her to stay still, but she did. Hattie and Eli had promised Jack they would not answer any questions Lawrence might have about her or allow him to get close to her until they were on the Double-O Ranch, and only then when they felt the time was right. Abby had known deep down that Lawrence could be trusted, from the moment she first saw him years ago. She hung her head in shame when she heard him ask Eli about her, and Eli shook his head and moved away. She knew he wanted to ask Momma Hattie something, but she never left her side long enough for him to make any inquiries.

Lawrence stood on the deck and looked around at his motley crew: an old woman who been on the Bradley Plantation since she was a girl, a mute and mentally challenged girl, and a strong quiet young man about his own age, who exuded confidence and wisdom. As far as Lawrence knew, none of them had been off the plantation before. He shook his head. A laugh escaped his lips as he bent forward over the rail. His thoughts were interrupted by his wife's loud voice. He was glad he'd made arrangements to secure the boat for his private use only. He turned to go to her but heard Hattie say in a soft voice, "Hush, child, let's get you downstairs for a nap and give that husband of yours a little rest. He's been waiting on you hand and foot ever since you left home."

Lawrence mouthed a thank you to Hattie and the girl. *The girl...* He lowered his head in shame. He hadn't bothered to ask Hattie her name. He looked at his wife as the women made their way to the cabin below. She had been sullen, cross, and complaining from the time they left the dock in Mason, and Hattie's ministrations did little to change that, even after they pulled in to the dock near Darin.

When the group finally arrived on the Double-O Ranch, Lawrence heard an intake of breath behind him and, turning found his wife's eyes and face gleamed. It was clear she was dazzled by the beauty of the place. His heart thumped as the wagon jostled up the drive. His sister's and brother-in-law's hands danced in the air with greetings as they stepped from the porch, and Lawrence bounced from the wagon before it came to a full stop.

"Lawrence, Lawrence!" Kathleen squealed as she picked up her skirt and ran into her brother's arms. He kissed her cheek and twirled her around, sending her skirt billowing in the air. He grabbed Adam's hand and slapped him on the back after he set his sister back on the ground.

"Glad you got here safely," Adam said, squeezing Lawrence's hand as he shook it. "We want to hear all about your adventures, but right now we want to meet your beautiful bride and your other guests."

The couple followed Lawrence to the wagon.

"Adam and Kathleen, I would like for you to meet my bride, the former Elizabeth Bradley." Elizabeth bowed her head in greeting.

"This is a magnificent place. Thank you for inviting us to come live here."

"These are our guests," Lawrence said with chagrin. "Hattie, her daughter…"

"Abby." Hattie supplied her name.

"And this is Eli," he finished.

A few pleasantries were exchanged before Kathleen interjected, "Lawrence, you need to get your wife and your guests home to rest and unpack. The house has been cleaned, and food has been prepared for everyone. We hope you will find everything in perfect order."

"You always think of everything, sis. Thank you." He kissed his sister on the cheek.

The group followed the road down to their home, and Elizabeth held her husband's arm tightly.

"Oh, Lawrence, the house is beautiful. It's a bit small, but we can make it work."

"I promise you, sweet wife," Lawrence said, tapping the end of her nose as his guests exited the wagon, "when we start a family, I will add on to it."

Sadness clouded her features. "I am sorry," she said, pressing one hand to her chest.

"Sorry about what?" Lawrence pulled his wife close to his side.

"For not giving you any children," she said softly, sucking on her bottom lip.

"Oh, sweetheart, don't think like that. When God is ready for us to have children, he will bless us with some."

"But we have been married eight months, and I know how much you want children."

"When the time is right, sweetheart, God may bless us with a dozen children. If he does," he said, twitching her nose, "you are not to complain."

Elizabeth laughed and kissed her husband's lips. "I am the luckiest girl on earth."

"Yes, you are." Lawrence helped her down from the wagon.

Chapter Seven

Lawrence absentmindedly tapped the pencil on the desk, his mind reviewing the details of his first month on the Double-O Ranch and the speed at which it had flown by. He rested his hands behind his head and leaned back in his chair. He still couldn't believe the ease with which Elizabeth had established a routine for the household, plus going horseback riding and visiting with Kathleen and the baby. He smiled when he pictured the shocked looks on the faces of his guests when he told them they would be earning wages for performing their duties in their new home.

He left his chair to walk over and stare out the window. Furrows formed between his brows as he puzzled over his own duties and responsibilities. He had been excited when Adam first asked him about using his knowledge of business to help the ranch turn a profit. He knew that wouldn't be a big challenge for him. He had created a successful business model for his father's floundering businesses when he was fifteen. All his business enterprises were using a version of that model today and turning huge profits every year. But what he hadn't counted on was going on business trips for this new venture. Adam had laughed when he voiced his objections to traveling and being away from his wife. He'd slapped him on the back, assuring him that his feelings were normal and every newly married husband felt the same way he did about leaving his bride. Now Lawrence blew out a breath and whispered, "If you only knew, brother Adam." He rocked on his heels in thought as he looked out the window. Elizabeth was enjoying life right now. But knowing what had happened in Philadelphia, Lawrence was sure the chances of that holding true in the future were very slim. He shuddered when he thought of his wife's behavior while visiting his parents. She had been irritable, demanding, and…frightening. He whispered a prayer that her present excitement and contentment about life wasn't a false euphoria. He threw the pencil back on the desk. "I have four people I am responsible for, but here I am talking to myself."

Lawrence stood at the stable door and watched Elizabeth as she walked alongside Hattie and Abby in the garden. He shook his head. He never thought he would see the day his wife would work alongside her former slaves and get her hands dirty, but there she was with a smile on her face. He gave her an enthusiastic wave when she turned around. She waved back and made her way over to him.

Behind her, Hattie muttered, "If that child had stayed here a minute longer, I was going to take her in the house myself. Hmph! The nerve of her, trying to show us how to plant flowers like we don't know what we are doing."

In reply, Abby giggled at her mother's impatience.

"You know what, Abby-girl? I think it's high time we talk to Mr. Lawrence. It's not right that we've been here for over a month and told him nothing." Abby nodded her head in agreement.

"Besides," Hattie added, giving her daughter's

hand a squeeze, "we don't want these good people to think there is something really wrong with you. You are free now to live the life I have dreamed for you."

At the stable, Elizabeth greeted her husband with a kiss, pulled her gloves off, and deposited them in the basket on her arm.

"Dinner will be ready in an hour," she said as she headed for the house. She had started serving her husband his meals, saying it was what a good wife did. Lawrence offered no complaints.

During dinner, Elizabeth stared at the pictures on the wall and turned up her nose. "Lawrence, do you think it will be all right if I make some changes to the house? Father has sent some of Mother's things, and I would like to add them…"

Lawrence kissed his wife's hand. "Darling, this is your home. You can do what you like to it."

"Oh, Lawrence, you are so good to me." She took his hand and cradled it to her cheek.

"Sweetheart, you remember I will be leaving for Rome, Georgia, in a few days on our business trip?"

She nodded. "Eli is going with you."

"Yes. We'll be gone for almost two weeks."

Elizabeth wove her fingers through her husband's. "I will be just fine. I have a lot to do to keep me busy, rearranging the house and getting ready for our first dinner party when you get back."

Lawrence let out a sigh. "Darling, won't you wait until a few days after I get back to have the party?"

Elizabeth snatched her hand from Lawrence's. "No! I'd set the date before you decided to go out of town on your old business trip, and I will not change it."

A line of muscles twitched in her husband's jaw.

****

Lawrence stared out across the room as Adam went over the details of their upcoming buying trip first and then the plans for a proposed general store on the property. "Many of the black ranch hands still don't feel comfortable leaving here other than for occasional trips to nearby farms on Sundays. Kathleen and I thought starting a general store for them would be a good idea. That way they don't have to go into town unless they want to. We will stock everything from sweets to small furniture." Adam pulled a piece of paper from the desk drawer. "Take a look at the list we put together." Adam held the paper out to Lawrence, who made no effort to take it. "Lawrence, are you listening?"

The sound of Adam's voice brought him out of his trance. He looked at his brother-in-law with a lopsided smile. "I'm afraid you caught me." Lawrence stood and walked the length of the study several times with his hands in his pockets before he continued. "Adam, I just can't figure out that girl."

Adam frowned. "You mean Hattie's daughter?"

"She's supposed to be mute and mentally challenged, yet she seems alert, and follows explicit directions without fail." Lawrence took a seat across from his brother-in-law and leaned forward in his chair. "I have seen her and Hattie with their heads together as if they are engaging in conversation." He looked at Adam. "And there's another thing. Sometimes she appears to be just a kid, but other times, with certain mannerisms, she seems a lot older. Have you seen those ridiculous black gloves she wears?" Lawrence said, pacing the floor again.

Adam leaned back in his chair. "Wouldn't you expect a mother to learn to communicate with her own daughter?"

"Now, Adam." Lawrence looked at his brother-in-law through slit eyes. "You know as well as I do there's no way Hattie is that girl's mother, old as she is."

Adam rubbed his chin thoughtfully. "Do you know who her parents are?"

Lawrence flopped down in his chair and shook his head. "I thought maybe it was Jack, but now I'm not sure."

A servant entered the room with a tray of refreshments. Adam motioned for him to place the tray on the table by the settee. He gave the servant a nod and smile as he left the room. "If you are this concerned, why don't you just ask Hattie?"

Lawrence got up from his chair and began pacing. "That's the thing. They avoid me at all cost. I don't know whether it's by design or by coincidence."

He rubbed the back of his neck and let out a whistle. He wanted to tell Adam that he was sure he had met that girl somewhere before. The way she held her head, with her nose tilted up like she was royalty, was familiar to him, but he didn't want Adam to think he had become obsessed with her and observed her every move. But he had. He swiped a scone from the tray and stuffed a bite of it into his mouth before turning the conversation back to the upcoming business trip.

****

Lawrence rubbed his hands down his trouser legs as he sat on the seat waiting for the wagon to pull off. He was having second thoughts about leaving Elizabeth alone, even though her eyes sparkled and her voice bubbled with excitement as she stood by the wagon waving goodbye and reminding him about the dinner party. He worried she might have a relapse and he wouldn't be there to protect her from herself—and the others from her. Her voice invaded his thoughts. "Lawrence, don't forget about the dinner party."

He blew her a kiss. "I won't forget, sweetheart."

Eli proved to be a faithful companion, and he never used that baritone voice of his unless he was spoken to, giving Lawrence the solitude he desired. His wife's state of mind took up most of his thoughts. He worried about her and wondered if she would indeed be all right. His thoughts lingered on Hattie and the mute girl; there was something very perplexing about those two. He gave his head a curt nod and said to himself, "I'm getting to the bottom of their mystery as soon as I get home."

****

Abby stood behind the worktable in the kitchen, crushing herbs and thinking of the freedom she would soon enjoy. She smiled. Soon she would be able to visit the other people on the property, freely walk through the woods, go searching for nuts, berries, roots, and special leaves she needed for her cooking herbs and medicinal tonics. She swallowed a laugh when she thought of the possibility of making friends. She had never had a real friend except for her momma, Mr. Jack, and Eli. They were good to her, but she wanted someone she could share secrets with, share dreams with. A smile crept across her face when she thought of marriage. She wiped the perspiration from her hands onto her apron as that possibility entered her consciousness.

Her thoughts were interrupted when Elizabeth stormed in, face flushed, fists clenched. Hattie turned from the stove and moved close to Abby. "What's wrong with you, child?" Hattie asked, keeping her voice calm.

Elizabeth pounded her fists against her hips. "Since I have to serve my husband, I will be making all meals from now on! Do I make myself clear?"

Hattie and Abby stood with their mouths hung open as they stared at Elizabeth in utter shock. They finally nodded their heads.

Elizabeth looked Abby in the eyes before she turned her attention to Hattie. "You slaves have it good here. From now on, I'll decide how much food you eat and when you eat it." Those words hung in the air as Elizabeth waltzed from the room.

Abby whispered to Hattie, "What do you think is wrong with her?"

Hattie shook her head slowly. "It's not good, Abby-girl. It's not good. I was afraid this might happen, one day, but not this soon."

Elizabeth kept her word, and for the next week she was in the kitchen every day preparing the morning, midday, and evening meals. She would not allow Hattie to add special herbs to her food, and she would not take the tonic Hattie had prepared for her. She became quarrelsome, demanding, and suspicious of everyone. Hattie and Abby quickly realized that the real danger they faced was right in the house where they lived instead of an enemy in their past.

One evening, while sitting on the garden bench, Hattie became deeply troubled. "Abby-girl, there's no doubt it's time for us to stop our ruse and tell Mr. Lawrence the truth. He's a good man, and I think he will protect us, if it comes to that."

Abby placed her hand over Hattie's. "Whatever you think, Momma."

"Oh, child." Hattie leaned close to Abby. "Everybody has always called me Momma Hattie as long as I can remember." She swallowed, trying to choke back tears. "But when you say just the word 'momma,' it warms my heart so much." Abby kissed Hattie on her black wrinkled cheek. "You are my mother. You are the only mother I have known, and you have loved me and put your life in danger to save me. You couldn't love me any more had I been your natural child. You've taught me all about healing and herbs. You've taught me how to read and write." Abby gave Hattie a wicked smile. "You've taught me how to pretend."

"Yes," Hattie said with a teasing tap on Abby's nose. "I think it's time for you to stop pretending and be the wonderful person God intended you to be."

Abby looked out on the garden. "What do you think Mr. Lawrence will do when he finds out I am not mute or slow?"

Hattie squeezed her daughter's hand. "I don't know for sure, Abby-girl, but I got a good feeling things will be fine. Maybe, more than fine," she said in a whisper. She patted Abby's hand. "We'll tell him as soon as he gets back from his trip."

****

Abby clamped her mouth shut as Elizabeth pushed and pulled unwanted household furnishings into the bedroom Abby and Hattie shared, just off the kitchen.

Elizabeth had demanded her help. Hattie burst through the kitchen. "Miss Elizabeth! What are you doing?"

A ray of light reflected in Elizabeth's green eyes gave her the appearance of a woman possessed. "You slaves"—she looked from Hattie to Abby—"don't need a big nice room like this. You belong down in the slave quarters." Disbelief marred Hattie's and Abby's faces. Abby's eyes grew huge, then quickly flashed in Hattie's direction. She wondered what her momma was going to say.

Hattie had learned from caring for Elizabeth's mother that a soothing tone and a pretense of going along with the patient's plan worked sometimes, if no one was in immediate danger. "Miss Elizabeth," Hattie said in a soft cooing tone, "if we move to the slave quarters, who will help you in the house? Suppose you need something during the night, who will be here to help you?" Elizabeth cocked her head, considering the question, then waved her hand. "You two can stay in the barn." Abby's hand flew to her mouth. Hattie nodded her head, trying to hold back her surprise. "Surely you don't mean that, Miss Elizabeth. We just can't stay out in the barn," Hattie said with a small smile.

Elizabeth rolled cold calculating eyes. "Okay, okay." She threw up her hands. "You can stay in Eli's room, in the carriage house." She sashayed from the room as if she had given them a great gift of some sort. Not only were Hattie and Abby receiving food rations...now they were no longer sleeping in the house.

By the next week Hattie and Abby were back cooking, but Elizabeth watched to be sure that no herbs or tonics were added to the meals. The morning before Lawrence was due to come home, Elizabeth entered the kitchen, her skin pale, dark circles surrounding her sunken eyes, her shoulders slumped. She held a crumpled piece of paper in her hand. Hattie leaned over in her chair and whispered to Abby. "She looks the way I feel."

"This came yesterday." Elizabeth fanned the paper in the air. "Four of my guests are unable to attend the dinner party tomorrow night." Her voice quivered. She blinked back tears.

"That's good that you are going to postpone your party. You don't look so good. Come here and sit down." Elizabeth took a seat at the table and closed her eyes. Hattie put her hand on top of hers. "You need to take a nap. You look awfully tired."

Elizabeth pulled her hand from under Hattie's. "I'm still having the party. It will just be Kathleen and Adam, and me and Lawrence." She stood to her full height. "So you slaves get busy and get everything ready." Hattie and Abby were dumbfounded by the sudden change in her behavior.

They got straight to work preparing everything they needed for the dinner party. Later that afternoon, Hattie heard Elizabeth screaming and rushed into the house to see what was happening. She found Elizabeth stretched out on the settee in the parlor, hitting and swinging her arms in the air, apparently having a bad dream. Hattie bent over to wake her. Elizabeth woke up, saw the bloodstains on Hattie's apron from butchering a hen, and became hysterical. She jumped up from the settee, grabbed the poker from the fireplace, and began swinging it toward Hattie, all the while yelling, "Stop it, stop it! Don't, don't!"

Abby heard the commotion coming from the house. She dropped the herbs she had gathered and hurried inside. Her eyes stretched as big as a Liberty coin when she saw the scene before her. Elizabeth's green eyes were wild with fire, and she swung the poker like she was trying to protect herself from a raging wild animal. Hattie stood frozen by the settee. Abby debated whether she should try talking to Elizabeth to calm her down. Hearing a mute girl speaking could cause more damage to her already fragile condition. Hattie sensed the dilemma. She spoke to Elizabeth in a slow, soothing tone as Abby carefully approached her from the side. She said whatever popped into her head.

"Miss Elizabeth, I found the fattest hen for your dinner party tomorrow night. I can tell it's going to be juicy and tender. It's right outside the kitchen door… Oh," Hattie continued, "Look at me! I came right on in this fine house without taking off my stained apron. Oh, Miss Elizabeth, I am so sorry."

Elizabeth stopped swinging the poker and stared at Hattie's apron. Abby grabbed at the poker, and after a brief tussle she took it from Elizabeth's grasp, but not before she and Hattie were hit several times on the legs and arms. Abby's dress had been ripped at the neck and sleeve, too. Hattie calmed Elizabeth down and led her to the settee. She placed Elizabeth's head in her lap and wiped away her tears with her handkerchief while speaking to her softly. Elizabeth cried like a baby until she fell asleep. She slept for a while. Hattie eased her head up while Abby tucked a pillow under her. Hattie struggled to get to her feet. She limped to the kitchen, where Abby took charge of taking care of her injuries. "Oh, Momma, your leg is already swollen."

"I know, child, and it hurts something awful. What about you, Abby-girl?"

"My shoulders hurt, but I will be fine." Abby got cold water and a towel to wrap Hattie's knee, and then she made willow bark tea for both of them, to ease their pain.

A few hours later Abby tiptoed into the parlor carrying a tray with Elizabeth's midday meal. She needed to not frighten her yet wake her up gently. Quietly she walked over to the settee—and stopped in her tracks, looking around the room. No Elizabeth. She plopped the tray onto the table and dashed room to room, searching for Elizabeth in all the downstairs rooms. No Elizabeth! She rushed upstairs to Elizabeth's room and knocked on the door. No answer. She took a deep breath and cautiously pushed open the bedroom door. Elizabeth wasn't there. She searched the other rooms upstairs. No Elizabeth. She ran down the stairs to the kitchen. She skidded to a stop when she saw Elizabeth entering the kitchen from the back door, a huge smile on her face. Hattie and Abby looked at each other with raised brows. They both knew Elizabeth was up to something.

That night they found out what she had been up to. She had locked them out of Eli's room.

"Momma, we have to go get help."

"I know, child, but neither of us can walk to the common house or up to Miss Kathleen's. Don't say you can, because I've noticed you trying not to limp. Besides, I don't want anyone to know you can talk until we tell Mr. Lawrence our story. Let's not bother anyone tonight. Mr. Lawrence will be back tomorrow." Hattie grimaced.

"But where are we going to sleep, Momma?"

"I guess we'll sleep in the barn." Arm in arm they slowly made their way to the barn. Abby found two horse blankets hanging on the rail, heaped up a mound of hay in a stall, and spread the blankets on top.

"Here, Momma, this is for you."

"Where are you going to sleep?"

"I'll sleep in the loft so I can keep an eye on the door, just in case Elizabeth comes in."

"That's a good idea, but can you climb up there?"

"Yes, I think I can. I'll be careful, Momma."

****

"You are late," Elizabeth screamed as she entered the kitchen the next morning. "Do you need the whip to make sure you get here on time? I have a dinner party this evening."

Hattie spoke softly. "Miss Elizabeth, it's still dark out." She cracked two of the four eggs Elizabeth had set aside for breakfast and plopped their contents into the hot skillet. Soon the smell of eggs, bacon, and biscuits filled the kitchen. "Miss Elizabeth, sit down here and have some breakfast." Abby poured the steaming coffee into her cup.

"We'll have everything ready by this evening."

"You'd better," Elizabeth said as she pushed her food from one side of the plate to the other. Soon she left the room in a huff. Hattie clutched the kitchen chair and sank down into it.

"Abby-girl, I think we are in terrible trouble. Elizabeth is getting more irrational every day. This dinner party is a big mistake. I'm glad those other guests are not coming. Her state of mind is too fragile for this. I'm afraid of what might happen to her. We have to let Mr. Lawrence know what's been going on here, and hopefully he can get Elizabeth to call off this party tonight." Abby nodded in agreement.

Abby pushed the kitchen curtains back for the twentieth time as she paced back and forth, trying to get a glimpse of Lawrence. Even the smell of her beloved herbs didn't calm her spirit. She had heard the wagon and the men outside around noon.

"Abby-girl, sit down before you wear a hole in that floor. I am just as anxious as you are for Mr. Lawrence to come inside." Hattie put the finishing touches on the apple, bearberries, and herb centerpiece artfully arranged in a large silver bowl and platter.

"I was sure he would come in for lunch. It's a good thing we got everything ready for that dinner party, anyway. Isn't it, Abby-girl?"

Abby barely heard her mother over the rapid beating of her heart. The butterflies in her stomach were about to take flight as she wrung her hands, racking her brain trying to think of the right words to tell Mr. Lawrence about their deceit. *What if he puts us out?* She trembled at the thought. She sat down in the chair and absentmindedly added leaves to the centerpiece. *Maybe Momma and I could go to some place out west, where Mr. Lawrence talks about.*

Hattie's words invaded her thoughts. "I'm not sure how I will hold up at the party," she heard her momma say with anguish in her voice. Abby stopped her woolgathering and looked at her. "My leg hurts something awful. What about you, Abby-girl? How's your shoulder?"

"I'm all right, Momma," she whispered before glancing over at the back door.

"I don't know what we're going to do about your dress. We can't get to the other one in our old room. Hmph. The way that girl is working us, I don't know when we will have time to mend the one you are wearing, before the party."

Before Abby could respond, Elizabeth swept into the kitchen with a pout on her face. She stomped her feet several times when she saw Hattie and Abby at the table with the centerpiece between them. "I need that finished now!" She flung the back door open and headed out to the barn. They stared at her back.

Elizabeth had waited since noon for Lawrence to come to the house. Unable to wait any longer, she leapt from her seat by the window and rushed through the kitchen, stopping only long enough to make sure everything was ready for the dinner party. When she located him, Lawrence held several bolts of fabric in his arms. "Sure hope the women at the sewing house will make new clothes for Hattie and the girl." He shook his head and chuckled. They wear the ugliest dresses I've ever seen."

"Did you say something, Mr. Lawrence?" Eli asked, coming around the wagon.

"No, I was just thinking out loud."

Lawrence had caught sight of Elizabeth as she rounded the corner of the barn, her clenched fist swinging in rhythm with her march-like gait. He knew she was not a happy woman. He had meant to go home as soon as the wagons pulled in but had gotten busy rearranging the store to make room for the new merchandise. He laid the fabric back in the wagon, wiped perspiration from his face, and headed in his wife's direction with outstretched arms. He hugged her tightly, lifted her off the ground, and spun her around.

When she pushed on his chest, he set her on the ground, and she gave him a kiss on the cheek, then immediately pushed him away to tell him all the details about the dinner party and how he needed to get dressed. She went on and on until he kissed her on the lips to prevent her from speaking further.

"Elizabeth," he said, "I promise as soon as I finish here I will come to the house, get washed up, and get dressed in plenty of time for your dinner party."

He kissed her again before he sent her back to the house. She marched back to the house in a huff, talking under her breath. Eli chuckled.

"Don't worry about unloading the wagons, boss. I will get everything done, even if I have to spend the night in the store." Lawrence slapped Eli on the back.

"You're a good man. Come, let me help you while I can."

Chapter Eight

Lawrence was relieved to see that Kathleen and Adam were the only guests at the dinner party. He was worried about Elizabeth and how rattled she had been when he returned home to get dressed, but he hoped it was just nerves and her desire for everything to be perfect for tonight.

The group enjoyed a great time in the parlor, talking and laughing about some of Lawrence's adventures, before they moved into the dining room for dinner. Lawrence and Adam seated their wives and then took their own seats at the table.

"Elizabeth, this centerpiece is beautiful. The mint..." Before Lawrence finished the compliment, Hattie entered the room, struggling to carry a large dish of food. The woman looked a hundred years old. She was extremely thin and walked with a pronounced limp. Her face revealed she was in great pain. Lawrence was so dumbfounded by her appearance he could only sit and stare at her, speechless, while Adam jumped up and took the dish from her and set it on the table. She tried to smile and thank him, but the words were barely audible. Lawrence wondered what had happened to this vibrant woman. She was old, yes, but she was spirited and certainly had not been that thin; and the limp—why had he not noticed it before? Then he tried to remember the last time he had seen her and the girl... It must have been at least a week before he left. Elizabeth had started serving his meals herself, saying that was her duty as a good wife. He had been happy because she was happy. His brow creased. He had been so concerned about his own happiness and peace of mind that he was oblivious to what was going on in his own home, right under his nose. Lawrence could see the look of horror on Kathleen's face, but she remained quiet. He finally found his voice and turned to his wife.

"Why didn't you tell me Hattie was ill?"

Elizabeth waved her hands in the air. "Don't be silly. There's nothing wrong with her. She just doesn't want to work. You know how slaves are." Disbelief was evident on everyone's face, and Kathleen covered her open mouth with her hand, then lowered her eyes.

A moment later, as Abby came in, her heel caught in the dress she was wearing. Kathleen gasped. Lawrence jumped up and grabbed the glass pitcher from her hand, while Adam caught her before she fell to the floor. Lawrence frowned. "Why in tarnation are you wearing that dress? It's clearly too big and too long for you." Abby lowered her pale face and left the room, holding the hem of the dress up to just above her black boots.

Lawrence slapped his palm on the table. "Elizabeth, I demand some answers. What is going on here?" She jumped up with an unintelligible exclamation and flung her hands out, knocking over the centerpiece and glasses and upsetting dishes before she ran upstairs screaming and crying. Lawrence followed after her, apologizing for his behavior. Before he could reach their bedroom, she had dashed in and locked the door behind her. Lawrence shook the knob. "Elizabeth, please, I am sorry for upsetting you." He tempered his voice, hoping the soothing tone would calm her. "I just want to know what is going on. Please let me in." He knocked...and knocked. He begged and begged. She wouldn't open the door.

He sank to the floor, his head in his hands. His pulse pounded in his head; his stomach felt sick. "I shouldn't have pressed her for answers the way I did, especially in front of guests. God, please help her...help me." Lawrence leaned his head back against the bedroom door and wept. He dried his tears with the back of his hands and tried the knob one more time. It was still locked. He headed downstairs. He knew he had to explain to his sister and brother-in-law what was going on. He blew out a breath. In a way he was relieved they had witnessed this side of his life.

He found Kathleen and Adam tidying up the kitchen and putting food away. When he came into view, Kathleen rushed into his arms. He held her in an embrace for a long time. Adam hugged his shoulders. When Kathleen pulled away from her brother, she looked deep into his midnight black eyes. "I am so sorry. What can we do to help?" Lawrence disengaged himself from his sister and brother-in-law, looked over at Hattie and Abby's bedroom door, and requested, "Let's go into the parlor. I need to talk to you."

Kathleen wove her fingers into Adam's as they sat side by side on the settee, waiting for her brother to speak. Lawrence's watery eyes held pain, hurt, and disbelief. He paced the floor, fingering his thick black hair.

"I...I mean...Elizabeth..."

Not able to witness her brother's agony any longer,

Kathleen spoke. "Lawrence, we know about Elizabeth's condition." He stopped mid-stride and turned to face her. His Adam's apple bobbed in his throat as he fought to speak. "How did you know? When did you find out?"

"If you remember"—Kathleen looked down at her hands—"I've spent a lot of time with Elizabeth. I have seen the mood swings. I know how irritable she can be." Tears felled down her rosy cheeks. "There were times when she didn't remember me or where she was."

Lawrence collapsed in the nearest chair and wept out loud. Kathleen went over to him and hugged his shoulders. "I knew you would tell us about it when you got ready."

When he had gained control of his emotions, Lawrence told them all about Elizabeth's episodes and their trip to Philadelphia. Sharing the burden of his wife's condition gave him more peace than he could have ever imagined.

After Kathleen and Adam left, Lawrence went back upstairs to see if he could talk to his wife. The door was still locked, and he could hear her soft cries. He sat outside the door until the crying stopped. He knew she had fallen asleep. He pulled out his watch to check the time. It was still early enough to call on Hattie and Abby. Curious about Elizabeth's state of mind while he was away, Lawrence went in search of them. He knocked on their bedroom door, the one right off the kitchen, several times. No answer. He didn't know whether they were sleeping or too embarrassed to talk to him. He paced the kitchen floor, wondering whether to bang on the door until someone answered. He decided against it. When no one answered his second knock, he swallowed his irritation and went outside to get some fresh air and to clear his head. As he neared the barn, he heard a moaning sound. He slowly opened the barn door, and the sound grew louder. Someone was crying, someone in the loft. *Who in tarnation would be in my barn, crying, and at this time of the night?* He grabbed the pitchfork hanging by the door, crept over to the ladder, and quietly climbed it. Once at the top, he shouted, "Show yourself now, or I'll find you with this pitchfork." He heard soft muffled words coming from the stacks of hay.

"It's me, Mr. Lawrence. I'm over here."

Lawrence was thunderstruck. A thousand thoughts assailed his mind. *Who is in my barn calling me Mr. Lawrence with a voice as sweet and melodious as a songbird? Hattie and Eli are the only two people on the ranch who call me Mr. Lawrence. It can't be the mute girl; she doesn't speak, or…does she?* Finally, he found his voice. "Abby, is that you?"

"Yes, sir."

"What are you doing out here?" His voice was harsher than he intended. Her cries grew stronger, and she began to hiccup. He followed the sound, to see only her head peeking out of a mound of hay. "Are you hurt? Did someone attack you?" Lawrence asked in a soft, kind voice. No answer. He took two tentative steps toward her, asking several questions as he went. He stopped, waited for her to say something, anything. She didn't.

Feet planted apart, his fists clenched at his waist, Lawrence asked, "Are you out here with someone?"

He received a face full of hay and a loud clear "no" as the response. That was followed by more crying. He tried to get closer to her, but she began kicking hay in his face. "Calm down, girl. I'm not going to hurt you. I'm sorry I accused you of being with someone." He folded his arms across his chest and stared down at her.

"You are full of surprises." His tone was laced with indignation. Their gazes locked. Neither spoke for a few minutes, but finally he shifted his weight from side to side and used a more amiable tone. "I just wanted to know why you are out here instead of in your room." His boots touched the mound of hay. He could have grabbed her out of the hay and demanded answers, but he didn't. At that moment she seemed so innocent, so frightened and vulnerable. He knelt beside her. "Abby, I just want to find out if you are hurt and why you are in the loft."

That's when he noticed she had changed back into her own dress. The sleeves and neckline were ripped, and there was a big stain of food in front. He guessed the food had been thrown at her. His stomach churned. He knew his wife had something to do with this. Without thinking further, he grabbed Abby up close to his chest and began rocking her back and forth like a baby. She melted against him and cried for a long time, as if a floodgate of emotions were finally free to escape. Her crying finally stopped.

"Let's get you back into the house where it's warm." Without thinking, he gently lifted her out of the hay, and she wrapped both her arms around his neck as he climbed down the ladder still carrying her at one side.

Before they reached the back door, she whispered, "We have to get Momma." She pointed to the garden shed. Lawrence stopped in his tracks, muscles tightening in his stomach. "She couldn't make it to the barn tonight because her knees are so swollen."

What a horrible nightmare, and Elizabeth is responsible for this bad dream. He carried Abby into the parlor and laid her on the green velvet settee. She curled up in a fetal position, shivering from the cold. "I'll get a good fire going as soon as I get back," he told her.

When he went back to get Hattie, he found the old woman lying in the middle of the shed floor on a mound of hay, wrapped in two blankets. He gently picked her up. She moaned from the pain but offered no protest. He carried her into the house and placed her on the cushioned settee opposite Abby. She whispered, "Thank you," then closed her eyes. As soon as he had added more logs to the fire, he went upstairs in search of blankets.

Within an hour, the room was warm and the two were fast asleep. After another hour or two spent in his study, mulling over the situation, Lawrence went to the kitchen to make tea. He heard someone come up behind him. "Abby, what are you doing up?"

"I heard someone in the kitchen. I thought it was Miss…"

"No, it's only me. I think Elizabeth is still sleeping. I…um…I can't get into the bedroom where she is."

Abby went to the cabinet that held the silverware. She opened a drawer and pulled out a five-inch skinny metal rod with a hook at one end and a sharp point at the other.

"This will open all the inside doors." She walked over to the kitchen door. "Just stick the pointed side in like this and turn." The lock clicked. She opened the door and handed the tool to Lawrence.

He stuck it in his pocket and nodded his thanks. "I was getting tea ready to take into the parlor, just in case you and Hattie woke up."

"Can I help you with something?"

"No, I can manage." He carried the tray into the parlor. When they entered the room, Hattie was already sitting on the edge of the settee.

"Stay put," Lawrence told her. He put the tray on the table and poured tea for the three of them, then took a chair across from the settee. After they drank their tea and ate the tea cakes, Lawrence leaned forward in his seat and released a huge sigh.

"Will someone please tell me what's going on here?" The women looked at each other.

"There's a lot to tell, Mr. Lawrence." Hattie folded her wrinkled hands together. "Where do you want me to start?" Abby moved closer to her mother on the settee and laid her head on her shoulder.

Lawrence looked at Abby. His kind and gentle black eyes never left her face. Color rose in her cheeks, and her neck and ears grew hot under his scrutiny.

"I would like to know about *her* miraculous healing, but right now I need to find out about my wife." He turned his gaze to Hattie. She cleared her throat and then relayed every detail about their two weeks with Elizabeth. "She stored so much stuff in our room that there was no room left for us. She wanted us to go to the slave quarters." Lawrence's eyebrows pulled together as he repeated after her, "The slave quarters." He stood as though to go to his wife and deal with her on the matter.

"She rationed our food," Abby said in her small

musical voice. At that, Lawrence dropped down into the nearest chair and held his head in his hands. The only sound in the room for a long time was breathing.

"Mr. Lawrence, I have something else I need to tell you." Hattie looked down at her wrinkled hands. "Miss Elizabeth's mother...well, she..."

Lawrence slowly shook his head and blew out a slow breath. His piercing gaze locked on Hattie's big, teary eyes.

"Miss Elizabeth's mother suffered from a mental condition." Lawrence stood so forcefully his chair almost toppled over. He slowly sat down again as Hattie clasped her hand together and licked her lips. "Elizabeth had problems with forgetfulness, moodiness, and irrational behavior on and off since she was sixteen. She hadn't had any spells until your wedding trip. I am telling you the truth, Mr. Lawrence. We thought she had outgrown them."

"So Jack knew about Elizabeth's condition but conspired to keep it from me by sending you three to keep me from knowing the truth. Jack said I was a good man. Now I know why—I took his daughter off his hands."

"Oh, Mr. Lawrence, please don't say such a thing."

"I've heard enough." Lawrence stood and walked out of the room.

As soon as he walked out, he knew he should go back and apologize to Hattie and Abby. He had known all was not well with Elizabeth shortly after they met, but he didn't want to admit it because he was so eager to get married and start a family. *She was so beautiful. Her moodiness and melancholy only made her more intriguing...at least that's what I thought in the beginning.*

Abby held Hattie's hand as she watched Lawrence leave the room, tears rolling down her cheeks. "Do you think Mr. Lawrence will turn us out because of our deception?" Hattie patted her daughter's hand.

"No, Abby-girl, I don't think so. He's just hurt right now. He's grieving the loss of a dream. The Lord will heal his heart in time."

Lawrence stretched out on the leather couch in his study after checking on Elizabeth, hoping to get some sleep. But sleep eluded him, and finally he sat on the end of the couch, trying to process all he knew about his wife's condition and what she needed in order to get better. The herbs, tonics, and massages seemed to have worked when she was taking them. He shook his head and blew out a whistle. That she was not taking them now was the problem. An idea came to him, and he jumped from the couch, went to his desk, found paper and pen, and wrote a letter to one of his solicitors in Boston, explaining Elizabeth's problems and asking him to search and obtain the best doctor in the country, one who knew how to treat people with her condition. He stared at the letter in his hand, praying he would be able to find help for his wife.

He continued to sit at his desk, in deep thought, and his thoughts wandered to Abby. Something awful must have happened in her life for her to pretend to be mute and slow for so many years. He tapped the letter on the table. "Did Jack know she could talk? Elizabeth certainly didn't know she could." He folded his lips together and hunched over the desk.

"What about Eli?" he whispered. "Did he know?" A muscle twitched in his jaw, and he threw the letter down on the desk.

"I've got to find the reason behind her hoax."

He was on his way to check on Hattie and Abby in the parlor, hoping they had slept better than he had, when a knock sounded at the kitchen door.

Who could be calling this early? It's barely light outside. When he opened the door, his sister fell into his arms. Then she pushed back from him to get a good look at her baby brother. "You look awful! Did you sleep at all last night?"

"No, ma'am, I didn't." He suppressed a yawn as he moved aside to allow Adam and Cookie to enter.

"What do you have here?" Lawrence said, looking at the dresses in his sister's arms. She held the dresses up.

"These are two of my dresses. They are for Hattie and Abby. I worked on them last night. If they don't fit, we can make more alterations. Cookie is here to prepare breakfast for everyone. Hattie and Abby may not be up to the task for a few days."

Lawrence looked over at Cookie, who was busy locating everything she needed to start breakfast.

"Let's go into the study. I have something to tell you."

Once everyone was seated, Lawrence told them all that Hattie and Abby had shared with him about their two weeks of anguish with Elizabeth.

"Elizabeth thought they were slaves, rationed their food, and later filled their room with all the household furnishings she didn't want. She made them sleep in the barn."

Kathleen blinked back tears and took hold of Adam's hand. "We're so sorry, Lawrence." Her husband nodded in agreement.

They prayed and wept over the crisis they faced, and Lawrence was glad his family could love and support him during this, his darkest times. The group came up with a plan. The first thing was to get Elizabeth back to drinking the tonics and eating the specially prepared foods with various herbs. They agreed that Lawrence would be the person to get her to do that, for now, at least until a doctor was found who could cope with the situation. Lawrence decided to hire two women from the common house to help care for his wife around the clock and hire someone to cook and clean until Hattie and Abby were back on their feet.

"There's more." Lawrence stood to his feet and massaged the back of his neck. "Abby can talk." Kathleen raised an eyebrow.

"How?" she asked.

Lawrence reclaimed his seat. "It seems that everything was a ruse. She could talk all along, and she is perfectly normal."

"You suspected as much, didn't you, Lawrence?"

Lawrence nodded, and Kathleen shook her head slowly. "Hattie and Abby seem so innocent. Why would they purposely deceive everyone?" Lawrence propelled himself to his feet with a fierce grip on the arms of his chair. "I don't know, but I'm going to find out now."

"Lawrence," Kathleen said as they were leaving the room, "it might be a good idea for Abby to continue her role as a mute when she encounters Elizabeth. The shock of her being able to talk might be too much for your wife's fragile state of mind right now."

Lawrence nodded. "That's a good idea."

"Hey," Adam said. "Why don't you let Hattie and Abby sleep as long as they can? I'll get Eli, and we can move the stuff from their bedroom."

"That's a wonderful idea, and I'll go along to supervise." Kathleen gave her brother a peck on the cheek. "Once they get up and have some breakfast, we'll hear what they have to say about their ruse. Meanwhile, you need to get a little sleep yourself."

Lawrence gave his head a tiny shake. "Okay."

A few hours later, all unwanted items had been removed from Hattie's and Abby's bedroom, except a few items Kathleen left to make the room more cozy and comfortable. Breakfast had been served and dishes put away. The group moved to the parlor while Cookie sat with Elizabeth.

Lawrence cleared his throat and looked at Hattie and Abby, huddled together on a settee opposite the one Kathleen and Adam occupied. "I've asked my sister and her husband to stay so they could hear about your"—Lawrence cleared his throat again—"about…"

"Our deception," Abby added. Her voice was low and melodic.

"Yes, Yes." Lawrence's words came with a forced cough as he sat in the green floral spoonback chair facing Hattie and Abby.

"Does Elizabeth know you can talk?" Kathleen asked.

Abby shook her head.

"Does Eli know?" Lawrence injected.

"I've never spoken in his presence, but I suspect he knows." Abby searched for Hattie's hand without taking her eyes off Lawrence.

"Mr. Jack is the only one who knows everything.

We planned the ruse together." A gasp filled the room, and all eyes locked on Hattie. "Before you think evil of me or Mr. Jack, we did what we did to protect my Abby." Hattie squeezed and patted Abby's hand and blinked back tears before she continued. "Mr. Jack has become a Christian man. But for too long he followed the traditions of his family instead of living his life the way God desired."

She waved a hand in the air and looked around at the group. "Enough about him. You want to hear about my Abby Rose." She cleared her throat. "Abby's grandfather, John Wesley, is a wealthy plantation owner in Virginia. He's been seeking Abby, to kill her, since she was born eighteen years ago."

Kathleen sucked in a deep breath. Lawrence and Adam each raised a curious brow. But no one was truly surprised by the attempted murder. It was not uncommon for white men who fathered mixed race children to kill the offspring, before or after the birth; or, in some cases, to sell the child to another slave owner to cover up their indiscretions. But what surprised them about this case was how relentless Wesley had been in pursuing a granddaughter…for eighteen years.

Lawrence's heart tightened in empathy for her. He spoke in a low voice laced with disbelief. "She's eighteen?" Abby lowered her head.

"I kept her in bindings to disguise her true age."

Kathleen and Adam tried not to stare at her at that moment, and Lawrence's mouth formed an O. "Please continue," he said as he looked at Abby.

Hattie glanced at her small audience. "Abby's mother ran away from home because she was pledged to marry a wealthy man older than her father. It was some type of business arrangement," Hattie said, flinging a hand in the air. "She fled to Chesapeake, where she met and married a free black man. He was a schoolteacher, and they were very much in love. Things went well for the couple for a while, until the girl's daddy found out where she was and had her forcibly taken back home. The husband followed her the whole sixty miles back. Her daddy soon found out she was with child, and she confessed she was married...to a black man."

All eyes were riveted on Hattie, except Abby's. She sat with her head down. She had heard the story before and didn't wish to hear it again, but she knew these people deserved to know the whole truth. She excused herself and went into the kitchen to get refreshments for everyone. When she returned, she put the silver tray carrying iced tea and sandwiches on the table between the two settees and served everyone.

Hattie continued her story. "Wesley spewed out a string of curse words that would make the devil himself blush." She smiled at Abby and took the glass she offered and sipped a bit.

"How did you learn all this?" Adam asked, setting his glass back on the tray.

"Abby's mother told me this before she died."

"I see."

"Well, to make a long story short, the girl's brother helped her escape from their father. They made their way to the Virginia coast, and again the husband followed. From there a childhood friend, Malcolm, helped the couple get to Mason, Georgia, with the intention of taking a riverboat up the Tennessee River to Indiana, where the couple could live in peace, they hoped. Abby's mother and Malcolm posed as a couple traveling with their slave. The plan was working well until they were spotted by the bounty hunters her father had hired to kill her, her husband, and the unborn child. The men were to cut the baby from the daughter's womb and take it back to Wesley as proof that the awful deed had been done." Hattie paused as a loud gasp filled the room.

Kathleen's hand flew to her chest, her eyes as large as a half-cent piece as she sputtered out in shocked horror, "They were to cut the baby from the girl's womb?" She reached for her husband's hand, and her words rushed in disbelief. "How could anyone do such a horrible thing? Let alone a father hiring someone to perform such a ghastly deed on his own daughter!"

"He hired bounty hunters to kill his daughter and her unborn child?" Lawrence's voice was loud and filled with incredulity.

Adam repeated the words, "bounty hunters" in a whisper.

Lawrence glanced at Abby, a muscle tightening in his jaw. He lowered his head and bared his teeth. "The man put out a bounty on his own daughter," he repeated. "I can't fathom how a father could orchestrate such a cruel and hideous plan against his own child."

Adam swallowed the surge of anger in his voice. "Only an insane man would put a bounty out on his daughter and hunt her down like a wild animal and order her unborn child to be cut from the womb. That's just plain evil," he added, cracking his knuckles.

"Sorry, I got ahead of myself," Hattie said, returning to her story. "The three were hunted down like animals, and they were beaten. Her friend Malcolm died from his wounds." Hattie took a deep breath.

Abby hugged herself as she left her seat and walked over to the window. She knew what was coming next. She felt heaviness in her chest as she listened to the tale that she had heard before. *My grandfather hates me because of the black blood that runs through my veins—blood that was mixed because two of God's children dared to fall in love.*

Lawrence watched Abby as she stood by the window, her arms wrapped around her waist, and he could see her down-turned lips and the anguish on her face. Should he ask Hattie to stop the story? He could kick himself for not asking Abby to leave the room earlier; she must have heard the story before, and it wasn't easy to hear even once. How could a man have that much hatred, to hunt down his own daughter to kill her? He pounded his fist on his knee as he brought his attention back to Hattie.

Hattie spoke in a whisper and wiped tears from her eyes. "They cut off her husband's head, hung his body from a tree, and made her watch, just like her father had ordered. They had been told to cut the baby out of the mother's womb and bring back the body as proof that the deed had been done." Hattie shook her head. "None of the hired men had the stomach for the ghastly deed. So they kicked the girl around and left her for dead. I found her when I was out hunting my herbs, and I did what I could for her, but she died giving birth to Abby."

Adam held his wife; her body shaking from her cries, while he and Lawrence gave up all pretense of concealing their freely flowing tears. Abby slipped back to the settee, where Hattie hugged her and held her tenderly.

After wiping his face with his handkerchief, Lawrence slammed his fist into his hand. His heart ached for the things Abby had gone through, living in constant fear of an unknown enemy and living the life of a slave. Jack had tried to do the right thing by her, but she still had lived as a slave...the only life she'd ever known. Lawrence found himself wanting to make up for the life she had lost.

Kathleen cleared her throat and interrupted his thoughts. "Oh, Abby, I'm so sorry for what you have gone through. I am truly sorry." She wiped at her eyes.

Abby said nothing.

Adam struggled to speak past the lump in his throat. He cleared his throat several times before he spoke. "Who educated you, Hattie?"

Hattie smiled. "Mr. Jack did when he was a young boy. We kinda learned together." The old woman looked at Abby with pride. "We taught my Abby Rose and Eli to read, write, and do sums, too."

Lawrence nodded his head slowly and grinned. "So that probably was a book I saw him quickly tuck in the hay when I was out in the barn. I thought there was more to Eli than he was letting on."

"Mr. Jack thought since Abby's grandfather is a wealthy man and her father was a teacher, it was only fitting that she be educated. And that Eli has a strong faith in the Lord." Hattie beamed with pride.

Lawrence's brows pulled together. "Why did he send you and Abby with me?"

"Mr. Jack is not well. He has awful pains in his stomach that keeps him in bed for days with fever and chills. My remedies were helping him less and less. He felt that you would do all you could to help keep us safe."

"Safe from everyone except my wife," he whispered. When Lawrence pulled his watch from his pocket, he was surprised at how late it had gotten. "I need to go check on Elizabeth."

"And we need to check on Raymon," Adam said, taking hold of his wife's hand.

They left, leaving Hattie and Abby in the parlor. Hattie hugged Abby again and looked her in the eyes. "Abby-girl, the ruse is finally over. You are free to be the person God intended you to be. You can talk, laugh, and make friends. You can wander around on this big place without having to look over your shoulder."

Abby smiled, kissed her momma's cheek, and released a big sigh. "I'm glad Mr. Lawrence isn't going to make us leave for tricking him."

"So am I, Abby-girl. So am I. I think he took it quite well."

"Momma, let's go to Sunday service at the common house so we can get to know the other people on the ranch."

"That's a good idea, Abby-girl." Hattie gave her daughter another hug.

Chapter Nine

Lawrence watched Abby from his study window as he had done so many times before, and as the sound of her perfectly pitched voice floated in the air, a smile tugged on his lips. He shook his head and marveled at the miraculous change that had taken place in her over the last few months. Since the night he rescued her from the barn, she had felt comfortable with him and become quite chatty. They interacted like friends, close friends. He delighted in the thought as he turned back to resume his paperwork.

Abby and Hattie's friendship had become a healing balm for his spirit. The three of them, along with Eli, had started a routine of meeting in the kitchen after Elizabeth's needs were taken care of and she was safely tucked away in bed. They read the Bible together, and the scripture readings gave him the strength and hope he needed to be a good caregiver to his wife. Lawrence would occasionally read from his collection of books, also, for the general education of all.

Feet propped up on his desk, Lawrence leaned back in his chair, staring up at the ceiling with his arms crossed on his chest. Before long, his ears tuned to the sound of giggles and the words "unc' Lawind," accompanied by his sister's voice. He dashed from the room and into the parlor, plucked his nephew from Kathleen's arms, and smothered his neck with kisses. A gentle toss in the air was followed by louder giggles from the toddler. Lawrence loved the feel of the little one in his arms, an invisible band tightening around his chest every time he saw his nephew because he knew that he and Elizabeth would never have children. He played with Raymon while his sister went upstairs to visit with his wife.

Kathleen read some of Elizabeth's favorite scriptures aloud before they started their knitting project. They had worked on the blanket for an hour before Lawrence entered the room with a giggling Raymon in his arms. Elizabeth's face lit up, and she put down her knitting, opened her arms, and let Raymon toddle into them. She scooped him up and gave him a kiss and began singing to him. Tears shimmered in Lawrence's eyes as he watched his wife interact with the baby. He only wished… He didn't complete the thought. Kathleen understood the scene before her and gave her brother's hand a gentle squeeze. Elizabeth looked at Kathleen and wrinkled her nose.

"Who's that nice man whose hand you're holding?" Lawrence's face went pale when he heard those words. Kathleen turned to Lawrence with tear-rimmed eyes.

"He's taken me on walks in the garden and to see horses, but I don't know his name." She bounced the baby on her lap. "Sometimes when I wake up he is sitting in the chair by my bed." Lawrence moved closer to his wife and knelt down in front of her. He hoped his pasted-on smile would not falter. He took her hand and kissed it. "Now, Elizabeth, who did I say I am?" She hid her face behind Raymon and smiled. "You're Lawrence."

"Yes that's right." He patted her hand, still on one knee before her. He thought about the doctor's advice about putting Elizabeth in a newly established home in Boston for people with mental disorders. He had vehemently opposed the idea. He hoped he had made the right decision, for now he was committed to taking care of her at home with the love and support of his family and friends.

After his sister's visit, Lawrence thumped his fingers on the desk, staring at the paper and pen in front of him, contemplating what to put in his letter to his father-in-law. As he dipped the ink into the inkwell, his mind drifted to the progress his wife had made over the last several months. She was eating the specially prepared food and taking the tonics. Her massages soothed her when she became a little agitated. But how could he tell a father that his only child was no longer connected to the present world, didn't recognize her husband, and might not recognize him? Lawrence thought as he tapped the pen on the desk. Then he began to write. Jack would understand. He had gone through the same thing with Elizabeth's mother. He dipped the pen back into the ink and wrote and wrote. Finally, Lawrence reread the letter, put it in the envelope, and addressed it.

A movement outside caught his eye, and he stepped closer to the window to get a better look. Abby was twirling around with outstretched arms, her nose pointing to the sky. He knew she was thanking God for the freedom she now enjoyed. He had heard her many times before. The smile on her lips gave way to infectious giggles that made him laugh out loud as he watched her. He returned to his desk, put aside the letter he had written to his father-in-law, and thumbed through some other correspondence, but his mind returned to Abby. A slight grin danced on his lips as he thought about how much she loved being outside. She and Hattie had been flabbergasted when he announced he'd hired four women to take care of the chores around the house and they were free to explore the ranch, work with their herbs, and spend time with the other people on the ranch. Lawrence had seen the pain in Hattie's eyes many times, even though she fought to keep her suffering from Abby. She had come to him later and thanked him for his kindness.

Every chance Abby got, she was outside searching one place or another for special wild flowers, roots, nuts, or something else she needed to make her special tonics. Lawrence had occasionally accompanied her and Hattie on searches in the woods by the creek, and he had seen firsthand her uncanny ability to recognize various plants, flowers, and roots and name their potential healing power.

He had watched as she busied herself with the plants, humming while she worked. Each plant she found she treated as if it was a treasure. Her face beamed as she told him the name of each one and how to prepare it for healing. Thinking of her, he put his long legs on top of the desk and leaned back in his chair, until an idea sprang to his mind and he smiled to himself. "The creek...Abby would love exploring the creek bank by the meadow for plants and other things she needs for her tonics. She's never been that far on her searches." He jumped from his chair, rushed out of the room...and bumped into her in the hallway.

He grabbed her with both hands to keep her from

toppling over. When he put her aright, he couldn't help but stare into her enchanting chestnut eyes. She no longer wore her headdress below her eyebrows, so he examined every inch of her oval face as she tilted her head up to look at him. Her lightly tanned skin was flawless; thick lashes gracefully moved up and down as she looked at him. Her straight nose spoke of loyalty, and those rosy lips... "Mr. Lawrence, you can let go of me now. I'm fine." Her musical voice broke into his thoughts. He quickly let go of her and put his hands behind his back to resist the temptation of touching her again. He couldn't help but stare at her for a moment longer. He grunted, trying to force the words out of his mouth to ask her if she would like to explore the woods by the meadow. A smile creased her lips as she waited for him to speak. Lawrence cleared his throat once...twice...three times before words poured from his mouth. "Would you like to search the creek bank by the meadow for things you might need for your tonics and herbal collections?" A flush rose to her cheeks. Her face beamed as she looked up at him.

His palms grew moist as he waited for her to answer.

"Yes," she said, with a smile as big as the outdoors. "But Momma isn't here. She is visiting at the common house and won't be back until later this afternoon."

"I will be more than happy to accompany you."

Abby's smile brightened. "I'd love to go. Just let me tell Betsy where I'm going."

"Don't bother," Lawrence said as he turned to go upstairs. "I'll tell her when I go up to check on Elizabeth."

"Thank you, sir."

Abby's heart drummed in her chest, and she fanned herself to calm her nerves. She hoped going to the meadow alone with Lawrence would give her the courage to tell him that they had met several years ago by a creek. She was giddy with excitement as she gathered the things she needed for the search.

White puffy clouds littered the blue sky, and birds chirped and fluttered in the air. Abby closed her eyes and took in a deep breath, enjoying the smell and sound of being outside. The pair walked in silence as they took the path behind the store, then turned right and followed a less traveled, grassy path that took them up a slight hill with open fields. Majestic mountains filled the background, while a grove of trees stood erect on the other side of the path.

Lawrence studied Abby, who was practically dancing as she went ahead of him. She was an amazing girl. Her years of self-imposed solitude and shyness had not dulled her personality or her sense of humor. She was smart and curious and had a wealth of knowledge on many topics. She was a slip of a thing yet with female curves that let you know she was not a child. A smile formed on his lips.

The sound of his name brought him out of his trance. "Mr. Lawrence, this is so beautiful!" Abby spun in her tracks and faced him on the path as she took in the beauty of the trees and the yellow and blue wildflowers scattered throughout the field.

"It is a beautiful view," Lawrence said, not taking his eyes off her. Abby smiled and lowered her lashes. "Just wait until you see the place where we're going," he added.

"Race you to the curve in the path."

Before Lawrence could respond, Abby lifted her yellow dress sprigged with tiny green leaves well above her ankle-high boots, exposing bare shapely legs, and dashed up the path. Lawrence took in the view with a smile and made a mental note to ask his sister to speak to her about proper undergarments. He raced after her.

Bent and panting, Lawrence looked up. Abby was covering her mouth with her hands, trying to hold back a laugh.

"You know you cheated. Before I realized a race was on, you were halfway up the path." Abby set her basket on the ground. She was laughing so hard tears ran down her cheeks.

"I do believe you are a sore loser." Her voice bubbled between words.

Something stirred in Lawrence's heart, and he smiled at the sensation it gave him. "If you are done humiliating me," Lawrence said, trying to hold back a smile, "I'll show you the spot I was telling you about by the creek." Abby curtseyed before him. "I'm ready, sir." She sucked on her bottom lip to keep from laughing as she stooped to retrieve the basket.

"Where are my manners?" As Lawrence took the basket from her, their hands touched. Abby's skin tingled where Lawrence rested his hand on top of hers. Her cheeks grew warm. She looked into those seductive black eyes. She filed away the strange sensation to examine it later when he was not watching her so intently.

He looked deep into her chestnut eyes but made no effort to remove his hand. He cleared his throat and found his voice. "This is heavy. What's in here?" He pushed back the rolled-up blanket, uncovering an apple, some cheese, and a pint jar of lemonade. He waggled a brow and cleared his throat. Abby lowered her head and kicked at the grass on the path.

"I see, Miss Abby, you didn't consider the fact that I might get a little hungry." He tried to suppress a chuckle.

"I thought I might stay a while, after you show me the spot, and have a bit of lunch." She wiggled a pebble from the ground with the toe of her boot.

"So you want to steal my spot for yourself." He tapped his chin with his finger. "I knew you couldn't be trusted, ma'am. So I'll just stay around to protect my interest."

Abby stuck her in nose in the air and, with a slight shake of her head, she replied, "Have it your way, sir. But you only get half of the food." She tried to look serious. The gleam in her eyes gave her away.

The pair walked another hundred yards. Abby's steps slowed as she heard the bubbling, rushing water, frogs croaking, and insects buzzing. Blue, violet, and white flowers were scattered among the tall trees that lined the winding path that led them to the creek. Her fingertips brushed the petals of the blue flowers decorating the foliage among the trees. The smell of fragrant flowers tickled her nose as she made her way down the path.

"I can't imagine heaven being more beautiful than this."

"Nor I," Lawrence said as he surveyed the place. "This is enchanting."

Abby's eyes lit up when she saw the spotted yellow and blue gentians and the chicory plants. She eagerly raced ahead of Lawrence to get a better look at them.

By the time he reached her, she was kneeling down, examining the plant leaves and bubbling with enthusiasm. "These are perfect!"

Lawrence set the basket down next to her, then took out the blanket and handed it to her. She pulled out her herb shears and snipped off some leaves from the chicory and put them in her basket. "These will be good to ease Momma's swollen joints."

"What else can you use them for?"

"Mainly for digestive problems, jaundice, and heart problems." She used her hands to push dirt away from the plant, then reached into the basket to retrieve the trowel. Lawrence reached for the trowel at the same time, and again their hands touched. Abby slowing raised her head, only to see clear midnight black eyes staring back at her. She smiled. That smile took Lawrence's breath away.

They spent the next few hours collecting leaves, flowers, pods, and roots.

"Miss Abby…" Lawrence chuckled and pointed to the basket. "This is going to be so full the two of us won't be able to carry it back to the house."

Abby knew she had probably gathered too much, but she was trying to find the right moment and the courage to mention to Lawrence that they had met before, a long time ago, by a creek, when she lived on the Bradley Plantation.

"Let's rest awhile and enjoy the view before we head back. I'm still willing to share my lunch," Abby said.

"I gladly accept."

Truth be told, Lawrence wasn't ready to leave the company of the charming beauty. After they found a spot under a big tree near the creek and spread the blanket out, he pulled out his pocket knife and cut the big green apple in half. Continuing preparations for their picnic, he opened the cloth containing the cheese and removed the lid from the lemonade that had been cooling in the creek. Meanwhile, Abby took off her black gloves, washed her hands in the creek, and joined him on the blanket. Lawrence propped his back against the oak tree, while Abby sat cross-legged facing him, her dress tucked carefully around her knees. The two laughed and talked for a long time, their conversation taking a variety of twists and turns. Abby felt the time was right for her to tell Lawrence they had met before. She tilted her head, raised her nose, and looked up at him. That's when it hit him. There had always been something familiar about Abby, especially the way she tilted her head with her nose turned upward in a pleasing, aristocratic way.

"You...you are the little girl I met at the creek years ago!" He bobbed his head, waving a finger at her, a wide grin on his face. "You are that little girl. I remember clearly now. Your head wrap almost covered your eyes, and you wouldn't talk to me."

A flush crept across Abby's face. Her heart raced in her chest at the thought that he remembered her from so many years ago. She smiled up at him. "I didn't think you would remember."

"I did. I always felt we had met somewhere before."

He leaned forward and arched an eyebrow. "I was lost, and you wouldn't help me."

Abby laughed so hard tears flowed down her face. "I couldn't help you because I didn't know where *I* was!"

Lawrence told her all about getting lost from his friend Paul while looking for firewood. He talked about his leaving home at seventeen, to the consternation of his parents, with so many funny stories included that their laughter rang through the woods. Lawrence couldn't remember the last time he had felt so happy.

Lawrence's gaze fell on Abby's black gloves lying beside her on the blanket, and he picked them up and examined them. They were made of fine leather. Jack must have paid a pretty penny for them.

"Tell me the story behind these gloves." He turned them over in his hand.

Abby got a faraway look in her eyes, and her smile begin to quiver. She looked at her hands as she spoke.

"When I was about five years old, two of my grandfather's men came looking for me. They headed for our house, where I was sleeping. Momma saw them coming and ran inside and hurriedly covered my head with a bonnet and painted my face and hands with black soot. Within minutes the men came bursting into our house demanding to see me. Mr. Jack came before they found me and ran them off his property."

Lawrence could see the wetness in her eyes. His heart broke. He vowed then and there he would do everything in his power to protect her all the days of his life. Abby looked up at him, her mouth stretched into a crooked smile even as she continued.

"They—Momma and Mr. Jack—wanted people to think I had some type of disease in addition to being mute and slow. They thought people would assume that my face was the only part of me that was white-looking and regard me as some type of…freak," she said the last word almost under her breath. "They hoped no one would be interested enough in me to harm me or ask questions about me. Wearing my wrap low on my face, the big dresses, the binding, and the drooling was all part of the disguise."

"Oh, Abby." Lawrence took both her hands into his. "I'm so sorry you had to go through so much." As Abby looked at his hands holding hers, the same sensation engulfed her as when he'd touched her hand before. She decided she liked the feeling...she liked it very much.

****

Lawrence shifted his weight on the hard bench in the common house. He caught sight of a young ranch hand still staring at Abby after he had given the man his best scowl. Before Eli could properly close out the service, the young man was standing in front of Abby, asking to walk her home. Abby looked at Lawrence as if seeking his permission. He wanted to yell at the young man and tell him, "No, Abby can't go walking with you, now or ever; and furthermore, don't ever talk to her again." But who was he to stop her from being courted by someone? He furrowed his brow and bit his bottom lip to keep from speaking. Instead, he went to compliment Eli on his powerful sermon. As Lawrence moved away, he heard Abby ask Hattie for permission to accept the young man's invitation.

Abby could tell by Lawrence's curt nod and tight fists that he was not happy Hank had asked her on an outing. His scowls had frightened other potential suitors away, but not Hank; he was quite persistent. She found herself wanting Lawrence to tell her she couldn't go, but he had walked away without saying a word.

Later, at home, Lawrence stood by the window in his study and let out another heavy sigh. He was hoping to get a peek at Abby and her caller…to make sure she was all right, or so he told himself. If they took the longer, more scenic route from the common house back to his, they would have to come into his view, he reasoned. He waited and waited…no Abby. He pulled out his pocket watch—more than two hours had passed since the church service was over. She had never been out that long with one of her callers before. He rubbed the back of his neck to ease the built-up tension.

Laughter bubbled from the kitchen, bringing Lawrence out of his gloom. He made his way in that direction and heard Hattie regaling Eli and the servants with tales of her life in Africa before she was stolen away, and stories about her first slave master. "We were forced to entertain our slave master and his friends." Lawrence heard her say as he approached the kitchen door. "Mr. Lawrence, come over here and sit down. I'm sure Hank is looking after my Abby-girl."

He blinked several times at her words and tried not to show surprise that she knew he was worrying about Abby. Eli gave him a nod as he sat at the table, and Hattie continued with her stories. "We would do dances that made fun of the master and his friends, but he didn't know it. They would cheer and congratulate us on our exotic, high-spirited African dancing. We would laugh for days about the trick we had played on them." Lawrence tried to laugh along with Hattie and the others, but the smile didn't reach his eyes. He pushed his chair back from the table with more force than he intended, and left the room.

Abby sat on the stone bench in an alcove in the

garden under the cascading vines of the white Cherokee rose bush, rubbing her hands together, recalling her walk with Hank. "He wants to ask Momma's permission to court me," she said to herself, biting her bottom lip. "I never thought I would ever get married, and now I have hope. But why am I not happy?" A door slammed, and she jumped and looked up. Lawrence came striding in her direction from the kitchen. She scooted deep into the alcove as he marched past the garden with clenched fists, set jaw, and flattened lip. Her body tensed; her heart raced; she could tell he was upset. She knew she should have gone into the house as soon as she returned, hours ago.

As darkness fell, Lawrence paced the floor in his office at the store, stopping every so often to stare out the window to see if he could spot Abby. She had been gone all afternoon, and now it was almost time for supper, and she still wasn't home. He slammed his fist into his palm. "Where is she? If he so much as lays a hand on her, I swear I'll…I'll…" Lawrence let out a loud breath. "I'll do what?" He stopped pacing, wove his fingers through his thick curly hair, and slowly sank into his chair. "What can I do? Could I deny Abby a chance for true happiness, to marry, have a family? Can I watch her marry someone and bear his children?" The thought made him ill. "I have to get control of myself. That kind of thinking is completely out of line. I have a wife."

Chapter Ten

As summer faded into fall, a dark cloud fell over Abby's heart. Her Momma Hattie's health was failing, and Abby's sense of identity faltered, as well. Lawrence spent many sleepless nights worrying about her. She was slowly slipping back into the quiet, stoic girl she had been when he first knew her. He almost but not quite wished she had continued receiving callers. He did the best thing he knew to do for her and hired someone to help her take care of Hattie, and they all continued the nightly meetings over the Bible, with Hattie there when she was up to it.

The screeching of the rocking chair could be heard as Lawrence approached the bedroom door; he smiled. He knew Hattie was having a good day...she was out of bed. He tapped on the door and entered the room. The frail woman looked like an African queen, dressed in white from head to toe, sitting on her regal oak rocking chair throne. He recognized the white knitted shawl as one Elizabeth had made. A smile danced on Hattie's lips as her crooked fingers beckon him to sit. Lawrence smiled and took the chair across from her, like he always did during his visits. She moved the rocker back and forth for several minutes before she spoke. Lawrence didn't mind. He knew wherever the conversation took them it would always end with praises to God.

One day during one of Lawrence's many visits to Hattie, she talked about how God had blessed her abundantly over her ninety-six years. Frowning, he sat staring at Hattie dozing in her chair, trying to analyze all she had said. It was difficult for him to fathom all the blessings she spoke of. She had been taken by force from her home to live in a foreign country with never any hope of seeing her family again. She was married once to a man she deeply loved. He was taken from her and given to another because she was not able to have a child in the time period her master had dictated. The man was finally sold, and she never knew what happened to him. She had been sold three times herself, once to a cruel master who whipped his slaves for his personal entertainment. Lawrence was shaking his head when Hattie resumed the conversation as if no time had elapsed between her last word and what she spoke now.

"Blessings are not always what you can see in the natural, Lawrence, but what happens supernaturally from the inside out. I am blessed. God loves me and chose me to be a part of His family. In the natural, He gave me the desires of my heart, and the ability to read His Holy Word for myself." She paused, and tears rolled down her cheeks as she croaked, "He gave me a child, my Abby Rose, and a friend like Mr. Jack."

Moved by Hattie's words, he took her calloused black wrinkled hand in his own, slowly moved it to his lips, and kissed it tenderly. He had never met anyone like Hattie before. With all the horrible things that had happened to her, she chose to focus on her blessings instead of dwelling on her tragedies.

****

Elizabeth was like a child who had just had her

first lick of a peppermint stick. Her green eyes grew large. She squealed and bounced up and down when she saw the carriage pull up to the front of the house. "Oh, Mister...I mean, Lawrence, he's here. Papa is finally here!" She swung Lawrence's arm in the air like she was getting ready to jump rope. It had taken Lawrence a while to adjust to his wife's childlike behavior. Her childish temper tantrums were easier to handle than those of a strong-willed, uncontrollable woman. As soon as Jack entered the house, Elizabeth ran to him and threw her arms around his neck. Jack gave her a one-handed hug and a kiss on each cheek.

"Oh, Papa, I missed you so much! What did you bring me?" Elizabeth danced on her tiptoes. Her father's smile never left his face as he pulled out one of Elizabeth's favorite dolls from childhood.

"Oh, Papa, you found her."

Elizabeth hugged the doll to her chest as Lawrence motioned for his father-in-law to follow him into the parlor, where Jack and Elizabeth chatted for a while. When Elizabeth saw Evelyn, her childhood personal maid, she bolted from her chair and rushed over to her.

"Where have you been? I've been waiting for you." Before Evelyn could respond, Elizabeth took her hand, pulling her toward the stairs. "Let's go to my room and play with my doll."

Lawrence quickly excused himself and followed the two upstairs to make sure Elizabeth would be okay. Jack lowered his head, covered his face with his hands...and wept.

Abby hung her apron on the peg by the pantry door and sped to her bedroom to see if Hattie was awake. She tiptoed in and, thinking her momma was asleep, was about to leave when she heard Hattie ask, "Is Mr. Jack here?"

Abby turned in her tracks, went back to the bed, and knelt on the floor. "Yes, I was in the back garden and saw his carriage come up the drive. I came to see if you are up to seeing him just now."

A deep, throaty chuckle rang out from the doorway. "Of course she wants to see me," Jack said with a smile as bright as the sunshine. "My, my…look at my girls! Abby, you are as pretty as a picture." He gave her a hug. Jack took the chair beside Hattie's bed. "How's my angel?"

"I was worried you wouldn't be able to come." Hattie's voice was weak.

"It took me a while. I thank God for giving me strength to get here. We have a lot of catching up to do." Jack patted Hattie's hand. "It looks like my girls are being well taken care of." He glanced from Hattie to Abby.

Lawrence, witnessing the scene from the doorway, was humbled that Jack had trusted him with his girls.

****

Soft giggles could be heard throughout the house whenever Elizabeth was with her father. He didn't deny her anything if his health allowed it. They walked in the garden and visited the stable. She had even talked him into going on a short horseback ride around the stable and house. But what surprised Lawrence the most was when she talked Jack into taking her to Darin for a festival in the town, one Adam and Kathleen had discussed over dinner one evening. A traveling troupe would be putting on a magic show in addition to a song-and-dance act. Fireworks were to end the performance, and Elizabeth loved fireworks.

One night, after Elizabeth had gone up to bed, Jack sat gazing at the fire as it flickered and danced in the fireplace. He cleared his throat several times. Tears flowed freely from his eyes. He looked at Lawrence, who sat motionless across from him in a spoonback chair.

"Thank you for taking such good care of my Lizzie. I appreciate your keeping me informed of her condition." He stared at his hands. "Please don't think I tried to pawn her off on you to make my life easier." His gaze met Lawrence's. "I know it's hard to believe, when I did that with Hattie and Abby. Well, I didn't send them here to make my life easier but to keep them safe. I should have told you the truth about them from the beginning, and for that I am deeply sorry."

Lawrence gave his head a slight nod while rubbing his forehead. "Hattie and Abby told me all about Wesley and his pursuits."

"Let me tell you about Elizabeth." Jack took out his handkerchief and wiped the tears from his face. His voice was shaky. "I had hoped Lizzie—Elizabeth— would have a normal life. I wanted her to have a chance at happiness. She did so well for such a long time, I wanted to believe…I had convinced myself she was all right and wouldn't experience what her mother went through." He dropped his head. "I am so sorry."

Lawrence leaned close to Jack. "I love your daughter. The signs were there from the beginning, but I chose to ignore them. I had spent almost three years roaming the countryside, searching for adventures, when I worked for the magazine company. Sometimes I would go months without seeing a female of any kind.

When I saw Elizabeth, and how beautiful she was, my only thought was claiming her for my wife...and fulfilling my dreams of having a family."

Jack's voice was low and labored. "I am sorry that didn't happen for you, but you are still young; it's not too late for your dreams to come true. It simply won't be with Elizabeth, is all."

Lawrence looked at Jack's pale face. "You are tired; let's continue this conversation another time."

The next day Lawrence found Jack sitting on a bench in the alcove in the garden. The Cherokee rose bushes crept over the trellis, making a nice secluded place. Lawrence gave a slow chuckle. He suspected Jack was hiding from Elizabeth to get some rest. She had been very active so far during his visit, like a young child with endless energy.

"Lawrence, my boy, come join me." Jack slid down the stone bench to make room. "It's sure beautiful out here." He waved a hand to indicate the view of the garden. "Knowing Abby as I do, I know she spends a lot of time out here."

Lawrence nodded. "Hattie did too, when she was able."

Jack turned to look at Lawrence. "Do you think Abby will be all right when Hattie's time comes? She's been her whole world. They were inseparable at my place."

"I'm not sure. She's had a hard time already but seems to be better now." Lawrence stretched his legs out. "They both have made many good friends in the months they've been here. You can tell by the number of people coming to visit Hattie."

Jack shook his head thoughtfully, and the two sat

in companionable silence for a while, until Jack cleared his throat. "I do owe you an explanation as to why I sent Hattie and Abby with you."

Lawrence held up his hand. "It's all right, Jack."

"Please let me tell you anyway," Jack said with a pleading look in his eyes.

Lawrence nodded.

"I know Hattie has told you the story of Abby's birth. Well, a few months after Hattie brought the baby back to my plantation, Abby's grandfather came for a visit. He was a despicable, prideful man." Jack shook his head.

"He told me the story of his daughter and her marriage to a black man. He berated his men for being miserable cowards for not cutting the baby from the mother's womb to make sure it had no chance of surviving." Jack drew in a deep breath and blew it out. "That man didn't want the blood of a Wesley running through the veins of a... I will spare you his vile language." Jack massaged his temple. "You know what he said to me?" Jack looked at Lawrence. "He said I should understand the need to exterminate anyone who has mixed blood running through their veins, being a Southern gentleman myself. He said it was people like us, me and him, who had the responsibility to keep the white race pure."

Lawrence's chest grew tight as he listened to his father-in-law. "How did you respond to that?" Lawrence gazed at Jack with raised eyebrows.

"I sat in my chair in a daze, stunned by what I heard, almost physically sick. Then I shook my fist in his face and told him to get out of my house and off my property and to never come back." Jack looked down at his hands before he spoke again. "Lawrence, I tell you the truth—what Wesley said did make me think."

Lawrence gazed at his father-in-law. "What do you mean?"

"After my head stopped pounding and my dizziness passed, I sat in my chair for several hours, just staring out the window, thinking. Would I have done the same thing to Elizabeth if she had married a black man? Do I have that much hatred for people who are different from me?" Jack looked off into the distance. "I tried to pinpoint the time when I embraced the idea of slavery just like my father and my grandfather had." He paused for quite a time with his lips pressed in a tight line, eyes glistening. He spoke slowly. "I never wanted to be a farmer or a slave owner. I just didn't have the guts to go against family tradition."

Lawrence reached over and gently squeezed Jack's knee.

"I certainly didn't want to be the man Wesley took me to be. I decided that I could stand up for what was right even if I could only help one person at a time—in this case, two people at a time."

Lawrence nodded his head in understanding.

Jack pressed his hands together as he stared out into the garden, a slow smile stretching over his lips. "I moved Hattie into an overseers' house, and our attempt to keep Abby safe began. You know, Lawrence…" Jack looked at his son-in-law. "For the first time, I really felt good about myself."

A sense of sadness and silence hung between the two men. Then Lawrence slowly reached over and squeezed Jack's shoulder and gave it a pat.

"God can change the willing heart of any man or

woman, and I can tell you are a changed man, Jack."

****

Lawrence sat behind his desk, thumping the letter with his fingers, as Jack came into the study with a smile and said, "I want to thank you for getting Elizabeth to understand that I am not a young man anymore." He chuckled as he took the chair next to the desk. "I told her I have to have my rest so we can go to the festival."

Lawrence rubbed his chin and held up the letter. "I have to go to Rome on business in a few days. I will probably be there for at least a week. If this weren't urgent, I wouldn't go. But I will do all in my power to get back so I can accompany you and Elizabeth to the festival."

Jack rubbed the back of his neck, twisted the ring on his finger, and then looked at Lawrence. "Will it be all right for me to take Elizabeth to the festival even if you don't make it back in time?"

Lawrence thought for a moment and then quietly nodded his head.

"We will be just fine," Jack continued. "Evelyn will come along, plus your sister and brother-in-law, and according to Elizabeth, everyone is going. I thought we might spend a few nights in town so Elizabeth will not get overly tired."

Lawrence leaned forward in his chair. "Jack, I know your health is failing, and who am I to deny you private time with your only child." He placed his hands on Jack's shoulders and gave a gentle squeeze. "I hope the two of you will have lots of fun."

****

Two days after Jack and the others left the ranch

for the festival, Hattie passed away in her sleep, with Abby holding her hand. Abby looked at Hattie's smiling face and gave her a kiss on the lips. "Goodbye, Momma."

Abby pulled the white sheet up over Hattie's face and left the room. That afternoon, Eli officiated over a very emotional ceremony for Hattie in the common house. She was laid to rest in one of her favorite spots by the creek. Everyone had known Hattie was dying, but that didn't make her passing any easier for anyone, especially Abby.

That evening, the house was empty. Abby paced the floor, wringing her hands, regretting that she had insisted upon being alone. She held the cool doorknob in her hand, debating whether to go out to the carriage house to talk to Eli. He had been in the house several times to check on her. She closed her eyes and leaned her head against the door frame. "I can do this. I can stay here alone." She released the doorknob and returned to her bedroom.

****

When Lawrence returned the next morning from his trip to Rome, he was met at the gate by Eli, who told him Hattie was dead and Abby had spent the night in the house alone. Jack and Elizabeth and the others had not yet returned from the festival in town.

Lawrence wasted no time but rushed to the house and called, "Abby? Abby where are you?" He checked the kitchen and was just ready to look for her in the garden when Abby ran from her room and into his arms. He hugged her tight and kissed her forehead as she wept in his arms.

A flame of deep desire kindled inside of him,

frightening Lawrence so much that he suddenly pushed her aside and left the room. Her mouth flew open. She blinked her wet thick lashes several times as she stood like a statue watching him leave. She sank into the nearest chair, wondering why he had left so suddenly. She covered her face with her hands and cried.

Lawrence raced to the study and closed the door behind him. He paced the floor, threading his fingers through his hair. He felt pain in his gut. He knew he had hurt Abby by leaving her so abruptly, alone in the kitchen.

What was I thinking, to hug her? She's just an innocent girl. In her time of grief, she needed a friend, not confusion. He slammed his fist down on the desk. Abby didn't see Lawrence the rest of the day. She and Eli waited for him to come to the kitchen for their nightly reading. He never came. She slowly got up from the table, dragging her feet as she went to her bedroom. She closed the door with a thud. She had the sickening feeling that not only had she lost Hattie but her friendship with Lawrence as well. The next day, Lawrence had all his meals served in the dining room. He wanted to avoid Abby, but at each meal he sat at the long table staring at his plate. He couldn't eat or sleep for thinking of her. He put the fork down and pushed the plate aside. The image of her dark sunken eyes, ashen skin, and slumped shoulders invaded his mind. He threw the napkin on the table, leaped from his chair, and went in search of her. He needed to apologize.

Chapter Eleven

Wide grins, sparkling eyes, and laughter greeted Lawrence as he stood by the walkway waiting for the carriage to come to a full stop. The excited chatter about the festival continued until Kathleen took notice of her brother's clenched jaw and bloodshot eyes.

"Lawrence, what's the matter?" Kathleen asked with wide eyes and arched eyebrows. Lawrence pinched his lips together, then told her, "Hattie passed away two days ago." A collective gasp filled the air. Kathleen immediately deposited her sleeping toddler in his father's arms and rushed from the carriage to find Abby. Lawrence could see the tears filling Jack's eyes when he heard the news. Elizabeth seemed to be the only one not affected by the news. She went on and on about the performance, telling Lawrence and anyone else in hearing range all about the festival. Lawrence spoke quietly to his wife. "Elizabeth, did you hear? Hattie is dead."

"Yes. So?"

Lawrence stared at his wife. The others in the group dropped their heads in embarrassment. Everyone had loved and respected the old woman, even though they had known her for less than a year. Her healing ability was legendary, and everyone had come to her for advice about one thing or another.

Later that evening, Elizabeth continued to be

animated and very excited as she shared with Abby and the housekeeper the highlights of the festival. After she finished her story, she kissed her father and Lawrence each on the cheek and headed up to her bedroom. She hadn't given her husband a kiss in a very long time. He watched her as she practically danced from the room. Lawrence took one look at Jack's pale face and moved to sit on the upholstered stool in front of him, just as Jack was taken by a violent coughing spell. Finally his cough eased enough for him to speak.

"Thank you, Lawrence." His voice was raspy. "Thanks for allowing me time with my little Lizzie. You can see she had a wonderful time."

"There is no need to thank me, Jack. Elizabeth is still your daughter." Before Jack could say another word, he slumped over in his chair. Lawrence touched him and found he was burning up with fever. He carefully stretched him out on the settee before he sprinted from the room to get Abby.

Abby was standing before the mirror brushing her hair when she heard Lawrence calling her name. She could tell from the sound of his voice and the quickness of his steps that this was not a social call. She opened her door just before he knocked. He stood looking at her with wide eyes and open mouth. After a few seconds she spoke. "Yes, Mr. Lawrence, do you need me for something?" He continued staring at her, speechless. She was like an angel standing before him: her long, light-brown hair went all the way to her waist, and the auburn streaks highlighted the reddish flecks in her eyes...her warm, seductive eyes... The sight of her took his breath away.

The housekeeper raced into the kitchen. "Abby,

come quick! It's Mr. Jack." Abby ran past Lawrence and followed Betsy into the parlor, with Lawrence coming behind. Jack was gasping for air.

Abby quickly took charge of the situation, untying his wide cravat so he could breathe more easily and issuing orders. "Betsy, I need for you to dip the white tablecloth in a bucket of cold water, wring it out good, and bring it upstairs to Mr. Jack's room." Betsy left to do what she was told.

Looking at Lawrence, Abby said, "Let's get him upstairs to his bed." The two of them struggled under Jack's weight. Once upstairs, they laid him gently on his bed. "We have to take his clothes off." Abby began unbuttoning his shirt. "He has a dangerously high fever. When Betsy gets here with the tablecloth, you are going to wrap Mr. Jack in it for about a half hour. It will help to reduce his fever."

Lawrence didn't respond.

"Do you hear me, Mr. Lawrence?"

He nodded.

"In the meantime, I'm going downstairs to make some tea with feverfew, to bring his fever down, and aniseed to ease his cough." Abby dashed from the room without looking back.

Several hours later, Jack's fever was down, and he was resting quietly. Lawrence sat in a chair next to his bed, trying to make sense of what had transpired earlier that evening. Thanks to Abby's quick actions, Jack was alive. She had been confident and authoritative as she assessed the situation and determined what course of action to take. He couldn't believe how inept he had been, standing there staring at her instead of explaining Jack's condition. It was as if he had seen her for the first time as she stood with her hair down, looking so beautiful. He had never thought about what her hair might look like, with it always under the wrap she wore almost all the time. He unconsciously rubbed the tips of his fingers together. They itched to become entangled in that long, light-brown, auburn-accented hair. He shook his head gently to bring himself back to the present. She was gorgeous. She was a stunning picture of true innocence. He blew air out of his lungs and shook his head. "Abby is a beautiful young woman," he said just above a whisper.

Jack moaned and coughed a few times. "That's why I sent her here. My cousin wanted to sell her to a brothel."

Lawrence went pale. His heart galloped in his chest. He bounced to his feet and shook Jack. He was desperate for more information. "What did you say?"

Jack's eyeballs rolled under his closed lids, but he didn't answer.

Lawrence fell back into his chair. Disbelief surged through him. "A brothel... Someone wanted to sell Abby." The word "brothel" left a sour taste in his mouth as well as in his gut. He slammed his clenched fist into his palm. "The impertinence of this...man. The scoundrel! I've got to get to the bottom of this." He jumped to his feet and started pacing the floor.

"Why didn't Hattie and Abby say anything about this?" He wiped his fingers through his hair. A thought crashed into his mind and his pacing came to a halt. "Maybe Hattie never mentioned it because she didn't want Abby to know." He sank down in his chair, muttering. "Abby has a grandfather who wants to kill her and someone else wants to sell her to a brothel. Oh,

God."

When Jack was sleeping peacefully, Lawrence left his side, determined to find Abby and learn more about the brothel. Approaching the kitchen door, he heard singing. He gently pushed the door open, and a grin lifted his lips.

Music swirled in the air as Abby raised her voice and belted out an African hymn while she crushed Cherokee rose leaves with the pestle. A smile sashayed around her mouth, and then she set aside the mortar and pestle and danced around the room. She was thinking of his apology after he'd left her so abruptly after trying to comfort her for the loss of her momma. Their eyes had met when he apologized, and his midnight-black gaze was warm and kind. His lopsided grin had taken her back to the boy she had met by the creek years before. She stopped dancing and remembered the kiss he'd planted on her forehead. It wasn't a kiss of love, just sympathy, but it still was her first kiss. She covered her forehead with her fingers and began singing and dancing again.

When she caught sight of Lawrence, propped against the door frame, his arms folded over his chest, enjoying the view of her dancing, her hand flew to her flushed cheeks. "How long have you been there?"

"Long enough to see your fancy footwork." He chortled.

Abby bowed her head and smiled. She turned her back to him, walked to the worktable, and resumed crushing the herbs. Lawrence came up behind her. His closeness made her stomach flutter like a swarm of butterflies. He reached from behind her, and their arms touched as he picked up a rose leaf from the mortar. He spoke into her ear. "You smell like mint and a hint of sweet roses." Abby sucked in a long breath as heat engulfed her. She thought she was going to faint. Lawrence went over to the stove and lifted the lid from the pot. She looked at him through thick lashes.

"That smells good. Beef stew is one of my favorites," he said. He walked around the table and stood in front of her, and she spoke without looking up at him.

"I'm afraid it will be only the two of us for dinner, sir." He quirked an eyebrow and smiled, then went out the door to the rest of the house. His stride was jaunty as he walked down the hallway to his study, whistling and smiling. He knew his behavior in the kitchen had rattled Abby, but when he saw her dancing, his heart had hammered in his chest like a herd of stampeding horses. He walked over to the window and peered outside into the garden. He smiled. He knew after their encounter in the kitchen he would never ask her about the brothel. She was so innocent and sweet he doubted if she knew the meaning of the word.

****

During Jack's time of recuperation, Elizabeth never left his side. When he was too weak to go downstairs for dinner, she joined him in his room to keep him company during the meal. She hovered over him when he woke. Her soft whimpers could be heard throughout the upstairs when Jack was too tired to muster the energy to interact with her. "Papa, Papa, wake up." Elizabeth's words echoed through the house many days and nights.

Over the next few days, Jack's chronic stomach issues flared up. Even as the older man slept, Lawrence saw him shake, wince, and squeeze his eyes trying to get through a wave of pain. The pain was excruciating at times, but Jack tried to hide it from everyone, especially Elizabeth. Lawrence sent for Jack's personal physician, even though Abby cared for him like a loving daughter. He hoped the doctor's presence would ease the burden on Abby. He could see weariness on her face. Her once bright and vibrant eyes were now sunken and outlined in dark shadows. He tried to convince himself that the sadness she wore like a cloak of armor was because of her grief and concern for Jack, that it had nothing to do with him withdrawing from her and not attending the nightly meetings they had once had with Eli in the kitchen. He tried to console himself by remembering he had apologized to her.

He also worried about Elizabeth's mental state and hoped she would benefit from the doctor's visit. She had become depressed and lethargic and spent most of her time curled up on Jack's bed, unless Lawrence carried her back to her bedroom. Lawrence sat with his wife and Jack for hours, all of them tended by the servants who took care of them around the clock. Elizabeth was a shell of the woman she used to be. Dark circles surrounded her once-beautiful eyes, and her glowing skin was wan. Her rosy cheeks were now hollow. He kissed the top of her head and gently eased her sleeping form down on the bed before he slid from the mattress.

Eli entered the room carrying a tray of food for Lawrence and Elizabeth. "I'm afraid, sir, that Evelyn and the other servants have nerves that have gotten the better of them. The tray was dropped twice before it left the kitchen." He put the tray on the table. "Do you need help to get her to eat some broth when she wakes up?"

Lawrence sucked in his bottom lip and didn't answer.

Eli looked at his boss. "You need to eat something yourself, sir." He handed Lawrence the plate. The roast beef sandwich was piled high, and the mint tea was hot.

Lawrence took a bite of the sandwich and a sip of tea before placing the food and drink back on the tray. "I'm worried," Lawrence said as he rubbed the stubble on his chin.

Eli arched a brow. "What concerns you, sir?"

Lawrence went to stand by the window, his face downcast. "I wonder what life will be like for Elizabeth…and me, when Jack's time comes."

Eli gave no response.

The tension drained from Lawrence's body and he released a huge sigh when Jack's personal physician arrived. The man examined Jack and announced that the worst was over for now.

"You old coot," the doctor said to Jack as he put his instruments back into his black bag. "You may be around for a while yet." He chuckled.

"I'm not worried about me." Jack's voice was thick with emotion. "I know I don't have much time left. What about Elizabeth?"

The doctor looked at Lawrence sitting at the foot of the bed. "Just like I told your son-in-law, physically Elizabeth will recover, with good food and those herbs." He snapped his bag closed without taking his eyes off Lawrence. "But you need to consider putting her in that home we talked about, the one in Boston."

Lawrence jerked to his feet. "I will never do that. I don't care how nice it's supposed to be."

Chapter Twelve

By late fall, laughter, singing, and gleeful chatter had replaced worried faces and whispers in Lawrence's household. Jack's condition improved enough for him to take short walks. Elizabeth's tantrums were manageable, at least most of the time. Lawrence was hopeful. Jack extended his stay for another two weeks to make sure he was well enough to make the journey home. Elizabeth fussed over him, barely allowing him from her sight.

One day, Jack planned an escape. He sneaked from the house, went down the path a distance, rounded a corner, and disappeared into the store. "There you are, Lawrence, my boy," Jack said, entering the store breathing heavily and wiping perspiration from his brow. "This is a fine idea, having a general store on the property."

Lawrence smiled. The man said the same thing each time he visited the store.

Jack spotted the jar of peppermint sticks and winked at his son-in-law, so Lawrence pulled out two sticks of candy and handed them over to Jack. "You have everything in here from candy to small household items," Jack said between licks. He grunted as he took a seat by the fireplace. He dabbed the back of his neck with his handkerchief.

Lawrence moved closer to him. "Are you all

right?"

Jack muttered under his breath, "I will be, if Lizzie stops all her mothering. Lawrence, my boy, let's go for a ride, get some fresh air, and…"

Lawrence chortled. "I would love to go, but I have to get these books balanced." He walked over and sat behind the desk tucked away in the corner of the room by a window. "Why don't you ask Eli? I know he'll be glad to spend some time with you."

"That's a good idea." Jack gazed off into the room with a peppermint stick dangling from his lips. "That Eli is something, isn't he? There is a depth about him that draws you in—it makes you want to be a better person. It's as if he can see right into your soul."

"I know," Lawrence said, putting his pen down on the desk.

"I knew my cousin would never appreciate that quality in him. That's why I sent him with you and didn't ask for him to be returned. I thought he might make a good match for Abby," Jack said, smiling and bobbing his head. Lawrence strangled on a cough. "Are you all right, my boy? You look a bit pale."

"I'm fine. Let me go tell Eli to get the carriage ready so you can go for your ride."

Elizabeth got wind of her father's plan to go for a ride. She decided to go with him and turn the outing into a picnic. A lunch was packed, and within an hour, they were on their way.

****

The house was quiet. Lawrence made his way to his study, his mind reeling. Jack's words about Eli being a good match for Abby had rattled him. He paced the floor of his study. Did Eli really have an interest in

Abby other than that of a brother or friend? All kinds of thoughts exploded in his head. A knock on the kitchen door brought him out of his rumination. The knocking grew louder. Lawrence rushed to the door and yanked it open. Hank, a persistent suitor of Abby's but one Lawrence thought had been thoroughly discouraged, stood on the other side with a bucket of dandelion roots.

"Is Miss Abby home?" Lawrence gave the man a long hard stare. His voice was gruff. "No, she is not."

Hank's gaze never left Lawrence's face. "I dug these for her..." Before Hank could finish his sentence, Lawrence grabbed the bucket from his hand and closed the door in his face. He dropped the bucket on the worktable and marched back to his office, muttering something about the nerve of that man.

Lawrence frowned when he thought of Hank. The man had had the audacity to ask permission to court Abby a few days after Hattie's death. He said she needed someone to look after her, since Hattie was gone. Lawrence slammed his fist against the door frame. He walked over and took a seat behind his desk, muttering under his breath.

He pulled out the correspondence he had received from his solicitor in England concerning trouble at the silk factory he owned. Lawrence tried to work, but he could only think of Abby. Every time she entered or left a room, he noticed her. He watched for her when she went by the store on her way to gather herbs and roots. A slow smile formed, and he leaned back in his chair. He had accompanied her on her searches too many times for his own good. He had become possessive of her, thinking of her as his own. He swiped his hand through his hair. *What is wrong with me? She is just an innocent girl under my protection.* He finally gave up all pretense of working. He threw his pen down on the desk and walked over to the window.

Lawrence saw Jack and Elizabeth's carriage rolling to a stop and went to meet them. Before Jack climbed out of the carriage, Elizabeth leaped down and ran up the walkway where Lawrence stood. "Papa is going to take me home to my old room. Isn't that wonderful?" She beamed and called to her father down the walkway, "Can we go home tomorrow, Papa?" Elizabeth bounced on her toes, waiting impatiently for Jack and Evelyn to make their way up the walkway. Jack, bent from pain, mopped perspiration from his pale face. Lawrence's eyes met his, and a knowing look passed between them. He knew how much Jack wanted to die at home, and he knew he had to do all in his power to make it happen. He cleared his throat and tried to smile. "Elizabeth," Lawrence said, "it might take us a few days to get everything ready for us to leave." She folded her arms across her chest and stomped her feet.

"Elizabeth, that's enough!" Lawrence voice was stern. She rolled her eyes and dashed into the house and up the stairs to her room.

Abby heard Elizabeth when she stormed through the house muttering something about going home. Jack had already mentioned to her his desire to be home when his time came. She knew his time was near, but she wasn't prepared for his leaving.

****

Elizabeth fell across her bed, grumbling and crying about going home. Evelyn rushed to her side. "Lizzie, Lizzie," she cooed, rubbing her back like a mother comforting a fussy baby. Elizabeth lunged to her feet, locked her arms across her chest and pouted her lips.

"I want to go home!"

"Now, Miss Elizabeth," Evelyn said softly, cupping Elizabeth's chin in her hand. "We are going home as soon as Mr. Lawrence makes the arrangements."

"We are going home soon?" Elizabeth asked, sniffing. She cocked her head to one side and stared at the woman for a moment. "I'm going home."

"Yes, you are. Now, let's take a nap before dinner."

When Elizabeth woke from her nap, her gaze traveled the length of the room and landed on the empty chair that was usually occupied by one of her caregivers.

"Papa, where are you?"

Her words jammed in her throat. She pulled the covers up to her chin.

"Papa, Papa, where are you?" Her breath was quick. Her eyes darted across the room again and again. She fidgeted with the bedcovers, scrunching the sheet in her balled fist. She stared at the open door. Tossing the covers aside, she yelled, "Wait for me, Papa! Wait for me! We're going home!" She dashed from the room, heading for the stairs.

She made it halfway down the steps before tripping. Cries and gut-wrenching screams rent the air as she tumbled down the staircase, landing in a quiet heap at the foot of the stairs.

The household buzzed with fright as Lawrence and the others instinctively charged to the source of the noise. He reached his wife first. His body trembled, his heart hammering in his chest. His eyes filled with unshed tears when he saw Elizabeth's still form. Lawrence dropped to the floor, tears blinding his sight. He raised her limp hand to his face. "Elizabeth! Oh, Elizabeth!" he cried.

Abby pushed through the small crowd, fell to her knees, and began examining Elizabeth. She put her ear to Elizabeth's chest, then to her mouth and nose. She slowly raised her tearstained face. She looked up at Lawrence and shook her head. "I'm sorry," she said, choking back tears. Tears dripped from Lawrence's cheeks. He fell back on his heels in shock. A loud gasp came from the parlor, where Jack slid down the doorjamb, muttering, "Lizzie, Lizzie, my little girl…"

****

Lawrence stared out the store window, eyes filled with unshed tears. He bit down on his bottom lip, determined not to let his mind consume him with grief and sadness today. Ever since Elizabeth's death, two weeks before, there had been a strange silence in his house. He knew his staff was thinking of him and Jack. He knew it was time to take Jack home, if he was going to honor his father-in-law's wishes to be home when his time came.

A smile pulled at the corners of his mouth when he thought of Abby and how she had showered them both with love and kindness during the weeks since Elizabeth's death. He knew then that he loved her. He caught sight of movement in the corner of his eyes. He stretched his neck to get a better look. It was Abby returning from her herb garden. Out of nowhere a conversation he'd had with Hattie popped into his head. *Couples on the plantations where I've lived marry by simply jumping over a broom and exchanging vows.*

An idea sprang into his mind. He rushed out of the store, heading for the house. He needed to see Abby. Lawrence skidded into the kitchen.

"Mr. Lawrence, you are just in time for dinner," the cook said. He looked around the room. Abby was nowhere to be seen. He wanted to tell the woman that dinner could wait. He had important business to discuss with Abby, but he wouldn't dare hurt the wonderful lady's feelings. "We were getting worried about you," she said. "Go ahead and get cleaned up. Mr. Jack is waiting for you in the dining room."

Silverware and porcelain clinked as servants stood ready to refill glasses and serve the platters of steaming baked fish, boiled white potatoes with chives, young sweet peas, and chocolate pie. All Lawrence's favorites, but he had no appetite. His mind was on Abby. The spattering of conversation gave him ample time to think of ways to persuade her to jump the broom with him. The ideas brought a smile to his lips. He cleared his throat, laid his fork down, and looked at his father-in-law. "Would you like to leave for Mason the day after tomorrow?" The older man beamed.

****

Abby rubbed her upper arms as she paced the floor in her room, distress and uncertainty plaguing her. She had heard Lawrence tell the household staff he would be taking Jack home day after tomorrow. "What am I to do?" she said, lovingly caressing Hattie's rocking chair. "I can't go back to the plantation. I don't want that life again."

She rubbed her temples. "The people will be wondering about my miraculous recovery." She sank into the chair and set it in motion. "What if my grandf—" She corrected herself. "What if John Wesley hears about a girl on the Bradley Plantation that was once mute and slow but now is fully recovered? That might bring him back searching for me." She stopped the chair with her feet, grabbed its arms, and shot to her feet. She began pacing again.

A knock sounded at her door. She jumped and mopped tears from her face with the back of her hand. Before she reached the door, it swung open. Lawrence stood before her with a broom in his hand.

"We need to talk." His eyes were pleading, his voice soft.

****

Abby hummed a jolly tune as she prepared lunch. She sat at the kitchen table, staring dreamily at the back of her hands. She had slept with one hand tucked under her chin and the other over her heart. Last night, Lawrence had stared lovingly into her eyes when they had shared their vows and jumped the broom. He had only kissed the back of her hands that night before he left her standing in the doorway of her room. She giggled. "Let me stop this woolgathering and take him lunch."

She stepped into Lawrence's study. His face lit up as though his heart did a flip in his chest at the sight of her. "I waited for you in the kitchen, but you never came," she said as she entered his office carrying a silver tray with his lunch. "That was about an hour ago, so I decided to bring lunch to you."

He pulled his watch from his pocket. "I didn't know it had gotten that late. I'm glad you thought to bring me lunch, my sweet wife." He whispered the last three words. They had vowed to keep their marriage secret for now.

A flush suffused her face, and her lips curved upward, transforming into a blinding smile. Lawrence moved back from the desk to give her room to work. He watched her closely as she placed the lunch tray on his desk. Several times their gazes met. She gave him a bashful smile as she placed the bowl of chicken and vegetable soup, slices of sourdough bread, and fruit on the placemat she had tucked in her pocket. She snapped her fingers. "I forgot your hot tea and dessert."

"Hot tea with mint, I hope."

Abby smiled and went to get the tea and a big slice of chocolate pie. She returned with the tea and pie and set them on the desk. He laughed.

"This is fit for a king." He watched her leave the room. His mouth watered, but not for food.

About an hour later, she returned to pick up the dishes.

"Excuse me, I thought you had finished."

"I have." He slid the dishes toward her just as she was reaching to pick them up. Their fingers touched. A desire as hot as a bolt of lightning shot through him. Lawrence gently and slowly rubbed her long fingers. A spark ignited a desire in her beyond any she had ever known. A soft moan escaped her lips. Lawrence pulled her down into his lap. He softly kissed her forehead, then her eyebrows, and as his longing grew, he kissed her cheeks. At last his lips found hers. He kissed them gently at first. Then, as passion exploded in him, he deepened the kiss. Abby's passion matched his, and they lost themselves in their desire and loneliness.

****

Lawrence spent the rest of the afternoon and most

of the next day making arrangements for his trip to Mason, Georgia. He sat at his desk, head throbbing from thinking of the best way to tell Abby she wouldn't be going with him. He closed his eyes and massaged his forehead. He didn't want to leave her behind, but he needed to protect her from John Wesley and Jack's cousin.

His rational thought and his emotional thought warred within him. He paced the length of the floor. Tears of despair filled his eyes. He slammed his balled fist into his palm. "It's for her own good. She must understand that." He threaded his fingers through his hair. *Why didn't I think of Abby's safety before I talked her into jumping the broom with me?* The muscle in his square jaw twitched. "I will not and cannot put her life in danger by taking her back to that place, not when Jack fought so hard to get her away from it." He dropped down in his chair. "I've already asked her to keep our marriage secret."

He lowered his head in shame. "Now what will she think of me when I tell her I'm leaving her behind?" He jumped to his feet. "I have to find Abby and explain things to her." And he had to make her understand that he had not used her for his pleasure and then abandoned her.

****

Abby packed herbs in a basket. Her mind exploded with thoughts of Lawrence. She had gotten only glimpses of him since the day they'd shared their love. That was what it was…love. She loved him. An icy dread suffused her.

"I have to tell him I cannot go back to the plantation." She blinked back tears. "I just can't do it."

She busied herself with the herbs. *Lawrence shouldn't be gone for long, but I don't know for sure. Mr. Jack's resilience has surprised us all.* She smiled at the thought. She stopped her work and stared into the room, wondering how Lawrence might respond to her news.

From the corner of her eye she caught sight of him leaning against the door frame of the kitchen, gazing at her. He walked up behind her and the mere closeness of him sent a delightful shiver over her entire body. She didn't turn around to face him but continued her task.

His warm breath tickled as he whispered in her ear, "I will always take care of you, Abby."

She turned to face him and wrapped her arms around his waist. She closed her eyes, enjoying the feel of him. She finally spoke. "I know you will, Lawrence."

They stayed in each other's embrace for a while, until finally Abby stepped away and turned her back, tears pooling in her eyes. She spoke just above a whisper. "I can't go back."

She turned to face him, tears rolling down her cheeks, and choked out, "I just can't go back to live that life again. I know Momma wouldn't want me to, and I don't think Mr. Jack does either."

Lawrence covered her lips with his finger. "I know, and I don't want you to." He held her tight, caressing the top of her head with his chin. He lifted her head, wiping her tears away with the pads of his fingers. "I understand, sweetheart. I understand." He made a trail of kisses down her cheek, then moved away from her just enough to look into her chestnut eyes, seductive, with just a hint of amber outlining the rim. He opened his mouth to speak.

Abby covered his lips with her finger. She looked deep into his eyes, blinked several times, and turned away from him. She traced the smooth wooden worktable with her finger. "I have made a decision."

A frown formed on Lawrence's face, and his heart slammed against his ribcage. "What decision is that?"

"I'm getting a room at the common house." She went on talking so he wouldn't interrupt. "Mr. Jack gave Momma and me some money, just in case we needed it. I can use that money to take care of my needs."

Lawrence took hold of both her arms. He stared at her in disbelief, wondering if he heard her correctly. "You want to live in the common house?"

A picture of Hank popped into his mind. He was a fine-looking man. He and Abby could pass as siblings. *Hank has a bright future, but not with my Abby.*

"You're not going to live in the common house!" The words came out more sharply than he intended. Abby's eyebrows soared to the top of her forehead like a bird taking off in flight. Her mouth fell open in shock, and she wiggled from his hold. She put her hands on her hips and, in words laced with outrage, she asked, "You're going to force me to go back to the plantation?"

"Oh, sweetheart, it's not that way at all." Lawrence took hold of Abby's hands and brought them to rest on his chest. She was crying again, and he rubbed her back and spoke softly to her between his kisses.

"I have arranged for you to stay with my sister and her family. You will have the third floor of the house to yourself. That's one of the main things I have been doing in getting ready to leave. You will be a companion to Kathleen. You can help her with the baby and whatever else you girls want to do." Abby's eyes shone with tears as she looked at Lawrence with love in her eyes. "You did that for me?"

"I want to do more for you, sweetheart." Abby wrapped her arms around his neck.

"Oh, Lawrence, thank you. I'll love being with Kathleen and Raymon." She kissed him deep and long.

Early the next morning, before Jack and the servants were out of bed, Lawrence hitched the horse to the carriage and drove it around to the side of the house. Abby was waiting for him outside the kitchen door. He helped her into the carriage, loaded her things, and then drove slowly up the lane to the main house. He felt as if he was going to a funeral...his funeral. Leaving Abby was like burying the best part of him in a box to be dug up after it had decayed.

Lawrence found her fingers beneath the folds of her skirt and caressed them tenderly all the way to the main house. Abby's heart skipped a beat when she glanced over at him. Oh, how she was going to miss this man...her first, her only love. Once they reached the house, Lawrence jumped from the carriage. He walked around the conveyance, put both hands around Abby's tiny waist, and slowly and gingerly lifted her down. She could feel the strength in his arms, and it sent tingles through her body. They stood for a while looking longingly into each other's eyes.

Kathleen cleared her throat as she approached the pair. "Abby, I'm so happy you will be living with us. I know we will have great fun together."

"Thank you, Miss Kathleen."

"Please, just call me Kathleen."

Lawrence released Abby's waist but folded her fingers around his arm and escorted her into the house. Kathleen left them in the foyer while she went to alert the staff to take Abby's things up to her room. Abby laced her fingers into Lawrence's as he led her up the stairs to the third floor—her new home. He opened the door and allowed her to enter first. Her hand flew to her opened mouth, and she turned in a slow circle, taking in the beauty of the lavishly decorated room. The mahogany four-post canopy bed stood against a long wall decorated with intricate stenciling. Various paintings of outdoor scenes of meadows, flowers, trees, animals, and winding rivers hung on the walls in ornate picture frames.

"I know how much you love the outdoors," Lawrence whispered in her ear. A dark blue upholstered settee was home to several stuffed pillows of various designs and shapes that gave it a comfortable, cozy look. The two Victorian spoonback chairs covered in blue floral design completed the seating arrangement.

"This is gorgeous!" Abby picked up a pillow and squeezed it to her bosom. Lawrence led her over to the double doors at the opposite side of the room. He flung them open to show her a balcony beckoning to be sat on, overlooking the magnificent garden and its gazebo tucked near the back gate. "Oh, Lawrence, this is amazing! It's fit for a queen."

He came up behind her and kissed her on the neck. "You are a queen, my sweet. Go look in the closet." Abby crossed the room, glancing back over her shoulder at Lawrence. He smiled and rocked on his heels. She opened the closet and gasped.

"These dresses are beautiful! When did you do all

this?"

"It's a long story, but I don't want you to ever wear another ugly dress."

Abby giggled and, running to him, she fell into his arms. Before she could say a word, Kathleen called from the second floor landing. "Lawrence, come down here and let Abby get settled in." He held Abby's hands and stared into her lovely face. Her brown eyes sparkled with unshed tears, and he lowered his head to her lips and kissed her deeply. At that moment, Abby wanted to tell him that she would go with him; she'd go with him anywhere. She didn't know whether she spoke the words audibly or if she only thought them.

When he broke the kiss, he traced her chin and then her lips with his thumb. He cupped her chin in his hand. "I have too much on my mind to constantly worry about your safety. I need for you to stay here." She nodded. He kissed her once more on the cheek. Then he turned and walked from the room without looking back.

Abby stood, hands at her lips and tears in her eyes. She whispered, "Goodbye," as he disappeared from sight. Minutes later, she walked to the window and watched Lawrence as he drove down the lane. He turned, looked back at the third floor window, and smiled. She pressed her face against the window panes and mouthed, "I love you."

Later that morning, Lawrence sat on the carriage seat, staring at the house he'd come to love, not for the structure itself but for the two wonderful ladies who had made the spacious house a home—Abby and Hattie. Water shimmered in his eyes. He didn't know when he'd be able to come back to his home and to Abby. Lawrence wished there were another road they could take that wouldn't lead them by the main house. "I might be tempted to jump out of this carriage and go get my..." The thought spilled from his lips.

"Did you say something, boss?" Eli asked. Lawrence shook his head, and the carriage pulled off, leaving behind trails of dirt...and his heart.

Chapter Thirteen

The first leg of the trip was uneventful, each person lost in his or her own thoughts. As the miles stretched before them, worry nibbled at the edge of Lawrence's mind as he observed Jack's pallid complexion, wrinkled facial features, and white knuckles gripping the seat cushion. "Don't worry about me, my boy. Just get me home."

Lawrence admired the man's courage. He would do all he could to make him comfortable. He was determined to have Jack's physician at his side during his final hours.

It was not long before the carriage rolled to a stop in front of the Bradleys' home. Jack was ushered into the house and upstairs to his bedroom, but not before Lawrence reminded him that Eli would be staying in the main house. Jack had no objections.

After Jack was settled, Lawrence went for a walk. He followed the path that led around the property, then circled back to the farm cottage where Abby and Hattie had once lived. He stood facing the small two-story house, thoughts of Abby and Hattie filling his mind. "My Abby, oh, my sweet, sweet Abby, how I miss you already," he moaned.

His longing for her overwhelmed his thoughts. He closed his eyes and relived the time they'd had together. When guilt forged through his mind for loving Abby so soon after Elizabeth's death, he lowered his head in shame.

Eli came up behind him, clearing his throat. "Mr. Jack would like to see you right now, sir."

Lawrence immediately followed the man into the house and upstairs. His footsteps slowed when he drew near the room he and Elizabeth had shared. He leaned his tall frame momentarily against the doorjamb, thinking of Elizabeth as the woman she had been, filled with vigor and sass. His smile faded and his eyes glassed over when he thought of what their lives could have been. Releasing a heavy sigh, he continued to Jack's room on the front hallway.

Jack was sitting up in bed surrounded by a mound of papers when Lawrence entered the room. His skin was pasty and his voice weak and raspy but with an anxious pleading tone.

"Lawrence, I want to change my will, and I know you are the person to help me get things in order, with your expertise in handling great amounts of money."

"How do you know that?" Lawrence said, pulling a chair up closer to the bed. Jack smiled weakly and continued thumbing through papers. Lawrence knew that Adam and Kathleen were the only people who knew the extent of his wealth, and that was the way he wanted it. He didn't want to live a life encumbered by the social norms of the wealthy, which dictated where to live, how to live, and with whom you should or should not associate.

Jack cleared his throat, bringing Lawrence out of his musing. "I'm sorry, Jack. What were you saying?"

"About my will…"

Lawrence nodded. "I'll do all I can to help."

"Good, my boy. I knew I could count on you. I'm breaking the Bradley family tradition. I'm freeing my slaves, something I've wanted to do for a long time but didn't have the courage for."

Lawrence gave his father-in-law a broad smile. "That's the right thing to do."

Through pain and determination, Jack outlined an impressive plan to free his slaves and to prevent his property from ever being worked by slave labor again. Jack's blue-veined hand trembled as he handed Lawrence the papers. Lawrence took the will and perused the contents. His eyes widened. A smile tugged at his lips. "You're being very generous. The provisions you are offering the slaves and Eli are impressive."

Jack squirmed from pain. "That's the least I can do. Eli should be more than able to provide a comfortable living for Abby anywhere they go. I told you before she will need someone solid, trustworthy, and smart to take care of her now that Hattie is gone."

Jack's words were like a dagger thrusting into Lawrence's heart. He began perspiring. He struggled to keep his composure. "I'll get to work on this right away." Lawrence swallowed the lump in his throat and quickly left the room.

Over the next few weeks, the new will was finalized, while Jack's health steadily declined. He needed more opium to endure the acute pain that was now his constant companion. Everyone knew he would not be much longer on this earth.

****

Lawrence walked with his chin lowered to his chest, hands tucked into his pockets. He kicked hickory nuts from the well-worn path that led to Abby and

Hattie's old cottage. He went to the house whenever he wanted to feel close to Abby…and to agonize. Jack's death had just added to the misery deep in his soul. The same questions inundated his mind day and night. *Did I jump the broom with Abby for the right reasons? Was it for lust or love? Who grieves for his wife, yet desires the affection of another? Did I take away her innocence just for my pleasure?* The thoughts ripped through his mind, shattering what was left of his dignity. He was consumed with guilt for loving Abby and sharing marriage vows with her so soon after Elizabeth's death. *Abby must think I'm a hard-hearted person.* He could barely look at himself in the mirror.

Lawrence stepped into the cottage, took a deep breath, and the smell of mint, clover, and onions greeted him like an old friend. He stroked the worktable in the middle of the room, surrounded by its four spindle-backed chairs.

He flopped down in a chair and covered his face with his hands and cried out in a loud voice, "I'm a wretched man…a wretched, wretched man." Eyes red rimmed, Lawrence stood and beat his hands to his chest. "I was a failure as a husband. I'm a failure as a Christian…and a failure as a friend." His insides shook from the force of his anguish.

He whispered, "Abby deserves better than me. Her love for me is probably out of obligation for the freedom she and Hattie enjoyed under my care and has nothing to do with true love."

He looked at the stairs. Abby had always said she found comfort in the upstairs room. "Lord, you know I need comfort." Lawrence walked slowly up the stairs, avoiding the third and sixth steps.

A smile tried to creep across his face when he thought of Abby and how she used to avoid the screeching of those two steps. She would walk on the right inside of each one, with her right shoulder rubbing against the wall. He tried it. No screeching.

When he reached the top of the stairs, his gaze roamed the open shelves. Each shelf held crocks containing various herbs. He fingered the one that read Mint and inhaled a deep, satisfying breath. He whispered, "Abby."

He lost track of time as he paced back and forth in the room, avoiding the screeching floor boards. He made a decision—freeing Abby of her obligation to him was what he needed to do.

Later that afternoon, Lawrence sat hunched over his desk. Balled-up sheets of paper littered the floor. He was writing Abby, struggling to describe his feelings— his guilt, his shame, and the war that raged inside of him. Finally, he gave up. He crumpled the stationery, tossed it aside, slumped over his desk, and began writing, this time to his sister.

The next few months were a blur for Lawrence. He lost himself in his work and grief as he went about fulfilling the provisions in Jack's will. He'd petitioned friends, investors, and his law firm for help in accomplishing Jack's last wishes. Lawrence and Eli met with the slaves often to educate them on life beyond the plantation and what it meant to live as free people. His friends were able to help the former slaves find jobs. Work ranged from skilled laborers to housekeepers in Christian businesses and homes throughout the north and Canada. A few brave men decided to venture out west to seek their fortunes. All were given monetary compensations for their years of toil. An old couple and a sick woman stayed on at the farm, unable to travel. A young girl stayed to care for them and to be a housekeeper for one of Lawrence's solicitors, who would be living in the main house and managing the farm. The land had been divided and rented to local farmers who did not hold slaves, with the stipulation that no slave labor could ever be used to work the land. It took longer than Lawrence had expected for all the provisions of Jack's will to be carried out. The plan to free the slaves had been successfully implemented, and the Bradley Plantation had been renamed the Bradley Farm. Lawrence had free time to think, but that was not what he needed.

Not long after everything for Jack's estate was settled, Lawrence sat at the table in Abby and Hattie's old house. He pulled a letter from his pocket, one of several from his solicitor in England. He turned the letter in his hands, thinking about its contents. "Maybe I should go to England and handle this business myself," he said, tapping the letter in his palm. He nodded his head and sat in silence for a time. "That's what I'll do." He left the cottage with a purposeful stride.

****

Kathleen sat motionless in the gazebo with Lawrence's open letter in her lap. Tears streamed down her cheeks and onto her blouse. She didn't bother to wipe them away as her husband found her.

"Darling! Darling, there you are. I've been… What's wrong?"

Adam quickly went to his wife and knelt before her. Kathleen pushed the letter in his direction, and he took it and sat next to her on the bench. He read the letter, with its details about Lawrence's agonies, as well as about Jack's suffering and death, details he hadn't included in his previous letters. Adam blew out a breath. "Poor Lawrence. He's been through so much."

Kathleen wiped the tears from her eyes. "He's going to London. He doesn't know when or if he'll ever come back to the ranch." Her voice trembled.

Adam hugged her. "Darling, he needs time to grieve and to decide what he wants to do with the rest of his life." He kissed the top of her head.

"I guess so." Kathleen wiped away her tears. *Abby will be devastated.* "There's something I must do," she said in a whisper as she rested her head on her husband's shoulder.

****

Abby stepped out onto the balcony, where the blackness of the moonless sky brought joy to her heart and praise to her lips. The blackness no longer reminded her of her beloved and guilt, but of God's love. She rubbed the swell in her belly. She never grew tired of thanking God for mercy and grace. She knew He'd forgiven her that instead of turning to God she had turned to another for comfort and companionship after her momma's death. She looked up to the sky.

"Momma, I have lived off your faith for so long, but now I have faith of my own. Thank you for teaching me and pointing me in the way I should go." She smiled and went back inside, where she yawned, stretched, and settled herself on the settee. Tucking her legs under her, she watched her light cotton gown move from the force of several kicks. "Hold on, little one," she said, rubbing her abdomen. "It's not time yet." Abby pulled a pillow to her chest and hugged it.

Tears filled her eyes. "What will Kathleen and the others think of me when they finally learn that I am going to have a baby?" She covered her face with the pillow. She had grown to love the people on the ranch. Kathleen had become a true friend, Raymon a nephew, and Adam like a big brother. The household staff was her family, as well. She frowned. "Will Kathleen and Adam turn me out? Will they order me to name my baby's father?" She bit down on her bottom lip in thought. From the moment she discovered she was pregnant, she had vowed she would not speak of her baby's father. His identity was between her and God. She buried her head in the pillow. Then, with a determined stride, she walked over to the chiffarobe and pulled out a heavy cloth bag. She carried the bag over to the bed, and dumped the contents. The coins jingled and thumped on the bedcover. She sat on the edge of the bed next to the money and stared at it. "Momma, you said I'll know when to use this." Abby fingered the money with tears streaming down her cheeks. *Maybe it's time for me to leave, and find my own way in this world.*

The next morning she overslept. She hurried to dress. Abby's full shirts and shawl had hidden her condition during the winter months. Now the weather was turning warmer, she had to do something about clothes. She could no longer fasten her skirts, and her blouses were getting snug. She adjusted her clothing the best she could, covering everything with her bib apron, before she went down to the kitchen.

As she stepped through the kitchen door, surprise lit her face as she saw Kathleen and the household staff—Cookie, Betsy, and Cedric—standing behind the table smiling at her. She stopped in her tracks and stared. Cookie and Betsy each laid a beautiful dress on the table, large enough to fit her new form. Cedric helped Kathleen lift a handsomely made mahogany baby bed onto the table. It was filled with various baby items and clothes.

"I can't have my little niece or nephew going without." Kathleen smiled and kissed Abby on the cheek. Abby's body shook from the force of her crying. Kathleen hugged her and whispered in her ear. "I love you, little sister," and led her to a chair to sit.

"You all know?" Abby asked between sobs.

Cookie spoke up first. "We ain't blind, child." She gave Abby a kiss on the cheek and a motherly hug. "This was all Miss Kathleen's idea, and we're glad to be a part of it." Cookie smiled at Kathleen with love in her eyes.

"But I…" The group stopped her attempt to speak by offering her one bit of baby advice after another. Warmth flowed through her, and she silently thanked God for her new family.

Two months later, Abby gave birth to a healthy baby girl. She named her Mercy, because God had been so merciful to her: loving her, forgiving her of her sins, and giving her a family that loved her. Mercy was a beautiful baby with shiny, curly, black hair, and eyes as black as soot. Every time she looked into her baby's eyes, she thought of her beloved and the possibility that she might never see him again.

One day a few weeks after Mercy's birth, Kathleen sat in the parlor, fidgeting with her hands, waiting for Abby. Her eyes were puffy, and her heart raced as she contemplated how to tell her that Lawrence would not be coming home any time soon, if ever.

Humming preceded Abby as she walked into the parlor with her herb basket on her arm, and her eyes lit up with a smile when she saw Kathleen in the chair by the window.

Kathleen's attempted smile faltered. Sorrow filled her heart when she saw how happy Abby was and thought of how happy she'd been since the baby's arrival. She hated to be the one to extinguish such happiness, but Abby needed to know Lawrence's plans.

The humming stopped as soon as Abby looked closely at Kathleen's face. "What's troubling you?" Abby hurried to her friend.

Kathleen patted a space on the settee next to her for Abby to sit, sucking on her lip before she spoke.

Abby's brows crinkled. "What's wrong?" She set the basket by her feet, folded her hands in her lap, and waited for her friend to speak.

Kathleen cleared her throat and looked down at the floor. "I've gotten a letter from my brother."

Abby nodded and gazed at her friend with a puzzled expression.

Tears formed in Kathleen's eyes. Silence fell over the room. She blew out a slow breath. "Lawrence and Eli have completed all the details stipulated in Jack's will—freeing the slaves, finding them jobs in the North, and renting out the farm."

Abby's eyebrows pulled together in confusion. "That's good, isn't it?"

Regret etching her face, Kathleen took hold of Abby's hands. "Lawrence is on his way to England. He doesn't know when or if he will ever return to the ranch."

Abby's legs grew weak. She was glad she was sitting down; otherwise she might have collapsed. She fought to keep the hurt of Lawrence's decision from playing out on her face and tried to smile, but the corners of her mouth wouldn't cooperate. She squeezed Kathleen's hands. "I know you are going to miss your brother very much." Those words hung in the air as she excused herself.

She left the room with her head held high and calmly climbed the stairs. When she reached the second floor landing, she dashed up the remaining steps to her room, threw herself on the bed, and cried for a long time. *He doesn't want me. What a fool I've been, thinking a man like Lawrence Mallory would want someone like me—a former slave with mixed blood.* She threw herself back on the bed and cried until there were no more tears left. The sun was low in the sky when she finally rose from her spot on the bed. "What a fool I've been, Momma. You always said, 'Know your place, child. Know your place.' I'm sorry I forgot."

Abby took a deep breath and went to peer out the balcony window. "I will continue to trust you, Lord, with my future and for all my needs."

****

Eli accompanied Lawrence to London. He proved to be a good companion and tolerated Lawrence's crankiness with compassion. For over a year and a half Lawrence threw himself into his work, trying to salvage his silk operation's good name. Even though his company produced the best quality of damasks, velvets, satins, and brocades for clothing and furniture in London, its managers had become slack and had greedily deprived the silk weavers of accurate pay. The weavers were on the verge of a strike. After much negotiation, Lawrence's company gave its workers fair wages, improved their working conditions, and hired new managers. Once again the company was thriving, and Lawrence had nothing more to do.

It seemed to Eli that Lawrence spent the next few months pacing back and forth in their apartment, except on those rare occasions when he was needed at the silk factory. Finally Eli couldn't take it any longer. He snapped his book shut with a thump, moved from behind the desk, and leaned against it with folded arms. "Boss, is there something you want to get off your chest?"

Lawrence stopped pacing. "How many times have I told you not to call me that?"

Eli smirked.

"Why are you asking me a question like that?" Lawrence took a seat by the fireplace.

"May I speak freely?" Eli still leaned against the desk with his arms folded.

"You must be kidding me. Can you speak freely?" Lawrence sneered and turned his head slightly to get a better look at his friend. "Who can stop the famous reverend from speaking?"

Eli chuckled. He had gained quite a reputation as a street preacher and humanitarian since his arrival in London. Lawrence had repeatedly stated how proud he was of his friend and attended as many of his sermons as possible. Eli straightened. "All kidding aside, Lawrence, you haven't been yourself since we left the ranch, almost three years ago."

Eli held up his hand to stop Lawrence from commenting. "I know you have grieved over the loss of your wife, your father-in-law, and Hattie."

Lawrence nodded slowly. Sadness washed over him, and he blew out a harsh breath before speaking quietly as if only to himself. "I impulsively married a woman I'd known for two weeks. I was drawn to her for my own selfish reasons. I was in love with the idea of marriage and family. I thought Elizabeth was the most beautiful woman in the world, and I wanted to make her mine." He looked at Eli. "I was so desperate for a wife and a family of my own." Lawrence pounded the arm of his chair. "I didn't know how to give her the care she needed." He left his chair and stood by the window.

Eli came up behind his friend and laid a hand on his shoulder. "You can't blame yourself for Miss Elizabeth's condition."

"I blame myself for everything." Lawrence rubbed his hand through his hair. He wanted to tell Eli about another quick marriage, but he didn't. He couldn't.

Eli walked across the room and lifted his Bible from the desk. "Blaming yourself is not going to give you the peace you need. Your peace can only come from the Almighty." Eli cleared his throat to break the silence that had formed between them. "I don't want to overstep my place, but maybe what's really wrong with you has to do with Miss Abby."

Lawrence whipped his head around so quickly he felt pain in his neck. His eyes widened and his eyebrows shot up. He opened his mouth to deny what Eli said, but then clamped it shut. There was one thing he knew about Eli: he was a very perceptive man.

Eli continued talking, ignoring Lawrence's reactions to his statement. "You speak of Miss Abby often in your sleep. I have awakened you many times from dreams where you were calling out to her." Speechless, Lawrence returned to his chair and sat down. Eli put the Bible on the side table where he sat. "You need to spend some time with the Lord to get the peace you need. We all make decisions that sometimes hurt others." Lawrence stared at him.

Eli slapped his friend on the shoulder. "When you do your reading, look at Psalm 139 and First Samuel 25, verses 40-42, and see what Abigail did." With that, Eli left the room.

Lawrence stared at the Bible in a daze. "Eli knows," he mumbled. Lawrence's fingers trembled as he flipped through the Bible, searching for the verses Eli had recommended. He didn't know how long he stayed on his knees praying, but he knew he had a peace he hadn't known for a long time.

The sun was beginning to rise as he finished reading Psalm 139. "Oh, Lord," he prayed, "thank you for reminding me that you know my heart and I cannot flee from you. In the story of David and Abigail, you helped me to understand that we all grieve differently and I am the only one who knows when it's right for me to love again. Thank you for your abundant mercy and grace."

When Eli walked into the parlor the next morning, Lawrence's hands were folded behind his back as he stared out the window. "Did you get any sleep last night?"

Lawrence grunted as he turned to face his friend. "Thank you for getting me back on the right track."

Eli smiled, and Lawrence turned back to the window. "I've been running for a long time…three years," he said just above a whisper. He paused for a few moments. "It's time for me to go home."

Eli squeezed his pal's shoulder. That afternoon, Lawrence began making preparation for him and Eli to go home. He was through running.

****

Abby smiled at her three-year-old daughter, who sat on a blanket in the herb garden, playing with a doll Kathleen and Adam had given her for her birthday. They had acted as aunt and uncle to Mercy from the moment she was born. Raymon had taken on the role of big brother, and Mercy followed him almost everywhere he went.

Soon it will be Mercy's turn to play big sister when Kathleen has her baby. Abby smiled again. The support and love she'd received from her friends at the ranch over the years had made her life happy. She was content even without her beloved. She would never forget him because looking in her daughter's face was like seeing him face to face.

"Mommy, come see." Abby put her basket down and went to sit next to her daughter on the blanket. "Look." Mercy showed her three worms she had found and put in a dish. "Dolly wants to eat."

Abby laughed and kissed her daughter on the nose. "I think you are the one who's hungry."

Mercy giggled, and Abby gathered up their things and headed back to the house with her.

The place was in a joyous uproar. Abby put her basket down on the kitchen table to help Mercy clean up for lunch. "What's going on? Everyone looks so happy."

"Mr. Lawrence is through with his wandering and

is coming home." Cookie said, busy pouring the cake batter into the greased pans before she turned to Abby. "What's wrong with you, child? You look as pale as that cat that runs around here."

Abby's hands trembled as she tried to dry Mercy's fingers on the towel hanging by the pantry door.

Cookie popped the cake pans into the oven, wiped her hands on her apron, and rushed to Abby. "Have you been toting that child around again? She's 'bout as big as you are. Go on over there and have a seat. I'll get this little angel her lunch."

Abby moved stiffly to the chair and plopped down. She took several deep breaths trying to calm her racing heart. She finally got enough courage to speak. "Will Mr. Lawrence be staying long?"

Cookie put Mercy in her special chair and placed a bowl of potato soup with chives in front of her before she answered.

"Umm," Mercy said with a giggle.

"I don't know how long he will be staying. Miss Kathleen only said he will be coming home in three weeks."

Abby could barely contain her joy at the news. Then she wondered if he would be staying. How had he changed? She had so many questions, she wondered if she would like the answers when she got them.

Over the next three weeks, everyone worked to get things ready for Lawrence and Eli's return. Lawrence's house was aired out and cleaned. Many of their favorite foods were prepared in anticipation of their homecoming. Abby hummed as she worked in the kitchen alongside Kathleen, Cookie, and Betsy. Abby smiled as she mixed the batter for the chocolate pies, one of Lawrence's favorite desserts. He liked the pies when the chocolate didn't curdle but remained the same smooth consistency from the top of the pie to the bottom. She followed Hattie's recipe with precision. She wanted the dessert to be perfect.

Chapter Fourteen

Lawrence was filled with anticipation as his carriage pulled into the lane to the Double-O. He couldn't wait to see his sister and her husband, but the real reason for his return was to properly claim Abby as his own. The ranch was more beautiful than he had remembered. It was good to be home.

His carriage was spotted as it traveled up the lane to the main house, and by the time he and Eli reached the house, a welcoming committee had assembled. Lawrence was moved by the affection that was shown to him not only by his sister and brother-in-law but by the entire ranch family. Yet the one person he craved affection from was not there. He wondered where Abby was.

Kathleen must have noticed the perplexed look on his face, because she blurted out, "Abby and some of the others are at your house making sure everything is in order for you."

He nodded. He could hardly wait to get away from the crowd. When he was finally able to excuse himself and make the short journey to his own home, he jumped from the carriage as soon as it pulled up to the barn. As he dashed up the walkway that led to the back door of his house, he heard giggles and a male voice coming from the garden. He turned to see Abby in a man's embrace. He could tell by the broad shoulders and muscular arms that it was Hank. The same man who had asked permission to court Abby a few years back.

At that moment, Abby looked up and saw him, and her mouth flew open, her eyebrows crinkled, and she quickly dropped her hand from Hank's shoulder as she stepped out of Hank's arms.

Her reaction alarmed Hank. He turned and instantly dropped his hands to his side. He looked at Abby's stunned face, then went to greet Lawrence, extending his hand. "Mr. Lawrence, welcome home."

Lawrence didn't respond. His gaze never left Abby. Hank touched the brim of his hat, nodded in Abby's direction, and left. Abby and Lawrence stared at each other until he abruptly turned and went into the house.

"What must he think of me?" Abby said as she slowly sank down onto the garden bench, crying.

Lawrence gripped the table with all his might. Tears pooling in his eyes, he hung his head, and the tears dropped. He banged his fist on the table.

"Oh, Lord, I'm too late."

Eli entered the back door. "You're too late for what, boss?" Eli grinned, but when he turned and looked into Lawrence's face, he knew that statement had nothing to do with him but everything to do with Abby. She had run into him as she raced toward the main house.

****

The men were invited to the main house for a welcome-home supper that evening. Eli and the servants declined to join Kathleen, Adam, and Lawrence in the dining room. Lawrence wished he could have declined also, but he made the best of the situation by recounting his work at the Bradley Farm and in London. There was a lull in the conversation. Adam took that moment to comment on how delicious the food was. Lawrence had hardly tasted anything even though all the dishes were his favorites. He was still upset by the scene he'd witnessed earlier that day—Abby in the arms of another man.

Kathleen insisted the servants join the family for dessert. Abby was still shaken by what Lawrence must have thought he saw in the garden. She would stay in the kitchen to tidy things up while everyone else went into the dining room, but Cookie wouldn't hear of it.

"Why don't you all go ahead? I'll stay…"

"You will do no such thing!" Cookie said in a tone louder than she meant. "You made these delicious pies for Mr. Lawrence because you know he loves them. You are coming with us so we can see how much he enjoys them." She shoved a pie into Abby's hands.

Abby tried to compose herself before she entered the dining room with the pie, but when she saw the scowl on Lawrence's face, her composure dissolved.

Kathleen was making a major issue of the pies. "Lawrence, Abby was beside herself when she thought we didn't have enough chocolate to make your favorite dessert. Ever since she found out you were coming home, she's been talking about how much you love chocolate pies and how much she wanted to make them for you." Kathleen beamed.

Abby walked slowly over to Lawrence to serve him. She selected the largest slice in the pan for him. He stared at her, then covered his plate with one hand.

"No. I don't want anything from you." Abby's bottom lip trembled.

"Sorry, sir," was her only reply.

Everyone was taken aback by Lawrence's remark, and Kathleen gasped. "Lawrence, what is the matter with you? You've hurt Abby's feelings."

Abby blinked back tears, but with much aplomb, she lifted her head and immediately excused herself and left the room.

"You need to apologize to Abby, right now." Kathleen threw her napkin on the table. Lawrence jumped from his chair, threw his napkin on the table, excused himself, and left the house.

An audible gasp filled the room.

****

Abby was proud of herself for not running up to her room crying. Instead, she checked on her sleeping child, in Cookie and Cedric's room, and then went back to the kitchen to clean up. Just then Kathleen and the others came in to check on her.

Kathleen rushed to Abby and began apologizing for her brother's behavior. "He must have been tired from his trip. I should have waited to…" Her voice faded in the air. She stopped speaking, gave Abby a hug, and left the room. The others gave her an understanding look and busied themselves in the kitchen.

****

Lawrence was ashamed of how he had responded to Abby in front of everyone. He had to get a grip on himself. He paced back and forth across the floor. He thought about leaving the ranch and going back to Philadelphia, but Adam had told him he was concerned about Kathleen's health. Her pregnancy was not going well. She was having serious complications in her fourth month. Adam had also told him about the important work God had called him to do, to become an abolitionist. After hearing the details about the work, Lawrence knew he and Eli would like to be a part of it. He couldn't leave.

"I can't run away again. I just have to deal with Abby's choice…somehow." Just then Eli entered the room carrying a chocolate pie. "Everyone lost their appetite for pie after you left." He set the pie on the table.

"I did behave reprehensibly, didn't I?"

Eli nodded his head in agreement and left the room for bed.

****

Over the next few weeks, Lawrence buried himself in his work and saw very little of Abby. When he did see her, they had very little to say to each other, if anything at all. He visited Kathleen regularly. She was having more complications from her pregnancy. During one of his visits, Abby served tea to him and Kathleen in the parlor. She poured a cup for Lawrence the way he had always liked it, with one teaspoon of sugar and mint. He tasted it, spit it out, and demanded that she make him another cup. Kathleen intervened.

"Lawrence, what has gotten into you? You have always liked your tea with sugar."

Abby arched a brow at him, then left the room with her head held high. "You need to stop whatever is going on between you and Abby."

"There's nothing going on between us."

Kathleen turned cold eyes to her brother. "Things are not always as they appear. Promise me that you will keep that in mind."

All during his visit with Kathleen, Lawrence thought how he had asked God to forgive him of his sins and lead him in everything he did. Surely God wasn't leading him to treat Abby so abominably. He felt awful.

He decided to find her and apologize. He went into the kitchen, but no one was there. He looked out the back window and saw Abby playing with a child. Cookie came up behind him. "What are you looking at?"

"Who is that child Miss Abby is playing with?"

Cookie moved the curtain aside.

"Oh, that's Miss Mercy, Abby's baby. Isn't she the cutest thing? I don't know why she insists on toting that child around." Cookie smiled. "She's about as big as she is." When Cookie turned around, Lawrence was gone. "Where did he go?" She raised a brow. "Humph!" She let the curtain fall back in place and resumed her work.

Lawrence had to get out of the kitchen before he made a complete fool of himself. He couldn't believe it. "Abby has a baby? My Abby Rose…has a baby?"

Blood rushed to his head, and he sat down on the front steps. He was there for a long time, shaking his head in absolute disbelief. "It can't be true," he said out loud. Still stunned by the news, Lawrence finally made his way home.

"What's wrong, boss? Are you sick?" Eli asked when he saw Lawrence's face.

Lawrence didn't answer. He went directly to the house, into his study, and closed the door. He stayed locked in that room all night.

The next morning, he decided to go for a walk,

hoping the fresh air would help him make sense of the situation with Abby. He found himself at the big barn where most of the Canadian stock was kept. As he approached the barn, he heard a familiar giggle. His blood began to boil in fury. When he turned the corner, his eyes grew big and his mouth flew open. He couldn't believe the picture before him: Abby was sitting on top of a light brown horse with a long white mane, and Hank stood beside her, looking up at her with admiration—or was that love in his eyes?

Lawrence rushed over, grabbed Abby by the waist, pulled her from the horse, and set her on the ground. "What are you trying to do, fool woman? You're going to break your neck."

Abby slapped his hands away from her waist. "What do you think you are doing?" she huffed. "You don't own me!"

"Oh, yes I do," Lawrence blurted out. "I never granted you your freedom."

Abby's hands flew to her mouth, and she ran toward the main house crying. Hank started to run after her, but thought better of it, while Lawrence marched back to his house in a fit of rage.

Adam and Kathleen turned their heads at the sound of Abby's soft cries as she made her way through the house heading for her bedroom, and Kathleen called out from her seat in the parlor, "Abby, what has happened? Are you hurt?"

Adam got up, went to Abby, and invited her to sit with them. "Tell us what this is all about."

Still standing, she spoke between sobs. "Lawrence is impossible, and I don't ever want to see him again. He wouldn't let me go riding with Hank. He said that he owns me and he can tell me what to do."

Kathleen and Adam stared at each other with curious looks. "Abby, come over here and sit down." Kathleen reached for her hand. "My brother knows this is a slave-free ranch. He doesn't even believe in the practice of slavery. I don't know what possessed him to say such a thing."

Adam sighed and shook his head. "I don't know what has gotten into Lawrence. I know he has had his share of trouble lately, but to say something like this...it's not like him."

Kathleen was sure she knew who was responsible for her brother's strange behavior.

A few more words of comfort were spoken before Abby left the room, heading upstairs. Adam took a seat next to his wife. "What has gotten into your brother?"

Kathleen pursed her lips. "I have an idea, but I am not exactly sure, yet."

"Do you think you can tell your dear husband, darling wife?" He kissed his wife's pouty lips.

****

Kathleen was five months along in her difficult pregnancy when she had a miscarriage. She struggled with low-grade fevers and bouts of fatigue. Her illness was a source of concern for everyone. Abby was her nurse as well as her constant companion and best friend. She could be found at Kathleen's bedside when she was not taking care of Mercy and Raymon. They had become more than friends; they were true sisters.

Abby was worried about Kathleen's illness and had gone out to gather more snakeroot to help reduce her fever. While she was gone, Kathleen woke up asking for her. She had decided it was time to tell Abby that she knew Lawrence was Mercy's father. It was time for her brother and her friend to call a truce and begin working out the problem between them. Lawrence was on his way to see his sister when a little boy who lived on the ranch stopped him. "Mr. Lawrence, do you know where Miss Abby is? Miss Kathleen is looking for her."

"I don't know," he told the boy. "But I intend to find out," he said under his breath. Leaning forward in the saddle, he galloped his horse up the road to the main house, walked briskly up the steps, and then took the stairs two at a time to Kathleen's bedroom, where he knocked on the door.

When he entered, she was struggling to sit up to get a drink of water. His sister could tell by the set of his jaw and the way he walked that his dander was up. She didn't have to guess who was responsible. Before she could speak, Abby came in, carrying a tray and chattering away about something. When Abby saw the expression on Lawrence's face, she stopped in her tracks.

He walked up to her, pointing his finger angrily in her face. "My sister needed you. Where have you been?" His voice was filled with sarcasm. "Oh, let me guess, you were with your lover. You little trollop!"

Kathleen screamed, "No, Lawrence! You have gone too far!"

The shock of his words gave way to fury that could be seen in Abby's face as she threw the tray at him. She raced from the room.

"Lawrence, have you gone mad? What you just did is incomprehensible! You must talk to Abby so you two can resolve whatever is going on between you."

"Who said there's something going on between

us?" he replied. His tone was curt, but then he gave a slight smile.

"Little brother, do you think we are all blind?"

Just then Adam, who had heard the tray crash to the floor and had seen Abby charging from the room, stormed into the room. Kathleen's arms were folded across her chest, and she was giving her brother a cold hard stare.

"What in blue blazes is going on here?" Adam's brow furrowed as he turned to Lawrence. "I will not have you or anyone else upsetting my wife!"

Kathleen's voice was weak. "It's all right, sweetheart."

Lawrence apologized to his sister and brother-in-law and quickly left the room.

****

Abby threw herself on the bed and buried her head in the pillow. To herself she muttered, "He said he owns me. Does he think of me only as his slave? Was our marriage only a master-and-slave union? Was that why he could leave me for three years and never write?" She hiccupped between sobs. "He called me a trollop. Oh!" She hugged the pillow and listened to the silence in the room. Her thoughts lingered on her future.

"It's obvious I can no longer stay here, since Lawrence thinks so little of me. But where will I go? I have Mercy to think of now." She pounded the pillow with her fist, and her thoughts went to Hank. He had asked her to marry him right after Mercy was born, but she had refused.

She snorted. "I may have vowed to never marry again, after Lawrence abandoned me, but that was before I knew I was pregnant with Mercy. I need to think of Mercy now instead of just me. I do enjoy the times with Hank, walking around the ranch and so forth." She smiled. "Mercy adores him and begs to go on another picnic with him. Maybe I should consider his marriage proposal…but I don't love him." She sighed. "Do my vows to Lawrence mean anything?" She knew that most people on the ranch assumed Hank was Mercy's father, everyone except Kathleen and maybe Adam.

Still, even though she was infuriated with Lawrence for making those accusations, she would not use Hank as a means of escaping her situation. It would be unfair to Hank.

She thought about pretending like she had done for so many years when Hattie was alive. She would pretend Lawrence didn't mean anything to her and go on about her daily life. Then she vowed she would continue to let God work her situation out the way He saw fit, and she didn't think using Hank or pretending Lawrence didn't exist would be part of God's plan. She dropped back on the bed and covered her face with the pillow.

Meanwhile, Lawrence mounted his horse and slowly rode down the lane to his house. He couldn't believe he'd called the woman he loved a trollop and put his own sister's health in danger because of his insane jealousy. He was so driven by the fear of losing Abby that he'd tried to handle things himself.

"All I did, God, was to make a bigger mess of things. I will lose her for sure now." He dismounted and led the horse into the barn, where Eli stood by the stall waiting to take the animal so he could brush him down and give him some feed. "That's all right, Eli. I'll take care of Chester myself. At least I can do that right."

"Mr. Lawrence, we need to talk."

Lawrence nodded his head. "Yes, we do."

Eli peered at Lawrence from the other side of the horse. "Hank is planning to ask Abby to marry him again."

"Again?" He repeated the word as he quirked an eyebrow.

"Yes, she refused his first offer, right after her baby was born." Eli emphasized the words "her baby."

Lawrence's eyebrows pressed together. "Her baby."

Eli pretended he didn't hear Lawrence and kept talking.

"It seems that Hank had once asked your permission to court Abby, but you denied him. Since you were gone for so long and it looked as if you weren't going to return, he started spending time with Abby whenever she would allow him to. He loves her and wants to take care of her and her baby."

Lawrence leaned against the stall and repeated the words again. "Her baby." A myriad of thoughts skirted through his mind, and when realization dawned on him, he sank down in the hay like a man who had been punched in the stomach.

"He's planning to ask her to marry him again soon," Eli said, taking the horse's lead rope from Lawrence's hand. Lawrence looked up. His watery eyes met Eli's. "He has been saving all the money he has earned working on the ranch, plus extra he's made from making furniture. He thinks he can comfortably take care of Abby and Mercy on the ranch or move north or out west, wherever Abby wants to go."

Lawrence covered his face in shame. He could only focus on one thing: Abby's baby. "Eli, do you know how old Abby's child is?"

"She is three."

"Eli…"

"Yes, boss?"

"I never asked Abby about her child. I didn't care. I was so hurt because I thought she had betrayed me. Oh, Eli, what a wretched man I am." Lawrence's face was devoid of all color, and he sat in silence for a long time.

Eli put his hands on his friend's shoulders and prayed for him while Lawrence hung his head and wept out loud.

Over the next few weeks, Lawrence decided that whenever he saw Abby he would be the picture of gentleness and kindness. The only problem was that he rarely saw her. Every time he entered a room she would excuse herself and leave, but he didn't let that bother him. He knew he had to win her trust again…and her love.

He decided he would use another tactic: get to know Mercy. The moment he laid eyes on the little girl fully, he understood why Abby had kept her away from him. He would recognize his daughter anywhere, and he loved her right away. He vowed then and there he would be a good father to her. Whenever Abby was busy with his sister or other chores, he would seek Mercy out and spend time with her. She was bright, curious, and a delight to be around.

Kathleen was weak and tired most days, but she managed to confront her brother on one of his many visits. She leaned back against the mound of pillows. "Lawrence, sit down." She gestured to the chair next to her bed. "I don't have much time left on this earth." Lawrence was about to protest, but Kathleen stopped him with the light shake of her head. "I have something I want to say to you. I know you are a fine Christian man, even though you have not been acting like one for the last few years." She let out a soft snort. "There's something I must say to you, and the best way I know is to say it out right. Mercy is my niece and your daughter."

Lawrence got out of his chair to go peer out the window. *Should I break my promise and tell Kathleen that Abby and I said vows together over three years ago?* After a few minutes he turned, went over to Kathleen's bed, and knelt beside it. He took her hand in his and kissed it gently. He finally spoke.

"I know, dear sister. I figured it out a few weeks ago. I have behaved like a complete fool."

"Yes you have," Kathleen agreed wholeheartedly. "What are you going to do about it? Before you answer," she said, giving her brother a stern look, "I want to say one more thing. I love Mercy, and I love Abby as a sister, and I will not have you hurting her anymore."

Lawrence smiled and kissed his sister's cheek. "I hope to…I hope to marry Abby legally, if she ever talks to me again." If his sister noticed his use of the word "legally," she didn't let on.

"It won't be easy for you, since people think the way they do about…" Kathleen didn't finish her sentence.

Lawrence gently massaged the back of her hands

with his thumbs. "We know that God is not behind prejudice. It's a ploy used by Satan." Kathleen nodded. "Prejudice keeps people divided," Lawrence added. "And it keeps us from experiencing the true joy of God's love and grace. He sees us all as equals, and that is how I see Abby, Eli, and the others."

"Now I know my brother is back." Kathleen gave a weak smile and kissed Lawrence on the cheek before she closed her eyes from fatigue.

Over the next few weeks, Kathleen's condition became grave. The doctor only confirmed what she and Abby already knew. Childbirth fever was fatal. Adam, Raymon, Lawrence, Abby, and Mercy kept a vigil by her bedside. The group had wonderful times together praying, praising God, and reminiscing about times gone by. Early one Sunday morning, Kathleen passed away in the arms of her beloved husband.

Chapter Fifteen

Lawrence peered out the side window of the store to the herb garden, his lips pressed into a smile. He had waited half the morning to get a glimpse of Abby when she came to the garden. He laced his fingers behind his back and took in the view. Abby was on her knees, clipping leaves from the plants. He was happy the men had followed his directions and put the garden where he could view the entire plot from the vantage point where he now stood. His gaze roamed every inch of her, and he loved what he saw.

His eyes twinkled when he noticed she was wearing one of Kathleen's straw hats with a wide rim to shield her face from the sun. She had added flowers to make it her own, and no doubt there was a sprig of mint somewhere in the arrangement. He remembered how her brown eyes had widened and her lips formed a perfect circle when she first saw the yellow dress with the tiny green leaves. She now wore it as a work dress. It was a perfect color for her light tan skin. It was worn, but still serviceable enough to wear under her green bib apron.

He shook his head, his eyes glowing. "Abby loves bright colors. They match the brightness of her spirit. The brightness of her spirit..." He repeated the words in a slow monotone. A tingle of guilt assailed him. "Abby's spirits haven't been that bright lately, with the passing of her first best friend Kathleen, and with me behaving so badly. God, please help me win back her affection… No," he corrected, "win her love again. I'll do anything."

The jangle of the bell over the door broke into his thoughts, and he walked away from the window to see who had entered the store. The giggles and laughter gave the person's identity away. There stood a three-foot-tall miniature of himself—of course a lot cuter. She was as beautiful as her mother. But she had her father's black eyes and black curly hair that protested being bound into a braid. There was no doubt she was her father's daughter. Lawrence went over and scooped her up in his arms and gave her a kiss on the forehead.

"What brings you here this morning?"

"Miss Betsy is going to buy me a treat since I've been good." Lawrence nodded for the clerk to give Mercy a peppermint stick. "Why don't you go over and get your treat while I talk to Betsy. Don't forget to get something for Raymon."

"Okay." Mercy hugged Lawrence and gave him a kiss on the cheek before she skipped over to the clerk.

Lawrence whispered to Betsy. "Do you think I can keep Mercy with me for a while?"

She smiled. "Yes, Miss Abby will be busy most of the morning." She gave a conspirator's wink.

Lawrence and Mercy spent the morning together playing games. He read to her and told her stories about his childhood. She helped brush and feed his horse. He knew Mercy enjoyed being with him as much as he loved being with her. This was confirmed while they were in the kitchen washing up from being out in the stable.

"Papa, I love you." As soon as the words came out of her mouth, her eyes grew wide and she covered her mouth with her hands. "Sorry," she said slowly, looking up at him with sad adorable black eyes. "I have a papa. He's gone away. I wish he was here," she said with a whimper. Lawrence felt ashamed. He got down on his knees in front of his daughter. "I will be proud if you called me Papa." He didn't know what else to say.

"Since you have a papa, maybe you can call me Papa Lawrence when we are together." Mercy gave him such a big hug that it knocked him off balance, and they both fell to the floor in a heap of laughter.

****

Abby hummed as she clipped leaves from the parsley, basil, and rosemary plants. Cookie wanted to use some of the herbs for the evening meal. The rumbling of a carriage drew closer. Abby looked up, and her heart dropped in her chest like a rock that had been thrown into a creek. "Widow O'Toole," Abby said through clenched teeth.

Abby continued her work. Before she knew it, small shiny black boots stood inches away from her dress, tapping on the ground, sending little puffs of black dirt into the air. The widow cleared her throat. "Girl! Girl, I say."

Abby slowly looked up to see the woman standing before her with both hands on her hips.

"Why didn't you answer me?" Before Abby could speak the woman continued. "Never mind." She patted the bun on the back of her head. "It's Abby, isn't it?" Abby stared at her, then slowly nodded and stood to her full five-foot-two-inch height. "I hear you are an expert with herbs. I thought you could clip me some."

Abby stared at the Widow O'Toole.

The woman smiled, but it didn't reach her eyes, and her voice was filled with a cool warning as she spoke. "Don't you think it's time for you to move out of the house since Mrs. O'Daley has passed away? I'm sure Mr. O'Daley and Mr. Mallory can manage without you." The widow's gaze bored into Abby. "As a matter of fact, my mother-in-law can probably use a companion, someone like you. I might be getting married soon," the widow added. She blinked her lashes as she patted her blonde bun again without taking her eyes off Abby.

Abby's eyes widened and her eyebrows shot up. She gripped the shears she was holding with both hands. Her fingers ached, but she didn't care. The pain kept her hands from doing something she might regret later. "Excuse me," Abby said. She walked away, leaving the widow staring after her, and the herb basket on the ground.

****

A smile lingered on Lawrence's face as he took the path that led to the store, remembering the time he had spent with Mercy. He wondered if her mother was still in the garden. He walked to the right side of the store to get a peek. "Oh, no!" Lawrence clenched his hands into fists. Distress etched his face as he sprinted toward the garden just in time to see Abby marching away, leaving her basket behind and the Widow O'Toole staring after her with her hands on her hips.

****

Lawrence moved his laced fingers up and down his unshaven chin as he and Adam sat in the study discussing the army contract they'd received for the purchase of a large quantity of horses, harnesses, and saddles. The conversation shifted to the Widow O'Toole's unwelcome visits to the ranch. They thanked her for her thoughtfulness and acts of kindness after Kathleen's death but had assured her their friends on the ranch were taking good care of them. Nevertheless, the visits had only increased. There was no longer a doubt that the widow had set her cap for one of them. She wanted a husband.

"That woman has upset everyone in the household," Adam said, leaning back in his chair. "She told the household staff the place needs a woman's touch." Adam smirked. "I'll never forget that day. Cookie, Betsy, and Abby all stopped their work at the same time, faced the widow with hands on hips, fingers balled into fists, all eyes shooting daggers in her direction. If I hadn't come into the kitchen when I did, I don't know what the women would have done to her." He chuckled. "Maybe I shouldn't have intervened." Merriment danced in his eyes as he looked at Lawrence with a grin. Adam put his elbows on the table and turned serious. "When she told me my son needed a mother, she went too far. I knew it was time for us to put a stop to her visits."

Lawrence nodded his head and tapped his fingers on the table. "I know the widow must have said something to Abby last week when I saw her in the herb garden." Lawrence blew out a long slow breath. "I am worried about Abby. Her stoic silence reminds me of how she once was, living her life as a mute slave. It breaks my heart, and I won't tolerate it." Lawrence punctuated each word with the slamming of his fist on the table.

Adam's gaze locked on his brother-in-law. Lawrence didn't try to hide his feelings. He had never told Adam that Mercy was his daughter, but he was sure Kathleen had. He thought it was a good time to tell him now and consult with him on his plans to ask Abby to marry him legally.

****

It was Tuesday, and gloom fell over the ladies in the main house. The Widow O'Toole would arrive at the ranch soon. She seemed to like to visit in late afternoon so she could be invited to dinner. Lawrence and Adam had made up their minds that tonight would be the last time the O'Toole woman would visit the ranch to carry out her scheme to find a husband. The two had devised a plan to put a stop to those visits.

After dinner, Lawrence escorted the young widow out to the gazebo to have a final talk with her about her visits. Cookie and Betsy peered out the window to see the young woman snuggling close to Lawrence.

"Can you believe that?" Betsy said. "Do you think she has finally gotten her hooks into…?"

Abby entered the kitchen smiling. "What are you two looking at?"

Cookie and Betsy jumped and quickly dropped the curtain back in place. Neither of the women spoke but hurriedly busied themselves in the kitchen.

Abby raised a brow. "What did you two see out there that made you so jumpy and quiet?" She walked over to the window, and pushed the curtain aside. She let out a loud groan before she covered her mouth. Lawrence was kissing the Widow O'Toole!

All night Abby was haunted by the scene of Lawrence kissing the attractive widow. She woke with a headache, still pondering the question that had invaded her dreams all night. *Could she stay on the ranch and watch her beloved in the arms of another? Oh, God, what do I do now?* She finished her chores in record time and searched everywhere for her daughter. She just wanted to hold her close as she contemplated their future. On her second trip through the kitchen, she found Cookie and Betsy coming in the back door.

"Have you two seen Mercy? I have searched all over for her."

The two women looked at each other, but as they didn't answer her right away, color drained from her face, and her legs became wobbly. "Has something happened to my baby?" Betsy rushed to grab her by the arms before she fell.

"Oh, no, Abby, it's nothing like that." Cookie twisted her apron string.

"Where is she? I've looked everywhere!"

Cookie laid her hand on her arm. "She's with Mr. Lawrence."

"She's where?" Abby quickly pulled her arms from their hold and ran out the kitchen door, straight to Lawrence's house. She muttered all the way. Abby's steps faltered when she saw her daughter laughing, sitting in the saddle in front of Lawrence as they rode around in a circle on the back of his Canadian horse. When Lawrence spotted Abby approaching, he made his way toward her. He could tell by the tilt of her head she was not happy. With much chagrin he reined Chester in right in front of her. He slowly handed down the rosy-cheeked, giggling child to the waiting arms of her mother.

"Did you see, Momma? Did you see me?" Mercy's

words tumbled from her lips.

"Yes, I saw you, baby. You did a good job riding Chester." Abby put Mercy down and held out her hand; she intended for the little one to take hold of it and go with her, but her daughter pulled away and walked back to the horse.

"Momma," she said, bouncing up and down. "I have to brush down Chester and give him some oats. You have to do that after you ride."

Abby looked at Lawrence, who had by now dismounted. He grinned and took Mercy's hand and guided her and Chester into the barn. Abby followed behind in a huff. Once in the barn, Lawrence signaled Eli to help Mercy with Chester. "Mercy, will you stay here with Uncle Eli? I need to talk to your mother for a moment."

"Sure, Papa..." Her eyes grew wide and she covered her mouth with her hand. Lawrence smiled down at her, pulling on one of her curly braids and putting her in Eli's care.

Abby followed Lawrence into the house. Once the door closed behind them, she pointed her finger in his face. "You thought I was going to, as you said, break my fool neck, when I was riding with Hank. But now it's okay for my four-year-old daughter to ride on your big ol' horse?"

Lawrence smiled down at her and covered her lips with his finger. Abby blinked. His finger made her feel uncomfortable. She felt a sensation that she didn't want to feel at that moment.

"Shh! Let's go into the study."

Abby continued her tirade about the horse as soon as the door there was closed. Lawrence walked over, sat behind his desk, and casually leaned back in the chair, watching Abby with a smug look on his face. Abby crossed her arms over her chest and gave him a hard look. "Did I hear my daughter call you Papa?"

Silence stretched between them.

Lawrence got up from his desk, slowly walked around, and stood in front of her. She turned her back. "When were you going to tell me about Mercy?"

Abby turned and looked at him with raised eyebrows. "Tell you what?"

"You know exactly what I mean, Abby. You can't deny that I'm Mercy's father."

There was a hitch in Abby's breathing, and she stiffened. She started to deny what Lawrence had said, but instead she sank into the chair next to the desk. Lawrence knelt beside her and took her hand. Immediately heat rushed through her body, and she could barely concentrate.

"Abby, I am so sorry for the way I have treated you. I know the words I spoke to you were hurtful and upsetting. I am so sorry; truly I am. I never meant to hurt you." He gently caressed each of her fingers. "When I first came back, all I could think of was seeing you and being with you. Then I saw you in Hank's arms, and I lost all hope. I never dreamed you would betray me."

Abby snatched her hand away from him. "Stop right there." She stared into his eyes. "I was not in Hank's arms, and furthermore, why were you kissing Widow O'Toole?"

"She was kissing me," he said with raised brows.

Abby put her hands on her hips. "So that makes it all right?"

"No. I took her out to the gazebo to tell her that her visits had to stop. But she mistook our stroll to the gazebo as me finally giving in to her scheme."

"Scheme?" Abby repeated.

"Yes, she and her mother-in-law wanted her to marry me or Adam. Lately, she had set her sights on me. But I am taken."

Abby quirked an eyebrow, and her voice dropped intimately low. "You are taken?"

"Yes, taken." Lawrence cupped his fingers around her hands and looked deep into her eyes. She could feel his love for her, and her breath caught in her throat.

"Now, what about you and Hank? Do you love him, Abby?"

"No!" Abby replied, still mesmerized by what she saw in Lawrence's eyes. "I know what it must have looked like," she said, gently freeing her hands from his and twisting them in her lap. "I lost my balance when I was getting up from the bench. Hank caught me."

Lawrence took hold of her hands, rubbing the backs with his thumbs. "I was so blind with jealousy I never considered that possibility." A smile tugged at his lips. "I'm sorry for jumping to the wrong conclusion. Will you ever forgive me?" Abby folded her hands in her lap, but Lawrence took them and kissed her palms. "Abby, I know it will take time for you to trust me again. I behaved abominably. I'm so, so sorry I abandoned you." He choked on his words. "Will you please give me another chance?" Lawrence looked deep into her eyes while caressing her fingers. "I love you, my Abby Rose."

Their gaze connected and held for a long moment.

Abby's heart fluttered for a minute before returning

to its normal cadence. "I forgive you, Lawrence."

He raised her hands and kissed each of her fingers. Delightful tingles ricocheted through her body and left her speechless.

****

Lawrence took a deep breath, and the sweet smell of Cherokee roses put a bounce in his step and a whistle on his lips as he walked by the garden, heading to the main house. He had decided to walk the mile today because he had a lot to think about. A big smile spread across his face when he thought of Abby. He knew she still had affection for him by the way she responded to his finger kisses. He whistled a little tune, then stopped suddenly. *Does she love me enough to let the whole world know?*

His eyebrows knitted together, and a frown erased the smile he once wore. *Widow O'Toole spewed her venom about marrying beneath one's station. And according to her, marrying outside your race is absolutely scandalous.* "Who would subject themselves to such ridicule?" she had said in the presence of Abby during one of her visits. *Will Abby allow the prejudice of others to keep us apart in order to protect me? Knowing Abby, she just might, thinking she'll be protecting me from ridicule, slander, and hatred by narrow-minded people.* Lawrence rubbed his hand across his chin. He shook his head. *Wait until she finds out about all my businesses and investments. She will definitely not marry me then, thinking our marriage will put my life's work in jeopardy.* He stuck his hands in his pocket. *What's the use in having riches upon riches when you can't share it with the people you love? I'll just have to keep my business affairs and my net worth a secret until our marriage is legal and binding in all states. I can't wait until the world knows that the beautiful and wonderful Abby Rose is my legal wife.* The thought sent shivers down his spine.

Lawrence resumed his leisurely pace up to the main house. His thoughts were interrupted when wild laughter reached his ears. He turned to the sound of the laughter and saw his sweet daughter and his nephew running toward him.

"Uncle Lawrence, Uncle Lawrence!"

"Papa Lawrence! Papa Lawrence, look what we found!"

"It's an arrowhead," Raymon added. "Can we go to your house to see if you have this one in your book?"

Lawrence tousled his nephew's hair. He took hold of his daughter's hand, and the three went back to his house. For over an hour, the little group searched through Lawrence's drawings. Cheers erupted when they saw a drawing of their arrowhead in Lawrence's collections. When Raymon heard his father and Eli outside, he dashed from the house to show them the arrowhead. Mercy had fallen asleep in her father's lap. He tickled her under her chin. "My little sweetie didn't get enough sleep last night, hmm?" Mercy struggled to open one eye. She spoke between yawns. "Momma kept me up again. She was crying in her sleep." Mercy stretched like a kitten. "I finally woke her up, but then I couldn't go back to sleep." A flash of confusion crossed Lawrence's face.

"How often does your momma cry in her sleep?"

"Mm, I don't know, but I hear her sometimes."

Lawrence cradled the child in his arms and didn't say anything for a while. His face contorted into a grimace. He knew his actions were the reason for Abby's unhappiness, but not anymore. He was determined to do all he could to win her love. His lips creased into a smile when he thought of their moment together in his study. He kissed the top of his daughter's head and wound around his finger a curl that had escaped her braid.

"You know what, little one? I think it might be time for you to have a room and a bed of your own."

Mercy's eyes grew big, and she clapped her hands together. "Do you think so, Papa Lawrence? Wait till I tell Momma."

"I tell you what, sweetie, let me tell her. It will be our surprise for her." They shook hands on the agreement.

After she left, Lawrence sat in the study, tapping his fingers on the desk in a rhythmic cadence. He remembered that Eli had said Hank was a furniture maker.

"Hank," Lawrence said the name slowly as he increased the cadence of his tapping. "It's time we meet anyway and clear the air between us." He left the room with a confident stride and headed outside to Hank's room in the common house.

On the way, Lawrence decided to ask him to make a bed, a night stand, and a trunk for Mercy. Moments later he tapped on the door. It slowly opened. Confusion clouded Hank's face when he saw Lawrence standing before him, but he took Lawrence's proffered hand.

An awkward silence fell between the two men. At last Lawrence cleared his throat. "Eli told me that you are an excellent furniture maker."

"So is Mr. Adam," Hank said.

"Yes, I know, but Adam doesn't have the time to make what I need, since running the ranch takes up most of his time. Mercy's birthday is coming up, and she would like to have her own bedroom. I would like to commission you to make a bed set for her." Hank's suspicious eyes slowly roamed Lawrence's face. Lawrence's penetrating eyes never left Hank.

Hank said nothing but pushed the door open and allowed Lawrence to enter his workshop. He walked over and uncovered a bundle on the floor. Lawrence's eyes widened. He was speechless when he saw a stunning bed set already made. The wood was carved into a braid that went from one side of the head and foot boards to the other side. The matching dark-stained night stands were true works of art. The same carved-wood braid served as a finish on the night stands. Hank's work was just as splendid as the finest furniture Lawrence had seen in some of the wealthiest homes in America and England.

"Who did you make this for? I would like to purchase it from that person, if I can."

A muscle tightened in Hank's jaw. "I made it for Abby."

Lawrence said nothing.

"May I speak freely, Mr. Lawrence?"

Lawrence nodded.

"I don't know what your intentions are toward Abby, but if you only plan to toy with her, I would like to marry her and raise Mercy as my own."

"What do you mean, 'toy with her'?" An angry tone laced Lawrence's voice.

Hank held up his hand to stop him from speaking

further. "I told Eli about my plans so you would know that I'm serious about marrying Abby. I'm in a position to provide her with a comfortable living here or wherever else she might want to live. I know I can't provide her with the luxury she's used to, but I hope I can one day. I will do all I can to make her happy."

Lawrence was silent for a moment. "I admire your boldness and honesty, but I have not and never will 'toy' with Abby as you say. I have loved her in the shadows, but no more. I plan to marry her, if she will have me, and the three of us will be a family." He almost told the man he had been married to Abby for years, but he didn't dare. He would have to answer the questions that were sure to follow: Why did you abandon her? And will you do it again?

Embarrassment filled the air between the two men for a time. Lawrence finally cleared his throat.

"Hank, I know you planned—"

Hank stopped him. "Mr. Lawrence you can have this set for Mercy. It's my gift to her."

"Oh, no." Lawrence waved his hand. "I would never dream of taking this without paying you what it's worth. This kind of furniture is what the wealthy would pay handsomely for. I will pay you for it."

Hank nodded.

"How long have you been making furniture?"

"Ever since I was big enough to hold the tools. My father was a freedman. He was a furniture maker in Charleston."

"I see." Lawrence rubbed his chin. "Have you thought about opening your own shop?"

"Yeah, I thought about it. I was on my way out west when I came here, about five years ago. I stayed because of…" His voice trailed off.

"I would like to talk to you sometime about your future," Lawrence said, looking into Hank's eyes.

Hank gave a curt nod.

****

Lawrence had the furniture delivered to the main house close to Mercy's fifth birthday. As soon as Abby walked into the kitchen from tending her herb garden, Mercy jumped up and down and grabbed her hand. "Come with me, Mommy, come with me."

"Where are we going?" Abby asked, looking at her daughter with love in her eyes.

"I want you to see my birthday surprise."

"It's a bit early for a birthday present, isn't it? You have two more days to go." There was a twinkle in Abby's eyes. "Give me a chance to put my basket down."

The basket had barely made contact with the table before Mercy started pulling her mother to the stairs.

"Your present is upstairs?" Abby gave Cookie, Betsy, and Cedric a questioning look.

When the two reached the third-floor landing, Lawrence was waiting with a big grin on his face. He picked up the giggling birthday girl, cradled her in his arms, and gave her a kiss on the neck. The picture of the two of them caused a deep yearning in Abby's heart. Abby looked around their bedroom in bewilderment, but she saw no evidence of a birthday present anywhere. Lawrence and Mercy watched her in amusement.

Mercy couldn't contain her eagerness any longer. She dashed over to the once spare room and threw open the door. Abby walked over cautiously, while Lawrence followed with a very satisfied look on his face. She put her hands over her mouth when she saw the exquisite bed set with matching night stands. "When…? How…? It's beautiful!" Mercy jumped up and down on the bed.

"I have my own room now, and you won't keep me up crying, Momma."

A flush crept up Abby's neck and onto her cheeks, but she gave no reply to her daughter's comment. "This beautiful bedroom is just what a princess like you needs." Abby gave her daughter a big hug and kiss. "Happy birthday, Princess."

Mercy showed her mother every inch of her new room, including the present she had gotten from Lawrence and the household staff. Mercy told how Eli and Lawrence set up the bed and how Betsy, Cookie, and Cedric helped decorate everything. She grabbed her new doll and books.

"I need to show my birthday presents to Raymon." She darted downstairs.

"Oh, Lawrence, you shouldn't have. This room is gorgeous, just like mine." Lawrence came up behind her. She could feel his breath on her neck, and it sent delightful shivers down her spine.

"There's nothing too good for my girls." Abby turned in his embrace to stare into his velvety-black eyes. All the years that had kept them apart faded away, and she wrapped her arms around his neck, a fiery passion ignited in her. Their lips met, and they kissed hungrily. Abby pulled away first when she heard two pairs of fast footsteps coming up the stairs.

Chapter Sixteen

Lawrence watched his brother-in-law pace the floor in the study as he went on and on about Raymon's need for a formal education.

Adam tugged on his mustache. "You know Kathleen wanted him to have the finest education money can buy."

Lawrence smiled. He'd heard the same speech for over an hour.

"That boy has an insatiable appetite for learning. I'm having trouble keeping up with his studies since I'm off the ranch so much." Adam paced some more and again fingered his mustache. "I think the best thing for me to do is to send him to Philadelphia to live with your folks, so he can get the education he deserves."

From his seat by the fireplace, Lawrence asked, "Are you sure you want to do that?"

Adam gave a slow nod. He tucked his fingers in his vest pockets and gazed out the window.

"Raymon has an uncanny ability to understand and apply scripture, for someone his age. He sure will be missed during our worship," Lawrence said.

Adam turned and looked at Lawrence. "Do you think I'm doing the right thing?" He took the chair opposite Lawrence, and the discussion continued.

****

Abby turned slowly in her beautiful third-floor

room. "No," she corrected, "my third floor home." Tears starred her lashes, and her stomach twisted in knots as she stroked the fine furnishings and thought of what the Widow O'Toole had said to her about moving out of the house. "It won't be proper for me to live here any longer, since Raymon will be gone and I won't be needed to help with his care." Abby let out a sigh.

She took one last look at the room, stiffened her spine, and left the room, looking for Adam. Abby swallowed a couple of times while she stood in the open study door waiting for him to acknowledge her presence. She knew that he, Lawrence, and Eli had recently returned from helping escaped slaves to a safe house. She was proud of all the work they did.

Adam looked up and smiled. He gestured toward the chair. "I didn't know you were there. How long have you been waiting?"

"Not long. I didn't want to disturb you."

"You don't disturb me. I always have time for you, no matter what."

Abby propped her hands under her chin and lowered her head. "I know you and Raymon will be on your way to Philadelphia soon," she began.

Adam grunted.

Abby gripped her hands in her lap. "By the time you get back, Mercy and I will be moved into the common house." He rolled out of his chair and took her hand.

"Abby, this is your home. Why would you want to leave?"

"You won't need me to help take care of Raymon any longer."

"That doesn't matter. This is still your home." He

patted her hand. The two chatted for a while longer. Adam was not able to convince Abby that it was right for her and Mercy to stay in the main house. He finally gave up trying and asked her to discuss the matter with Lawrence.

Abby hummed as she hurriedly put the last dish in the cupboard. She was anxious to talk to Lawrence about her plans to move to the common house. She darted back and forth through the kitchen, helping the others with various chores, until Lawrence came in, praising Cookie for a wonderful meal as had been his routine every night since Mercy's birthday.

"It's a lovely evening. Would you care to sit with me a while, Miss Abby?" A shiver coursed through her as she took Lawrence's offered arm. He escorted her to the gazebo, and as soon as she sat down, he put his arms around her and pulled her close. Abby nestled her head on his shoulders. They sat in companionable silence for a while.

"Lawrence, I have been thinking about moving." Lawrence stopped her. He turned her head so she could face him.

"Adam told me all about it." He fingered her flushed cheeks. His voice was husky. "If you want to move, then move in with me." He kissed her lips with a passion that tingled throughout her body. "I love you, Abby. Will you marry me, again? This time with a preacher and witnesses?"

Her heart hiccupped at his words. "Oh, Lawrence, I love you too, and yes, I will marry you, again."

"You will?"

Abby smiled at him and nodded her head eagerly.

Lawrence let out a loud whoop. "Let's get married

tonight! We have witnesses and a preacher just a yell away."

Abby giggled and threw her arms around his neck. "Oh, Lawrence, you are incorrigible."

Someone cleared a throat in the shadow by the kitchen door, and the couple stilled. Betsy stepped out into the light from the window. "Excuse me, Miss Abby, but Mercy is sick, and she is calling for you," she said, biting her bottom lip.

Abby got up quickly and ran to the kitchen with Lawrence close behind. When they reached Cookie and Cedric's room, they found Mercy lying on the little cot they kept for her there. After examining her and talking to her, Abby determined that she only had a bad stomach ache caused by eating too many unripe persimmons.

"It seems she and Raymon made a pact to get sick, hoping this would keep him from going to Philadelphia in the morning," Abby told the others.

Their little trick would have been very amusing, had Mercy not gotten so sick.

Lawrence lifted the miserable child from the cot and carried her upstairs to her room while Abby made an herb potion for Mercy in case she needed it during the night. When Abby arrived upstairs, she saw Lawrence curled up on the bed with Mercy asleep in his arms. The picture of the two of them brought tears of joy to her eyes.

The unripened persimmon had no effect on Raymon. The next morning he visited Mercy before leaving for Philadelphia and apologized for letting her eat the unripe fruit. The two shared a very tearful goodbye, and Mercy begged him not to forget her.

After a few days of recuperation, Mercy was back to her old self, creating stories and looking forward to riding Chester as Lawrence had promised.

Eli was walking Chester around the small paddock for the third time when he looked up and saw a group of men coming toward the house. His attention immediately fixed on the fine carriage. There was something very familiar about the man seated next to the driver. As Eli continued to watch the carriage come down the lane, he remembered where he had seen that familiar figure. He took Mercy hastily from the horse and handed her over to a nearby ranch hand with the firm directive, "Keep her out of sight, no matter what!" And then rushed into the house.

Lawrence and Abby were sitting at the kitchen table enjoying their tea and discussing plans for the wedding.

"Lawrence, we have trouble." The alarm in Eli's voice and the expression on his face let them know something serious was going on. Lawrence and Abby both leapt to their feet, and Abby took hold of Lawrence's hand.

"Has something happened to Mercy?" they said in unison.

Eli stepped closer to Lawrence. "It's Miss Abby's grandpa."

Abby sucked in a gulp of air as the color drained from her face. Her heart raced in her chest. She trembled all over, and her knees gave way. Lawrence swept her up in his arms before she collapsed to the floor.

Eli motioned for him to hurry as he opened the door to his bedroom right off the kitchen. Eli whispered, "Mercy is hidden away."

Just as Lawrence set Abby in a chair by the bed, a loud, impatient knock sounded at the kitchen door. Eli went to open the door.

Lawrence put a finger to his lips, signaling Abby to keep quiet. He kissed her hand and whispered, "Pray, sweetheart, and don't worry. I will not let any harm come to you. I promise." He patted her hands as he placed them in her lap, then got to his feet and went to stand by Eli as he opened the door.

A very distinguished-looking gentleman stared at Eli with disdain. His eyes were the color of Abby's, and traces of brown could still be seen in his thick gray hair. Lawrence looked at his distinctive nose, the tilt of his head; there was no doubt he was related to Abby. "I saw your boy here come to this door, so we just followed him."

Lawrence interrupted the man before he could say another word. "This *man* here"—he motioned toward Eli—"is named Eli." Lawrence rocked on his heels. "State your business, sir."

"I am John Wesley from the Wesley Plantation in Virginia." He offered his card.

Lawrence kept his hands by his side. "And what do you want from me, Mr. Wesley?" Lawrence asked, planting his feet in a wide stance.

"We were told by an old man at the Bradley Plantation..." He cleared his throat. "I mean, the Bradley Farm, that you were the proprietor of the property and could perhaps give us information about some of the slaves that used to live there. May I come in to discuss this matter in private with you?"

"This is fine right here." Lawrence crossed his

arms in front of him. "There are no secrets between me and Eli." Mr. Wesley's eyebrows shot up to his black hat. He rocked back and forth on his heels with agitation.

"As you wish, sir," Wesley said in a mocking tone.

Eli turned to Lawrence and, with his eyes, pointed toward his room where Abby was hiding. "Mr. Lawrence, sir, perhaps you and your guest would be more comfortable in the parlor. I will serve you all refreshments there."

"Very well, Eli," Lawrence said, a knowing hint in his voice. "Please forgive my poor manners, Mr. Wesley." Lawrence led Wesley into the parlor.

The man stopped in the middle of the room, his jaw dropped, and a smile of approval lit his face.

Lawrence motioned for him to sit in the chair across from the settee.

"You have exquisite taste, Mr. Lawrence."

"About your business, sir?" Lawrence's question was terse. He took a seat on the settee.

Lawrence's obvious hostility informed Wesley he would need to use a different approach to get information from him. "As I was saying, I hope you have information about a midwife or healer who used to live on the Bradley Plant— I mean, Farm."

Lawrence's eyes were as cold as ice. "What is your business with her?"

Wesley thrust his chest out. "I believe she might have stumbled across an expecting white woman in the woods some time back."

Lawrence frowned. "Why do you think that?"

"I understand this woman spent a great deal of time in the woods."

As Wesley spoke, Lawrence was nauseated just thinking about how much hatred must be in the heart of the old man. After all these years, he had traveled all the way from Virginia to seek and kill his own daughter's child, because of the black blood running through the child's veins. Lawrence crossed his legs and stared at Wesley. He asked one question after another in rapid succession. "Is the woman who was expecting a child related to you? Why was she in the woods instead of in her home? Did you do something to her to make her go into the woods? Or did she run away from someone…her husband…you?"

Wesley's palms grew sweaty at the barrage of questions. He was not conversing with an ordinary rancher but a very skilled conversationalist and debater, perhaps a lawyer or politician. Wesley rubbed his chin. It didn't matter how he tried to disguise his true intentions or his plans for the child, this man could see right through him. Finally, growing weary of playing games, the red-faced, angry Wesley leaped from his chair, almost overturning it, and pointed a finger at Lawrence. "I tell you what, sir! If I find out that the child is alive, I will kill anybody who harbors it and burn down all they own."

Lawrence jumped to his feet, but before he could speak, Eli came into the room with a tray of refreshments. He calmly turned toward Wesley, "Refreshments, sir?"

"Our guest is just leaving, Eli." Lawrence's pulse was thundering in his head as he moved closer to Wesley.

Their gazes locked.

Eli put the tray on the table, and he and Lawrence

escorted John Wesley out the front door. Wesley's nostrils flared as he climbed into the carriage in a huff. The horses hurriedly pulled it away, leaving a plume of dust behind as they sped down the road. Eli ran for his horse and followed the carriage to make sure the men left the Double-O Ranch without talking to anyone.

Lawrence rushed back into the kitchen to find Abby. His mouth went dry, and his alarm grew when he opened the door to Eli's room and didn't see her. He called out and immediately began searching the house. He found her sitting in a chair in his office, staring out into the room as if in a trance.

Lawrence slowly walked to her and knelt before her. He took her hands in his. "You heard, didn't you?"

Abby was motionless for a moment. Finally she nodded.

Lawrence kissed her hands. "Things will be all right, Abby. We have to put our trust in God, not in our situation." Silence swept between them.

"Yes, I know." Tears rolled down her cheeks.

Lawrence dug into his pocket and handed her his handkerchief.

She looked up at him. She fidgeted with her hands. "We can never live together as a married couple. No one must ever know our secret."

Lines formed between his eyebrows. "Why not?"

"You heard what my...Mr. Wesley said. He promised to do harm to anyone who harbored the child or withheld information about the child's whereabouts."

Abby twisted the handkerchief in her hand as fresh tears flowed down her cheeks. Lawrence folded her into his arms and held her close until her crying subsided.

"Wesley is an evil man. We can't let him control

our lives—your life—any longer. We are going to have a wedding and invite our friends." He lifted her face so he could look into her eyes. "We will live as husband and wife. I will not have you shamed any longer."

Abby squirmed from his embrace and paced the floor. She inhaled a deep breath. Her voice was filled with tears. She spoke without looking at him. "Mercy and I can go away somewhere."

Lawrence rushed to her side and pulled her toward him. "You will do no such thing!"

She lowered herself onto the settee. Tears flowed down her cheeks. "I don't know what else to do. I will not put the lives of people I love in danger."

Lawrence sat beside her, lacing his fingers through hers. "I don't care about me. I only care about you and Mercy."

"Then you have to agree we cannot live as husband and wife."

Lawrence couldn't understand how not living as husband and wife would keep Wesley from carrying out his threats if the man knew his grandchild was living on the ranch.

As the debate continued, regarding whether to marry in a public ceremony or continue to live their separate lives based on the threats made by Wesley, Eli walked into the room. He cleared his throat. "Wesley and his men are gone. I'm glad Hank went with Adam to Philadelphia. Wesley and his men might have spotted him and thought he was the person they were looking for."

Abby's eyes grew large, and she covered her mouth with her hands. "I never thought of that."

Eli took a seat by the fireplace. "I couldn't help but

overhear your debate. Miss Abby, you have to marry him. He will be impossible to live with if you don't. Believe me, I know what I'm talking about. But I have an idea. Instead of getting married in the common house like you want, you can get married here with only a few witnesses. You can wait until the time is right to tell Adam and the others."

Silence fell over the room for a space of time.

Abby folded her lips and turned pleading eyes to Lawrence and spoke slowly. "Will you please do it for me?"

Lawrence grimaced and crossed his arms over his chest. "I just don't like it."

She looked at him through thick lowered lashes. "Once you asked me to keep a secret. I did. Even now I keep that secret."

Lawrence gave a quick nod in agreement. He drew her close and kissed her cheek. "I'll do as you say, sweetheart. But I want the wedding to be tonight." Abby arched a brow. "Okay, tomorrow, and that's that."

Abby kissed his cheek. "Tomorrow, then."

Eli breathed a sigh of relief. "You can get Cookie, Cedric, and Betsy to be witnesses." He looked from Abby to Lawrence.

"Will that be all right with you?" Lawrence asked, dabbing tears from Abby's cheeks. "We will have to tell them the truth about your past, Wesley's threats, and Mercy. Although I believe they have guessed the latter."

Abby smiled. "The three have been my family since Momma passed away. They will keep our secret as long as we want them to."

"They can even help with the planning," Lawrence said. "I know what the women are going to say." He laughed and tapped Abby's nose. "They'll say, 'We can't plan a wedding overnight.' " He kissed his soon-to-be-bride with a passion that promised greater things to come.

Eli cleared his throat. "Are we having a wedding, or what?" Abby and Lawrence broke their kiss with laughter. The rest of the afternoon was spent preparing for the wedding. Everything was arranged. The wedding would be in Lawrence's parlor at two o'clock in the afternoon, during Mercy's naptime and while she was under the watchful eye of the housekeeper. Cookie and Cedric and Betsy arranged to take care of Mercy for two days and nights to give the couple some private time.

Unbeknownst to Abby, Lawrence had arranged for Cookie and Betsy to press out and make any alterations on a gown he had purchased for her while he was in London. He thought it would make a beautiful wedding dress. Abby had just stepped out of the porcelain clawfoot bathtub when a knock sounded at the door. She dried herself off quickly, wrapped a large towel around herself, and went to the door. Her eyes sparkled with delight when she saw Cookie and Betsy holding the most beautiful dress she had ever seen. The white silk empire-style gown had a square neckline and capped, tight sleeves. Abby was momentarily speechless.

Cookie smiled. "Mr. Lawrence bought this for you when he was in London. He thought it would make a beautiful wedding dress." Abby looked over at the blue muslin print dress she had laid out on the bed.

"London?" Abby repeated. The shimmering fabric with its crisp texture was smooth to her touch. She closed her eyes and brushed the fabric across her cheeks. Just touching it made her feel pretty. "Well," Betsy uttered, "are you going to wear it or just look at it?"

They all laughed. Abby put the dress over her head, and Cookie and Betsy pulled it down over her. It was a perfect fit, just like they expected.

"It's amazing how Mr. Lawrence was able to choose a dress that fits you perfectly," Betsy said, smoothing the dress down over Abby's slight but feminine figure.

"You look like a princess," Cookie said, kissing Abby on the cheek like a proud parent. Cookie and Betsy brushed her hair until it shone and decorated it with the diamond hair clips Lawrence had given to her as a wedding present. He wanted her to wear her hair down for the wedding and whenever they were alone.

Betsy opened the door to the chifforobe so Abby could look at herself in the mirror. She couldn't believe the person in the mirror was her. Cookie and Betsy turned her around to face them. "You are gorgeous," Betsy said.

"Just wait until Mr. Lawrence sees you," Cookie added.

The very idea sent delightful chills through Abby.

****

Lawrence rubbed his sweaty palms together and wiggled his shoulders to loosen the tension in his neck. His heart was racing. He was anxious to get the ceremony over with and begin his new life with his bride. He grew somber as his mind took him back to another time. "Thank You, God, for Your grace and a second chance at love…true love, not the kind I experienced before, when I was in love with the idea of marriage and a family."

Soft voices from the top of the stairs interrupted his prayer, and Lawrence beamed as he looked up, anticipating a view of his bride. His face fell when he saw it was only Cookie and Betsy. "Just a few minutes longer," the older woman said with a smile as she descended the stairs.

Meanwhile, Abby looked at herself in the mirror one last time. She quickly batted her eyes to keep the tears from falling. "God, thank you for this day, I wish Momma was here to be a part of it. It's what she's always wanted for me, to be happy and have a normal life. Lord, you know that's what I've dreamed of and prayed for all my life. Thank you for making it possible." She opened her eyes and took one last look in the mirror before she left the room.

Her eyes twinkled when she saw the white and yellow ribbons decorating the stairs. As she glided down the steps, she drank in the sight of her handsome groom. Lawrence's slim, muscular frame was accented by his tailored black tailcoat, white linen shirt, and light gray trousers. His wide black-and-gray-striped cravat added sophistication to his already dapper attire.

Lawrence couldn't take his eyes off Abby. She was stunningly beautiful. She looked like a fairy princess…*his* princess. His fingers itched with the anticipation of running his fingers through her long hair, now adorned with the diamond hair clips. The diamonds paled in comparison to her beauty. A smile spread across his face when he thought about his fingers caressing her hair and…more. He followed her every move until she came to stand by him in front of Eli, and his nostrils took in the flowery scent she wore—it brought delight to his senses.

Abby gasped and could barely concentrate on what Eli was saying when she saw the ring Lawrence was about to slip on her finger. The silver-and-ruby ring was stunning. Lawrence kissed his bride's ring finger, and then the couple jumped the broom to symbolize the start of their life together and legitimize their marriage, this time before witnesses. Eli finished the ceremony with a heartfelt prayer for the couple's happiness and protection in the years to come. Lawrence kissed his bride with all the fervor that decorum would allow, and Abby responded in the same manner.

Congratulations from the others were followed by light refreshments in the dining room. The room had been decorated like the parlor with cut flowers, candles, and yellow and white ribbons. Tears came to Abby's eyes when she saw the two-tier white wedding cake on the table. She hugged Cookie and Betsy. She knew the two had probably stayed up most of the night making sure her wedding day was special.

Lawrence was happy about all the fuss the women had gone through to make the day special for Abby, but he was eager to be alone with his bride. When the couple was alone at last, Lawrence turned his bride in his arms and basked in her beauty. "You are dazzling, stunning, and gorgeous," he said between kisses in his wife's ear.

"The dress is exquisite and a perfect fit, husband," Abby said breathlessly.

"I can tell, my wife." Lawrence lifted his bride in his arms and walked upstairs to their bedroom.

****

While Abby was still sleeping, Lawrence slipped downstairs to make breakfast. The rich aroma of coffee and ham greeted him as he descended the stairs. A peek into the parlor and the dining room caused him to smile. His friends had cleared away all the decorations from the wedding and put everything back in order. He whistled as he made his way into the kitchen, He found the kitchen clean and breakfast warming in the oven. Lawrence returned to the bedroom, placed the silver tray on the table next to the bed, and woke his bride with a kiss on the forehead.

"Look what I have for you, sweetheart."

Abby sleepily rose up on one elbow. "Oh, Lawrence, you are so good to me. I should have been up making breakfast for us."

"I want to serve the one I love," he said, kissing his bride on the forehead again. "Besides, our friends did this for us." He motioned to the food. After they ate, he took Abby in his arms and they shared a time of delicious intimacy. Later that morning, propped on pillows in her bed, Abby held her hand up, admiring her wedding ring. "This ring is exquisite. I don't want to lose it when I am working in the herb garden."

Lawrence kissed her fingers. "Sweetheart, you don't have to do any work around the ranch. You never had to. I saw to that a long time ago."

"I know, Lawrence, but I want to be useful." She laid her head on his chest.

"I'm going to arrange for someone to help you with your herbs."

"I'll gladly accept," she said, gazing into her husband's seductive black eyes.

He reached over and took a box from the nightstand. "You can keep your ring right here with mine until the time comes when we can tell the world that we are husband and wife. I will contact my lawyers to draw up the necessary paper to make our marriage legal and binding in any court of law. And everything I have will be legally yours. No one can ever take it from you."

"How can you do that?"

Lawrence kissed Abby on the cheek. "I have my ways, sweetheart. You have married a very wealthy and influential man, my dear," he said with a tease.

"I have married a wonderful, God-fearing man." Abby kissed her husband, took the ring box, and took out a silver band with the same design as hers—two interlocking hearts with the letter A in one heart and the letter L in the other. "That is so clever, having our initials engraved in our rings. When did you purchase these?"

"When I was in London," he said, giving his wife a peck on her lips.

"So you got my wedding dress and the rings when you were in London." She turned the ring gingerly in her hands.

Lawrence nodded, kissing his bride on her neck.

Abby giggled and moved her head slightly to look into her husband's eyes. "Mr. Mallory, you were pretty sure of yourself after being gone for so long, weren't you?" Abby wrapped her arms around her husband's neck.

He smiled. "I thought so, until I came back." He kissed his wife deeply.

****

Three weeks after Abby and Lawrence's marriage, Adam returned to the ranch, unable to leave his nine-year-old son in Philadelphia for a formal city education. The couple told him about John Wesley's visit and his threats, and about their marriage. For Abby's peace of mind, the men agreed, reluctantly, not to make the marriage public knowledge for a while.

Chapter Seventeen

Over the years, Abby's niggling fear of her grandfather's threats still kept the couple from living as husband and wife. They became masters of creative ways to spend time together. They enjoyed enchanting nights together when Mercy slept overnight with Cookie, Cedric, and Betsy. It was sheer delight when Lawrence spent the night at the main house and the two would sneak away to share their marriage bed. They stole time alone when Mercy was busy trying to keep up with her best friend, Raymon.

One day, the couple sat cuddling on the secluded stone bench in the garden at Lawrence's house. He kissed his bride of eight years. "Happy anniversary, sweetheart," his voice was seductively low.

Abby's eyes were filled with love. "Happy anniversary to you, my beloved. I didn't think it was possible to love you more now than I did eight years ago, but I do."

"I love you so much." Lawrence covered his wife's lips with his.

Eli cleared his throat as he approached the couple in the garden. "You asked me to remind you when the soldiers arrived for the military purchases."

Lawrence snorted. "Are you sure I said that?"

Eli laughed. "Yes, you did."

Lawrence pulled Abby up from the bench with

him. "When you finish up here, tell one of the ranch hands, and he will drive you back to the main house."

"Oh, Lawrence, you don't have to fuss over me. I can walk back to the house."

He kissed Abby on the nose. "Sweetheart, we've had this conversation before."

Eli chuckled. "This is where I'll leave you two." He turned and went back around the house, heading for the store.

Lawrence hugged his wife tight. "Remember—keep close to the house. There'll be many soldiers here today." He tapped her on her scrunched up her nose. "I'm only concerned for your safety."

"I know you are, and I love you for it." Abby playfully pushed Lawrence away. "You get back to work, and I will do as you say." She stood on her tiptoes and gave her husband a kiss on the cheek.

****

Abby inhaled a deep breath, taking in the sweet smell of the apricot pink roses as she made her way down the path to her herb garden. She thought the ranch was just as beautiful as the English gardens Lawrence had described to her. Her steps slowed when she thought of how it had changed over the years. People far and near came to the ranch to purchase Canadian horses and fine leather works made in the leather shop. She shuddered when she thought of one of the patrons, an army lieutenant who had thought the ranch sold illicit entertainment. Abby remembered her encounter with the man. His eyes had roamed the length of her, and his snide remarks were laced with sexual overtones. Lawrence's intuitive conviction that there was something unprincipled about the man had saved her from his intentions. She pushed the unpleasant thought from her mind when her herb garden came into sight and, in the distance, she caught a glimpse of Lawrence and Eli making their way to the store. As she worked in the garden, she sent up a silent prayer of thanksgiving for their safe return from one of their trips.

****

Lawrence slapped his brown trousers with his dusty, wide-brimmed hat, trying to dislodge the week-old dust before entering the store. The three men—Lawrence, Adam, and Eli—always met in the store for debriefing whenever they returned from one of their abolition campaigns, as they called them. Today was no different. Lawrence was tired and needed a bath, but he knew he needed to share with Adam what he and Eli had learned.

A lump formed in his throat as he thought how the news might affect Abby and her sense of freedom, but she had to know for her own safety. When the men entered the store, Lawrence noticed the gloom on Adam's face as he sat behind the desk with his head resting on his folded hands. His eyes searched Raymon's face and saw the same kind of gloom.

"What's wrong?" Lawrence and Eli asked at the same time as they walked closer to the desk. Adam pushed back in his chair and rubbed the wrinkles that had formed in his forehead.

"I hope you and Eli have better news than I do."

Lawrence pulled out his dusty handkerchief and wiped the sweat from his neck.

"I wish we did. It seems that some farmers and ranchers are making huge profits these days, but not from buying and selling horses, cotton, or tobacco."

"They are turning to stealing slaves, and selling them for huge profits," Eli added, pulling up two chairs to face the desk.

"The practice is becoming widespread." Lawrence also took a seat. "This is happening from Virginia to Louisiana. So far, our small community hasn't succumbed to the greed, and I hope it stays that way." Lawrence rubbed his chin. "We still need to inform the hands so they know what is going on and can be vigilant as they travel."

Adam nodded.

Silence and gloom fell over the room. Lawrence's stomach felt queasy. He didn't relish the idea of telling Abby about the vigilantes that were stealing free blacks and slaves to sell for profit. There was no doubt she needed to know, since she occasionally went to visit the midwife on the next farm when her herbs and medical advice were needed. Lawrence shook his head. Knowing Abby, she would still insist upon going if the need was serious. "That fool woman," he said to himself with a smile.

"Did you say something else, Lawrence?" Adam asked as he walked over to the window. When there was no reply, he didn't turn around as he went on,

"I got a report from one of our informants." He paused. "Several free blacks were captured while they were traveling from Darin to Savannah." He turned to look at Lawrence and Eli.

Disbelief clouded their faces.

"You mean...it's happening this close to home?" Lawrence said slowly.

"I'm afraid so." Adam shook his head slightly and returned to his seat behind the desk. "That's not all.

Maxwell told me that a cargo ship came into port in Savannah a few weeks ago. It carried over a hundred slaves. According to him, their condition was horrendous."

Raymon propped his head up with his hands as he listened to his father share the story with his uncle and Eli from his side of the desk.

"He said their naked, emaciated bodies were covered with bruises and scars. None of them were able to walk more than two feet before collapsing on the ground." Adam shook his head. "Maxwell said he had never seen so much misery and uncertainty in the faces of human beings before. The stench alone made him retch several times. And another ship is scheduled to come in soon."

Lawrence blew out a whistle.

Eli dropped his head.

Raymon pounded his fist in his palm. "This despicable practice is gaining more of a stronghold here in the South. It will be years before I'm in a position to bring an end to slavery."

Adam put his arms around his son's shoulders.

"Son, we all believe that all people are created equal, and that all mankind should be treated with decency and respect, as God ordained. I know you believe God has called you in particular to stand against the inhumane treatment of slaves and others, but this is not your fight alone. Remember Elijah?" Raymon nodded.

"He thought he was the only person left that was true to God, but God had seven thousand in Israel that had not bowed their knees to Baal. We have to believe that God has men and women all over the States, and across the ocean, fighting to help put an end to the horrible practice of slavery. I know you believe that it's God's will for you to become a lawyer to help fight against the injustice. But remember, God's idea of how to accomplish His will may be different from your own. Promise me you will not forget this." Adam smiled at his son. "I'm humbled..." He looked from Lawrence to Eli and corrected himself. "We're humbled by your youthful zeal and passion."

****

Fear no longer kept the residents on the Double-O Ranch looking over their shoulders. It had been six months and no word of slave hunters had been reported within a hundred miles of Darin, Georgia. Life on the ranch was back to normal, but Abby and Lawrence had new worries. Their hearts were troubled over their thirteen-year-old daughter and how she would handle the news that her best friend, Raymon, would be leaving the ranch...maybe for good. This time it was definite. He would be leaving for Philadelphia within the month to study law under the famous attorney Henry Clark.

Lawrence and Abby stood by the fence, watching Mercy and Raymon mount their horses to go for a ride. Abby leaned close to her husband.

"Do you think he will tell her the news today?"

"I sure hope so. She will need some time to get used to the idea."

Abby gave a slow nod, thinking how much she still missed Kathleen, her first best friend. "I wish he had allowed me to tell her first."

"The news will be difficult for her no matter who tells her," Lawrence said.

The swaying of the horse and the clip-clop of the hooves didn't do much to lull Mercy from her melancholy. She gave Sheba, the horse Papa Lawrence had given her for her seventh birthday, a pat on the neck and glanced over at Raymon. He was staring straight ahead with an unreadable expression on his face. She knew he had something important to say to her. Her heart dropped. She had a good idea what it was.

The two dismounted by a small cave in the cleft of two large rocks near the stream they visited often, searching for treasures. Over the years, they had found interesting rocks, Indian arrowheads, and bits of pottery there. They sat in their favorite spot, on a rock overlooking the stream. They both stared into the slow-moving water. Raymon picked up a pebble and threw it into the stream. Mercy picked up a stick and made marks in the dirt.

"You're going away, aren't you?"

He tossed another pebble in the stream before answering.

"I'm going to Philadelphia to study law. I will be leaving in less than a month. Father and Mr. Wainwright have made all the arrangements." He could tell by the tilt of her head and the look in her eyes that she was struggling to be happy for him.

She struggled to keep her emotions under control, but she could not stop the flow of tears that streaked down her cheeks and landed on her riding habit. She stood, folded her arms around her waist, and took a few steps toward the stream.

"Will you ever come back?"

Raymon moved to stand in front of her. "Of course

I'll come back, you silly goose."

The moment between them grew tense.

"Why are you going all the way to Philadelphia to study law, when there is an attorney twenty miles away in Darin?"

"My father and Mr. Wainwright thought that, given my conviction about slavery, studying in a Free State would be my best option." He laughed. "Mr. Wainwright said that my beliefs about slavery might get me hanged in the South, but only ostracized in the North."

Mercy rolled her eyes. "I don't see the humor in that."

"Anyway, Attorney Henry Clark is a prominent attorney and abolitionist. He's a champion against injustice and inhumane treatment of blacks, the poor, and the immigrants. He works behind the scenes to end the practice of slavery. He will be training three of us students in law. We will be studying and working with him for two years. If we prove ourselves capable, we will work in his practice for a year before we go out on our own."

"So you will be gone for three years?"

Mercy jabbed the stick she was holding into the ground.

"You will be twenty when you return."

"Yes, Mercy." He laughed softly. "But I plan to come home many times during those years."

"I'm so proud of you for wanting to dedicate your life to fight for the justice of others. I'm so thankful God has given you such a caring spirit. I wish you didn't have to go so far."

He looked off into the distance. "I know it's a long

way to Philadelphia. It will take weeks to get there. Mr. Wainwright and Uncle Lawrence will accompany me. Father is expecting his friend, General Scott, who's purchasing a large number of horses. Father plans to visit me after that, in the fall. I'll be staying with my uncle and aunt in Philadelphia, mother's sister and her husband, and my grandparents, of course."

Mercy sat back on the large flat rock. Tears formed in her eyes again. "Who will take care of the ranch while both Uncle Adam and Papa Lawrence are away in Philadelphia?"

"Mercy, you know that Maxwell and Gabe will, like they always do when Father and Uncle Lawrence are away."

Raymon sat back on his rock. "Besides," he continued, "Uncle Lawrence will only be staying for a few weeks. He will return home long before Father leaves for Philadelphia. I know what you are thinking about the slave hunters. Right now, they are not close to Darin. God will look after you. His word says that He will never leave you nor forsake you. You do believe that, don't you?"

Mercy nodded.

"I have something for you that will keep all of God's promises alive for you." He pulled his Bible out from under his shirt and handed it to her. Her eyes grew big from disbelief. She shook her head.

"No I can't take this. This is precious to you. You have all your favorite passages marked. You will need to take it with you." He handed her the Bible.

"Now all my favorite verses are marked for you."

Mercy stared at the Bible, then pulled it to her chest and whimpered.

Raymon put his arms around her shoulders. "This is my going-away present to you. Read it, and remember all the things we've talked about. And remember me."

Mercy finally found her voice. "But what about you?" she said, still hugging the Bible to her chest. "How will you remember all of God's promises?"

He pointed to his head and then his heart. "I have them here. Besides, I will be taking Mother's Bible with me."

They sat by the cave in silence for a long time. He remembered the warning his father had given him several months ago about spending so much time with Mercy now that they both were on the verge of adulthood. He smiled. *Old habits are hard to break.* He broke the silence between them.

"We should be getting back."

They mounted their horses and rode back to the barn in silence.

****

Concern etched Lawrence's and Abby's faces as they stared at Mercy from the third floor bedroom. Ever since Raymon told her he would be leaving for Philadelphia to attend law school, she had been moping around the ranch. Now she sat on the floor of the gazebo, dragging the heel of her black boots back and forth on the wooden floor. Abby stifled a cry.

"Oh, Lawrence, I am worried about her. I don't know what she will do with herself when Raymon leaves."

"I know. They are great friends, and they have been inseparable. But I think our daughter's greatest problem is envy."

Abby blinked. "You think she is jealous of Raymon's opportunity to study and pursue his dreams?"

Lawrence let out a huge sigh. "Yes, I do. Remember how upset she was when Wainwright wouldn't let her sit in on his classes with Raymon? He thought girls didn't have the mental capacity to learn like boys." Abby rolled her eyes and smiled.

"You showed him." She snuggled up to her husband. "Thank you for teaching our daughter."

He kissed the top of her head. "You've done a good job yourself, my love."

"She has a thirst for knowledge."

Lawrence turned his wife in his arms. "I have an idea that just might put a smile on her face again. I'm going to find her a tutor!"

"Do you think she needs one?"

"No, I don't," Lawrence said, chuckling. "But she thinks she does."

The next day, Lawrence knocked on Raymon's bedroom door, and when the door opened he noticed his nephew's stooped shoulders and splotchy skin. He didn't have to ask what was wrong; he knew. He and Mercy were both unhappy about his leaving. Raymon sat on the side of his bed while his uncle pulled over the chair from the desk. Neither spoke for a while.

"You want to talk about it?"

Raymon let out a huge sigh. "I've always wanted to be a lawyer. I hoped with the right connections I would someday be in a position to help enact laws that would stop the practice of slavery. But now I'm not too sure."

"What do you mean you aren't so sure?"

Raymon didn't want to mention the strange feelings and thoughts he was having about leaving Mercy...thoughts he didn't want to explain. He moved from the bed and began pacing the floor.

"My position on slavery hasn't changed. You know that. And it isn't that I don't think I'm not prepared for the academic challenges that lie ahead. Mr. Wainwright has prepared me well." He snorted. "He said I have wisdom and knowledge far beyond my years." He laughed, but then his voice faded.

"It's Mercy, isn't it?" Lawrence said.

Raymon stopped pacing and flopped down on the bed.

"I'm going to miss Father and everyone on the ranch, but with Mercy..." His voice trailed off. "I'm leaving my best friend." Lawrence laid his hand on his nephew's shoulder.

"She's missing you already." Raymon nodded his head slightly.

"I've been encouraging her to write down all her stories. I hope this will keep her occupied while you are gone. Well, at least for some of the time while you are gone. I hope my other idea will cheer her up and give her something to look forward to."

Raymon's face brightened. "What do you have in mind?"

"I'm going to write some friends up north to see if I can't find a female tutor for her."

His nephew's eyes stretched. "You'll do that for her?"

"I sure will. When one is found, I will have you interview her to see if she will be a good fit for Mercy."

Raymon beamed.

"I will be glad to do anything that will make Mercy happy."

After Lawrence left, Raymon lay on his bed, put his hands under his head, and allowed his mind to wander in all directions. A grin stretched across his full lips when he thought about the game of chase he and Mercy used to play. He would allow her to win, most of the time. But as she grew she became a fierce competitor, and he had to run with all his might to keep up with her. His mind traveled to the many scavenger hunts they'd gone on in the woods. They would sometimes spend the whole day searching for fruit trees and other treasures. Sometimes, if they were lucky, they would find a peach tree with large sweet orange peaches. They were always ready to sample their find, and Mercy would always complain that the fuzz on the peach made her lips tingle even after she wiped the peach on her dress to remove the fuzz.

She would smile up at him and say, "My lips don't tingle as much when you wipe the peach off on your shirt."

He laughed and shook his head at the time when they'd dared each other to eat unripe persimmons. He could still feel the chalky taste in his mouth. Oh, how awful! He remembered how their eyes watered and their jaws locked up and they were unable to speak for a while. They had never tasted anything so sour—and they had never laughed so much.

He sat up on his bed when he thought about the time when he and Mercy ate ten green persimmons each to get sick so he wouldn't have to go to Philadelphia. Every time he remembered the incident, he felt ashamed because it was his idea to eat the unripe fruit, but Mercy was the one who got sick.

Raymon sprang from his bed like a wildcat leaping on its prey when he heard his father calling him from downstairs. He had to get those ridiculous thoughts of Mercy from his mind. As soon as his feet hit the floor, he started stuffing clothes into his trunk.

"Son, you need to hurry down. It is almost time for our guests to arrive for your going-away party."

He put the last article of clothing into his leather valise and looked around. Lying on the dresser was the leather pouch Mercy had made for him. She had stitched the pouch for him on his twelfth birthday. She had carefully stitched his name on the front and two hearts on the back. He remembered how proud she was of the job she had done and how straight her stitches were. Without thinking further, he tossed the pouch into his suitcase before dashing downstairs to greet his guests.

The house and grounds had been transformed; the large dining room had been turned into a grand banquet hall. Some of the furniture had been removed to allow room for six square tables that seated six guests each. Some tables were scattered out on the veranda, as well. They all were covered with tablecloths, either blue or white. The yard took on a carnival atmosphere, with places designed for games, horse racing, and dancing. Loud happy voices, laughter, screams, and giggles filled the air. Music clashed with the neighing of horses and enthusiastic voices calling, "Come! Try this!" Raymon's eyes lit up with pleasure, and a smile stretched across his lips as he stepped out onto the veranda.

"Son, come over here and say hello to our guest."

As he conversed with his father and other guests, children played games of tag, hide-and-seek, hopscotch, and marbles. High-pitched screams whirled through the air as others participated in the three-legged races, games of horseshoes, and horseback racing.

Later, Raymon participated in the horseback racing. It was invigorating. His mind didn't linger on his troubles with the feel of Oscar under him as he raced up and down the field, jumping over the different hurdles. Oscar was the best when it came to jumping hurdles. He was strong, reliable, and even-tempered, like all of their Canadian stock. Raymon felt so alive on the back of Oscar—but truthfully, his mind did stray once or twice to his best friend as she stood by the finish line cheering him on.

Just before the dinner, some of the ranch hands performed a cakewalk dance in Raymon's honor. The dancers included old and young black couples, a few white children, and Abby and Mercy. They were all decked out in fancy clothing, waving colorful scarves as they performed the elegant, high-kicking, prancing, walk-around dance to banjo music. It was energetic and breathtaking. But Raymon had eyes for only one person, Mercy. She was dressed in a light green linen dress with white flowers and little white round buttons coming down to the v-shaped waist. The collar of the dress and the short puffy sleeves were trimmed with white lace. Her long black curly hair was braided and wrapped into a bun on the back of her head. A matching scarf adorned her hair and ended in a bow at the side of her face. She wore no shoes because the African dance was done in bare feet. Mercy looked beautiful. He was aware that several of the young boys were watching her. He also noticed his Uncle Lawrence watching Mercy and Abby with love and pride. Maybe what Mercy suspected about him was true.

The dance ended with enthusiastic applause and whistles. It was customary to present the cake to the best dancer. Instead the cake was given to Raymon as a token of love. He accepted the beautiful cake with much appreciation, and the crowd cheered.

Singing and banjo music trailed the guests as they moved inside to the dining room or to the tables outside on the veranda. The long, elegant dining room table that seated ten was still in the middle of the room. Large candelabras flanked each end of the table; in the center of the table was a replica of Oscar, Raymon's horse. He was surrounded by miniature horses, a barn, trees, and a stream flowing through hills. All these were made from various confections. He knew instantly who was responsible for the elaborate, delicious-looking art work: Abby and Mercy, and he now understood why he had seen very little of Mercy in the last few days. His heart sang with joy to know that all the time and effort they had put into this masterpiece was done out of love for him, pure and simple. He had no doubt that the dessert was going to be his favorite part of the meal. The intricately detailed centerpiece captured the attention of all the guests. He could tell they appreciated the artful designs almost as much as he did. His mother's prized imported blue-and-white Wedgwood china added its own elegance to the large dining room table where he, his father, his uncle, and special guests sat. He knew his mother would be pleased. Raymon wished she were there to share the special occasion with him. His eyes met his father's, and he knew he was thinking the same thing.

Lawrence looked over at Adam and Raymon. He could tell by the look in their eyes they were thinking of Kathleen. Their happiness was shrouded in sadness because of her absence, he knew, and he had that same sadness in his heart for his sister, but more so for his own family, Abby and Mercy. Abby had talked him into letting her and Mercy help with the serving. He gritted his teeth until his jaw ached. His chin felt like hard marble. *This will be the last time, the very last time, that my wife or my daughter play the role of servant to anyone.* His hands were balled tightly into fists. He wanted to yell out to everyone that Abby was his wife and Mercy his daughter and not servants. Adam gave him a stern look. He didn't think he'd spoken the words out loud, but he must have, for his brother-in-law to respond the way he did.

Abby and Mercy's appearance in the large dining room earned them a scowl from Lawrence when he saw they had changed from their beautiful linen dresses to servant clothing, at a celebration where they both should have been sitting at the table of honor as aunt and cousin instead of acting as mere house servants. There was nothing wrong with being a servant; he loved and cared for all the servants on the ranch. They had chosen their jobs and were being well compensated. He just didn't want his wife and daughter to be thought of as merely hired hands. He had to get control of his emotions. He didn't want to ruin his nephew's party. Raymon watched Mercy as she entered the room with the other servants. Her beautiful green linen dress had been replaced with a loose-fitting, dark blue, long-sleeved dress such as was worn by the servers on special occasions. The dress was covered by a white bib apron that crossed over the shoulders and tied into a big bow in the back. She looked so solemn, as if afraid she would make a mistake or spill something. Each servant carried a steaming platter of succulent food. The smell alone caused a few stomachs to growl and groan. The three-course meal consisted of fish chowder, roasted wild turkey, chicken fricassee, boiled corn on the cob, steamed cabbage, pickled beets, white diced potatoes, and more of Raymon's favorite dishes. Adam tapped his glass with a spoon. He stood and bowed his head to bless the food. "Heavenly Father, we thank you for the friends that have gathered here today. I ask that you bless this abundant meal and use it for the nourishment of our bodies. In Jesus' name, Amen."

For a moment, the only sound to be heard in the room was the click and clatter of silverware. Later, polite conversation filled the room. Raymon noticed that Mercy and the servers stood in the back of the room, waiting to meet all the needs of the guests, which they did with quiet formality.

After everyone had had their fill, the tables were cleared and dessert plates placed on the table. When Mercy came over to place the dessert plate in front of him, he breathed in the scent of her, the sweet flowery aroma of lilac that reminded him of their times spent in the flower and herb gardens. He smiled and quietly thanked her for the food and the fabulous centerpiece creation. He thought everything had gone extremely well. The only thing that could have made the afternoon more perfect was having Mercy, his best friend, sitting beside him instead of serving him.

Serving. His smile faded, and his eyes grew wide. He struggled to open his mouth to speak. No words came out.

Mercy set the dessert plate down on the table with so much force that it clinked and wobbled before it came to rest in front of him. She dashed from the room without looking back. The hurt look in her eyes made him lose his appetite. He threw his napkin down on the table and half stood, with the intent of going after her, but he heard his uncle saying, "Are you going to eat Oscar, or what? We are ready for dessert."

The guests roared with laughter as they helped themselves to dessert.

Raymon felt sick to his stomach.

What have I done? What was I thinking?

Before he could finish that thought, his father stood.

"Friends and neighbors, it has been an honor having you in our home today. Please join me in wishing my son much success in his endeavors. We pray that he will remain true to his calling and that God will use him in a mighty way. Have a safe journey, son."

The room erupted with cheers and best wishes.

Lawrence, Adam, and Raymon stood outside saying goodbye to their guests. More than two hours had passed since dinner. When the last guest finally left the ranch, Raymon was anxious to find Mercy, to talk to her and try to make things right between them. Before he could make it to the first steps, Lawrence stopped him.

"Mercy needs time. Her mother is with her right now."

He stumbled to the steps and sat down. Lawrence and Adam sat also, one on each side of him. For a long time no one spoke.

Raymon's voice came out strangled. "Abby and Mercy should have been sitting at the table with us as family instead of serving us." Lawrence nodded his head and stared at his hands.

"They are part of our family. Abby has been like a second mother to me for the last ten years. She saw to it that I kept up with my studies and Bible reading before Mr. Wainwright came. She knew how important it was to Mother. She loved me like her own. Other than you," he said, looking at his father, "and you, Uncle, Abby and Mercy care more for me and my dreams than anyone else." He let out a big sigh. "But their role at my farewell dinner was nothing more than as slaves at any master's table. I'm ashamed."

All color drained from Lawrence's face.

"Is that how you saw it?"

Raymon's voice was just above a whisper. "That's what I saw in Mercy's eyes."

"You both are too hard on yourselves." Adam snorted. "You know how Abby can be. She can easily fall back into a servant's role. We've allowed her to do that too much over the years." Adam looked at his brother-in-law. Lawrence twisted his lips with disgust and clenched his hands into fists.

"I'll put an end to this." Lawrence jumped to his feet, leaving Adam and Raymon on the steps.

After a minute, Adam scooted closer to his son and laid his arm across his shoulders.

"I'm afraid we have gotten so used to Abby serving us that it didn't feel awkward for her to be serving us at your party. I'll speak to her and Mercy. I know Lawrence will, but knowing Abby, I'm sure Mercy was following her mother's wishes. But we all should have insisted that they join the celebration as family. For that oversight, I am truly sorry."

Father and son sat in companionable silence, each lost in his own thoughts. Adam cleared his throat and glanced at his son.

"Son, I'm sorry I won't be accompanying you to Philadelphia."

"I understand, Father. I really do. Uncle Lawrence hasn't seen his parents in forever. Besides, you will only be delayed for a few weeks." Raymon smiled.

Adam rubbed his chin slowly. "I might be delayed a little more than a few weeks."

He looked his son in the eyes.

"Eli and I have been called away to check on one of our safe houses. We need to see if the owner's identity has been compromised. If so, we will need to get them out of the South as soon as we can. You know a Southern abolitionist can be in great danger."

Raymon nodded. "Please be careful, Father."

Chapter Eighteen

Abby's heart was heavy and filled with regret as she slowly dragged her way up the flight of stairs to the third floor. She could hear her daughter's cries and hiccups when she reached the third-floor landing, and her heart ached when she remembered how Lawrence had tried to convince her that she and Mercy should be seated with the family instead of serving them. She tried to stifle a sob as she entered the room and went to her daughter's side. "Oh, baby, I am so sorry. Please forgive me. I didn't realize what I was asking you to do. Please forgive me."

Abby grabbed her daughter and rocked her back and forth in her arms like she had when she was a baby. Both of them cried for a while.

Mercy finally pulled away. "I can't believe I ran out of the dining room with a room full of guests." She wiped tears from her eyes. "Oh, Momma, when Raymon whispered his thanks, I just could not go on. I don't know what came over me."

She threw herself back on the bed and started crying again.

Abby rubbed her back. "I'm sorry, Mercy, for asking you to step in and help out with the serving. I wasn't thinking."

Mercy peeked at her mother as her crying subsided. "I remember something you told me when I was about four years old. It came back to me when I was serving."

"What is it, sweetie?" Abby asked from her perch on the edge of the bed.

"You said that I should always remember my place."

Mercy sat up and propped herself up on the pillows.

"You told me I was smart, that I can read and write better than most white children and some grownups. But you said I will still be regarded as inferior because of the black blood that runs through my veins. And then you touched my nose and said, 'We are just as good as anyone, and God loves us all the same.' "

Abby straightened, dread filling her heart. *Oh, Lord what have I done?* The words thundered in her head. Abby knew exactly when she had uttered the words, and why. She'd had no idea that a four-year-old would remember the words and take them to heart.

But Mercy had, and continued with recounting what her mother had said that day. "You told me, 'White folks don't see us as their equal, and until the good Lord chooses to change their hearts, they will always believe that. There aren't many white people like Mr. Lawrence, Mr. Adam, and Raymon, but they are still white, and they don't see us as their equals either. They treat you one way when their white friends are around and another way when they aren't. You best learn this right now,' you said."

Mercy looked over at her mother, her eyebrows scrunching together when she saw tears spilling from her eyes. She moved over to sit next to her mother on the edge of the bed.

Abby held her daughter in her arms and cried

uncontrollably.

"What's wrong, Momma? Did I say something to upset you? Are you ashamed of me for running out of the party?"

Abby could only shake her head and sob into her hands.

Mercy continued to embrace her mother. She was puzzled by her behavior.

Abby cried until she had no more tears to shed. She took hold of her daughter's hand and kissed it.

"I'm so sorry for what I have done to you. It was out of my own jealousy and misunderstanding that I spoke those words to you. Please forgive me."

A knock at the door lessened the tension in the room. Mother and daughter dried their eyes but made no effort to answer the door.

Raymon tapped lightly on the bedroom door again, and then waited on the first step like he had when he was younger. When Abby finally opened the door, he stood, and she walked past him, wiping tears from her eyes. He touched her arm. "Please forgive me. I'm so sorry."

She nodded, and then made her way downstairs.

Mercy slowly walked out of the room. Her gaze met his before she lowered her head.

Her red, puffy eyes caused an ache in his chest. His throat tightened, and he could barely choke out his words. "Mercy, I am so very sorry. Please forgive me. You are my best friend, yet I didn't…" He lowered his head in shame. "I didn't think about it until later"—he lifted his head—"but we should have insisted that you and Abby join us at the family table."

Mercy kept her eyes lowered.

"Mercy, look at me? Say something."

She finally looked up. "I understand, and you don't owe me an explanation."

"I don't think you do understand. I treated you abominably. My behavior was no better than that of any slaver."

Mercy gasped. "Raymon, please don't ever say a thing like that. Don't even think it. It's not true. You are a fine person and a wonderful fr...friend." She couldn't quite get the last word out. "I will always remember all you did for me. You taught me to read and write." She quirked a brow and gave a wicked grin to lighten the mood.

Raymon chortled. "If I remember correctly, you were making good progress on your own."

She smiled, but it was tinged with sadness. "Thank you for sharing your books with me. They have taken me to places that I never knew existed. Our time studying the Bible has given me hope and insight that many people don't have. You see, you owe me no apology. I owe you a thousand thanks for what you have given me."

The pair moved over to sit on the steps. Mercy put her hands in her lap and turned to face Raymon. Her gaze moved slowly across her best friend's face, and she looked deep into his hazel eyes. She wanted to memorize every inch of his face so she would never forget him.

Raymon smiled. "You don't have to memorize my face. I'm coming back."

Neither spoke for a while.

Raymon gently touched Mercy's fingers. "You mean a lot to me."

They sat looking at each other for a moment. Sadness clouded Mercy's pretty face. She drew her knees up to her chest.

"I wish I had a future."

He frowned. "You do have a future."

"What is it? Cooking, cleaning, and tending the herb garden?" Her lips twitched into a half smile. "I do enjoy teaching the people on the ranch, and I am writing my stories down like Papa Lawrence suggested." After a moment, she continued, "What will become of me?" She stretched her legs out in front of her and let out a big sigh. "I've only been off this ranch twice, and that was when Mother and I went to the Hadleys' to help care for a sick friend of Grandma Cookie's. I have no idea what lies beyond this ranch…what life is like beyond the South."

He let out a soft chuckle. "You are not being held here against your will. You are not a slave."

She was silent for a moment. Tears streamed down her cheeks. "Am I not?"

Raymon's eyebrows knitted together in surprise. He took her hand in his and rubbed it lightly.

"How long have you been feeling this way?"

"I don't know, for a while. I suppose when I found out you were leaving and may never come back. I know you said you would, but things change, and so do people."

"I will return."

She looked in his eyes. "Then what? Will we continue with our scavenger hunts and exploring the woods, playing tag and horseshoes?"

He knew instantly what she meant. He dropped her hands and spoke just above a whisper. "I don't know."

****

Abby closed the door to Lawrence's bedroom on the second floor in the main house, threw herself on the bed, and wept. She knew she had made a mess of things by telling Mercy that all whites feel superior to people with mixed blood and to blacks, and that even when whites are nice, they treat you one way when their white friends are around and a different way when they're not. She pounded the pillow and wept out loud.

"Oh, Lord, please forgive me! I was just trying to protect my daughter. I was hurting so badly when I thought Lawrence had rejected me."

Lawrence stepped into the room with a determined set of his jaw. He intended to tell Abby once and for all that he was going to tell everyone they were husband and wife and Mercy was his daughter. He would no longer allow them to be thought of as just servants. His starched resolve crumbled when he saw his wife stretched out across the bed crying. He rushed over and scooped her up into his arms.

"Sweetheart, what's wrong?"

She didn't speak.

Again he asked, "Oh, sweetheart, what's wrong?" He stroked her long hair that had escaped from its pins.

She laid her head on his chest and cried more as she tried to tell him what had happened.

"Sweetheart, just take your time and tell me what has upset you so."

"I should have listened to you when you asked for Mercy and me to join you at the party as family. I had no idea my decision not to do that would hurt our daughter so much." She started crying again.

Lawrence kissed the top of her head, rubbed her

back gently, and spoke words of comfort to her. Between hiccups, Abby told him about Mercy running from the dinner party and feeling inferior. And how she had shared her own prejudice about whites with her long ago when she thought she had lost him to the Widow O'Toole.

"I had no idea that at four years of age she would understand my angry babbling. My careless words have festered and grown in her heart. Don't you see what I have done?"

"Shh…shh, I know you and Mercy don't really feel that way. You both were responding to being hurt."

He pulled a handkerchief from his pocket and dabbed her tears away.

Abby's voice cracked as she continued, "I didn't want Mercy to be hurt the way I was hurting when you went away and I thought you were never coming back."

She looked up into her husband's eyes. "Will you forgive me for misguiding our daughter?"

Lawrence pulled his wife closer to his side. "Oh, sweetheart, I was the one who acted so foolishly. Please forgive me for hurting you so."

Silence and sniffles filled the room for a time.

"We can't change the past, but we can change the future." Lawrence lifted his wife's chin with his finger, and she gazed into his eyes. "You are the best thing that ever happened to me. I want to spend all my days and nights with you. I won't go on loving you in the shadows." He tried to lighten the mood of their conversation. "Besides, we are getting a little too old to be sneaking around."

Abby laughed and playfully hit him on his arm. "Speak for yourself, husband. I am only thirty-one."

She spoke between sniffles.

"I stand corrected, sweetie. Since I am four years older than you, I am too old to be sneaking around."

Lawrence's impish comment was followed by an ardent kiss on his wife's lips. He became serious.

"I know you still think about the baby we lost."

Abby's eyes were downcast as she nodded. He lifted his wife's chin to look into her eyes.

"We still want to have other children, don't we?"

"Yes." She nodded and smiled, remembering the note she planned to slip into his bag.

"I want our marriage to be public knowledge, at least to everyone on the ranch, before we have more children. I don't want you to be ashamed and carry my child in secret like you had to do with Mercy." He kissed his wife's hand.

A light tap sounded at the door, and Abby wiped away the remnants of her tears as Lawrence eased from the bed and opened the door slightly. Cedric stood at the door, smiling.

"Mr. Adam would like to see you in the study."

"Thank you, Cedric. I'll be there in just a few minutes."

He closed the door and turned to Abby and gave her a cross-eyed look. Laughter bubbled from her lips, and Lawrence's heart danced in his chest. He didn't like to see his wife so sad and brokenhearted as she had been. He kissed her soundly on the lips.

"I've been summoned by my dear brother." He snuggled with his wife for only a few minutes longer.

She gave him a peck on the cheek. "I'll get your things packed."

Lawrence held his wife and gave her a kiss so

intense that it left her breathless and yearning for more. Then he left the room.

Abby pulled the leather valises out of the closet and smiled. It seemed that she was always packing a bag for Lawrence for one reason or another. Sometimes he, Adam, and Eli would be gone for days with only the clothes on their backs. She prayed for her husband more fervently during those times. He had told her long ago that he was about the Lord's work and it was for her own safety not to know many details. She had accepted that without hesitation.

She placed the valises on the bed, and as she packed the last one, her thoughts went to Mercy.

"Oh, Lord, how am I going to tell my daughter that I have been secretly married to her Papa Lawrence for eight years?"

"What will she do when she finds out that Raymon is really her cousin, and she can't have the future she has dreamed of having with him?"

****

When Lawrence stepped into his brother-in-law's study, he was surprised by the melancholy he saw on Adam's face. Of course Adam was disappointed at not being able to go with Raymon to Philadelphia and had mixed emotions about his leaving, like any loving parent would. But there was something different in his mood that Lawrence couldn't quite identify. He cleared his throat and went to sit in a chair next to the desk. Adam twirled a pencil in his hand. Neither man spoke for a while.

Adam finally turned concerned eyes to Lawrence. "Do you know your daughter feels like a slave on this ranch?"

Lawrence propelled from his chair so fast it threatened to topple over. "She what?"

"I've been trying to make sense of it ever since Raymon told me."

Lawrence swiped his fingers through his thick curly hair and began pacing the room. He let out a long, exaggerated sigh. "I've made a mess of things. This is my fault. If I hadn't been so impulsive, if I hadn't abandoned Abby…"

"Lawrence calm down. What's done is done."

"But I set everything in motion."

"Lawrence, please sit down."

Lawrence's jaw twitched as he sat in silence.

Adam propped his elbows on the desk. "Everyone on the ranch thinks of Abby and Mercy as part of the Mallory and O'Daley family."

"I know," Lawrence responded. He chewed on his bottom lip absentmindedly. "Abby never wanted to leave the ranch because of Wesley's threats. I never thought of Mercy. She always seemed happy and content to stay here. Of course, she knows nothing of the threats."

Adam nodded. "I've been thinking about that."

Lawrence gazed out the window, then turned slowly to his brother-in-law. "I wish I had known how Mercy felt. I would have taken her and her mother to town with me." Lawrence looked at his brother-in-law. "Would you do me a favor? The next time you go into Darin, will you take the girls?"

Adam rubbed his chin. "What about Wesley?"

"It's been eight years. Hopefully the old man has given up the hunt by now. My investigators don't seem to think he and his men are threats anymore."

Adam leaned back in his chair and put both hands behind his head. "I wonder if the other ranch hands and workers still feel like slaves. We've asked them to be watchful when they leave the ranch, but that was for their own protection. I've noticed only a few leave the ranch these days, but it's not because we've prohibited them from doing so. I hope they understand that." Adam sat straight up in his chair. "I need to find out how they feel."

That night, Abby knocked on her husband's bedroom door around midnight. Lawrence couldn't believe the beautiful sight before him. His wife wore a long satin dressing gown with white lace on the collar and sleeves trimmed with white ribbon bows. She looked like an angel. He stood staring at her for a while as his thoughts went back to the night he had first seen her without her head wrapped. The picture of her standing there took his breath away just as it had those many years ago.

"Are you going to let me in, husband?" Abby batted her eyes seductively.

Lawrence chuckled and opened the door with a flourish. Abby swirled into his embrace, and the couple had an enchanting time on their last night together. They made plans for their future and discussed the best way to tell Mercy about her parentage.

Early the next morning, Lawrence kissed Abby as she snuggled in his arms.

"It's time to wake up, wife." Abby groaned but gave her husband a kiss before she got out of bed.

Lawrence went to the marble-topped dresser and pulled out the black velvet box that held their wedding rings. Abby blinked back tears when she saw the box.

She could count the times they had worn those rings in eight years. He opened the box, pulled out her silver-and-ruby ring, placed it on her finger—and then kissed it.

"I will never take it off. It's the symbol of our love. And I love you very much, Mr. Mallory." Abby slipped Lawrence's ring onto his finger. He repeated the words Abby had spoken as he gazed into her honey-brown eyes.

"We will make our announcement to the world when I return."

Chapter Nineteen

The next morning, the conveyance was packed and pulled up in front of the house. Lawrence peered into the carriage. It looked as if all their belongings had been packed, along with enough provisions to last a month instead of a few days. He smiled. He knew Abby was behind the abundance.

All the ranch hands had gathered in the yard at the main house to say goodbye. Lawrence made his way over to Abby, led her away from the crowd, and guided her to the corner of the house. He pulled her into his arms and crushed his lips against hers. The delightful tingle ignited an explosion of pure pleasure in his body that made him lose track of time and place. He wanted to shout to the world that this beautiful slip of a woman was his wife.

Abby pulled away from her husband, just far enough to lose herself in his glistening ebony eyes. All her fears faded, and she looked forward to telling Mercy and the world that this handsome, godly man was her husband and Mercy's father. She whispered into his ear, "I love you. I know Mercy and I will enjoy the outing you have arranged with Adam and Eli."

He grinned. "I love you, sweetheart. Thanks for agreeing to take Mercy to town."

The couple stood gazing in each other's eyes until they heard someone clearing his throat.

"Lawrence, I believe it's time for you to go." Eli slapped his friend on the back.

"Take care of my girls, my brother."

Raymon slowly made his way to the back of the conveyance, where he climbed into the second seat behind his uncle and Mr. Wainwright. He remembered the pouch Mercy had given him. He took it from his bag and put it in his pocket. Every time he touched it, he would think of her. He thought of the conversation he'd had with her. He hoped he had convinced her to use the gifts and talents God had given her for the good of those on the ranch. He noticed from the corner of his eye, while his father was saying his final goodbye, Abby and Mercy clinging to his Uncle Lawrence. There was definitely something between the two adults, but he would have to examine that later. For now, Mercy was upmost in his mind.

Abby's heart squeezed in her chest as she stood with the others, saying goodbye to her beloved. She watched the wagon until only a cloud of dirt could be seen.

As the wagon rolled down the lane, Lawrence and Raymon looked back at the crowd of people who had gathered. Raymon's eyes were fixed on his father and Mercy. Lawrence's gaze fell on Abby and his daughter until they were just silhouettes, among the crepe myrtles and sturdy oaks, against the three-story red brick colonial house. There was no doubt he was leaving his heart on the Double-O Ranch.

Raymon's eyes lingered on the wooden sign that hung above the fence. "Welcome to the Double-O Ranch," it said, and in small print, "Adam O'Daley and son." He wondered if he would ever take ownership, with all the changes taking place in the South. He wondered if he wanted to.

****

As the carriage rocked to and fro over the landscape, Lawrence relaxed against the seat and lost himself in thought. A grin lit his face as he thought of his lovely wife and the titillating night they had spent together. She'd looked like an angel in her white satin nightgown when she came to him in the middle of the night.

A snort from Mr. Wainwright brought Lawrence out of his rumination. "I do believe it's lunch time," Wainwright said, his jaws jiggling. "You and Raymon have been engrossed in your own thoughts almost all morning, oblivious to the jarring and creaking of the carriage, which only made me hungry."

Laughter rang out, and soon the group stopped for lunch in a grove of trees.

After lunch, Lawrence pulled his handkerchief from his pocket and a note came out with it. As he read the note, laugh lines stretched across his face, and his eyes sparkled. He shoved the note back into his pocket and walked with a skip in his step as he boarded the carriage.

The two-day trip to Rome, Georgia, was uneventful, and the group spent their time discussing topics from religion to politics.

They arrived in Rome just before time for the evening meal, and lodging was secured. Then Lawrence, Raymon, and Wainwright spent a little time touring the town. As the three strolled down the street, delicious smells of cooking beef drifted through the air.

"Gentlemen, I don't know about you, but my

stomach tells me it's time to eat," Wainwright said.

His belly jiggled from the force of his laughter as he guided Lawrence and Raymon to the dining establishment that issued such wonderful aromas into the street. The place was an explosion of conversation; politics was the topic of discussion. They followed the waitress through the crowded room and the maze of white-linen-covered tables until they reached a table in the rear of the room by the unlit fireplace.

Lawrence observed the patrons with disgust. He recognized many as wealthy plantation owners. He knew an election was coming up, and they had walked right into the middle of an election circus. He studied his nephew, who sat across from him, as they waited for their food. His facial expression remained neutral, like that of any good attorney in a court of law, even though Lawrence knew he recognized the situation for what it was. The Georgia political system was being played out in front of them. Food, drink, and promises were in abundance as wealthy slave owners wooed non-slave owners, persuading them to cast their vote with them. Slave owners had great political power in the state. Raymon shook his head slightly at the scene before him. He hoped he could make a difference in the political arena someday soon. Unfortunately, the scene repeated itself many times in the coming days as the three sailed down the Coosa River to Savannah.

The group spent two days enjoying the city of Savannah before boarding the steamship *Orion*, heading for Philadelphia. Lawrence was pleased with their rooms. He remembered the trip back home with Elizabeth and her hysteria over their accommodations, but he smiled as he looked at his companions' faces; he could tell they were very happy with their large stateroom, with its separate seating area, firm mattresses, dressers for storage, and a door that opened directly into a private salon where they would have their meals and socialize. This delighted Mr. Wainwright.

Lawrence toured the ship with his nephew, who hadn't been on a steamship since his trip to Philadelphia eight years ago. In some places they were halted temporarily by small crowds of people from all races and social status. Young children clung to their mother's skirts, and others saw the ship as their personal playground.

"There's so much to see and so many interesting-looking people to meet," Raymon said.

"I know. Why don't you get to know some of these people? I've seen several young men and young ladies about your age. I don't want you to feel you have to spend all your time with me or Wainwright."

Raymon took his uncle's advice and engaged in small talk with several people. He especially wanted to talk with some of the black passengers and workers. He wanted firsthand information about their lives, their experiences, and their plight. He felt the insight would be valuable to him as an attorney. He tried to solicit conversation from them, but to no avail. He was friendly and tried to put the people at ease, but they became as statues chiseled with emotionless faces, with heads and eyes downcast. He thought of Mercy. Even though some of the blacks on the ship were not slaves, they still followed the social rules and expectations of bonded men because their lives were so restricted by what they could do or say.

Is that what Mercy was talking about? he asked himself. *Do these people not feel truly free to be themselves, to pursue their dreams?* He hung his head. He knew the answers to his questions.

****

Raymon was reading in the salon, but his head snapped up at the sound of clinking glasses and dishes crashing to the floor. A soft but firm female voice captured his attention.

"You did that on purpose. You need to apologize, now."

The young blonde girl about his age stood with her fisted hands on her hips, tapping her toes while staring at a boy of about twelve. He had just tripped a black server as he walked past. The boy's eyes were big, but he squeaked out a weak apology before scurrying away.

"And what are you looking at?"

Raymon turned to see who was standing behind him. His mouth fell open when he realized the petite girl was speaking to him. "Oh, I...I was..." he stammered and held up the law book he was reading. "I was just thinking about what I've read."

A blush crept up her neck. "I'm so sorry I snapped at you. I can't tolerate meanness and rudeness perpetrated on innocent, hard-working people."

She lowered her thick lashes and tucked an errant strand of hair behind her ear.

"I did see what you did, but I was not staring," he quickly added. "That was very kind of you." He set the book down on the table and stood to his feet.

"Thank you. My name is Phoebe Brown." She gave a slight curtsy.

Raymon bowed. "It's a pleasure to make your

acquaintance, Miss Brown. I'm Raymon O'Daley. Would you like to sit?" Raymon waved his hand over the chair next to him.

"Yes," she replied, adjusting her skirt as she sat down.

Lawrence's eyes twinkled in amusement when he heard the beautiful young lady reprimand Raymon for something he hadn't done. The look of bewilderment on his nephew's face was priceless. He had planned to spend some time with his nephew but decided against it when he saw the young man invite the girl to join him. "Maybe talking to the young lady will help him get his mind off Mercy."

Phoebe fingered the book. "Interesting reading material," she said with a smile.

Raymon scrambled for the book. "Yes, I will be studying law in Philadelphia with Attorney Clark." Her lips formed a circle. "You mean Attorney Henry Clark?"

"Yes, do you know him?" Raymon leaned forward in his chair.

"Everyone in Philadelphia and the North knows him. You will do well under his tutelage, and will rise to prominence quickly after you complete your studies. You just wait and see, Mr. O'Daley." She gave him a coy smile. The pair talked for over an hour, covering subjects from horses to politics.

After Phoebe left, Raymon went in search of his Uncle Lawrence. He found him on deck talking to several black men. When he came up to the group, the men moved away. He leaned his back against the railing. "How did you get them to talk to you?"

Lawrence dangled his fingers from his vest

pockets. His brow furrowed. "What do you mean?"

Raymon rubbed his chin. "I've tried to talk to several of the blacks, and only one has talked to me so far. He's a freedman who owns his own wrought iron business. He's headed to Boston. He's been commissioned by a wealthy family to make a decorative wrought iron fence for their property." Raymon frowned. "Why won't the others talk to me?"

Lawrence tipped his chin up. "They've probably been watching you and can't figure out why you are trying so hard to talk to them. Besides," Lawrence said, folding his arms across his chest, "I know Micah from the Bradley Farm. He just completed some work in Savannah and is heading back home to Charleston." Lawrence gave Raymon a playful pat on the back. "Why don't you join me for a bit of exercise before dinner?"

As the two walked, Lawrence remembered Micah had told him they had "thought Miss Elizabeth had outgrown those spells." He shivered at the thought.

"Are you all right, Uncle?"

"Yes, I was just thinking."

Raymon stopped in his tracks. "I see some people I want to talk to. Will you excuse me?" Lawrence nodded and continued his stroll around the deck. As he walked, he touched the note in his pocket. *We're having a baby.* A chuckle rose in his throat. *This time things will be different. Abby will get the rest and care she needs and not spend all her time in that confounded herb garden of hers.* He shook his head and smiled. *Wild horses can't keep that woman from her garden.* He took a long look at the ocean. *I will be at her side, and she won't have to worry if I'm coming back or if I love her.* He made his way back to his room, where he stretched out on his bed, closed his eyes, and thought about how much he loved his wife and daughter. He thanked God for giving him a second chance at love.

****

The day before they were to disembark, Lawrence caught a glimpse of Raymon as he and Wainwright strolled around the deck. He was in a small group of black men. All heads were bowed, and his nephew was leading them in prayer.

"That's a fine young man," Wainwright said as he dabbed perspiration from his brow.

"Yes, he is." Lawrence spoke with pride in his voice.

"I want to apologize to you."

Lawrence raised an eyebrow and turned to face the man. "For what?"

Wainwright dabbed at the beads of perspiration that had formed above his lips.

"I was so concerned about my reputation as a tutor that"—he lowered his eyes—"I didn't want it blemished by educating a girl."

Lawrence crossed his arms over his chest and stared at the man.

"Mercy is a fine young lady," Wainwright added with a slight quiver in his voice.

Lawrence's lips twitched from trying to hold in a smile. This wasn't the first time John Wainwright had apologized to him, but more like the hundredth time since the man determined that Mercy might be his daughter. Lawrence had been furious at first, but his wife had reasoned with him, pointing out that no one knew their daughter had such a thirst for knowledge.

And besides, Adam had hired the man for Raymon, to prepare him to accomplish his dreams as an attorney, Abby had reminded him. Mercy's turn would come...*and it will*, he said to himself. A grin creased his lips, and his thoughts returned to Wainwright. "We thank you for the use of your books." He slapped Wainwright on the shoulders.

"Besides, I understand from my nephew that the schoolroom was often hot, and you had to leave the door open, especially if a certain young lady was lurking in the hallway," Lawrence said, giving him a sly grin.

The two men laughed.

Raymon looked up to see his uncle and his tutor in the crowd of people. After he finished the prayer and conversation, he joined them on the deck.

"I've made many friends," Raymon said, waving to the small crowd he'd just left. The three walked in silence for a while. "You know what I learned? It makes my skin crawl just thinking about it."

Lawrence looked at his nephew with a slight shake of the head.

"I've talked to a minister today, and he said that some of his brothers in the faith are being pressured by certain members of their congregation to select passages from the Bible that speak of slavery. This is to convince the slaves that it's their destiny to be slaves and obediently serve their white masters."

Disgust was written on the faces of his hearers.

****

Lawrence and his nephew stood on the deck, taking in the view of the city that would be Raymon's home for the next three years, at least. The shore was filled with people of all ethnic groups, some working as laborers, loading and unloading cargo, others cleaning and washing down boats. Some lurked in the shadows, their shifty eyes darting from side to side, trying to find a way to make quick money.

As they moved through the crowds, Lawrence recognized a lovely blonde as the girl Raymon had spent time with during their voyage. She waved her handkerchief and rushed over to them, pulling two adults along with her.

"Mother and Father, I would like for you to meet Mr. Mallory and his nephew, Raymon O'Daley. Raymon is here to study law with Attorney Clark."

Mrs. Brown's eyes widened with delight, and so did Mr. Brown's. "Mallory, did you say?" Mrs. Brown turned to her daughter and then back to Lawrence. "Would you be the son of Vincent Mallory, the wealthy…" Her voiced faded, and she cleared her throat. "I mean…the prominent businessman?"

Lawrence smiled, but didn't respond. That's what bothered him about most people. They judged by what you had or didn't have, never getting to know the person God created you to be. The conversation with the Browns ended when Lawrence heard Wainwright calling them. He moved in the direction of the voice, and the Browns followed, extending an invitation to dine with them on the next Tuesday. He wondered if Raymon would remember the information. He secretly hoped he wouldn't. As they boarded the hack Wainwright had secured, he heard Mrs. Brown calling that she would send their carriage for them. A grunt escaped his lips.

Lawrence gave his nephew a brief history of the

city as they traveled from the dock, heading toward Market Street, the home of his parents. He pointed out the numerous machine shops, iron shops, and lumber yards near the docks, strewn through areas occupied by sea captains, seafaring men, and their families. The carriage bumped over the stone pavers as they traveled past modest single-family homes nestled on small, neat yards.

When the carriage turned onto the street leading to uptown, the scenery and the smells caught Raymon's attention. People crowded into retail stores and farmers' markets. His nostrils filled with the sweet fragrance of freshly baked bread. He thought about the delicious bread Cookie had always baked, and a feeling of homesickness engulfed him.

In the metropolitan area, the yards became larger and filled with various kinds of blossoming trees and flowers, and expensive wrought iron fences encircled many properties. Lawrence pointed out houses of friends and distant relatives. Before long, they pulled into the brick driveway of a mansion, where Wainwright let out a slow whistle. The huge red brick structure boasted stately columns supporting an enclosed porch on the second floor. The house was surrounded by a decorative wrought iron fence, trimmed green grass, and mounds of flowers and flowery trees. Even before they could disembark, they were greeted with hugs, kisses, and an abundance of conversation from family members.

Chapter Twenty

Abby sat straight as an arrow on the hard bench in the common house. Tears pooled in her eyes as she heard the tremble in Adam's voice and saw the slight shaking of his hand as he stood and asked the people to stay after the Sunday worship. A hush fell over the crowd. He cleared his throat…once…twice…three times.

"It's been almost eighteen years since my wife and I first arrived here on the Double-O. We couldn't believe the deplorable condition the slave quarters were in. We set about making changes that are evident on the ranch today." Adam paused. "It took us over three years and plenty of hard work from all of us, but we created what I hope has been a comfortable community for us all. The most important thing my wife and I did was to give you your freedom." His voice cracked, and he choked on his words.

Abby saw heads nodding and heard murmurs of agreement throughout the room. Mercy gripped her mother's arm, and tears ran down her cheeks.

Adam continued. "Those who didn't want to stay on at the ranch were given wages, provisions, and their freedom papers. A copy of each of your freedom papers is still in the main house today." He dabbed his eyes with his handkerchief and gazed over the crowd. "I hope none of you feel like slaves today." His voice broke. "You are all family. I know we have asked you at times to be careful in your travels because of the slave traders. But I have never ever forbidden any of you to leave the ranch. Please know you are free to leave whenever you like."

For a moment, a hush fell over the crowd. Abby put her arms around her daughter, who was shivering and rocking with her tears. Everyone started speaking at once, telling Adam how much they appreciated everything he had done for them and that they didn't feel like slaves.

"Mr. Adam," an older man said, "it took me a long time to feel free, but I knew I was free when I got paid for the work I did, and I could work in my own garden to have food for my family. I was afraid for a long time that my family might be split up and sold, and we would never see each other again, but that never happened."

The man was so overcome with emotion he needed help as he sat down. Most of the people agreed that living on the ranch had given them a life they had only dreamed of and probably would not have been possible any other place. They thanked Adam for looking out for their safety and granting them their freedom. Others thanked him for allowing them to learn a trade and take care of their own families. One woman yelled out, "I'm sixty years old, and I never thought I could learn to read. But thanks to Miss Kathleen, God rest her soul, I can read. And thanks to Miss Abby and Miss Mercy for helping us to teach our young'uns."

Mercy laid her head in her mother's lap. Eli knelt beside them and prayed. When the crowd cleared out, Mercy rushed over to Adam. She threw her arms around his neck and wept.

"Oh, Uncle Adam, I am sorry for saying those words! I had no idea they would hurt you so. Please accept my apology. I was so jealous of Raymon for the education he is getting and his hopes and plans for the future. Please say that you forgive me." Mercy choked on her words.

"Oh, honey," Adam said, pulling Mercy close. "I forgive you. I had no idea you felt that way. I wanted to be sure that…" His voice trailed off, and he gave Mercy another hug. "Have you spoken to your mother and Lawrence about your feelings?" Just then, Abby came up. She hugged Mercy.

"Sweetie, we need to talk. There are things I must tell you."

Adam gave Abby a knowing nod. She and Mercy walked away arm in arm to the main house.

Abby twisted her hands together and paced the floor, muttering, "Oh, Mercy, I am so sorry."

This went on for quite a while, until Mercy spoke up from her chair by the window. "Momma, please sit down. I have an idea what you want to tell me."

Abby stopped in her tracks. "You do?"

"I know that you and Papa Lawrence are married."

Abby's mouth flew open, her heart raced, and she staggered over and plopped down on the edge of the settee. She spoke slowly as if in a trance. "You know?"

Mercy nodded.

Abby stammered, "But how did you… How long have you known?"

Mercy knelt before her mother and took her hand.

"I have known there was something between you and Papa Lawrence for a long time, even when you weren't supposed to like him."

Abby's eyes stretched wide, and her hand flew to her chest.

"You used to talk and cry in your sleep, Momma."

Abby sat in stun silence.

Mercy took a seat on the settee next her mother. "When I was about ten, I became very concerned about Papa Lawrence's health. He was often sick and needed us—well, he needed you to take care of him," she said, smiling. "We had been staying at his house for a few days when I sneaked to his room one night to check on him. He wasn't there, so I went downstairs. I heard laughter coming from the parlor. I was going to go right in, but I stopped at the door when I saw you dressed in the most beautiful blue gown I had ever seen. You and Papa were playing chess, and you won. He kissed your ring finger and called you 'wife' and you called him 'husband.' I wanted to come out of hiding and laugh with you because I was so happy to have a real family. But I was afraid I might get in trouble for getting out of bed and for spying." Mercy patted her mother's hand. "You were always so happy when you were with Papa. It was fun watching both of you pretend there was nothing going on between you. I was so happy to have a papa that I pretended, too, pretended I didn't know."

Tears fell from Abby's eyes as she spoke to her daughter. "Oh, Mercy, I am sorry about our deception. We never meant to hurt you. Do you know everything between Lawrence and me?"

"Momma, if you mean if I know that Papa Lawrence is my real father, the answer is yes."

Abby gasped. "How long have you known that?"

"I guess I have always known. When I looked in

Papa's face I would see me. Does that make any sense?"

Abby nodded. "Yes, baby, it makes perfect sense." She stood and hugged her daughter tightly. "Oh, Mercy, I am so sorry we deceived you. Please forgive us."

"Mother, there is nothing to forgive. I love you and Papa so much, and I know you both love me."

Abby massaged her temples. "Sweetie, we had our reasons for not telling you. There are things in our past, my past, that I didn't want you to know."

Mercy held her mother's hands. "Mother, you don't have to tell me anything. Whatever you and Papa did, I know you did it for my own good. You both have taken good care of me, and for that I'm grateful." Abby cried and hugged her daughter for a long time.

"Your father and I had planned to tell you about our marriage and your birth after he returned from Philadelphia. I'm glad you know." Abby hugged her daughter again.

****

Lawrence had time to do a lot of soul searching on his way to Philadelphia. Abby's note about being pregnant was all it took for him to think about moving his family from the South. Everywhere he visited in the city, he tried to look at it from Abby and Mercy's perspective. He was not convinced they would be happy living there. The blacks in the city went about their daily lives without the fear of being sold into slavery, at least not now. Some blacks owned very successful businesses. There were some aristocratic blacks, mulattos, and mixed-race couples who moved in and out of the white society with ease. The only thing that seemed to matter in those cases was how much money they had. Lawrence's interactions with his friends and acquaintances made one thing crystal clear to him: for the most part the good people of Philadelphia didn't necessarily want social and political equality for blacks, only emancipation. He was not surprised that this opinion was commonplace for most people, but he was disappointed that many Bible-believing and God-fearing people held to the same belief.

The smell of shortbread greeted Lawrence at the bottom of the stairs and interrupted his rendition of one of Abby's favorite songs. He took in a long, deep breath and followed his nose to the kitchen, but voices from his mother's sitting room made him stop in his tracks and lean against the door frame there as his mother and his sister Lauren fingered through papers sprawled out over the top of the marble tabletop. He ground his back teeth until his jaw hurt. He knew what they were up to. It was no secret that they thought he spent too much time around the house daydreaming and Raymon spent too much time studying. He cleared his throat.

"If you ladies are planning a party to introduce me to the city's most lovely and eligible ladies, you can count me out."

His mother and sister looked at him in bewilderment.

Lawrence stepped into the room. "I refuse to go to another dinner party or gathering where the hostess's only agenda is to partner me with more of the city's most eligible ladies." His tone dripped in sarcasm.

He went over to stand beside his mother's chair.

"I have something I need to tell you." He dropped his head. "As a matter of fact, I should have told you years ago, but I was held to a promise. But first, let me go get Raymon."

"What about Father?" Lauren said, alarm in her voice.

"Father already knows."

His sister and mother gazed at each other.

Lawrence returned with Raymon, then helped his mother to the parlor, where he stood and waited for everyone to be seated. He looked at their faces, smiled, and rocked back and forth on his heels. His heart felt so light he thought it was going to take flight and fly away.

"I'm married," he announced.

Raymon smiled.

His sister gasped.

His mother's eyes grew large, and she threw her wrinkled hand over her heart. "For heaven's sakes, you're married?" His mother's voice was weak but clear.

His sister fired one question after another. "Who is she? How long? Why didn't you tell us?"

"If you two calm down, I will tell you everything you want to know." Lawrence looked at Raymon. "You don't seem to be surprised by the news."

Raymon shook his head and smiled. "I'll be surprised if you're not married to who I think it is."

"Tell us who she is." Lawrence's sister leaned forward on the edge of chair.

"I'm married to Abby Rose." Lawrence held up his hands to stop any further questions. "We have been married for eight years."

Raymon raised a brow.

"Eight years!" they all repeated. "Why have you kept her a secret?"

His mother fingered the pearls hanging from around her neck. She had a faraway look in her eyes. Lawrence walked over and sat on the arm of her chair. He put his arms around her and kissed her on the cheek. As they gazed into each other's eyes, something passed between them. He squeezed her shoulders. He knew she was thinking about his marriage to Elizabeth. Lines formed between his sister's eyebrows.

"Abby, Abby," Lawrence's sister said slowly. "I know that name."

"I know Kathleen probably wrote to you about an Abby. That's my Abby Rose."

"Isn't she…?"

Lawrence jumped to his feet and stopped Lauren from speaking.

"Let's get one thing clear right now. I will not have anyone disrespecting my wife. I thought we believed that all people are created in the image of God and are equally loved by Him. Do we believe all of God's word or only the parts we like?"

Mrs. Mallory tugged on Lawrence's coat.

"Lawrence, calm down. I don't think your sister meant any harm."

Tears pooled in Lauren's eyes. "I was going to say…Isn't she the beautiful mixed girl Kathleen loved so much?" She sniffed. "You're not the only one who has grown up over the years. I have changed too, little brother."

Lawrence apologized to his weeping sister and to the others for his behavior. When the group was calm again, he continued his story.

"I also have a thirteen-year-old daughter named Mercy." Both his mother and sister gasped when they heard the news. Silence cloaked the room.

The distant sound of a cane tapping on the floor broke the silence. Mr. Mallory soon appeared at the entry to the parlor. He looked from his wife to his daughter.

"I suppose you all know." His thin lips widened into a smile. "Judge nothing before the time, God's word says." He laughed. "We have ourselves a granddaughter. Isn't our God good?" A collective sigh filled the room, and Mr. Mallory gave his son a wink as he went over to sit beside his wife.

Lawrence told his family about Abby and her grandfather's obsession with finding her.

"We kept our marriage secret, not telling even Adam at first, to protect him and everyone else on the ranch from Wesley's threats."

He sat on the edge of the French-style armchair.

"I found out last month that Wesley has passed away. I hope the threat to Abby and Mercy is over."

The group sat in silence for a while, trying to take in all they had heard, especially the part about Abby's grandfather. Raymon was the first to speak.

"Does Mercy know any of this?"

"Not yet," Lawrence said. "But she will know everything when I return home."

"I think she knows that you are her real father, but she didn't want to say anything."

Lawrence only nodded his head at the statement.

"I thought she had an idea. When she was young, she would often say that she would see herself in my eyes. I knew what she meant by that, but I would tell her, 'Of course you can see your reflection in my eyes.' "

Everyone began talking at once, asking questions about Lawrence's wife and daughter. The room filled with laughter and excitement as Lawrence and Raymon told story after story about the two. They told of Abby's love and knowledge of herbs, and Mercy's knack for storytelling. Silence fell over the crowd when Lawrence left the room. Seconds later, he returned with a portrait he had drawn of his wife and daughter. He slowly unveiled the picture.

"Oh, they are so beautiful," his mother and sister both said with tears in their eyes.

"Who's so beautiful?" Lawrence's nephew said, as he bounced into the room.

Raymon couldn't respond. He just sat staring at the beautiful girl in the portrait.

Lawrence nodded as he listened to his family's arguments about moving his family from the South. He agreed with them that the situation in the South was getting more dangerous for them and for the work he and the others were trying to accomplish. As they talked, he thought he might reconsider his first impression of the city and how his family might fit into the culture. There was no doubt it would be easier to find a female tutor in the city than to request that one to pack up and move to the ranch in the South, especially one that would be sympathetic to their cause. He and Abby had much to discuss and consider when he returned home. His sister's voice broke into his musing.

"You might want to convince our brother-in-law to come home, as well. He and Kathleen never wanted to live in the South anyway." Her expression was somber.

Chapter Twenty-One

Abby crushed the white envelope to her breast. Tears filled her eyes, and a longing for her beloved burned in her bones. Mercy wrapped her arms around her mother's shoulders.

"I miss Papa too, but he will be away just three more weeks." Mercy kissed her mother's cheek.

Abby smiled, rose to her feet, and turned around in a small circle. Mercy's hand flew to her mouth. "I love the new gown!" She fondled the soft ruffles that trimmed the large collar and went down the length of the dress. Abby beamed and showed Mercy the drawstring in the waist. "This will give me room to grow." The two giggled all the way downstairs, where Adam stood waiting for them. A smile tugged his lips.

"Don't you two look pretty? The carriage is here. We need to get going so we can get back before dark. I'm sorry the trip will be cut short today, but I have business I need to take care of." Abby touched Adam's arm. "We are glad you are doing this for us."

The girls were giddy with excitement as they boarded the carriage. They had taken several trips into town with Adam since Lawrence left. They knew he would be pleased to know they were having fun and getting off the ranch.

It was a beautiful fall day. The air was warm, and puffy clouds decorated the blue sky. Geese honked overhead, and Abby closed her eyes and took in a deep breath of contentment, with a mixture of sadness. She glanced at Mercy, who was chatting away with Eli. He rode alongside them, while another ranch hand rode along on the other side of the carriage. Adam and Maxwell chattered from the front seat, and Pete drove. She leaned her head back on the cushioned leather seat and thought of Lawrence. Before she knew it, they had reached Darin.

The rhythmic echo of heels tapping the boardwalk faded as Abby and Mercy went into the millinery. They were excited to see the finished straw hat Abby had purchased for a surprise birthday gift for Cookie.

"I hope Grandma Cookie will love her new hat," Mercy said as she stepped from the store holding the hatbox by its ribbons.

Abby smiled. "She's going to love it. This will be her first hat that was bought especially for her."

The two locked arms and crossed the street, went two blocks, and came to the mercantile located at the end of the street.

"We need to hurry; I don't want to keep Adam waiting," Abby said as they upped their pace.

The bell overhead jingled, announcing their presence, and the rich smell of coffee greeted them. The store stocked an assortment of items, from perfume and candies to dry goods and hardware, and it had a cozy feel that Abby liked.

"I will be with you ladies in just a minute," the clerk said, coming from the back of the store, where two men searched through an assortment of nails.

Mercy passed the knick-knacks and went straight to the quill pens she needed, while Abby picked out little items for the children and small gifts for the household staff, things the store on the Double-O did not carry.

When the clerk came around the counter smiling at her, he asked, "Are you finding everything you need?"

"Yes, thank you," Abby replied.

The clerk helped carry her items to the counter. Mercy came up a moment later and put her items next to her mother's.

"Will this be all, ladies?"

"Yes." Abby smiled.

The clerk wrapped their purchases and handed them over the counter. They were on their way to the door when Mercy stopped in her tracks, causing her mother to bump into her.

"Sorry, Momma. I forgot to get candy for the men."

Mercy rushed back to the counter, put her package down, and selected several peppermint sticks and horehound candy sticks. She paid for them, then plopped a peppermint stick into her mouth.

Abby laughed. "Is that candy for you or the men?"

Mercy giggled and tried to answer without taking the candy from her mouth.

The bell jangled as the ladies left the store, and Abby saw the carriage just a few yards down the board walk.

"I see the men are all here and waiting for us."

"Oh, I forgot my package!" Mercy dashed back to the store, and Abby followed. "Uncle Adam," Mercy called over her shoulder, "I'll be right back."

Just as Mercy reached the counter to retrieve her package, a man grabbed her from behind. She tried to call out, but a dirty hand covered her mouth. Mercy kicked, wriggled, and beat his hand with her fists, trying to loosen his strong grip. She couldn't. Her heart thundered in her chest as she struggled to get free.

Seconds later, Abby entered the store, and her packages tumbled to the floor and a scream escaped her lips when she saw her daughter dangling from the arms of a thin, dirty-looking man with terror in his eyes. Abby shook with fear, but she willed herself to move. She had to get to Mercy. She took two steps toward her daughter before she was snatched up in the arms of another man. His big hand covered her mouth. Abby kicked and struggled with all her might. She prayed for Adam, Eli, or someone to come through the door.

The men struggled to carry their unwilling burdens to the back door, and as they went Abby saw the boots of the storekeeper sticking out from behind the counter, where he lay very still. Her eyes met her daughter's. Mercy's fear and desperation mirrored her own. She thought about kicking items over as she struggled, until the man hissed in her ear, "Don't even think about it. I'll snap you in two right now."

Abby stiffened. As quick as lightning, she and Mercy were on horses in front of their abductors, racing through the alley to the outskirts of town and into the nearby woods.

****

Adam pulled out his watch for the second time. "What's keeping the girls?" he said in a tone more gruff than he intended. "I told Abby we needed to get home before dark."

The bell jangled, and the storekeeper stumbled out of the store, bleeding and dazed, and fell to the boardwalk.

"What in the blue blazes…?" Adam didn't finish his sentence. He jumped from the carriage, ran to the storekeeper, and knelt beside him. "What happened?"

The man didn't answer.

"Pete, take care of him." Adam ran into the store. "Abby, Mercy, where are you?"

Panic overcame him as he yelled their names and didn't see them anywhere. Eli pushed past him. He searched the back room and the upstairs area but found no sign of Abby or Mercy other than their packages scattered where they had been dropped. One of the ranch hands charged through the back door, carrying another of their packages. "I found this outside." He paused and looked from to Adam and Eli. "It was by fresh horse tracks headed toward the woods."

Color drained from Adam's face. He held onto the counter. "Merciful God, please help us."

The ranch men began searching every inch of the little Scots-Irish town, while Eli and Adam followed the horse tracks out of town. After several hours, it was too dark to continue the search. All the men stayed in town, with the exception of Maxwell, who went back to the ranch to get supplies, provisions, and more men for the search the next day.

****

Abby's heartbeat was in rhythm with the hooves of the galloping horses; she thought it was going to jump out of her chest. She had never been so terrified in her life. The fear she had lived with for most of her life was nothing compared to the horror she now felt for herself and her daughter. Tears fell from her eyes and onto her captor's sleeve, but she didn't care. She thought how her grandfather had finally accomplished his goal of finding her. She wondered whether the men had learned she was pregnant. *Pregnant!* She wailed. *Oh, God, please don't let them hurt my baby.* Loud sobs escaped her lips. *Will they cut my baby from my womb just as my grandfather ordered for his own daughter?* The thought caused her to break out in a cold sweat. Her teeth begin to chatter, and her body shook so hard she thought she would slip from her captor's grip. *Oh, Lawrence, our baby...our baby.* She began to pray fervently. *God, please let Adam and Eli find us before it's too late.*

The path grew wide, and the horses were able to gallop side by side. Abby could see her daughter through her veil of tears. Mercy's curly hair had escaped its pins and was hanging loosely from under her bonnet. Her shoulders were hunched, and her eyes were wide with fear. Even so, her lips were moving, and Abby knew she was praying just like she was.

Later, Abby noticed Mercy observing their surroundings closely as if trying to memorize landmarks, just in case they were able to escape. "Escape," she whispered. "Where would we go? We don't know our way around this country. We might be able to get away from our captors, but we might run right onto a slave plantation or slave traders. Oh, Lord, please help us!"

Their captors turned onto a narrow path that led deeper into the woods. The horses plodded up hills and down hills and over rough terrain. Sometimes the brush was so thick the horses had to walk one behind the other; other times they walked side by side. Their captors didn't speak and neither did Abby or Mercy.

Just around dusk, the captors brought their horses to a halt by a grouping of rocks. The men dismounted and lifted their captives down. Abby was surprised by the men's gentleness. As soon as her feet touched the ground, she grabbed her daughter's arm and willed her legs to stop shaking. The men led them around the rocks to an opening and pointed for them to go inside. Abby tried to hold back a sob, but she couldn't, and neither could Mercy. The scent of pine tickled their nostrils as Abby and her daughter entered the cave. Abby's eyes grew big when she scanned the space; pine needles lay scattered over the floor, and a fire pit was located just to the left of the entrance. Blankets and a few canned goods were stacked nearby. As she took in these details, fear brought Abby to her knees. Mercy lowered herself with her mother as she sank to the ground, burying her head under her mother's chin. Abby's mind wandered back to a time when she and Lawrence came across an escaped slave and his wife hiding by the creek on the ranch. The man's body was distorted by the bulging, crisscross scars of whip marks across his head, face, and back. She wondered if she and Mercy would be tortured in a similar way…or worse.

Later that night, when their captors thought they were asleep, Abby's fingers searched the dirt floor for something she could use as a weapon. She found a sharp stick and a flat sharp rock. She put the stick under her blanket and the rock in her pocket. She was ready to fight with all her might to save Mercy, herself, and her unborn child.

The two huddled even closer when they heard the men arguing.

"I'm telling you those women are not the ones we're looking fer. I ain't even sure they's black. Have you really looked at dem?" the tall man asked, looking down at his partner, who leaned in a leisurely manner against a rock, a pine needle stuck between his teeth.

"Yeah, I've looked at 'em." He glanced over at the two captives huddled together. "It don't matter," he said, looking up at his partner. "They still can bring a good price."

"Larry, are you crazy?" The man raked his hands through his stringy hair. "I ain't sellin' no white women or whatever they are into slavery." He balled and released his fingers several times. "We're in enough trouble already for sluggin' that storekeeper and robbin' the store."

"Jake, we didn't really rob the store; we just got ourselves a loan."

Larry tried to act calm, while Jake paced back and forth in the small space. He turned to look at Larry. His voice quivered. "Have you looked at how them women is dressed? They's dressed like rich folk. I bet somebody's lookin fer 'em right now...and us." He slammed his fist into his palm and resumed his pacing.

Larry rubbed his chin thoughtfully. "Maybe we oughta stay put fer a while and see if we been follered."

Abby and Mercy continued to listen to the men's whispered arguments until they fell asleep around dawn.

The men made no advances toward them that night, and for that they thanked God.

The next day, Abby awoke to the smell of smoke and of meat roasting over a fire. She kept her eyes half closed, waiting and fearing that the men might still make some kind of advances toward her and her daughter. To her surprise, the one called Jake walked over and shoved a tin plate of beans and meat to her, and set a similar plate down next to Mercy's sleeping form. Abby woke her daughter, and they ate the offered food.

Fear consumed every minute of Abby's and Mercy's waking hours. The men had been with their captives for a whole day and had made no effort to talk to them. Neither did Abby nor Mercy try to talk to them. But they did whisper to each other when their captors left them alone for short periods of time.

"Momma, do you think Uncle Adam and Uncle Eli are looking for us?"

"Yes, baby." Abby kissed her daughter's cheek.

"Do you think we will be home before Papa comes back?"

Abby released a sob and held her daughter tight. She was relieved that Mercy didn't know the story about John Wesley and his determination to put her to death. She looked into her daughter's eyes and whispered, "If we're not home when Papa gets back, you can be sure he will join the search. He won't give up until he finds us."

When the men let the captives out of the cave to get fresh air, Abby spotted some leaves she recognized as having a high nutritional value. She headed out into the woods to pick them. Before she reached the plant, Jake, the tall man, grabbed her by the arm. He dropped it as if it was on fire when Abby began explaining to him that she was not trying to run away but wanted the leaves to eat—but instead of her words coming out in English, to her amazement she spoke in French. Abby hoped her captor didn't recognize the tremor in her voice or notice the shaking of her limbs. She didn't know what was happening to her, but she had been praying for a miracle.

Mercy's eyes widened, and she covered her mouth to conceal her shock. She had no idea her mother could speak that language. She had shown little interest when her papa was teaching her. Not only did her mother speak fluently, but she had an authentic French accent. Mercy decided to converse with her mother in French.

Jake frantically called for his partner. He stood back from the women with his mouth gaping open as he waited for his partner to come. Larry emerged from the mouth of the cave, his rifle in hand.

"What's going on?" he asked, yawning and rubbing his eyes.

"I told you! I told you that these ain't the women we's lookin' fer! They don't even speak English!" Jake stuttered with alarm in his voice.

"They what?" Larry asked, staring wide-eyed at Abby and Mercy. The men grew more nervous and uncertain about what to do with their captives.

****

Terror consumed Cookie, Betsy, Cedric, and the whole ranch when they learned that Abby and Mercy had been abducted. They knew the perpetrators had to be some of Wesley's men. They fasted and prayed for their safe return. They also prayed for Lawrence. They didn't want to think how he would respond when he found out what had happened.

At daybreak, Adam and Eli formed two search parties. Eli and Maxwell's group went north, while Adam and Gabe's group went south. Many of the townspeople joined the search as well. They respected Adam and Lawrence, appreciated all they had done for their community, and wanted to do whatever they could to help.

After a week of searching, the weary men met in Darin. Adam leaned against the hitching post. His shoulders drooped as he listened to the report. Neither group had found any signs of Abby, Mercy, or their captors.

"Thank you for helping us with the search," Adam told the townspeople as he and Eli made preparations to rest and continue their search the next day.

Eli spoke to Adam as they entered their lodging for the night. "If their captors are slave traders, I think they might travel deeper south."

Adam nodded. "I was thinking the same thing." He flung his hat down on the bed. "We have to get them back, for their sake and Lawrence's."

"Lawrence…Lawrence." Eli shook his head and tried to hold back the tremor in his voice.

For the next two weeks, Adam and Eli stopped at several of the contact houses they'd established to help fugitive slaves escape north. They gave descriptions of Abby and Mercy and instructed their friends to pass the word along about the abduction. They were confident their contacts would do all they could to help find the girls. They just hoped it wouldn't be too late.

****

After spending three weeks in the cave, the captors moved Abby and Mercy to another hiding place. Abby felt they had been traveling in a circle, so the men could make sure they weren't being followed. They rested in the hollow of a tree before they made their way to an old dilapidated lean-to that jutted out from a huge rock. There was no doubt the men had planned the abduction and made simple provisions for whomever they had planned to take captive. That was evident by the extra canned goods and an effort made to clean the structure. But the smell of animal still lingered in the air.

"I just can't take this no mo'," Jake said, staring at Abby and Mercy where they sat on a log with their arms locked together. "I tell you, Larry, they's somethin' about them women. I don't know what it is abou' dem, but they make me nervous." Jake wrung his hands and gripped his wrist. "They seem to be prayin' or somethin' all the time, and talkin' that language. We gotta get rid of dem or somethin'."

Larry folded his arms across his chest. "What we oughta do then, Jake?"

"I don't know...somethin'. The older one is in the family way, just in case you haven't noticed. The other ain't nothin' but a girl."

"We woulda been back to our boat weeks ago if we hadn't brought 'em along."

Jake popped his knuckles in frustration. "You think we could leave 'em some place and hope somebody'll find 'em?"

"I don't know. I need to think on it some mo'."

The men had done a good job of keeping their captives out of sight. They allowed the girls more freedom to move around in the woods near the lean-to. Mercy watched her mother as she shook out their blankets. She was beginning to worry. Her mother tired easily, and her stomach seemed to have gotten bigger overnight. Mercy worried how their captors might respond to her mother's pregnancy. She was certain she could find her way back to Darin, and then the Double-O, thanks to what she had learned from Raymon. The mere thought of his name sent tears flowing down her cheeks. But if she did escape, she wasn't sure her mother could keep up, in her condition.

Abby moved slowly about the woods not far from the camp, gathering seeds from faded wildflower plants and leaves from various plants. She and Mercy chewed on them throughout the day to add nutrients to their bland diet. Abby hoped it would be enough to keep her babies alive. If she was not mistaken, she was carrying twins. As she watched their captors, she didn't think they were cruel men. If they were, she and Mercy would have been dead by now, or wished they were.

Nevertheless, they still had to be careful not to upset them or let them know they could speak English. They obeyed their captors, who directed them mostly by pointing or using simple words. The men communicated very little to each other—at least not in the hearing of their captives.

Abby knew her daughter was still trying to find a way to escape by the way she studied their surroundings. She was sure Mercy had landmarks memorized. Abby hoped it would be enough if the opportunity for an escape came. She didn't want to think of delivering her babies under a tree or in some damp cave. They just had to think of a way to get free and go home to Lawrence and their friends on the ranch. She wept over the predicament they were in.

A few days later, as the group made their way to where the men had hidden the boat, Larry and Jake argued about what to do with the women. After debating back and forth, they agreed to let the women go. They would sail to Mason and leave the women at the port.

Abby wove her fingers into Mercy's. She swallowed down a laugh when she overheard the news. She could see the joy in her daughter's eyes. They would only have to tell someone that they were from the Double-O Ranch and needed to get a message to Lawrence Mallory's solicitor, the one who managed the Bradley Farm.

Her heart did a flip in her chest, and she breathed deeply for the first time in weeks. Then she looked down at her clothes. Her new dress was dirty and stained. She and Mercy both needed a change of clothes and a bath. She hoped their appearance wouldn't keep someone from helping them.

As the men pulled the boat from under the brush, a few drops of rain fell from the clear blue sky. "Larry, maybe we oughta wait and see if a storm is comin'."

Larry stopped tossing sticks from the boat and looked up into the sky. "I don't think we got nothin' to worry 'bout. If it don't storm, we can be safe in Mason."

Jake rubbed his chin and arched his brow. "I don't know. I seen bad storms that start up from a clear blue sky."

Abby's gaze met Mercy's. She hoped Larry was right this time and they had nothing to worry about.

They had been on the water for about an hour. Suddenly gray clouds appeared on the horizon. The air grew cooler, and Mercy began to shiver. Abby hugged her closer to keep her warm. Jake tossed them a blanket, and she wrapped it around them. The world around them became silent as birds stopped singing;

frogs were no longer croaking or insects buzzing. Black ominous clouds rolled overhead. Lightning flashed from a distance. Thunder boomed with such force that it seemed to rock the boat. Everyone grabbed hold of the sides of the boat as it rocked and tipped from one side to the other, and their faces were chiseled with fear. Several fat raindrops were followed by a great downpour. As they sailed toward the Tennessee River, the storm became more menacing; the waves grew high and choppy. The men fought to keep the boat from capsizing, while Abby and Mercy clung to each other with all their might as the rain poured over them, and they prayed like they had never prayed before. Screams and cries were drowned out by the fierce wind. The boat swirled out of control, hit a rock, and broke apart, and the fury of the current took them all under the cold, cold water.

****

Mercy's teeth chattered from the cold. She wanted to pull the blanket up to her chin to get warm, but the pain was so great she couldn't. She shivered and tried to pull the blanket up with her left hand. She was expecting a soft blanket to chase the cold away; instead she got gooey mud, leaves, and sticks. A moan escaped her lips. She remembered the boat capsizing.

"Momma, Momma," she tried to yell through the excruciating pain in her head. Dizziness followed...then darkness.

The sun was low in the sky when she woke again. She opened her mouth to call out, but dryness kept her words trapped in her throat. Despite the pain in her body, she wiggled and wiggled to set herself free from the branches that partially covered her. She felt herself fading away. This must be what it feels like to die, she thought, before darkness overtook her again.

After a time, Mercy's eyes slowly fluttered opened. A wrinkled, bronze-looking woman came into view. An angel, Mercy thought. She squeezed her eyes shut, then opened them slowly. The angel was still there, smiling down at her. The angel spoke in words she didn't understand. Mercy called for her mother and tried to sit up, but the warmth of the angel's hand gently pushed her back down. Her nostrils flared and her stomach growled at the succulent smell of roasted meat, with onions, basil, and other spices. She heard voices and felt the presence of someone other than the angel beside her. She knew then that she was alive.

Someone kneeling behind her lifted her head; the angel spoke, then picked up a wooden bowl and lifted it to her lips. The tasty broth had bites of venison; it was warm and soothing. It calmed her growling stomach. After she had her fill, she collapsed on her pallet and fell into a deep sleep. The routine went on for days; eating…and then sleeping.

Days later, Mercy sat up on the pallet, waited for the dizziness to pass, then rolled over and sat up on her knees. She grabbed hold of a pole and pulled herself to her feet. She stumbled to the entrance of the little wooden hut that housed her. Her eyes widened with wonder when she saw ten or fifteen little wooden houses in a rectangle with a large rectangular building in the middle. Before she was able to take a step outside, a young beautiful Indian girl took her by the arm and led her back to her pallet. Mercy's eyes filled with tears, and she shook her head and planted her feet in the dirt.

"I need to go find my mother."

The girl patted her hand and spoke in perfect English. "Your mother is here. She is very sick."

Relief washed over Mercy even as tears rolled from her eyes at the thought of her mother being so ill. Mercy gave thanks to the Lord for saving her and her mother. "May I see her, please?"

The girl nodded and led Mercy to the cabin next door.

Mercy entered the dark cabin and, with the aid of the girl, made her way to her mother's bed, which stood a few feet off the floor. She held Abby's limp hand and kissed her cheek. Abby made no sound. Mercy turned glassy eyes to the girl.

"How long has she been like this?"

"She was like this when she was found, over a week ago."

Mercy wept.

Two days later, Mercy moved into the cabin with her mother to help with her care. She talked to her, told her how much she and her father loved her. She massaged her limbs, all the while begging her to live for them and for the babies. Later that evening, Abby groaned and thrashed about in the bed. Mercy rushed to her side, kneeling on the dirt floor beside her to hold her hand while speaking in a soothing voice. Abby wiggled her fingers, and Mercy beamed.

After two weeks of special herbs and loving attention, Abby and the babies were doing well, but still not strong enough to travel. Abby longed to go home. She wanted so much to be in her husband's arms and feel safe again. She grew sad when she thought how much Lawrence had wanted to be with her during this pregnancy. She had her doubts whether he would be present to welcome their twins into the world. She and Mercy had been gone for a long time. She had another disturbing thought.

Did he believe they were still alive? Was he still looking for them? Was anyone looking for them?

Chapter Twenty-Two

Lawrence's hands gripped the steamship railing as he looked out at the soft waves in the shimmering blue ocean. Abby and Mercy were on his mind. "They must have been upset when they got the message that I would be delayed because of a mysterious illness the captain and half his crew had contracted," he said to himself. He felt an uneasiness in his spirit that grew more intense as the days passed. He shoved his hands into his pockets and leaned his body onto the railing.

"It's unlike Adam not to answer my wire. Maybe he and Eli were called away on an emergency at one of our contact houses. But...let me stop this kind of thinking," he said. He gave himself a good talking to. "I'll be on the Double-O soon enough and find out what the problem is, or if there is a problem. If I don't stop talking to myself, people are going to think I've gone mad."

Lawrence could only think of Abby and Mercy and the possibility of moving them out of the South as he sailed to Savannah and then on to Mason. There he waited overnight for a carriage from the ranch to pick him up. He pulled his watch from his pocket as he stood in front of the inn. A frown formed on his face. It was well past noon. He snapped the watch closed. "My message to Adam said I wanted to get an early start this morning." He tried to keep calm, reminding himself

Adam and Eli must have been called away. He strolled down the street to pass time, looking in shop windows to see what else he could buy his wife and daughter. A familiar-looking ring caught his eye in the jeweler's display, but before he could examine it, he heard his name.

"Mr. Lawrence, I'm sorry to keep you waiting."

Lawrence turned, expecting to see their usual driver, Pete; instead it was Ed, from the saddle and harness shop. Lawrence shook the man's hand and slapped him on the shoulders. "Afternoon, Ed. I was expecting Pete."

"He was tied up, so I came instead. Would you be spending the night, or do you want to start back now?"

Lawrence laughed. "Let's start back now. I can't wait to get home…" He wanted to add, "to get home to my wife and daughter," but he knew it wasn't the time to say that yet. "I would have caught a boat, but none were going down river."

"Did you have a good trip, Mr. Lawrence?" Ed asked as he packed the last of Lawrence's things into the conveyance and stepped in himself.

Lawrence looked over at the man. "It was very good, and I had plenty of time to think and make plans for the future." Lawrence smiled and added a few more details about his trip before he asked Ed about the ranch. The man used the least amount of words possible to answer Lawrence's questions. Lawrence didn't mind; the man was known as a fellow of few words.

Ed began singing in his rich baritone voice as soon as they left town. Lawrence enjoyed the music, and the lack of conversation gave him time to think about the addition to their family Abby had written him about. He was looking forward to spending time with his wife and daughter. He no longer had to love his wife in the shadows; very soon all the people on the ranch would know he was married to the most beautiful woman in the world, his Abby Rose, and that the doll of the ranch, the vivacious Mercy, was his daughter.

The days it took to travel to the ranch flew by, and Lawrence was certain he would move his family out of the South. He would take his wife and daughter to Philadelphia to visit his family, and then... He blew out a breath. He was glad he had gone ahead with his plans to build a house in upstate New York, close to Canada. He chortled. Mercy might even enjoy going to a fine women's college in England. Before he knew it, he saw the sign ahead saying, "Welcome to the Double-O Ranch." He leaned over to Ed.

"You can take me home first."

Ed drove the carriage down the lane to the main house, ignoring the instructions. Lawrence looked over at Ed, who stared straight ahead. His brows knitted together. It was unlike any of the ranch hands to ignore a direct request. He looked out over the ranch—it was as beautiful as ever. He couldn't quite put his finger on it, but there was something different about the place. It felt as if something was missing. Before he could analyze the situation, Adam and Eli came out of the house to meet the carriage as it came to a full stop.

Lawrence stood to greet them warmly, but there was something about the men's countenance that gave him pause. He stepped from the carriage. "What's wrong, Adam?"

Before Adam could respond, Lawrence directed his question to Eli. "Eli, what is it? Has something happened to Abby and the baby? Where is Mercy? Has something…" Lawrence stopped speaking and stared at the two men as Ed left to put the carriage away. "For goodness' sake, will someone please answer me?"

Adam put his hand on his brother-in-law's shoulder. "Let's go inside, Lawrence."

"I don't want to go inside."

He wiggled his shoulder, dislodging Adam's hand. He stood with his legs slightly apart, arms across his chest. "Somebody tell me something—now!"

Neither Adam nor Eli responded; they turned and moved toward the house. Lawrence followed with fists balled at his sides. Eli closed the door behind them. Panic overtook Lawrence, and he broke out into a cold sweat.

"I'm not taking another step until someone tells me what is going on here." Anguish clouded his features. "Where are my wife and daughter?"

"Let's go in here and sit down," Adam said, taking his brother-in-law by the arm.

Lawrence entered the parlor. "I can't sit down! Tell me what's going on! Now! Where are my wife and daughter?" His voice grew shaky. His knees got weak. He turned pale as he looked from Adam to Eli, waiting for one of them to give him some answers.

Adam laid his hand on his brother-in-law's shoulder. His voice was foggy. "I'm sorry to tell you this, Lawrence, but Abby and Mercy have been abducted."

"Abducted?" The word came out as a whisper. Lawrence fell to his knees, covered his face with his hands, and let a wail out so loud it seemed to shake the room.

Adam and Eli knelt down on the floor next to him, wrapped their arms around him, and wept and prayed with him. Some time later, Lawrence was able to speak.

"What happened?"

"I took the girls into town for some shopping—with five escorts. Things were going fine, and the girls were having fun. They forgot a package in the general store and went back to get it. They must have walked in on a robbery. They probably spooked the men, who got scared and took the girls with them."

Lawrence looked from Adam to Eli. "Or," Lawrence said, "They were taken by slave traders."

He slammed his fist into his palm. Adam nodded.

"We know, Lawrence," Eli said. "We have been out searching for them for weeks. We have also petitioned our contacts for their help," Adam added.

Lawrence slowly stood to his feet. "I have to go search for my family myself." He headed for the door.

"Lawrence it's getting late, and you are tired from your trip. Why don't you wait until morning?"

Lawrence stopped, turned slowly, and looked Adam in the eyes. "If Kathleen was out there, would you wait?"

Adam shook his head.

"We thought you would say that," Eli said, making his way to the door. "The horses are ready. I'll go get them."

As Lawrence was heading out the door, Adam stopped him. "I'm sorry I couldn't keep them safe."

Lawrence turned and walked back to his brother-in-law. "I know you did everything you could, Adam." He placed both hands on his brother-in-law's shoulders. "I don't blame you, and please don't blame yourself."

****

Laughter rang out in the little wooden house as Abby sat on a stool listening to Mercy and their friends, the Muskogee women, telling story after story as they made blankets and baby clothes for her babies. She studied the faces of the people she had come to love and thanked God for them. She shuddered when she thought how she and Mercy would not be alive had it not been for the kind people in the village, who had rescued them after the boat capsized and the men left them, assuming they were dead.

Abby stopped her weaving, looked up toward heaven, and in a whisper said, "Oh, God, please protect these hard-working people. They just want to be left alone on their own land to live the life they have chosen. Instead, they are being hunted by soldiers who want to remove them from their homes and relocate them to a strange land in Oklahoma so the land of their ancestors can be divided into farmlands and towns."

Abby's thoughts were interrupted. A smile danced on her face as she listened to Mercy trying to converse with her "angel" in the Muskogee language.

"Momma, it's your turn."

Abby laughed and repeated the words the women told her. She heard Mercy telling her new friends how they spoke French to their captors and to each other.

****

Joy filled Abby's heart when she had given birth to two healthy baby boys in the little house that had become home during the last four months. She cradled the babies in her arms. A wave of sorrow washed over her as she thought of her beloved Lawrence. He had wanted so much to be with her during her pregnancy and the birth of the child—not knowing it would be more than one. She smiled and kissed her babies. She and her little family would be going home as soon as she was strong enough to travel.

Abby was cuddling her crying babies when Mercy came over to take little Joshua Lawrence from his mother's arms. She walked and cooed to the little one until he was asleep just like his brother Matthew Adam. Mercy had named the baby Joshua Lawrence because of his curly black hair and sparkling black eyes like hers and her father's. She was proud to be a big sister. She loved both of her baby brothers and enjoyed the feel of them in her arms.

"They're so adorable, aren't they, Mother?"

Abby nodded as she kissed the sleeping baby in her arms.

Abby was proud of her sons and her daughter. Mercy was wonderful with the boys and had been a tremendous help to her. She couldn't ask for anything more, except going home and being with her beloved.

****

Lawrence stood with his hands clasped behind his back, despair washing over him as he looked into the darkness. He had been so sure his instincts would lead him to his wife and daughter when he first arrived home more than four months ago. He knew from quick glances and the smiles that didn't reach the eyes that many, including Eli and Adam, felt it was time for him to give up the search and try to move on. But he couldn't, not until he had a confirmation in his spirit that it was time. He didn't have that confirmation yet. He moved over to the other window and looked out into the darkness.

A smile stretched across his lips when he remembered Raymon's commitment to finding Abby and Mercy. He'd left Philadelphia when his father sent a wire postponing his visit. Raymon had felt deep in his spirit that something was wrong. His father would never cancel his trip otherwise.

Lawrence rocked on his heels, remembering the disappointment on his nephew's face when Adam had to physically restrain him from going out on the last search. "You are too exhausted, son. You can't go on like this without rest." Lawrence knew the frustration Raymon felt. He felt the same thing each time Adam or Eli reminded him about his need for rest. He blew out a loud breath and whispered into the night, "Abby and Mercy, I know you are out there, and I will not give up until I find you…or learn what happened to you."

Lawrence prepared for bed. He sat at his wife's dressing table, as he had done many nights before. This time, he unlocked the drawer where she kept her jewelry and pulled out the velvet box that contained her ring. He opened the box—the ring was not there. He stared at the empty box longingly for a while.

"How Abby loved that ring," he said out loud. "Ring…the ring!"

He dropped the box, jumped from the bench, and ran downstairs, yelling for Eli as loudly as he could. Eli stumbled from his room, wide-eyed and half-dressed.

"What is it, Lawrence?"

Lawrence was breathless. He clutched Eli's nightshirt with both hands.

"Eli… Eli, tell me…was Abby wearing her wedding ring when she was abducted?"

Eli thought for a while.

"Yes, I think she was. Yes, she was! What does that mean?"

Lawrence's face went pale. He slowly released his hold and sank down in the kitchen chair.

Eli held onto his friend as he went down. "Lawrence what's wrong?"

Lawrence gasped for air. "I saw a ring in a shop in Mason that resembled Abby's. I didn't give it much thought at the time, and I didn't get a good look at it, but I remember that it caught my eye. You know I had our rings custom made when we were in London. There shouldn't be one exactly like ours anywhere."

He slapped his hands on the table and quickly rose from his chair.

"Eli, I have to get to that shop in Mason."

His friend placed a hand on his shoulders. "Lawrence, can we wait until first light?"

****

Lawrence and Eli reached Mason in record time. Weariness and dread consumed them. Neither man spoke as they dismounted in front of the little shop near the inn where they would spend the night. They had already discussed the possible reasons for Abby's ring to be in the shop, if in fact it was her ring. The possibilities had left them both distressed. A bell overhead rang out, and a cheerful shopkeeper greeted them.

Lawrence went immediately to the glass display case. "I noticed this silver ring in the window a few months ago. It's magnificent. I'm surprised it has not been sold already." Looking at the price tag, he gave a whistle. "It sure is pricey."

"It's beautiful, isn't it? I thought about reducing it,

but I can't bring myself to do that just yet. I know the right buyer will come along soon."

"May I see it?"

The shopkeeper eagerly opened the display case. Lawrence took the ring from the velvet box. His heart began to race as he slowly turned it from side to side. There were two interlocking hearts on both sides of the ring, with a letter L in one heart and an A in the other.

Terror seized him, his complexion was pallid, and his knees buckled.

Eli's strong arms kept him on his feet. Lawrence fought through the dizziness and disbelief to compose himself, and his gaze locked on the storekeeper. He leaned forward and in a stern voice demanded, "Sir, how did you get this ring?"

The storekeeper's eyebrows shot up. "Look here, sir! I don't like what you are implying."

Lawrence paused, trying to swallow the lump in his throat. "That ring belongs to my wife. I had it made for her when I was in London. There's not another one like it."

The man mopped sweat from his brow.

Lawrence slipped his ring from his finger. "Take a look at mine. The rings are identical."

The shopkeeper swallowed several times. He rubbed the back of his neck as he made his way to the door, where he pulled the "Closed" sign down. A forlorn look on his face, he walked back and sat on his stool.

His demeanor sent chills down Lawrence's spine. Eli moved closer to his friend.

The man cleared his throat...once...twice...three times. "The two men who brought the ring in didn't strike me as bad men, just a little down on their luck. I believe they are brothers. They mentioned something about trying to save their farm. The taller one was named Jake, and the other man was Larry."

The shopkeeper went on and on about everything he could remember about the men.

Lawrence looked at Eli. They could tell the man was stalling. Lawrence raised his hand to stop the man.

"The ring, sir. How did they get the ring?"

The shopkeeper looked directly into Lawrence's eyes. "I am sorry, sir. They said they got it off of a dead woman."

Lawrence gripped the glass case so hard he thought it might crack. Tears rolled down his face and splattered on the glass. Tension was high in the room, and no one spoke for a moment.

Finally Eli cleared his throat. "Do the men live around here?"

"I don't think so, but I have seen them a couple of times since they brought the ring in. That was late last fall."

"Mr. Mallory will be staying at the inn down the street. We will be in town for several days. If you think of anything else, or if you see the men, please let us know. You will be compensated for your troubles. Meanwhile, we will take the ring and pay you what you paid for it."

Eli paid the shopkeeper and bid him a good day before he escorted Lawrence out of the shop, down the boardwalk, and up to their room.

Lawrence sank down in the chair by the fireplace and stared into the flames for a long time. "Eli." He looked up at his friend from his place by the window and spoke slowly. "I can't accept the idea that Abby and Mercy are dead. I just can't. I still feel a connection to them, as if they are still alive." He paused. "Is it easier to live with the expectancy of hope or the certainty of death?"

Eli walked over and stood by his friend. "I think until the heart heals, one is just as devastating as the other."

Neither man spoke for a while.

"I was careless in letting the shopkeeper know that the missing woman is my wife."

Eli grinned, and his voice held humor. "Yeah, boss, you want to get us hung? What will the young ladies say when they find out the wealthy and dashing Lawrence Mallory has gotten married right out from under their noses to a lady whose complexion is like one who has been lightly kissed by the sun, and now that wife is missing. That would be scandalous! Tongues will surely wag."

Eli turned serious. "We do need to be careful about giving people just enough information to let them know we are looking for two young light-complexioned black women. Most people have heard about the two runaways from down the river, and it's easy for us to use their descriptions to get information about Abby and Mercy, knowing that the two runaways are safely tucked away in the north."

"I didn't think about the danger I might be putting us in as Southern abolitionists when I spoke so freely. It was hard for me to think rationally when I saw Abby's ring."

"I know." Eli squeezed his friend's shoulder. "I probably would have done the same thing."

"Eli, old friend, thank you."

Lawrence placed his hands on Eli's shoulders, and his voice cracked as he said, "Had it not been for you, I would never have made it through these last four months of waiting. Waiting for what I hoped would be the answers I wanted."

Eli embraced his friend.

Days turned into weeks and still there was no word about the two men who had brought in Abby's ring. Lawrence's voice lowered to a whisper as he stood with his hand on the mantel. He turned to look at Eli.

"Sorrow, fear, and anxiety have been my constant enemies during our stay here. Had it not been for you and your strong faith, I don't know how I would have stayed grounded in my own faith. Thank you, my friend."

Lawrence paced back and forth on the squeaky wooden floor. He slapped his fist into his palm. His voice quivered. "I think it's time for us to go home. We'll have to trust that the storekeeper will get as much information from the men as he can and send us word, if he sees them again."

Eli went to Lawrence and looked into his eyes. "Are you sure?"

Lawrence nodded and turned away.

The two men decided to search the port area one last time before heading home to the Double-O. Eli peered into the small crowd of men near the water. Just beyond them, a small boat pulled up to the dock. Eli called to Lawrence. "Boss, look. I think those might be the men we are looking for. They fit the description the storekeeper gave us."

"I think you are right."

309

Lawrence and Eli reined their horses to a halt near the men and waited until they had secured the boat before they dismounted and moved over to where the men stood.

"Good day, gentlemen." Lawrence's voice was kind but stiff. "May I have a word with you two?" Larry and Jake looked at each other.

"What fer, mister? We's payin' the last of our debts today."

"Oh, you have gotten this all wrong. I just want to ask you some questions about the two women you came upon last fall."

The men turned pale and started to run away, but Eli and Lawrence stopped them. Lawrence held Jake by the collar and shoved him a few times.

"You can tell me all you know about those women the easy way or the hard way. It's your choice."

Lawrence gave Jake a shake to emphasize his words. Jake's eyes bulged and his teeth began to chatter. He looked to his brother Larry for help. Lawrence tightened his grip.

"Okay, Okay, mister. We didn't do nothin' to those women! I swear we never laid a hand on dem women. They drownded when our boat broke apart in the river."

"Drowned?" Lawrence hissed, trying to keep the trembling from his voice.

"Yes, mister." Jake squirmed to get free of Lawrence's hold.

"Why were they in your boat?" Lawrence barked.

Jake's eyes got big, and he looked at his brother.

"Larry, I told you somebody was lookin' fer dem women."

Larry looked at Lawrence. "Let him go, mister, and

we'll tell you anything you wanna know."

Lawrence slowly released his grip on Jake's shirt, but his gaze stayed locked on him. Jake's fingers twitched as he straightened his shirt. Larry backed away from Eli and bumped into his brother. The jumpy men tumbled over their words as they told Lawrence and Eli about the robbery.

"We didn't mean to hurt that storekeeper in Darin," Larry said, squeezing his clasped hands together.

"Mister, we really didn't," Jake added. "And we paid him back. But...aah...aah...he didn't know it was us who slugged him or robbed him." He kicked at a pebble with the toe of his boot. He looked from Lawrence to Eli. "Dem two women surprised us and we got scared." His voice held remorse. "We never hurt anyone or stole anythin' in our life. Ain't that right, Larry?"

Larry gave a quick shake of his head.

"We was desperate for money to save our farm. Just lookin' at 'em quickly, we thought they was the two runaways from the Todd Plantation. Old Woman Todd had 'cided to sell the women after her brother died. Shucks, everybody knowed he was dem women's pappy. Just before the sale, the women ran away. Miss Todd promised if we found 'em she'd give us enough money to save our farm." Jake paused for a long time and lowered his eyes to the ground.

Lawrence folded his arms across his chest and cocked an eye at Larry. "Go on," Lawrence demanded. Larry cleared his throat.

"Well, we ain't never seen Mr. Todd's girls close up, and we never did look at dem women close until we was hidin' out for a while."

"You what?" Lawrence's eyebrows rose in question, and he roared with anger. "So you don't hurt anyone, you just abduct them!"

Larry face turned crimson, and he shook his head violently. "No, sir, that ain't what I mean."

Lawrence growled. "Make your point then, and make it quickly."

"Well, sir, we knew we had the wrong women when they didn't speak English, and Miss Todd ain't said nothin' 'bout one being in the family way."

Lawrence grabbed Larry by his collar. "What do you mean, they didn't speak English?"

"I tell you the truth, dem women didn't speak English, and the older one was with child. We got scared and started paying more attention to 'em. They dressed like rich folk. We knew we'd made a mistake and tried to figure out what to do with 'em."

Lawrence grabbed Jake's shirt again. "What *did* you do with them?"

Jake's eyes grew big; he chewed on his bottom lip. "We was gonna drop 'em off here at the port. But...but a terrible storm came up while we were on the Tennessee River, 'bout thirty miles from Darin. Our boat turnt over, and we was all throwed overboard."

A violent shiver moved throughout Lawrence's body at the possibility of his wife and daughter drowning.

"Me and Larry was able to make it out the river with only some bad bruises, but the women..." Jake's voice trailed off, and he shook his head. "Well, we found the older one. She was bleedin' from her head, and her body was real cold." Lawrence tried to steady his voice. He inhaled a shallow breath, then struggled for another. "What happened to the other woman?"

"We searched for her but couldn't find her. What we're tellin' you is the truth, mister."

"You didn't tell me how you got the ring."

Larry and Jake looked at each other. Finally Larry spoke.

"We took it from the dead woman's finger."

He started to say more, but after one look at Lawrence and Eli, he closed his mouth.

"What you gonna do to us?" Jake asked.

With no reply, Lawrence pushed the men aside and mounted his horse. Eli followed.

As he rode out of town, Lawrence struggled to keep his emotions under control as tears spilled from his eyes. He had thought his heart would burst as the men recounted what had happened to...those women. He couldn't say his wife and daughter's names. But he was confident from the descriptions the two men gave that the women were Abby and Mercy. When they were a distance from town, Lawrence reined in the trotting horse. He slid down, fell on his knees, and yelled at the top of his voice from the sorrow deep in his soul. Eli dismounted and knelt beside his friend.

"Oh, Lord, why my family?" Lawrence shouted. He put his face in his hands and wept. He opened his eyes and looked up to heaven for a long time. Then he muttered, "Why not my family? All your children are precious to you, not just me and my family."

He thought of Hattie and of all she had told him about being taken from her country and never seeing her family again. He thought of the many slave families torn apart almost daily. He asked God's forgiveness for thinking he should be exempt from suffering...and he wept. He wept for the injustice of it all.

Eli wondered how much more heartache Lawrence could endure. His own heart was filled with grief at what he had heard. He knew his friend's heart was beyond shattered. Mounted once again, they rode more than an hour before a word was spoken.

"Eli, I have to do one last thing before I can find something that resembles peace in my soul. I have to search the edge of the river near Darin again before I can give this up. Maybe then I can accept the fact that my Abby Rose and Mercy are lost to me forever. At the very least, perhaps we can retrieve their bodies and give them a decent burial."

As they rode, Lawrence glanced over at Eli several times, studying the tall, straight, muscular man riding beside him. He was beginning to understand why God had brought him into his life. He had known there was something special about this gentle giant of a man as soon as he met him years ago. Jack's words had proven true: he had said that looking into Eli's eyes was like looking into the face of God. The man had a depth of wisdom beyond that of most men anywhere, regardless of color. Lawrence cleared his throat, slow and long.

"You've wanted to say something for a while. What is it, my friend?" Eli asked, continuing to look straight ahead, swaying in the saddle.

"There is something that has been bothering me for years, but I have never spoken of it to anyone because I didn't want to give my words an audience, and I never wanted to question God."

Eli looked over at his friend. "God delights in his children asking questions so they may grow to be more like Him. What's the question?"

Lawrence took in a big breath and exhaled it slowly. "Why does God allow slavery to exist?" He rushed on to add, "We know that He could prevent it from happening or supernaturally free the slaves from their hopeless and cruel circumstances, but He has allowed the evil system to continue and flourish."

"Being a former slave, I've asked God that same question, many times. M-a-n-y times. And many other enslaved people have asked that very same question. Trust me; you are not alone in your thinking. This is what I think is the answer to your question and to many others like it." Eli pulled back on the reins and brought his horse to a stop.

Lawrence followed suit. Both rested their hands on the pommels as Eli continued.

"First of all, this is an evil world and mankind does evil things. Secondly, God loves mankind so much that He has given us free will; the right to choose right or wrong—good or evil. When man exercises his rights or his free will, he often takes away the rights and free will of others, especially when he chooses to do evil. This is the case with slavery. The whites are exercising their free will to enslave blacks. Black people's rights and free will are taken away because of the evil whites choose instead of good. Even though God has given us all free will or the right to choose, we must be sure that when we exercise those rights we are not hurting others."

Lawrence nodded.

Eli continued. "It helps to remember that God has a purpose and plan for everything, and he's aware of all things that are happening no matter how cruel or unfair things seem. I struggled with that truth especially when

I was enslaved. I believed that God was going to take care of me because I belonged to Him."

"I prayed that God would allow me to find my family unharmed."

Eli was silent for a while. Then, he spoke. "We will probably never know why God allows evil to prosper or bad things to happen to good people, not while we are on this side of heaven."

"You're right, Eli. People are blinded by evil, greed, and stupidity when they can look at blacks, people of mixed race, or anyone who's different from them and think they don't deserve the same right to be free and pursue life and happiness as they do."

Squawking of birds overhead interrupted the conversation, and the men moved on.

Eli adjusted himself in the saddle. "It's easy to take away people's rights and freedom," he said, "when you dehumanize, demoralize, and marginalize them in the eyes of the world; then the world becomes desensitized to a person's basic needs as humans and regards them as less than human. That's what has happened with the practice of slavery. People don't want to see blacks as humans needing and having the same rights as others do. If they did, they would have to put a stop to the cruel institution of slavery."

Lawrence pressed his lips together and nodded.

The clip-clop of the horses' hooves penetrated the silence as each man struggled to keep his emotions in check on their journey home.

Eli looked over at his friend's haggard face. "Let's go to the ranch and get more men to help before we search the riverbank down from Darin."

Chapter Twenty-Three

Lawrence was disturbed by tormenting and recurring dreams of a woman crying, begging him not to leave her. The dreams were so agonizing they woke him up at night and haunted him by day. Eli grew concerned about his friend's wellbeing and persuaded him to postpone their final search for his wife and daughter until Adam and his son returned from their interviews with their contacts.

****

Adam's mind whirled, thoughts exploding in all directions, as his horse trotted next to his son's. He wasn't looking forward to telling Lawrence that none of their contacts had information about Abby and Mercy. He grimaced when he thought how a few of their contacts were being harassed for their open opposition to slavery. One had tried to open a newspaper that spoke out against the inhumane treatment of slaves. His newspaper office and machinery was destroyed and he was dragged through the streets as an example to those that might hold a similar point of view. Adam was reminded once again about the danger of being an abolitionist in the South.

Raymon cleared his throat. "Father, I am beginning to understand what you have been trying to tell me for years: one person can't fight the wicked system of slavery alone." He paused and looked over at his father.

"It seems to be too much for a few good men."

Adam pressed his lips into a straight line and nodded. "But we put our trust in God, don't we, son? That He will end this cruel system of servitude in His timing and with the men and women he has put in place for such a time as this. We know that God's ways are not our ways. His thoughts are not our thoughts." Adam and Raymon solemnly repeated the words together. "Let's ride on down to Lawrence's house to see if he and Eli have returned from their search."

Raymon gave a nod, and the two rode on in silence. When they arrived at the stable, they dismounted and went into the house. Eli and Lawrence were sitting at the kitchen table having their midday meal. Adam looked from Lawrence to Eli, and his pulse quickened. He knew the news they were about to share was not good.

The next day more than a dozen men assembled by the main house, waiting for Lawrence to give instructions regarding their final organized search for Abby and Mercy along the banks of the Tennessee River from Darin to Mason.

****

Coos and loud cries filled the little wooden house as the Muskogee women put the fussy two-month-olds into their buckskin cradle boards. Abby and Mercy stood with their arms outstretched as the women secured the cradle boards on their backs. Abby's lips curled into a smile. Today she and Mercy would be going home. Her eyes filled with tears as she hugged her new friends, while Mercy said goodbye to her angel, the healer and midwife, in the Muskogee language. Warmth radiated through Abby at the thought of seeing her beloved husband and presenting him with their two beautiful, healthy twin boys. They thanked the wonderful people again for all they had done for them, and with more tears and goodbyes they followed their guide, Yaholo, from the camp.

The old Indian trail was rough, narrow, and a bit scary at times, but neither Mercy nor Abby complained. The babies found the jostling motion soothing and slept most of the time. It took the group only three days to reach the ranch. Relief and excitement were visible on Abby's and Mercy's faces that final morning when they came upon the familiar creek where both of them had spent so much time. As they walked up the hill to the ranch, their eyes overflowed with tears of joy as they took in the beautiful sight before them. Whispers grew loud as people spilled from houses to watch the three figures making their way up to the main house.

Abby's heart fluttered when she spotted a tall handsome man in the midst of a group of riders. Heat rose to her cheeks when he turned his head in their direction.

Lawrence stopped speaking in the middle of his sentence when he caught a glimpse of the three figures. One tall and two small figures were coming toward him. There was something very familiar about the two small figures. "It can't be," he whispered. His pulse pounded at the sight of them. He rubbed his eyes to be sure the three figures weren't a figment of his imagination.

The figures began running toward him.

"Oh, God, can it be, can it be?" He jumped from his horse and raced to meet them.

Abby and Mercy held their arms open, and

Lawrence flew into them, startling the babies. The three of them drank in each other's presence and collapsed into each other's arms. They were overcome with joy and relief. Words of endearment, hugs, and kisses flowed freely among them. Cries of joy could be heard throughout the crowd that had gathered. Cookie and Betsy fell to their knees to thank God for the safe return of the ones they had so dearly missed.

Adam and Raymon parted the crowd and rushed to their side. They gave Abby and Mercy each a big hug. Adam swallowed several times, trying to dislodge the lump in his throat. He held Abby's and Mercy's hands. "I'm sorry I didn't keep you safe."

Mercy stood on her tiptoes and wrapped her arms around her uncle's neck.

"Oh, Uncle, you have nothing to be sorry for."

Abby blinked back tears. "Mercy is right. Adam, Eli, everyone, please don't blame yourselves for any of this. It was not your fault."

While Abby and Mercy were still talking and thanking everyone, Lawrence and Eli took the cradleboards with the babies. Cookie and Betsy untied the leather straps that held the babies in place, and Lawrence lifted the babies up one at a time and wept tears of joy as he held each of his baby boys. He kissed his wife on her full, soft lips right there for everyone to see.

The cheerful crowd moved aside as Lawrence led his family to the main house.

Raymon took Mercy's hand. His grin stretched across his face. "I'm so glad you and Abby are safe."

"I am too. How long have you been home? And what about your education?"

Raymon tweaked her nose. "One question at a time, you silly goose. I came back right after your Papa Lawrence did—I mean, your father—almost six months ago."

"Six months!"

"We were all concerned about 'the girls,' as father would say."

Mercy lowered her head and looked up at him with a shy smile.

Raymon dropped her hand. "We can talk later."

Once inside, Cookie and Betsy took charge of the babies, while Lawrence spent some time with his wife and daughter before joining Adam and the others in the kitchen, where they were plying Yaholo with refreshments and questions. As Lawrence entered the kitchen he heard pleading.

"Will you reconsider and take something? We would like to show our gratitude to you and your people for taking care of our Abby and Mercy."

Lawrence shook the man's hand. "Please, what can we do for you and your people?"

Yaholo refused any payment but later relented when Lawrence and Adam begged him to take several horses. Lawrence would have gladly given the man the world, if it had been his to give, in return for having his family safely back home.

Before the evening meal, both Abby and Mercy enjoyed a luxurious bath and pampering. Lawrence supervised his wife's bath and massaged her tired body, enjoying the feel of her in his arms.

Later Mercy knocked on the bedroom door, and Lawrence opened it, with Abby joining him by the door. "I'll be sleeping in the nursery with the twins," she announced to her parents. "So there will be no need for anyone to be sneaking around tonight."

"Oh, come in here." Lawrence laughed and pulled her into his arms. Abby laughed and gave her daughter a hug too.

Earlier that afternoon, Lawrence had arranged for a wet nurse to take care of the babies during the night so he and his wife could share an enchanted evening getting reacquainted. He was so thrilled to have time alone with his wife to talk, to reconnect, and to make plans for their future. Abby cuddled with her husband in their bed.

"It feels good finally to be in your arms again," Abby said as Lawrence kissed the top of her head.

"And the best part is we can stay here until morning." He kissed his wife's lips. "We can stay here all day," he said between kisses.

Abby giggled and playfully punched him in the chest. "Mr. Mallory, whatever is on your mind?"

"You will soon find out, Mrs. Mallory." Lawrence held his wife in his arms and smothered her with kisses.

"There's something I need to tell you."

Abby looked up at her husband and kissed him on the lips. "What is it?"

He put his chin on top of her head. "I talked to Jake and Larry."

She turned in her husband's arms and looked up into his face. "You did? When?"

"I saw them in Mason."

"How did you know them?"

"I saw your ring in a store window and the storekeeper told me about the men who brought it in for cash."

"You saw my ring?"

Lawrence nodded. "The storekeeper described the men to me and Eli. Then we waited until they returned to Mason." Lawrence told Abby about seeing the men at the dock and persuading them to tell the truth.

Abby cuddled closer to her husband. "Did you and Eli punch them?"

Lawrence smiled. "No, we just roughed them up some."

"You know what, Lawrence, after a few days I didn't think they were bad men. Don't get me wrong— Mercy and I were terrified the whole time we were with them, and we didn't want to do anything that would upset them, but they didn't seem bent on harming us."

Lawrence rubbed his wife's arms. "Did they touch you and Mercy in any way?"

"No. I didn't sleep the first or second night at all, thinking they might try something. I was ready to fight to my death to protect us."

Lawrence squeezed his wife tight and let out a quiet hiss of relief. "Thank God you and Mercy are safe and unharmed."

He adjusted himself on the pillows. "Your captors said you and Mercy didn't speak English."

"Oh, Lawrence, that was the strangest thing. I was telling the one man, Jake, something—in English, I thought—but my words came out in French. I was just as surprised as he was. I had heard you and Mercy conversing in French, but I have only been able to speak a few words. I am far from being fluent. Anyway, Mercy and I decided to keep up the charade. If they thought we couldn't speak English we hoped to be able to learn what they intended to do with us."

"I'm so proud of you for your quick thinking. I love my clever wife," Lawrence said as he wrapped his arms around her and held her close. "I'm sorry you and Mercy had to go through that ordeal." He kissed her cheek. "I'm thankful God answered all our prayers and brought you both back safely." He kissed his wife with all the passion he had pent up for months.

Abby responded hungrily, and the couple enjoyed a delectable evening of intimacy.

Early the next morning, Abby sat at her dressing table, brushing her hair, when Lawrence pulled out the black velvet box and placed it in front of her, smiling. She turned to face him, her eyes sparkling with delight. "Is this my ring?"

He picked up the box, opened it, took out the ring, and placed it on his wife's finger. "I am so happy you are my wife. I'm the luckiest man in the world."

"It is I who is the lucky one."

Their lips met. Abby was the first to break the kiss. She stood on her tiptoes and wrapped her arms around her husband's neck. "I'm glad you were able to get my ring back. Did it cost a lot?"

"The storekeeper would have given it to me. He said he didn't want to profit from someone else's misfortune. We insisted on paying him what he had paid the men for it, though. It was only fair."

Lawrence kissed Abby on the forehead, then her ear. He folded her into his arms. "I don't ever want you, Mercy, or any of my loved ones to have to go through what you went through, not ever again. Never!" He pushed Abby back so he could see into her beautiful brown eyes. "I want to take you, Mercy, and the boys away from here—away from the South."

Tears rolled down her cheeks. "Oh, Lawrence, I do want to feel safe again."

Abby stepped out of her husband's embrace and walked over to stare out the window.

"Will we truly be safe anywhere we go...being the way we are?"

Lawrence turned his wife to face him.

"I promise you I will do all in my power to keep you and the children safe, with God's help." He stroked her long hair. "Sweetheart, we can't allow hatred to keep us from loving each other and living the life I know the Lord has sanctioned. The only blood that runs through your veins is red, the same as all people's."

"I know." Abby looked into her husband's eyes. "I love you so much."

He took his wife by the hand and led her to her dressing table. "Sweetheart, look in the mirror and tell me what you see."

Abby sat in the chair and stared at herself in the mirror for a while.

"So, what do you see?"

Uncertainty washed over her as she studied herself in the mirror. "I see me."

Lawrence nodded. "Tell me about the person you see."

She hesitated. "I have a wonderful, loving husband, three adorable children, great friends..." She continued to describe herself until reality dawned on her. She stared at Lawrence. "I never used color to describe myself, did I?"

"No, you didn't, because you are more than the color of your skin. It's who you are on the inside that counts...your character."

Abby walked out onto the balcony. "That was what Momma was trying to tell me all along when she said, 'Abby, remember your place.' She meant that I shouldn't try to fit into a black world or a white world, but my place is in the family of God. That's a place where *all* are welcomed and loved because they have accepted Jesus as their Lord and Savior. Oh, Lawrence, I finally understand."

She turned into her husband's waiting arms. She felt snug, happy, and secure wrapped in the warmth of his embrace. She peeked up at the bright sky through her long thick lashes. When she looked beyond the white puffy clouds that were gently floating through the crystal blue sky, she felt she saw the face of God, smiling down at her, giving her permission to enjoy the freedom she had wished for and prayed for all her life…a freedom not determined or controlled by man, but a greater freedom that can be found only at the foot of the cross.

****

Lawrence decided against moving his family to his house down the lane. He knew how much Abby and Mercy wanted to be with family—Cookie, Cedric, and Betsy. Even though he felt the men who abducted his girls had acted alone and were not really dangerous, he still posted armed men around the main house. He was committed to doing his part in keeping his family safe.

On one afternoon a few weeks after the family had been reunited, Lawrence paced back and forth in front of the unlit fireplace in the parlor. He stopped, smiled, and looked from his wife to his daughter.

"So it's decided. We'll go to Philadelphia to live with my folks until we can move to our new house in

New York, close to Pennsylvania and Canada." Heads nodded and faces beamed.

The family had spent many days making plans for their future. It was hard for Abby to imagine a life outside of the South. Mercy tried to hold down a snicker when she asked her papa to tell them about the land...again. He had spent several days describing the land and going over the blueprints for the house and other buildings, trying to convince them that the move would be good for everyone and they wouldn't want for a thing. Mercy's eyes flashed to her mother, who tried to hide a chortle behind her hand.

Lawrence, sitting next to his wife, leaned his head back on the settee. His eyes sparkled. "The natural beauty of the place took my breath away when I first saw it. The changing of the leaves in the fall months is spectacular, there is moderate snow in winter, and it doesn't get so terribly hot in summer like it does here."

Laughter seeped through Abby's fingers. Mercy hid her face behind a pillow.

Lawrence looked from Abby to Mercy. "My girls are laughing at me."

Abby snuggled close to him. "You don't have to sell us, Lawrence. We will follow you anywhere." She kissed his cheek.

Mercy let out a loud laugh from her seat across the room.

He threw a pillow at her. "Little missy, I guess I'll stop my search for a tutor."

"You're getting me a tutor?" Mercy screamed, jumped up and down, and hopped into her father's lap to hug his neck.

"I will also see about you attending college in

London, if you like."

"If…I would like? Of course I would love to go to college in London one day." Mercy kissed him on the cheek and then jumped up from his lap. "I have to go write Raymon and tell him all about my future."

Abby wove her hand into her husband's. "Thank you for what you are doing for our daughter. She's been beside herself ever since Raymon went back to Philadelphia a month ago."

Mercy took the steps two at a time. Her heart was light with joy as she thought of getting her own tutor and going to London to study abroad like her papa had done. But her thoughts lingered more on Raymon, her best friend, and the expectancy of seeing him every day in Philadelphia like she had done for all her life.

She sat at her desk and tapped the pen against her cheek and stared at the paper in front of her. A deep sadness overtook her, and she glanced out across the room, blinking back tears. "I had such dreamy thoughts about a future with you, Raymon, but now we are to have a different kind of future," she whispered into the empty room.

She had thought that pretending Lawrence wasn't her real father could make the realization of Raymon being her first cousin go away. Every time she thought of him being her cousin, it evoked a tremendous pain that started in her heart and moved down her body in waves that exited though her feet. It left her weak and chilled. She knew she had to let go of all the fantasies she'd had about their future, but it wouldn't be easy. She wiped her eyes, cleared her throat, and then set her pen in motion. She wrote and wrote.

****

Lawrence sat at the desk in the study with his head bowed and his fingers laced under his chin, trying to contain a smile.

Adam paced back and forth with his hands clasped behind his back. He stopped and rubbed his chin thoughtfully. "You think this might work?"

Lawrence smiled. His brother-in-law had asked him the same question several times during the last half hour. Lawrence leaned back in the chair. "The two hundred thousand acres I purchased in New York are not too far from Pennsylvania and extend across the Canadian border. I admit I'm talking about something that's never been done before. This just might make history." Lawrence smiled and tapped his fingertips together.

Adam continued his pacing. "Moving a ranch to New York will be history making, all right." He looked at Lawrence. "All the people here are like family; we certainly don't want to leave them in the South unless they want to stay, and I can't imagine any would want to do that." He was silent for a while. "I think it's a brilliant idea. First, we will ask who would like to go with us. Some might decide to settle in other cities in the north, which is fine. Those who go with us will help rebuild the ranch just like it is here, and maybe better."

"We can dismantle all the buildings that we can and rebuild them on the property in New York. We will load the furniture and everything else on the ships I will commission for the task," Lawrence added.

"What a wonderful idea. This will cost you a mint." Adam slapped his brother-in-law on the back.

Lawrence nodded. "What good is money if you can't spend it on the people you love?"

"Before we mention any of this to anyone else, let me see if Maxwell or Gabe would like to purchase the property here, or at least work it."

"You are right, Adam. I didn't take that into consideration."

Lawrence and Adam discussed the plan with the two men and everyone else on the ranch, and it was determined that no one wished to remain in the South. Over the next few months, groups met to decide the best course of action to take in dismantling the houses and the other buildings. Everyone agreed the project would best be done in phases. Maxwell and Clark would stay on to manage the ranch until everything was completed in New York. Additional men would be hired to get things ready on the northern property, and to help clear land and get things ready for the massive building project in New York.

Adam had been so moved by some of the stories from his contacts that he decided the houses and buildings that would remain on the ranch would be turned into an orphanage and a place of refuge for people like the widow of the newspaper reporter who had been killed because he printed articles that spoke out against the institution of slavery.

Chapter Twenty-Four

Abby hummed as she put her final items into her trunk. Lawrence came up behind her and grabbed her by the waist and kissed her on the back of the neck.

"Oh, Lawrence, you startled me!" Merriment danced in her eyes as she turned to face her husband and caressed the ring on his finger. She looked into his dreamy black eyes. Her lips trembled when she spoke. "Do you think your family will like me and the children?"

Lawrence chortled. "What about you and our precious children would they not like?" Abby smiled, and he traced her lips with his fingers.

"I don't know." Abby stepped out onto the balcony and looked out at the beautiful gardens. "Kathleen knew all about me. She loved me from the beginning, and she always referred to herself as Aunt Kathleen, even before she knew you were Mercy's father."

Lawrence walked over and stood behind his wife and kissed her neck. "My family knows all about you and Mercy."

She turned and faced him. "How do they know all about me?"

Lawrence smiled and rocked on his heels. "I told them when I was in Philadelphia."

Abby waggled a brow. "I thought we were going to wait and tell them together."

"Well, something came up." He quickly changed the subject. "Have you finished packing, sweetheart?"

Abby took hold of his lapels and playfully pushed him back into the room. "What came up, Lawrence?" She pushed him down onto the bed and sat on top of him, giggling. "Oh, wait." Her brows crinkled. "Don't tell me. Was she cute?"

Lawrence smiled and rolled over on top of her. "My family and friends thought an eligible bachelor like me should have his pick of lovely eligible ladies." He kissed his wife's eyebrows.

"They didn't!" Abby laughed.

"Oh, yes, they did. I finally had to put a stop to all the scheming and planning. That's when I told them about you and Mercy. I even showed them a portrait of the two of you."

Abby's eyes widened. "You did?"

"They think you and Mercy are beautiful, and that you are the luckiest woman in the world to have me."

Abby laughed as she pulled Lawrence's head down and kissed him with all the love she had.

****

Lawrence wove his fingers into Abby's. He brought her long slender fingers to his lips and kissed them softly, never taking his eyes off her trembling lips. He fingered a stray strand of hair that had escaped her bun and gently brushed her cheek.

She closed her eyes to his touch and kept them closed until the queasiness in her stomach subsided. It had been four months since she, Mercy, and the babies returned to the ranch. They both felt a bit nervous about sailing, after their ordeal in the river, but Lawrence had assured them that sailing in a large vessel like the

Voyager II was quite different from a small boat such as their captors had used. Abby could tell that some of the household staff shared her and Mercy's reservations about being at sea.

Mercy slid her hand around the wooden railing as she made her way to her parents, who stood just a few feet away from her. "Papa, when will we get to Philadelphia?"

Lawrence tapped her nose. "Sweetie, I'm afraid it will be a while." A groan escaped her lips as she made her way over to Adam, Eli, and the others. Lawrence smiled and shook his head. "She is so eager to see Raymon."

Abby locked arms with her husband and smiled. "I know she is." She leaned in against her husband as they stood watching the rise and fall of the white-tipped waves. She placed his palm on her stomach.

He slowly turned her in his arms. He pressed his nose against hers. His smile stretched as wide as the ocean. "Does this mean what I think?"

Abby nodded.

Lawrence let out a yell and twirled her around, her skirt billowing in the wind.

"Put me back down! Everyone is watching," she said, giggling.

"We're among family."

Abby's eyes twinkled. "You are right. We're so blessed to have such a loving family."

Abby folded Lawrence's arms around her waist. "Look at us. We range from white to brown to black, with all the shades between."

Lawrence kissed her on the cheek. "Yes, and that's the way God intended from the beginning of time."

A word about the author...

As a kindergarten teacher, Linda's mantra in the classroom was: You're only limited by your imagination. Now retired after thirty-seven years of service, she's discovering what an unlimited imagination can do for her, especially in writing.

Linda grew up on a farm in North Carolina. She resides in Charlotte, North Carolina, with her husband. She has two grown children and one grandson, and loves spending time with each one. She enjoys walking, biking, and reading—historical romance is her favorite genre.

She holds a BS degree from North Carolina A&T State University, a teaching certificate from Fayetteville State University, and a Master's degree from the University of North Carolina at Charlotte.

Thank you for purchasing
this publication of The Wild Rose Press, Inc.

If you enjoyed the story, we would appreciate your
letting others know by leaving a review.

For other wonderful stories,
please visit our on-line bookstore at
www.thewildrosepress.com.

For questions or more information
contact us at
info@thewildrosepress.com.

The Wild Rose Press, Inc.
www.thewildrosepress.com

Stay current with The Wild Rose Press, Inc.

Like us on Facebook

https://www.facebook.com/TheWildRosePress

And Follow us on Twitter
https://twitter.com/WildRosePress